Wonders of the Wilderness

by
Eric Carlton Neperud

This book is dedicated to the savages and the tourons.

By Eric Carlton Neperud

THE LIMBO CHRONICLES
     Trees And Weeds
     Limbo
     The Octagonal Knight
     Dragons And Golems
     The Brotherhood Of Giants
     Wizards And Druids

THE YELLOWSONE TRILOGY
     Wonders Of The Wilderness
     Fleas Upon Snow
     The Periphery Of Sorrow

Copyright © 2017 by Eric Carlton Neperud
All rights reserved.
ISBN: 0998383864
ISBN-13: 978-09983838-6-6
Published by Valhalla Books

Cover photo by Eric Carlton Neperud
Back cover photo by Eric Carlton Neperud

Cast of Characters

Steve Harrison...Bison
Magnolia Woods...Amber Fox
Kathleen O'Neel................................Poodle
Martha Devla.....................................The Wolf
Ryan Turner...Grizzly
William Soloman......................................Mantis
Charlie Peterson.....................................Cougar
Samantha Salsa.................................Diamondback
Andy Lincoln.....................................Bighorn
Christine Faith.....................................Rabbit
Alice Grunden.....................................Dish Dove
Barry Henry.......................................Bald Owl
Iris Douglas.......................................Mama Bear
Harry Douglas............................Rainbow Trout
Daphnee Delaware.............................Marmot
Rebecca Gar.......................................Terrapin
Tony Whitaker..............................The Mosquito

Wonders Of The Wilderness
by
Eric Carlton Neperud

The kids fought in the back of the car as I fought rush hour traffic. My wife coped the best she could: she put ear plugs in after taking a Xanax. On days like these my only comfort was remembering what my life was like before the chaos. It was fifteen years ago that I....

1. FOR THE BENEFIT AND THE ENJOYMENT

Livingston. Finally. But where was the sign for Yellowstone? I got off at the exit, then pulled off the road. My road atlas looked like someone had sat on an old, dilapidated telephone directory. The pages were curled, the cover ripped. Nothing was written on it. I took great pride in that, but I couldn't prevent it from aging. Every anticipatory glance added a wrinkle. Every course correction created sag. Damn. There was more than one exit for Livingston.

Who would have guessed a town that size would have been that complicated?

It felt good to be back on the freeway. It would feel better if I could continue driving. Did I really want to do this? I had signed a contract, and had to earn some money this summer. I had a hundred dollars in my wallet and twice that in the bank. Even being thrifty I barely made it through college---financially. My grades, although not stellar, were always adequate. I had student loans, but they didn't pay for everything. Incidentals added up. To save money I lived in a dorm---for four years. There had to be some good times there, but I didn't remember any of them. It was just a place to stay until I graduated. Now that I did, I wasn't sure what I wanted to do. If nothing else, college provided focus. I had planned to go on all those job interviews so many of my classmates did their senior year.

That was before my dad died. I no longer had the enthusiasm to drive to Portland or fly to Chicago. I liked to travel, the idea of it anyway. I never did much of it as a child. My parents were too poor to spend money on going to places like Disneyland. Once a year we made it to the coast, but for just the day. My dad was very careful with money. He held to a tight budget. If he rationed ten dollars for gas that was how much he would put in the car. He became irate whenever he pumped a penny over. My dad rarely cursed, but whenever he made a mistake like that I heard the same words I wasn't allowed to say. When I first heard them, I didn't know what they meant, but because I was forbidden to say them there must have been something special about them---like that candy put on the top shelf I wasn't allowed to eat. When I was alone I would say the words softly, like I was nibbling on one of those candies I climbed up to eat. In the manner my dad stretched out every syllable of those words I was confident he not only knew their meaning, but their origin and every alternate definition.

With my parents being as poor as they were, I was surprised they got divorced my freshman year of college. It wasn't that they

6

never argued. It wasn't financially prudent for each of them to pay rent.

Yep. There's the sign for Yellowstone. It was the second exit. I stopped for gas. Prices were higher in remote places, so I wanted to take advantage of the relatively cheap gas in Livingston. I topped off the tank, stopping when the numbers flipped to 10.00. Habits were hard to break. I walked into the gas station. I was tempted to buy a candy bar, but I didn't want to pay the fifty cents it would set me back. I was down to ninety dollars. When I returned to my car I had to roll a window down. I smelled that badly of second hand smoke. I didn't care if others died of lung cancer. I just didn't want them to stink, and from their proximity to me, for me to stink.

I returned to the two-lane highway. A few businesses and homes lingered. A couple of minutes later, just scenery. A river was left of the road, cottonwoods nestled along its banks. Beyond the irrigated farmland mountains rose, snow beginning at their bellies. So beautiful. I began to hyperventilate.

I began to think about being isolated in the wilderness, my only contact with civilization, cleaning dirty toilets and making beds. Could I really spend the entire summer doing that?

I turned into a parking lot and turned around. When I merged with traffic on the freeway it felt like the governor had given me a pardon on the day of my execution.

What was I doing? I couldn't return home now. Where was home? I lived with my dad during the summers, but now.... I could probably stay with my mom, but she had remarried. *He* was not only there, but his two kids. He was a nice enough guy, as were his kids. There just wasn't room---not really. If I asked they would make room somehow. I could sleep on the couch, but then what? I could work for a fast food restaurant while I looked for a higher paying job, something more related to my degree, or maybe work my way up to management.

I got off at the next exit and turned back around. If I was

7

going to make minimum wage for a while I might as well be doing it somewhere scenic.

I filled up my car again, this time in Gardiner, the last city before Yellowstone. I had driven just 80 miles, including the turn around, but it was my last opportunity for relatively cheap gas. I paid ten cents more---per gallon---than I did in Livingston, but that had to be twenty to thirty cents less than what I would pay in the Park. I paid the service station attendant five dollars. Four twenties and a five remained in my wallet.

To save money, the little I had, I intended to camp. My check-in date was tomorrow, in the morning.

My car, affectionately called the Lemon, because of its yellow exterior and its withering disposition, fainted at the northern entrance to the Park.

"The elevation probably caused the carburetor to flood," said the attending ranger. "Let it sit awhile. It should recover in a few minutes."

I handed him my employment agreement. "The letter I was sent said I could get into Yellowstone for free with this." It was ten dollars for a seven-day pass. I was already making money.

The ranger looked over the employee agreement, then handed it back to me. "Lake Hotel, huh. When you get to Mammoth you can go either direction around the upper loop. Just watch for the signs for Canyon. Once you reach Canyon Junction, head south. They'll be a sign if you get disoriented."

"Thanks." I tried to start the Lemon. Nope. Still flooded.

"You need to move your car out of the way." I gave him a perplexed look. "Just put it in neutral and push it."

If I did that how would I be able to steer? What if it got away from me? I did what I was told, but instead of pushing from behind I held onto the side of the vehicle with the door open. After the initial resistance, the car rolled easily. I reached for the steering wheel, guiding the car to the side of the road. I was quite pleased with myself. Who else would have thought to do it that way? With the clog removed the ebb and flow of recreational vehicles resumed.

How could all those people afford such luxury? My parents saved for months to buy their five-person tent.

To consume time---and to ease stress---I walked to the Gateway Arch. *For the Benefit and the Enjoyment of the People* was chiseled in the stone. That sounded like something in the preamble to the constitution. Maybe working in Yellowstone would be the start of something, something more than a place to hang out while I decided what I wanted to do with my life.

I walked back to the Lemon. It started up on the first attempt. The first six miles inside the park was through a box canyon. The road climbed steeply, first beside a frothing river, then above it. Steam rose. COULD IT BE A GEYSER?! A motor home whipped around the curve in front of me. I had to hug the non-existent shoulder to keep from scraping the two-feet of recreational opulence in my lane.

At the top of the canyon was a campground. And it wasn't full. It was beginning to get dark, and it had just started to rain. I paid the camp attendant eight dollars. That wasn't too bad, but it brought my cash down to 77 dollars.

When I used the bathroom, I found out why it was so inexpensive. There was running water, but no showers. Great. First impressions were supposed to be important, and the one I was going to make was of someone who didn't bath regularly. I washed under my arms, then put on fresh deodorant. In the morning, I intended to put on clean clothes.

I had helped my parents set up the tent, but not since high school. It was dark enough now that I had to shine my headlights on the uneven, damp track of land that was to be my campsite. The only thing that became clearer was the rain. The damp cold must have numbed my brain, because I didn't remember finishing setting up the tent. When I reclaimed my senses, I was lying in my sleeping bag eating cold pork and beans from the can.

I opened my water bottle, took a swallow, then set it down beside me. The incline was just enough to prevent the bottle from standing upright. The right side of my sleeping bag became soaked before I could put the lid back on the water. I might as well be back outside. The water was fresher.

I was becoming sleepy, but I had to pee again. I hated getting up in the middle of the night, so I always squeezed whatever was left in my bladder out before turning in for good. I could urinate from the flap of the tent, but I also needed to brush my teeth. Having dirty teeth was nearly as bad as having a partially full bladder. I had a phobia about leaving food debris in my mouth overnight. I envisioned little demons chipping away at my teeth as I slept.

I ran to the restroom, toiletry bag under my arm, like a running back carrying a football. Instead of being greeted by cheering fans at the end zone, I was tackled by the odorous remnants of men with too much testosterone. I hadn't noticed the odors the first time I used the bathroom. Either I had to go so badly that first time I didn't notice them, the odors occurred since I last used the restroom, or the exertion of running forced a more substantial amount of air into my nostrils. I became nauseous thinking about the offensive air particles entering my mouth as I brushed my teeth.

Becoming bored looking at my reflection I visually explored my surroundings. On the door was a poster warning campers to store food in their vehicles, and to dispose of refuse into bear-proof garbage cans. They looked like green mail boxes: a can with a swinging door on top.

I remembered to set my watch alarm. I had to check-in before 10 a.m. I planned to get there much earlier---to beat the crowd.

I slept with my head uphill, to prevent too much blood flowing into my head, giving me a headache. Or was it supposed to be the other way?

I couldn't fall asleep. If I was more comfortable I may have had a fighting chance. When my parents camped they brought mattresses, real ones, not the ones that inflated. My dad wasn't too happy when I dropped one on the way to the tent. That was when he stopped going camping. My mom attempted to take us camping by herself---my brother and me. Without mattresses---my father's decree. The combination of sleeping on the hard ground and struggling to set up camp soured us, as much as dirtying the mattress soured my father. Sleeping on the hard ground with the sound of the rain falling against the tent reminded me of that last time I went camping, which reminded me of my father dying.

I went to the cemetery the day before I left for Yellowstone. My dad's grave was on the fringe, where most of the new burials occurred. It was so desolate there. It didn't have any of the ornamentations the older plots had. No trees. Not even any shrubs. It was stark in its absence of character, like a vacant lot in a very developed part of the city. Without any barriers to break the wind on that side of the cemetery, it would often be chilly standing there, while I talked to my dad. My mom was concerned he would get cold. Although she had divorced him and had remarried she still had a fondness for him. A person couldn't suddenly hate everything about a person. There had to have been something there for them to have once been married.

As I left the cemetery I looked at the gravestones. They varied in size, texture, and shape. It was difficult to not focus on the larger ones. Did the people who erected these monuments appreciate their loved ones as much while they lived? Were they trying to make up for lost time? The smaller headstones weren't as bold, but they told the same story. Many of the older graves were either without headstones or too weathered to read. Are the people buried beneath them still remembered? If even the memories of us fade, then do we truly die? If we no longer exist, did we ever exist?

Before my dad died he laid in bed many weeks struggling for

his life. The cancer was incurable. The pain had progressively gotten worse. Periodically he would grimace, or his whole body would tremble. Everyone wished he would give-in to the death grip, so the misery would end, but he wanted so much to live. He had so much more to do. Why couldn't one of those people who attempted suicide take his place, so they could die rather than him, instead of being saved at the last instant. With so many people wanting to die, why should one who didn't have to? The morphine had to be increased daily. Why couldn't he just die? Occasionally he would recognize someone, but most of the time he was just too drugged to care. It was like he was dead already, and all that remained was his shell. Two demons fought for control of his body, one to retain it, one to take it away. If only the war could be over....

2. GLADIATORS

The only thing worse than putting up a tent in the rain was taking it down the next morning. The rain had stopped, but there hadn't been enough time for the tent to dry. It was soaked. After removing all the poles, I shook the canvas. Most of the water flew off it, but it was still damp. I rolled it up and shoved it in its case. Sometime, in the very near future, I would have to take it back out and dry it more thoroughly. My parents had once forgotten to do so. It stunk of mildew the entire time we had it up the following camping trip.

Keeping to my budget of not spending any money I didn't absolutely have to spend, I opened a can of cherry pie filling and finished the entire can as I sat on a mostly dry picnic table. Crap. It wasn't quite dry enough. My backside was wet. There was no way

I was going to check-in with a wet butt. I pulled a clean, dry pair of jeans out of my suitcase and took them with me to the restroom. I had to brush my teeth anyway, and use the bathroom one more time. A precaution to counter the potential long wait in line. I had been wearing shorts, but mornings in an elevation of more than a mile were brisk. Cooler temperatures moderated bathroom odors. Or maybe I was getting used to them. Or someone had recently cleaned the building.

I returned to Gardiner. I entered a building with a life size bear logo above its main entrance. A receptionist and arrows guided me to the end of a line. There was a distinct division between newcomers and old-timers.

The old-timers were talkative. They were enthusiastic to be there. They hadn't seen some of their friends for nearly a year. Their happiness accentuated my loneliness. A person couldn't truly be lonely until he saw others being sociable---unintentionally exclusionary.

The newcomers stood quietly, their thoughts internal. They looked around nervously, attempting to ascertain a hint of their surroundings, and their future.

Driver licenses were snatched as we waited in line. Names were called when someone was ready for us at one of the six counter spaces. I felt like I was waiting to see the principal. "Steve?"

I walked up to a slightly overweight, middle-aged woman. She had a file with my name on it in front of her. I began to fidget. "We're going to have to assign you to kitchen help. Too many room attendants were hired." I didn't care. Being a dishwasher was just as good---or as bad---as being a maid. But wasn't I hired as a room attendant. Could they just change someone's employment agreement like that without that person's permission? Could they also make me stay longer than I wished to? "You need to fill this out." It was a W-4 form. "Did your drive here?"

"Yes."

13

"Then you'll need this. It's a seven-day pass to enter the Park. You'll need to go to a ranger station and get a decal for your car if you don't want to pay after the pass expires." She set a white folder with the bear logo on top of my file. She removed an index card from it. "Sign your name, making sure you stay within the lines." She reclaimed the card, then explained the miscellaneous information about Yellowstone in the folder. My eyes were drawn to the small blue and white pen with the bear logo on it. "When you finish at Gardiner, you can eat lunch at Mammoth Hot Springs. It's just six miles inside the Park. Here's a map to show you how to get to the employee dining room." She pulled a park map out of my folder and showed me where Mammoth Hot Springs and Lake Hotel were located. "To pick up your uniforms, take a left once you exit the building. The uniform room is across the gravel parking lot. There will be a sign. We'll call you when we're ready to take your photo for your I.D. You may wait in the hallway." She handed me the white folder with the bear logo. "There is an orientation in this building at 10 a.m."

I got a drink of water from the fountain in the hallway, then sat on a metal folding chair. The chairs were aligned in two rows against the walls of the hallway, forcing the employees being processed to face one another, like gladiators in a holding box, waiting their turn to fight in the arena.

"Steve Harrison?"

I leaned against a blue tapestry. Flash. "Now just one more." Flash. "We'll bring you your I.D. when it is ready." I returned to the box, still alive after my first melee. A few minutes later my laminated I.D. card was handed to me. It was still warm. The picture looked great, not at all like a driver license photo.

I put my paperwork in the Lemon, then headed for the uniform room. As I opened the door it felt like I had walked into a building with an indoor pool. The chlorine bleach odor confirmed I was in the right place. Five people were ahead of me in line, giving me enough time to visually examine---and internally laugh---at the colorful uniforms. A young woman came out of the dressing room wearing black and white checkered pants and a white shirt. She looked like a little girl dressing up to go golfing with daddy. She frowned. "Do you have any pants that fit a girl?" She pulled at her pants where they were snug at her hips and buttocks.

"That's all we have."

"You better get me a twenty-six then instead of a twenty-four." I didn't want the girl to be uncomfortable, but I wouldn't have minded seeing her in pants a couple of sizes too small. I smiled for the first time since I left Seattle.

A couple of people in front of me were given maroon slacks and magenta shirts. The guy in front of me was given brown pants and brown and white checkered shirts. I pictured the people around me simultaneously wearing the black and white checkered pants and the brown and white checkered shirts. I smiled again.

I was given two checkered pants, two white shirts, and one white apron. One pair of pants had snaps that popped apart whenever I stretched too much. The other pair had buttons. There was enough space in the crotch to fill-out any man's boasting. I was becoming fatigued from all the running around, so I left with what I was given.

I threw my uniforms in the Lemon, then waited for the meeting to begin, sitting on top of a picnic table in front of the building. I had an hour to kill. I watched people come and go. Will any of them become my friends? Will I have any friends at all this summer? Maybe one of them will even become my girlfriend.

People began flowing into the orientation room at five minutes before ten. I followed them. The room was filled wall to wall with chairs. There were over a hundred of them, in a relatively small room. I wasn't clinically claustrophobic, but I did feel uncomfortable around that many people in such a close space. I never went to a movie on opening night for that reason. If a movie was particularly popular I waited a month or more to see it. There was a vacant seat next to a couple of beautiful young women. I

15

took advantage of the opportunity. "Hi," I said, trying to be friendly, but not wanting to come across as being overly so.

The girl seated next to me was very enthusiastic to see me. She gave me a wide smile. "Well, hello," she stretched out with a strong Southern drawl. Her blond hair was incredible. It was shaped like a willow. It arched from the top of her head, down to the middle of her back. Its body was as full as her figure. It was difficult to keep my eyes off her.

Her friend's face revealed little. Either she was bored with me or her surroundings. Her face had too much make-up on it, which may have been why it wasn't animated. She didn't want to crack the plaster. If she wasn't so young or attractive the make-up would have looked grotesque, but because she was beautiful, the make-up simply blunted the intricacies of her features and personality.

"I'm Magnolia," said the more natural girl. I would have laughed at her parents' choice of names if I wasn't so enamored with her. My pulse raced. Could I be in love already?

"I'm Steve." I extended my hand. She enthusiastically grabbed it like it was a game. Her hand felt like rose petals. I didn't want the contact to ever end. She was first pull away, I too enthralled to move. My hand continued to tingle.

"This is Kathleen." She cordially turned her head my way. She raised the corners of her mouth, then curtly dropped them. She turned to look ahead again, obviously fatigued from the effort.

It was ten after ten and people were still shuffling in--- mainly old-timers. They didn't seem too concerned. Ten minutes later a petite, athletic woman, about twice my age, stood in front of the room. She refused to speak until the room was quiet.

"Let me introduce myself," she began in her Boston accent. "I'm Martha Devla. I'll be Lake Yellowstone Hotel's location manager this summer. A location manager is like a mayor. I'll be in charge of all operations in and around Lake Hotel. You should feel proud to be part of the Yellowstone experience. Yellowstone is the world's first national park. It was established in 1872...."

I took out my notebook and began taking notes. Magnolia saw me and began to laugh. She whispered, "This isn't class."

The location manager shared more information about Yellowstone National Park, and the concessionaire which ran its food and lodging facilities. I compiled little of the information. My thoughts were of Magnolia.

"Are you guys going to eat at Mammoth?" I asked the girls when the show was over.

"The bus is going to stop there on the way to Lake Hotel, so I guess we will," Magnolia answered.

"You didn't drive?"

"It's a long way to drive when you're only going to be here three months. Are you going to eat with us?"

"Yes, if you wouldn't mind."

"Please do."

3.   TOP OF THE HILL GASPING

Half the cars behind me passed once the road straightened. I thought about pulling off, before I realized I was going the speed limit. I refused. They could pass me if they liked, but I wasn't going to go out of my way to satisfy their impatience.

I didn't see the bus yet, so I decided to do some sight-seeing. In the distance, steam rose from a white cliff adorned with boardwalk necklaces and pearl people. I felt I didn't have time to see it, so I climbed the hill overlooking the Mammoth Hot Springs Hotel instead. I would still be able to get a good view of the area. Every step felt like it would be my last. My throat was raw. I could taste blood. I had to make it to the top. How could I feel competent enough to join the Hundred Mile Hiking Club if I couldn't even climb a stupid hill? I couldn't be that much out of shape. It must have been the altitude. The higher the elevation the thinner the air. Mammoth was about 6300 feet above sea level. Lake Hotel 1500 feet higher than that. I reached the top of the hill gasping. Mountains surrounding me, most thousands of feet higher than my exhausting climb. How was I ever going to hike a hundred miles this summer? How could anyone hike that many miles?

The bus pulled in next to the Employee Dining Room, more often referred to as the EDR. People filed out. I took a minute more to catch my breath, then I ran down the hill, trying not to kick up too much dust. So far, the Park had been surprisingly arid.

My timing could have been better. I was at the end of a line forty bus riders deep. I was ravenous after the ten minutes it took me to get to the serving counter. The greatest appetizer was one's sense of smell. "May I see your ID card?" asked the first server behind the steaming serving line. She glanced at my card, then wrote down my employee ID number. The leakage from the steam baths caused the Plexiglas to become opaque. Instead of wasting time asking what was in each pan, I told the servers to give me everything. My loaded tray was topped off with a salad from the salad bar. If I was forced to pay for this stuff I was going to get my money's worth. There wasn't room left on my tray for a drink, so I had to carry the gold plastic tumbler filled with coke with one hand as I balanced the tray with the other.

There wasn't a single chair unoccupied in the dining room. A couple of newcomers were waiting at the edge of the chaos for something to open up. As I also waited I scanned the room for Magnolia. She was having a riveting conversation with a pretty-boy. I got depressed again. She probably didn't even like me anyway. I was only going to be here four months. It was better if I didn't get involved.

Someone finally got up. I grabbed the spot before anyone

else could. Most of the people at the table had plates instead of trays. Either the EDR had run out of clean plates, or it didn't wish to dirty them on newcomers. No one at the table even looked at me the entire time I was eating. The Mammoth employees must have seen so many new arrivals it was no longer a curiosity to them. I ate quickly, anxious to check-in at Lake Hotel, and feeling a bit out of place. My table-mates' plates had been nearly empty since the time I sat down. They had been consuming more gossip than food. I didn't blame them for not getting up while people were still standing. If I was in their situation I might do the same. They were probably tired of their location becoming a circus every time a new group of employees were processed. I would hate to work at Mammoth.

4. SOMETHING BIG AND HAIRY

The road climbed hesitantly through irregular rock formations, called hoodoos. At the summit of the rise was Golden Gate, the unmarked entry into the Yellowstone highlands. A veiled waterfall adorned the maw. Traffic was spat from the opening, accelerating to forty-five miles per hour onto the Swan Flats straight away.

The trip south was one thermal feature and beautiful landscape after another: lake begets forest begets river begets meadow begets hot springs. I was disappointed when the Grand Canyon of the Yellowstone River couldn't be seen from the road. A few miles later the Park made up for it.

Something big and hairy pulled out in front of me. I had to slam on the brakes, disrupting my tidy packing. I rolled down my window with one hand as I searched for my camera with the other. On cue, the beast walked to the driver's side of the Lemon. I shot half a roll of film. Fortunately, no one was behind me to get pissed at the traffic obstruction I created. I was actually looking at a buffalo. A BUFFALO!

Moments later I entered a sage-spotted meadow. Buffalo, or bison, as they were officially called, cluttered the green-tinted, rolling hills. How foolish I had been to stop for just one. I was proud of myself when I didn't stop to watch a buffalo cross the Yellowstone River.

5.   A WORKING VACATION

I checked-in with the Lake Yellowstone Hotel Personnel Manager. She directed me to Pelican Dorm, where the Resident Coordinator---RC---will assign me a room and distribute linen and a pillow. The employee compound consisted of an oblong circle of trailers and a basketball court surrounded by one small dormitory and three larger ones. The dorms were just two stories tall, but they looked nicer than the dorm I stayed in while attending college. Their brown exteriors fit in well with the sylvan environment.

The RC's door was open, but he wasn't present. I waited outside his door, not wanting to intrude. I became mildly upset for having to wait. From the hallway, I perused the RC's extensive possessions. Books, records, a stereo, games, and camping equipment filled his room. Without even meeting him I knew he would be the type of person who would want to make me feel at home.

Someone began walking towards me down the hall. He was

short, stocky, and looked like he had just gotten out of bed. His face erupted into a Cheshire grin when he saw me. "Would you like a room?"

"Very much so."

I followed the RC into his room. He had paperwork scattered all over his desk, and on the floor beneath it. He found a blank housing agreement and began filling it out. "Is there anyone you would like to room with?"

"Christie Brinkley."

"She'll be checking into the hotel in July, so we'll have to assign you another roommate until she arrives." Expressionless, he waited for my reply.

"I just got here, so I don't know anyone yet."

His broad grin returned. "How about I put you in room 218 then? There's a guy about your age in there already. His name is William Soloman." The RC gave me my room key. "My name is Ryan." He held out his hand. I shook it.

"I'm Steve." Ryan began to write my name down on the housing agreement. "Uh, Steve Harrison."

"Would you like linen?"

He led me to the linen room. He allowed me to pick out my own pillow, which I appreciated, since some of them looked nasty.

"You're going to have fun in a few minutes. Forty people are arriving on a bus."

"I'm looking forward to it. After they are all processed it's going to be kick back time until people begin leaving. You plan to do any camping this summer?"

"I guess, if I can find people who want to go."

"How about we get some people together sometime and go camping, then?"

"Sure."

Pelican 218 was much warmer and more welcoming than any of my dorm rooms in college. It was designed for pleasurable tasks, like sleeping and playing. In college, the rooms were designed for studying: a hard desk, an uncomfortable chair, ugly decor, a tile floor. They were made to be uncomfortable so people would study, not be distracted by decadence. In Yellowstone, everything was designed to promote a working vacation atmosphere. If employees enjoyed themselves while off the clock, they would be in productive moods when they returned to work.

William Soloman wasn't in the room. I unpacked hurriedly, wanting to finish before my roommate returned, so he wouldn't be looking over my shoulder and taking inventory of everything I owned. A pile in the Lemon became a pile in the middle of Pelican 218. Before my stuff was organized and put away, it remained undefined, without personality---like Yellowstone employees before they find their niche of friends and activities.

I got side-tracked when I became curious of my roommate. Initially, I just glanced at his side of the room, but the craving for knowledge became too great. There was a bible on his bed, tattered, with a dozen book markers sticking out of it. And a...Playboy?

I looked at the door, then back at the Playboy. Then back at the door. I leaned over the bed, careful to not make contact with the blanket on top of it as I opened the magazine. Shock. Disappointment. Confusion. There was a woman, but the parts of her that I was hoping to see were covered---with a black marker, very artistically drawn, looking like a bikini.

Someone put a key into the doorknob and turned it. I scrambled, closing the magazine as I darted back to my side of the room.

"Hello," I stuttered.

"You must be my roommate." The big hairy, bearded man smiled sincerely. "I'm William...Soloman." He put his hand out in front of him.

I shook it. Then glanced at William's bed, confirming that the magazine was in the location, and orientation, I found it. Noticing William noticing me, in particular, the direction of my focus, I said, "You read the bible?"

"Not as often as I should. Are you a Christian?"

"I was raised a Christian. I went to Sunday School as a child. I've read parts of the bible."

"Do you believe the bible is the Word of God?"

"I guess. At least most of it."

"You're more certain than I, then."

"I thought…."

"I read the bible. I study it. I just don't trust the people who wrote it---who interpreted the Word of God. There's too much to gain by corrupting it." William lay down. He placed the Playboy on his nightstand, then held and opened the bible. After reading for a couple of minutes he crossed something out with a black marker.

"Are you allowed to do that?" I asked him.

"Probably not, but Jesus did a lot of things he wasn't supposed to do."

"I guess I should get back to unpacking."

William smiled, then returned to crossing out verses of the bible he didn't agree with.

After dinner, I had to attend a series of meetings. Following another sermon by Martha Devla, the Food and Beverage Department showed a murder mystery video about an unsanitary man causing food poisoning. The acting and dialogue were so hokey I thought the video might turn into a porno. Kitchen help was divided into dishwashers, pantry, and EDR. Not having any restaurant experience I couldn't escape washing dirty dishes. The evening concluded with a tour of the kitchen. The part of the evening I despised the most was finding out I had to work at 8 a.m. the next morning.

6.   FELT TIP DECLARATIONS

I couldn't see a thing. I turned around. I could still see the lights of Osprey Dorm, the dorm closest to the trail. I turned back around. Just a couple of more steps until I reached the road. Then a couple more. My foot caught on something. I surged forward, stumbling, but never completely losing my balance. I became disoriented. I couldn't even see lights behind me now. The ground rose. My feet became bloodhounds, probing for evidence, following a scent that was just barely there. My right foot dropped farther than I was prepared for. I stumbled again. My feet slapped against a hard surface.

It was still dark. I could barely see the curve of the road. My shoulder bumped into something hairy and solid. It grunted. I rushed behind a tree. I could see light again. I listened. No more sounds from the animal. It must have been asleep. It was probably still asleep. I oozed towards the light, making sure I stayed behind trees. Seeing the road clearly now, I rushed towards it, walking briskly downhill to Lake Lodge. I could barely distinguish Lake Yellowstone behind it. I began to hear music and people laughing.

Above the door of a brown one-story building were the words *Employee Pub*. I opened the door. The music and laughing became much louder. A man with a tie-dye shirt put a large **X** on the hands of two girls. They scurried off, giggling like they were in middle school, which couldn't have been too many years ago. Did I look that young when I graduated from high school? The man looked up at me. "I.D. please." I showed him my laminated employee card. It was handed back to me.

"Don't I get marked?"

"Only minors do."

"If someone tried hard enough don't you think they could rub that mark off?"

"Every season someone does, but after they are caught---and they always are---no one else is stupid enough to try. The penalty is too great. If a minor is caught drinking alcohol in the pub his, or her, privileges are provoked for the remainder of the season. The same goes for the person giving them the alcohol."

I glanced around. To the left, up a couple of steps, people ordered drinks and pizza. To the right, people played pool and foosball. Scattered throughout were two dozen tables. Most were occupied. All ages were represented, but a majority of the people were younger than me. "You must go through a lot of pens."

"This summer I probably will. The drinking age was just raised to twenty-one in Wyoming. I'll actually have to earn my pay this year. There will probably be more drinking in the dorms now. I would hate to be an RC. Here, I can just kick people out, for the night, or for the remainder of the season. RCs have fewer options. Either they force the minors to dispose of the alcohol or they can recommend the employees be terminated. There is a drinking clause in the employment agreement."

Not seeing anyone I knew---being new to Yellowstone, acquaintances became significant relationships---I moseyed up to the bar. I was never the type of person to drink in excess. With my parents allowing me to sample beer and wine from a young age the novelty of drinking wasn't as great as it was for many of my peers. The flavor of alcohol was still unique enough to me that sometimes I drank it for its taste, but most of the time---like most adults, and kids pretending to be adults---I consumed it to modify my mood. Nearly everyone in the pub was talking to someone, even the newcomers. Social situations never came easy to me. I bought a beer to loosen up.

I stood by myself, leaning against a wooden post. I watched

the people around me enjoying themselves. I glanced at a mural: grim men in western attire. The painting reflected the mood of the building, my perception of it anyway. Gaiety was a façade, enhanced by alcohol and socialization. Wooden rafters filled the sky, oars reaching towards an aerial void. Graffiti besieged the walls in felt tip declarations of goodwill and self-gratification.

I wandered to where a crowd huddled around a foosball table. Two couples played against one another. One of the couples was flamboyant. He had little-boy charm. She had a trim, lightly curvaceous body, with a wicked Texan tongue. His entire body moved with every flick of his wrist. She moved her hips with every thrust. Steady, demure opponents faced them. He was awkward in his play, and in his appearance. She had a consistent smile, and consistent play----no errors, but no winners. The flamboyant couple lost the game. The boyish-man got so excited that he accidentally flipped the winning ball into his own goal. He screamed in anguish, but retained a smile. The excitement for him was in playing the game, win or lose.

There was a line of quarters on the table, each one representing a person or group reserving their play. Fame sometimes brought unwanted interest. The awkward guy didn't feel like playing with strangers, so he resigned. The girls, upon seeing the huge, gruff, unwashed men who were to play next, also chose to withdraw. The boyish-man still wanted to play, so he searched for a new partner. He turned to me. "Shall we?"

I didn't know how to respond. I knew some friendly people, but this guy...he acted like he had known me for years.

"I don't know. It's fun just watching."

"Come on." He shook me. "Watching is existing. Participating is living."

Afraid of what he may do next, I finally accepted. The boyish-man wanted to play offense. I didn't argue. His flashy style of play was perfect for scoring. A steadier hand and a more concentrated demeanor was needed to play defense, and I had that.

Having not played in a while, my reflexes were rusty. I let two balls go past me in the first thirty seconds. Surprisingly, my partner didn't condemn me. He remained jovial, laughing at lost points. "We lost that one, but we'll win the next." He encouraged me, making me want to improve, instead of just wishing the game to be over. He even congratulated his opponents when they made a good shot. We won, with the final ball.

The boyish-man hooted and hollered. "ICE CREAM AND ONIONS!" He put out his hand. "My name is Charlie."

"I'm Steve. Steve Harrison." Charlie grabbed my hand. He twisted it into a brotherhood handshake. He grinned as he shook my body at the shoulders. "Shall we continue?"

We played until the row of quarters were gone. I got better with practice. We won every game, which we had to do to retain the table. The consistent couple and the Texan returned with plastic tumblers of beer. Being distracted, we thoroughly lost our next game.

Charlie introduced me to his friends. "This is Andy Lincoln." I shook hands with the tall, awkward man. "And Christine Faith." The taciturn girl politely offered her hand.

"And I'm Samantha Salsa." The Texan wrapped her arms around me and squeezed. The tight shorts and tank top she wore left little to the imagination. After pressing up against her even less was kept secret.

"We ordered pizza," said Andy, "but they wouldn't let us buy you a beer. You'll have to get it yourself."

"You want a beer, Steve?" asked Charlie.

"I have one somewhere." Where did I put it? I wandered back to the foosball table, then changed my mind about halfway. Someone could have drank out of it. I didn't want the beer that much.

Charlie waited for me to return. "Gone?" I smiled uncomfortably as I nodded. "Let's get you another one, then."

27

"I think one beer is enough for me tonight. Payday is still a couple of weeks away."

"No worries, I'm buying."

"That's okay. I'll just get some water."

"You can't drink water with pizza."

I balanced being a moocher with depleting the little money I had. Mooching won.

I had to walk up to the bar with Charlie, so the bartender would know who the drink was for. I felt like I was Charlie's date, but I got a free beer out of it.

When we found Charlie's friends they were sitting at one of the tables on the upper level with a large, steaming pizza. Not wanting to barge into their clique, I sat in the chair at the end of the table.

The four of them dove into the pizza. Samantha only ate the crust, passing along the guts to Charlie. I wasn't sure if it was her attempt at dieting, or just a preference. She was trim, but not overly. She retained flesh in the areas most desirable to men.

Noticing I wasn't eating any pizza, Charlie said, "Help yourself. We're all friends here."

I begrudgingly pulled out two dollars from my wallet. The pizza did look and smell good, but....

"The pizza is already paid for," said Samantha. "You can chip in next time."

I bit into the tip of my slice, then slowly worked my way to the crust, relishing every bite. It might be another two weeks before I ate another pizza.

"So, where are you from?" Eating just the sloppy parts of the pizza, Charlie's mouth was oozing with sauce and cheese.

"Seattle."

"I'm from N'Awlins, as is Andy. We went to the same high school, and then roomed together at LSU. Samantha's from Austin, and Christine...."

"I'm from Iowa. It's easy to forget. If I was still there I

would probably be married by now---and pregnant. Farmer's wives raise a lot of children."

"And you are opposed to having children?" asked Samantha.

"I just want to see some of the world before that happens. Most people born in Iowa never leave."

"I always wanted to go to Seattle," said Samantha. "I've been to California a couple of times, but not up to Oregon or Washington."

"It rains a lot there," I responded without emotion. I didn't mind the steady nine-month long drizzle, but others did. I felt I had to make excuses, the weather becoming analogous to obnoxious relatives. "But it stays green because of it."

"I don't mind getting a bit damp."

"It must be great living in New Orleans. All that craziness on Bourbon Street. All that great food."

"I hate the humidity," said Andy. "When I lived there I was used to it, but after living out west, and returning, it feels like I'm in a sauna. Mardi Gras, that's something I miss."

"Do the girls really flash for beads? It's not some urban myth, is it?"

"Oh, they flash." Charlie looked at Samantha. She blushed. "Well, you do."

"But from the way you say it, it sounds like I expose myself every chance I get."

"Mardi Gras isn't the only time you expose yourself," Christine remarked.

"Hotpotting is like bathing. Who wears their bathing suit in a bathtub?"

"There are hot tubs in the Park?" I asked.

"Natural ones," said Charlie. "We'll take you to one soon." If people got naked in them, then soon wasn't soon enough for me. But that meant I also had to be naked, didn't it? It wasn't that I was embarrassed about others seeing me. But when girls were around, especially undressed girls, part of my body had a tendency to contort. I preferred others didn't see me like that. It was like going to the bathroom during one of those sit-down situations.

Christine wasn't finished with Samantha. "So, Mardi Gras and bathing---indoor or out---are the only times you get naked?"

Charlie looked at Samantha. "So, if I dared you to flash in the pub, you wouldn't do it?"

"Now if it was a dare…. But there would have to be some reward involved." Samantha began to lift her shirt. She exposed herself, but only those areas her bra didn't conceal.

Sweat began to bead on Andy's forehead. He did his best to block what was going on. He didn't want to be kicked out of the pub, especially on opening night. "Pull your shirt back down," he whispered as loudly as he could. Charlie laughed. The girls giggled, even Christine, who apparently took pleasure in the self-inflicted discomfort Andy's prudishness caused him. "We can't take you two anywhere."

"Then we should leave. Let's run through the Hotel." Charlie's suggestion didn't even raise an eyebrow. What type of things did these people do?

As an afterthought, Christine asked, "Won't someone care?"

"Probably. But how can something be fun if there isn't the risk of getting into trouble. Let's see how much we can get away with. You coming, Steve?"

Did I really want to get arrested during my first week in Yellowstone National Park? "Sure."

7. TOO MUCH TO OFFER

Charlie ran down the carpeted hallway as swiftly as he could. Andy and the girls chased after him. I lagged behind, being extremely self-conscious of how much noise we were making. One-hundred-year-old buildings had very loud aches and pains.

"Let's race, Steve," said Charlie.

I acquiesced, but hesitantly. Samantha removed the scarf around her neck. She stood in front of Charlie and me with the scarf raised. She waved it around like someone doing the fan dance, or turning letters on Wheel of Fortune. She continued until we were thoroughly aroused---her queue. She dropped the scarf. We charged past her, but were briefly detained when she used her body as a speed bump. With a mild frown, Christine shook her head. It was difficult for me to concentrate on winning, knowing that at any second we would get caught. Uninhibited, Charlie won by two door lengths. "ICE CREAM AND ONIONS!"

A short, angry woman in a fur coat entered the hallway from a room near the finish line. She obviously was wearing the coat as a bathrobe, because the only other noticeable article of clothing she wore were slippers. She was barely able to speak. "DOWNSTAIRS! NOW!" Somehow Charlie was able to retain his smile, which didn't please Martha Devla. I finally recognized the location manager. Embarrassment. Shame. I was going to have to return to Seattle, fired after the first day. I should have stayed in my room.

A security guard was in the lobby. "MIKE!" shouted Charlie. The security guard waved back.

Martha Devla guided us into her office. She held onto the

31

doorknob as she shut the door loudly behind her. "What can you say for yourselves, gentlemen?"

I didn't know what to say. It didn't matter. Charlie was verbal enough for both of us. "We were just having a little fun. No one was around."

"I was." The location manager opened a desk drawer and took out two pieces of paper. "If we had guests in the Hotel there would be hell to pay. Didn't you care that you might be bothering someone?"

"There isn't anyone around yet. If we felt we had to create some mischief, wasn't this the best time to do it?"

Martha Devla began filling out the papers. *Employee Incident Notice* was in bold print at the top. I read about them in the employee handbook. They were like demerits. If an employee got three of them they would be fired. "I know you, Charlie Peterson, but who is this young man you are trying to corrupt?"

My throat was so full of nerves-induced phlegm, I barely choked out, "Steve Harrison."

"You'll be proud to know that you two will receive the first Employee Incidence Notices of the season. I have a drawer full of them. It's usually empty by September. If another disturbance takes place in the Hotel, especially while guests are around, further disciplinary action will occur, up to termination. Do you understand? Now sign these."

I felt like I was signing my own execution. "Now, what specifically were you two doing? It sounded like large mice outside my door."

"We were racing," said Charlie, with a big grin on his face. "If you didn't catch us so quickly we may have also played hide-and-seek." The location manager rolled her eyes.

"Good night gentlemen. I don't want to see you back here. Yellowstone has too much to offer for you to throw it all away." She hurried back to her room, a smile plastered on her face. Either she was happy to be going back to bed, or she was thinking of her own impetuous youth.

Samantha, Christine, and Andy were waiting for us in the parking lot. Andy shook his head.

"We were seen. We were conquered. Simple as that," said Charlie. "Let's go down by the lake. It's so dark and clear tonight. Let's see some shooting stars."

"How can you be so certain?"

"When Charlie's around things like that just happen," Samantha stated.

8. YELLOWSTONE NAMES

Bear warning signs inundated both sides of the ten-foot-wide corridor that connected the employee compound to the Grand Loop Road. I felt exceedingly secure, considering how well trained the bears must be in Yellowstone for them not to go where they weren't supposed to go.

We walked past a wooden sign, *Elephant's Back* boldly heralding the inauguration of our endeavor. One-hundred feet down trail was a sign-in box. A name, a destination, a time, and a camping permit number, if applicable, were requested. I never liked writing down my name. It felt like I was signing away my life. People would also begin to know too much about me.

"So, this is your first hike in Yellowstone, Steve?" asked Andy. He was a couple of inches taller than me, but looked even taller when he was moving. He flopped his arms around like a monkey. Sometimes a trail enabled hiking side by side, but not next to Andy. It was also dangerous to hike behind him if you were going uphill. He kicked up rocks like he was tilling soil.

"This is my first hike, if you don't count walking to the pub last night."

"Walking *home* from the pub some nights might be considered a challenge," said Charlie. "Not sure about getting there. Certainly not something the Hundred Mile Hiking Club would sanction."

"Maybe the Rec Director will make an exception, considering the circumstances." I briefly lost my train of thought as I looked down. The trail's surface varied from damp, to muddy, to wet. I was mostly concerned with the wet parts. I scurried across a log atop a seasonal bog. I leapt from the wooden springboard to a soft spot that left my footprint, and nearly my sneaker.

"You took a particularly scenic route to the pub?" asked Andy. He was in front of me, a few steps behind Charlie. It made my life a lot safer, and drier, learning from my friends' mistakes.

"I bumped into a buffalo."

"YOU DID WHAT?!" Charlie's head looked back at me, but his feet continued forward, into a puddle. He stumbled to keep from getting completely wet. The only thing he prevented was a solitary soaking. Andy and I were both splattered with mud.

We shook off earth's excrement the best we could, then continued the hike. If a person turned around every time he had a mishap no one would get anywhere.

I continued my story. "It was dark."

"We have to give him a Yellowstone name, Cougar," Andy told Charlie.

"Agreed, Bighorn."

"What's a Yellowstone name?"

"It's a nickname we give to Yellowstone employees," said Charlie. "By we I mean those who have already been named. There must be a consensus. And the recipient must agree."

"Bison?"

"What do you think, Steve?"

"Not sure if I should feel proud or insulted."

"Then it's perfect."

"How did you guys get your names?"

Andy was first to answer. "Charlie's done a lot of stupid things, which he's survived, like a cat having nine lives. And there's that tomcatting thing."

"He marks his territory?"

"In a manner of speaking. By the end of the season most of the girls at Lake will be at least given the opportunity to have a relationship with him."

"It would be disrespectful for me to not make the attempt," Charlie explained. "All women are beautiful: blonde, brunette, redhead, black, white, tall, short, hard, soft...."

"What does Samantha think of your...activities?" I asked.

"We have an understanding. She also dates other people."

I shook my head.

"You don't approve?"

"Just debating whether dating that many girls would be paradise or too much work."

"I like to keep active."

"How about you?" I asked Andy.

"I only date one girl at a time."

"I was referring to the origin of your Yellowstone name."

Charlie answered for him by pointing at his nose.

Andy countered by pointing lower.

"How long have you been dating Christine?" I asked.

"I don't know," Andy responded, sounding confused.

"Andy and Christine have a...ambiguous relationship," Charlie explained. "As do many couples in Yellowstone. Uncertainty has a lot to do with it. How intense are you willing a relationship to get with a mandatory separation waiting at the end of the season? And one-night stands here are rarely anonymous. If you don't see the person at work the next day, you'll see them in the EDR that evening."

A half-mile into the hike the trail began to rise. Being out of shape, and unaccustomed to the elevation, I became fatigued. Charlie, not wanting to be detained by anything, pushed me uphill with both of his hands on my back. Feeling guilty, I reached deep within, forcing myself to plod along unassisted. I was in pain, but I was doing it.

When we hit snow Charlie and Andy didn't even pause. Charlie smiled. I patted myself on the back for wearing jeans. I would stay warm. There were footprints in the snow. We used them as stepping stones. After a while we fell into a rhythm. We became football players running through tires. Occasionally we hit a soft spot or missed the template entirely, causing a damp foot to become soaked and cold. My pants began to sop up the melted snow. Those pats on my back became slaps.

The trail gained enough elevation to reward us with spectacular views of Lake Yellowstone. Most of the ice in it had melted, but just enough remained to give a sparkle to the water. It was difficult to fully comprehend a lake so beautiful being twenty miles across. Beauty was supposed to be petite and mysterious. Hidden and arduous to find.

Not paying attention to my exertion helped me climb, but concurrently causing me to miss where I was supposed to step. Snow entered my shoes from the top, and in liquid form through the vinyl sides. Wet feet remained warm if enough body heat was generated. Sixty-degree air could be overcome, but not thirty-two-degree snow. I was freezing. How well was I going to move once my feet became numb?

I expected the trail to end once we reached the top of Elephant's Back. It didn't. In fact, the trail actually began to descend. The snow became deeper. The rim of the plateau bowl had protected the white crystals flawlessly. I no longer had islands of emptiness to fall back upon. I was stranded in an ocean bleached of color. Where was this trail leading me?

We entered a clearing on the elephant's brow. Two log benches were cleared of snow. We sat, taking sips of water, before permitting our eyes to feast on the panorama below. Lake Yellowstone was the backdrop. It covered nearly half the canvas. The water was framed in white, where ice had accumulated along its shore. The mountains across the lake were also white, but just upon their top-knots. The Yellowstone River escaped to the northwest. It passed beneath Fishing Bridge, a mile downstream. Pelican Creek flowed into the lake farther east. The valley at its headwaters was lush, florescent in contrast to the drab lodgepole pine forests so prevalent in the Park. Three clear-cuts scarred the woods below. The Hotel, at the perimeter of one of the clearings, rose to the height of the trees around it, not wanting to be outdone by them.

"How many trees did it take to build the Hotel?" I asked.

"Too many," Charlie answered, no longer his smiling self. "I'm speaking in general. Our old growth forests are becoming extinct."

"But we need the wood," Andy countered. "How can you condemn logging if you sit in a wooden chair, at a wooden table, in a wooden house?"

"I think some logging is necessary, as long as it's renewable, but if the remaining old growth forests are being harvested, logging can't be that renewable. We must be taking more trees than can be produced. We need to use less. We need to recycle. We need to use wood products longer, so we can harvest less.

"When I was in California all I could think about were the boulevards that have replaced orange groves. Pollution has seeped into the Sierras. When I was in Oregon some of the people there spoke about their love-hate relationship with California. They loved the diverse paradise it once was, but hated its people for what they have let it become. Did you know Oregon once had a sign at its border that said *Enjoy Your Visit*, implying spend your tourist money here, but leave afterwards."

"Washington isn't as anti-California," I claimed. "Or as environmentally friendly. We don't have a bottle bill. We aren't charged a nickel for each bottle or can we buy. Litter is more of a problem in Washington. Some of my college friends drove down to the Oregon Coast to participate in its annual litter drive. If you like Oregon so much, why don't you live there in the summer instead of Yellowstone?"

"Yellowstone is unique. I don't think there is a place on earth so diverse of landscape, flora, and fauna. Some places are more beautiful. The Canadian Rockies for one, or even the Tetons. But those places are one-dimensional. To see all Yellowstone has to offer, you'll have to go to half-a-dozen different parks. And there are also the people. Men and women, boys and girls, come from all over the country---from all over the world---to see Yellowstone, and to work here. The Park is a great melting pot, where the things thrown into it aren't required to melt. Most of the people who work here are individualists: free spirits, rebels, mavericks."

"It must be refreshing to live and work in an environment so idyllic."

"Even Yellowstone has its environmental problems---too many of them. Being the first national park, Yellowstone has been the test model. The environment must be weighed against the benefit to the people, and consequently to the almighty dollar."

"But they are trying to let some areas go back to nature. How about the bear restrictions?"

"Many of the restrictions are for safety, not for preservation. Less than a decade ago Grant Village was built, on five spawning streams. Swamp was replaced with concrete. How much wildlife was displaced? Grant Village was so sloppily constructed that its marina is already too dangerous to use. Sidewalks beside it are falling into the Lake. It's an ugly monstrosity, a tumor in the wild."

"How environmentally friendly is Louisiana? Don't people there leave rusting cars in their front yard?"

"Sadly, true," said Andy. "Where we come from people rarely think about the environment. I guess it has to do with having the muddy Mississippi and the swampy Bayou so close to us. It's not unusual to see someone dump toxic chemicals in their backyard."

"Like you dumping that dirty motor oil into the hole you dug in your backyard?" Charlie carped.

Andy looked stone-faced. "You do some things in New Orleans you would never think to do out here."

"That's no excuse."

"No, but it is an explanation."

Charlie dug into his backpack. He retrieved what looked like a mutated telescope. "It's half of a broken binocular. I call it a monocular." He took a quick look through it, then handed it to me. He was smiling again. It made me depressed whenever I saw someone always happy become solemn. Charlie didn't like being that way either. He knew how he could make himself happy again.

I saw trumpeter swans in the Yellowstone River. Across the river the grasses were lush, damp, refreshing. Tires screeched. A horn honked. My eyes attempted to connect an object to the sounds. In the clearing nearest to us, automobiles become insects, devouring the foliage. I passed the monocular to Andy.

After a quick look, he passed it back to Charlie, who plunged it into his backpack. Three black trash bags were pulled out. "Would anyone be interested in doing some sledding?"

We sloshed through the snow to where the trail dropped. It was remarkable how interpretations of conditions change. An hour ago, I used my full concentration to step concisely into the stepping holes, so I wouldn't get wet. Now that my feet were already soaked, and I was heading to a hot shower and dry clothes, I cared more for quickness. The next group of hikers up Elephant Back will have plenty of places to place their feet.

Charlie dropped his bag on the ground. He placed his feet at the far end of it, his butt on the near end. He pushed off, moving slowly at first, but picking up momentum. "ICE CREAM AND ONIONS!" was heard from somewhere down the trail. Andy went next. I followed, just seconds behind him. The trail was getting slicker upon each successive run. Andy was catching up to Charlie, and I to Andy. Charlie leaned in as he went around a switchback. He straddled the lip of the trail, barely staying upright. Andy hit the turn moving too fast. He rolled over the lip, but not completely. I somersaulted over Andy's legs. I didn't even feel the cold. I flapped my arms. I always wanted to make a snow angel.

9. TOURONS

I sat down next to Christine in the EDR. She looked worn and depressed. "How's the bed making going?" I asked her. "And the toilet cleaning?"

"I made two-fifty in tips this morning," she replied, brightening up.

"Is that a lot?"

"Not bad for housekeeping. Waiters and bellhops make that much in...ten minutes."

I glanced across the room to see what entertainment today's lunch had to offer. Two room attendants at the next table were discussing how they liked to watch women eat corn dogs. Christine pulled hers from its stick, placed it on her tray, then cut it with a fork and knife. The two gentlemen grimaced. I laughed. Christine looked up at me and smiled.

"Does it ever gross you out to strip messy sheets from beds?"

"Does it ever gross you out to clean off a plate after someone spits up something on it?"

"It seems worse to handle dirty sheets."

"The only thing I can't stand is when people throw things on the carpet instead of putting them in the garbage can. Sometimes people do leave good things behind: candy bars, pens, books."

We saw Samantha at the beverage station. We waved her over. She sure looked nice in her uniform. On anyone else the mauve blouse over the maroon slacks would look atrocious. On her, the girl next door all grown up. She could make a potato sack look like a cocktail dress. "Tourons can be so frustrating," Samantha said harshly through clenched teeth.

Touron was a combination of tourist and moron. They ask the stupidest questions like: "When do the deer turn into elk?" "Is Old Faithful turned off during the winter?" "Are the buffalo kept in cages at night?"

Samantha screamed silently.

10. CLEANSING TO THE SOUL

I put on a body length rubber apron. There were times it didn't completely cover me, allowing a sample of the scraps du jour to plaster my shirt to my upper torso. Spraying serving spoons were particularly troublesome. I normally let things like that soak, but occasionally I rushed. After getting a mouth full of recycled oatmeal I learned to keep my mouth shut.

Dishes were hot when they came out of the dish machine. I got used to them---eventually---like when I began drinking scorching coffee.

Silverware tended to pile up, because no one liked to clean it. It must be put through the dish machine twice, then sorted. Nothing felt hotter than 180-degree stainless steel.

41

Alice Grunden was the only person who truly enjoyed the dish room. It gave her time to think. She had long, straight, blond hair, and eyes that looked like they were looking somewhere else, even when she was looking directly at you. Beneath her white work shirt, she wore a tie-dyed tee-shirt. The colors leaked through, making her uniform appear on the edge of indecency. "My name's Alice," she said when she first introduced herself to me. "Like in the Jefferson Airplane song."

Alice began taking dishes from the dish machine. She placed them in their appropriate spots, on their proper racks, without pausing. Instinctively she knew where everything belonged in the universe, minute or grand. "Washing is so cleansing to the soul. Each plate, each glass, each bowl is unique. The dish machine washes away the sins committed upon them. It leaves the dishes warm, pure---eager to accumulate knowledge."

The dishes began to pile up. The waitri---the unisex name given to waiters and waitresses---were extremely busy, which meant they were extremely lazy when it came to doing anything that didn't contribute to a tip. When it was slow, waitri and bussers stacked dishes. Alas, the dish drop looked like a dump.

The chaos didn't affect Alice. "All things must pass. We are just a pair of chicken nuggets in one billion sold. Our planet will exist long after we're gone."

In a couple of hours this mess would be cleaned up, but I still dreaded doing it. Do the waitri realize dishwashers must stay an hour or two later than they do, and make a third as much as they make?

There were ways to fight back. When glasses were set in the dish drop right side up, instead of turned over to drain their contents, the dishwashers would tip them over, the tumultuous flow soaking the degenerates. There were limitations to their vengeance. Wine and coffee will stain---even coke---so they only tipped water glasses. If dinner rolls were left on plates, instead of throwing them into the trash, they threw them at the waitri. The same couldn't be said for blueberry pie. At times busser's alley was dirtier than the dish room.

It felt great to get back at the *Front of the House*, but in doing so we got behind. At midnight, the cooks and dishwashers were the only restaurant employs that remained. Music was blasted. Barry Henry, one of the cooks, sang loudly off-key. It was kickback time. We could go at our own pace now. If we wished to get out of there quickly we could jam, but if we wished to coast into the finish line after a hectic day, we were allowed to do that too, if the closing manager didn't have to open the next morning. Food Production Managers have worked in the inferno behind the cooks line and have scrubbed pans smelling like vomit.

Barry came into the dish room with a bucket in one hand. His grease-stained chef's jacket was off. He was black from balding pate to torn hiking boots. He looked like he had been working in a coal mine. "Would you like some beer?" he asked behind an insane grin.

"Now?"

"Why not? Hardly anyone's around, and we're not open. What better way to unwind than to drink some beer?"

I accepted, but Alice declined. "The gain doesn't outweigh the potential loss," she said.

Barry placed a water goblet on the dish drop. He poured the malted beverage from the bucket. "We use it to make beer batter for onion rings. It's flat, but is has alcohol in it." Barry scurried out with the bucket in one hand and glasses in the other.

I took a swig. With the fizz gone, it went down smoothly. It really hit the spot. I took another sip, then set the glass on the floor. I didn't want to tip it over while cleaning the dish drop. And I didn't want to get caught. Barry wasn't exactly an authority figure. Hey, I was almost out of here.

11.   ALREADY PACKED

Nearly everyone was in bed, their own or a neighbor's. I was still pumped up. I was hungry too. I wished there was something more nutritious than candy bars in the snack machine. Sugar only made me more hyper. Why couldn't a candy machine have fruit salad in it, not fruit cocktail, real fruit, ripe and delicious, and stored in their own natural juices? Even having juice in the beverage machine would remedy my craving for something nutritious, then I could chase it down with something more filling--- like a bag of chips. Chips weren't *that* unhealthy. But doesn't a coke sound good after work, and a big, chewy, chocolate candy bar? We were given what we really wanted.

I sprinted downstairs and bought another candy bar. Ryan beat me to it. He put his money in. He made his selection. Nothing happened. He kicked the machine, then tilted it. "I'm not making a very good example, am I? I better put a note on the machine." They were out of Snickers---DAMN!---so I had to buy a Baby Ruth. They didn't put enough sugar in them. It was like eating peanuts, not chocolate. DAMN!

Ryan returned with the note. A wad of tape was stuck to its backside. As his right hand placed it on the machine his left fist slammed it into place. "I'm ready to get away. Sure, I've only been here two weeks, but the first two weeks being an RC feels like two months. I bought a hiking book today. It describes all the trails in Yellowstone. Want to take a look?"

"Sure."

Ryan's books consumed more space than all of my stuff

combined. He put on one of his two-hundred records. It sounded like Diana Ross in *Lady Sings The Blues*, but squeakier. "Do you like Billie Holiday?" Ryan asked.

"It sounds eerie. Every time I hear dead people sing I get goose bumps."

Ryan retrieved the hiking book from atop his backpack. I had never seen a pack that large before. Sure, I had seen them on television and in stores. Mountain men and safaris used them, but not real people. It was nearly as large as Ryan. "I already packed it. I'm so anxious to go camping. I even have some food in it. I bought some of that dehydrated stuff that costs a fortune. I guess it's worth the cost if it reduces the weight of the pack."

"Doesn't Yellowstone supply us with sack lunches?"

"They're not hot. I like at least my dinners to be. And maybe some coffee in the morning. A sandwich can't be that appetizing after climbing out of a cold tent."

"I don't like the idea of paying for food twice. Six dollars is deducted from our pay every day, even when we don't eat it. The juices, cookies, chips, fruit, and sandwiches are appetizing enough for me."

Ryan thumbed through his hiking book. "This is where I want to go on my days off next week. Four lakes are connected by a ten-mile long trail: Cascade, Grebe, Wolf, and Ice. Can you imagine, hiking to four lakes in two days? Grebe Lake looks like the best place to camp. Are you still scheduled to be off Tuesday and Wednesday?"

"As far as I know."

"So, do you want to do this?"

"Sure."

The girl who sat next to Magnolia at the orientation came into Ryan's room. She gave Ryan an exaggerated hug. "This is my fiancé, Kathleen O'Neel."

"So, you're spending your last single summer together in Yellowstone?"

"We don't plan on getting married for three more years," Kathleen clarified. "That's when Ryan will graduate from law school."

"If I get accepted."

"You could have applied to more schools."

"I chose Yale because we're from Connecticut. Our families still live there. Once school begins I won't be able to spend that much time with Kathleen."

"We would be able to spend some time together. You could have applied to another couple of schools."

Ryan grimaced.

"When he gets accepted we'll have to leave---early."

"I signed an employment agreement."

"That only means something if you want to be rehired."

12. EVER WONDER IF YOU MADE A MISTAKE

There were some mornings I just hated getting up. I went to bed at a decent hour, but that was part of the problem. When I went to bed before I was sleepy my mind wandered. Lately I had been thinking about washing dishes. I even dreamed of washing dishes. I would wake exhausted, as if I had actually washed those damn dishes. It was better to go to bed when I was tired, even if that time never arrived.

The only good thing to wake-up to was Iris Douglas. She was scheduled to work just five days a week, but she seemed to always be serving meals in the EDR. She was in her mid-fifties. Considering how genuinely affectionate she was with people she had to have a herd of grandkids that loved her dearly. Her looks, build, and politics were unremarkably typical for her age and gender. She stood out by her warmth and general concern. She was a bartender who served breakfast instead of alcohol. She listened to anyone who wished to talk.

I ordered everything on the menu: pancakes, scrambled eggs, sausage patties, and home fries. I took the menu board's word, because the Plexiglas protecting the food was once again fogged from the steam tables. Considering how bent some of the pans in it were, it didn't surprise me that some of the steam would escape.

"Iris, do you ever wonder if you made a mistake coming out here, to Yellowstone?" Iris listened rather than advised, which was why people came to her. People didn't really want someone else to decide for them. They wanted someone to be supportive as they constructed their own conclusions. "I remember being so excited when I received my employment agreement. I would be able to play for four months---no deadlines, no obligations, no pressure. But when I got here, even while traveling here, I faced new obstacles. Life is never a vacation. I first had to push myself to drive those long miles to Yellowstone. Then I had to adjust to a new roommate. I spent hours deciding what to do. From brochures, it sounded like recreation was in abundance, and all planned out for us. I'm all alone here. I can't relax. I'm always on my guard. At least at home I had my own room to crash in. I can't even do my laundry when I want to. There are times I wait over an hour for an empty washer. And we must do our laundry twice a week, because we weren't given enough uniforms."

"Your food is getting cold, dear. Would you like to go hiking with Harry and me after dinner tonight?" Harry was Iris's husband, and Lake Yellowstone Hotel's assistant location manager.

"I would love to." Suddenly, I became cheery.

"Why don't you invite some of the people you know along. We will begin at the Storm Point trailhead at 7 p.m."

"Thanks."

47

"Why don't you help yourself to some fresh fruit salad in the breakfast bar. I added some strawberries this morning."

"Thanks."

13. DRENCHED IN HAPPINESS HEAT

Word of the hike spread. The Storm Point parking lot was completely full. Some of the people I recognized. Most I didn't. Charlie, Andy, Samantha, and Christine accepted my invitation. The five of us were at the tail of the herd. Fortunately, the trail wasn't particularly dusty. Iris and Harry were at the head of the procession. I thought I should force my way to the front to be with them, but I decided I could wait half an hour to talk to them, when we were expected to arrive at Storm Point.

Indian Pond was just beyond the trailhead. The Absaroka Mountains, on the eastern border of the Park, were reflected in the water. Sky blue icing trimmed with whipped cream lapped at their feet. The temperature was beginning to drop, but it was still warmer than cool. The sage was particularly fragrant. I felt completely at ease, wishing I could stay in this precise spot the remainder of my life.

A frisbee was thrown up and down the swarm. Hikers became obstacles, making play more challenging, and hiking more dangerous. Bison patties were bonus obstacles. A typical dropping measured a foot across. Being wet when they hit the ground, they splattered and spread. Bison, being herd animals, left their debris in bunches, like a mine field. It wasn't easy catching a frisbee while watching the ground. To maintain our interest, we made the game increasingly challenging. Andy could barely be seen behind a natural hedge. Like a surgeon with a scalpel he meticulously sliced the flying disc between two curtseying limbs. The arrival of the disc was so unexpected, I barely had time to jump at the forty-five-degree angle necessary to prevent the disc from landing in Lake Yellowstone. I landed sloppily on one of the aforementioned bison residues. I was coated to the top lace of my boot and splattered up to my knee. My friends laughed. I couldn't blame them. I shook my foot like a dog trying to dry off. Lugees of damp manure exploded from the limb. I tried to rub the remainder off in the grass, but too much had already soaked into the canvas and leather. My right foot felt twice as heavy as my left.

The trail fell into a dense forest, leaving Lake Yellowstone behind. At the base of the depression was a bridge over the memory of a creek. Charlie and the girls ran across a log. Andy didn't want to risk the five-foot drop. I was a bit more daring. I hit a damp spot. I stumbled, but did not fall. Charlie used the tip of the log as a spring board. His gymnastic dismount was perfect.

The trail took a hard left, contouring to meet Storm Point. The forest became denser. We had to walk single file. Fallen trees looked like a giant's game of pick-up-sticks. We heard a rustling ahead. A BEAR!? "Did you see the moose?" echoed down the hiking chain. It was gone by the time I was close enough to see it clearly. One of the disadvantages of hiking in a large group.

The trail entered a clearing. Small sand traps were scattered in the rough grass. Something large had been caught in one of them. Bones were half buried and copiously scattered. It was like we were in a graveyard that had survived an earthquake. "Bison come here to die," Christine announced ominously. "One day they will rise from the grave, during a new moon, when no one can see them."

At the end of the fairway, the land dropped. Beyond a sea of sand was a rock outcropping. A half-dozen large rodents laid jelly-like on the rocks. One couldn't help but wish he was in the animals' place at that moment. Their bodies were drenched in happiness heat. As the humans walked by, two of them lifted just their heads. The gravity of pleasure held them too tightly for a more pronounced reaction.

I sat next to the rocks to empty my shoes of sand. After the sand was dumped, my feet began to feel gritty, itchy, even sticky. I hated when a new pair of shoes got sand in them. They became ruined in a sense, because I could never get all the sand out.

A piercing peep was discharged from the rocks. "So, the beasts do mind that we are here," I announced.

"It's our chatter," Samantha hypothesized. "How would you like it if you were sprawling in bed, and someone walked by, stayed awhile, and even talked to you?" Why were there subliminal connotations whenever Samantha spoke? Maybe it was my mind that was in the gutter. I knew I would have a difficult time keeping quiet if I saw her sprawled in bed.

Charlie whispered loudly, "Let's be considerate. Just because some of us may feel a little superior towards the marmots doesn't mean we can't respect them, and their wishes." Charlie walked away from the rocks as quietly as possible. We followed, some of us stoically, in respect for Charlie, others snickering.

The human flock scattered when it reached the rim of the lake. Some hikers sat on the grass atop the bank, where they watched waves crash below them against boulders. Seagulls scattered at each exclamation. The most civilized of our group walked aimlessly down the lake shore, hoping to find something that would entertain them. The remainder, the most adventurous and self-motivated, completed the journey to the tip of the cape. It was concealed by a bushy stand of trees. For those who were courageous enough to venture through the jungle, they were rewarded by a rocky platform from which to view the lake from three elevated directions.

Christine removed a bottle of wine from her backpack. "Scat. I forgot the cork screw."

"Let me." Charlie put the bottle between his legs. He reached for a short, sturdy stick beside him. It was about half an inch in diameter. With the stick between his right thumb and forefinger, and his left hand on top of the bottle, he pressed against the cork. Slowly, the stopper was forced into the bottle. Pop. Kerplunk. Charlie handed the bottle back to Christine.

"I guess we're going to have to drink it all now," she said. The bottle was passed around the circle of friends as we watched the lake below. Many miles away was an island. It was just large enough for five people to get stranded on for a while. Hazily seen on the southern horizon were the south and southeast arms of Lake Yellowstone.

When it was my turn to drink, Christine shrieked. "WHAT ARE YOU DOING!?"

Samantha smiled wickedly. "You're going to make a girl very happy one day."

Christine blushed. "I didn't mean *that*. I was just worried about him adding contaminates with his tongue."

"I can't help it," I pleaded. "That's just how I drink, to control how much wine comes out."

"Don't apologize," Samantha chuckled. "I just wish more guys took the initiative to practice...their craft."

Charlie was uncharacteristically quiet. He was focused on something at the base of the promontory. His face transitioned from a quiet, hidden anger, to a twisted, grotesque fury. He looked like he was going to kill someone. He dropped down to the water, then bent down to pick up something. Then something else. He took his time returning, using the slow excursion to vent his emotions. In his raised hands, he held a beer can and a potato chip bag. "WHY DO PEOPLE COME *HERE* TO DO THIS?! There must be some place left on earth that remains untouched, that remains pure." Charlie placed the litter in Christine's backpack. He immediately began to cheer up. Sight unseen, sight forgotten.

Charlie's commotion attracted the Douglases. Seeing that everything was all right, they opted to quietly join the youngsters. Iris easily joined our conversations, but Harry was quieter. He spoke only when something truly interested him.

Harry was a couple of generations older than most of Yellowstone's employees, and even a decade older than Iris. He barely missed out on going to World War II. To appease his conscience, he declared he would rebuild post-war America. As a building manufacturer, he built the nation from the foundation up. His commitment in his self-proclaimed *paid vacation* earned him a promotion to Assistant Location Manager after only one year. He took pride in doing a job well done. Nothing could rile Harry more than talk about inefficiency.

"I'm not going to make any money at all this summer," Samantha declared. "I barely work thirty hours a week."

"We do worse than that in housekeeping," said Christine. "We're so overstaffed we're going to four-day---six-hour---work weeks."

"Some people are already thinking about leaving," said Andy.

"Overstaffing compensates for attrition," said Harry. "But at the cost of losing some of the best employees. They're the ones who can get another job easily. The company isn't looking at the long run. Look what happened to American industry. If no one lasts the season or comes back next summer, we'll have a staff of greenhorns every year. Experienced personnel are a company's greatest resource."

"Being in Yellowstone is such a wonderful experience," said Iris. "The scenery and wildlife are incredible. It's sad that work and money must get in the way."

"At least managers get paid a salary," I said. "They get paid for forty hours even if they work thirty."

"They're far more likely to work fifty---sixty at the beginning and end of the season," said Harry.

"It comes down to one question," stated Christine. "Are you going to return next year?"

Harry perused the Lake, then his wife. His smirk was answer

enough.

It surprised me how many people were down on the small beach west of the point. There was a much better view from where we were sitting. And these rocks had to be more comfortable than that gritty, semi-moist sand. People lay on the beach like they were sunbathing. It was nearly dusk, so it couldn't be that warm.

I walked to the beach to investigate. I sat on the ground, nearly burning my behind off. I bounced on my butt until I landed on a more moderate patch of sand. No longer painful, it still felt like I was sitting on California sand mid-afternoon.

"This is the life," said Andy, who, along with Charlie, Samantha, and Christine, had followed me to the thermal beach.

"It makes you want to go hotpotting," said Christine, "and camping. To become one with all the wonders of the wilderness."

The warm sand heated more than epidermises. Charlie and Samantha were going at it on the sand. It was said that women became more desirable when they were hard to get. Samantha had become uncharacteristically elusive. She put sand on her face, causing Charlie to get a mouthful when he kissed her.

Andy began to worry. "We better get going. It'll be dark soon." Charlie and I went with Andy, but the girls wished to spend a few more minutes in bliss.

"It's not safe for two girls to hike alone in the dark," Charlie stated. He was fearless when it came to his own safety, but practically paternal when it came to others.

"We have a flashlight." Samantha flashed it in Charlie's eyes to show that it worked.

"Don't stay too long."

Nature had set a trap and sunset was the bait. The return route was less interesting, but more direct. There were as many fallen logs as standing ones. Most of the logs that had fallen across the trail had their midsections removed. Those that hadn't made the return to the trailhead entertaining. Charlie thought it would be fun to run the obstacle course as fast as he could. Andy and I had to follow or be left behind. We jumped over, crawled beneath, and zipped around the never-ending logs. Visibility was becoming a problem as darkness overtook us, creating greater uncertainty in traversing the course. We had become characters in a video game, dodging and weaving at the last second.

The dragon at the end of the maze was in the form of a creek. Our means of crossing was a partially submerged bridge. We could rush the bridge, wading ankle high through the corrosive liquid, thereby weakening, but not killing us. Or we could try to leap across, saving ourselves completely. But if we fell we would become soaked, incurring enough damage to kill us. Charlie jumped across without hesitation. His back foot hit a partially submerged plank, which slapped the water noisily. Somehow, he was able to hold on, reaching the far bank after a couple of more steps.

Andy slowly pussyfooted across. The bridge sank a couple of inches lower when he reached the spot that was cracked. The water ate him up to his ankles. He sprinted the remaining ten feet. His abrupt acceleration caused him to slip. He slid back down to the bottom. He dropped to his hands and knees to catch himself. He crawled back up, this time permanently. The bottom of his shorts was wet where the water snuck in a blow.

I had been debating how I wanted to cross. Andy's demise made the decision for me. I backed up, giving myself plenty of runway space. NOW! I ran ahead as fast as I could. I panicked a step from the brink. Charlie and Andy were watching me. I couldn't chicken out now. I looked at where I must land. I chiseled the information into my brain. I was halfway across the creek before I left the ground.

"ICE CREAM AND ONIONS!" Charlie bellowed.

Only two-hundred yards of sage lay between us and the parking lot. Even under open skies it was difficult to see. The sage smelled wonderful. The temperature had dropped quickly in the last hour, slapping the vegetation into agitated aroma. The odors penetrated my body, creating a symbiotic relationship with nature. A whoosh of a car driving past the parking lot woke me from my stupor.

We waited for the girls. And waited. One by one the cars in the parking lot filled, then left. Iris and Harry walked up to us. "Waiting for the sunrise?" Iris asked.

"Christine and Samantha are still out there," I said.

"There was a grizzly spotted here two days ago," Harry warned.

"I'm going to look for them," said Charlie.

"I'll go too," I seconded.

"I'll wait here," said Andy, "in case they return before you do. We don't want them having to look for us."

"Would you like us to notify the rangers?" asked Harry.

Charlie shivered. His enthusiasm for mischief had forced too many unwelcome associations with the park authorities. "Let's wait. If Steve and I can't find them in an hour, *we'll* contact the rangers."

"Good luck," said Iris. The Douglases got in their truck and drove off.

"I SEE A LIGHT!" shouted Andy.

Charlie whispered, "How about us paying them back for worrying us."

"How?"

"Follow me, and keep quiet." We tiptoed a hundred feet down the trail. Charlie laid down to the right of the trail. Andy and I dropped to the left. "Shhh."

The light wobbled its way towards us. A murmur of conversation became nearly intelligible by the time the girls were upon us. Charlie leapt up. Andy and I followed his lead. Charlie growled. The girls shrieked. It took just a second for them to realize who the monsters were, but that second must had seemed like an eternity to them. They beat Charlie with their fists. He lost his footing. The three of them tumbled into the darkness. It didn't take any investigation to determine the instigator. Charlie screamed. The girls giggled. If only I could be a bad boy like Charlie.

14.   LIKE A SENTINEL

I was drawn to Willy's bed, specifically his Playboy. Even if the tantalizing parts were concealed, I could use my imagination. But…the bible was beside it. Not just beside it, but partially on top of it, like a sentinel guarding it. I was curious. What parts of the bible did Willy not agree with?

I heard Willy unlock the door. I rushed back to my side of the room.

Willy noticed my swimsuit. "You're not going to do something foolish, like jumping into Lake Yellowstone? Five minutes in that forty-degree water can kill you. God didn't give us life so we may haphazardly take it away."

"I'm going to Boiling River. It's a thermal spring. Want to come along?" Did I really want Willy to tag along? Too late now.

Willy smiled. "A Yellowstone baptism? A man ought to recommit every couple of years. Thank you for providing me the opportunity." Willy frowned. "You wouldn't happen to have another swimsuit I could borrow? Unless it's one of those clothing optional situations?"

"It's a very public place. Not sure tourists would appreciate your lack of attire. Or we theirs."

Willy smiled.

"It's a river, not a swimming pool," I added. "Shorts ought to suffice."

15. TOO HOT AT THE BRINK

I learned from Iris: If I wanted to have fun I would have to create the fun myself. She was kind enough to invite me along on her hike, so I decided I would reciprocate by inviting people along on an outing of my own design. What better way to get acquainted with people than in a natural hot tub. I invited everyone I knew, but only Charlie and his gang, Alice, and Willy, accepted my invitation.

The only vehicle large enough for the seven of us was Charlie's van. I was concerned Charlie might not approve of Willy and Alice. "The more the mightier," was his reply. "The more we weigh the less likely we will tip over when we round curves."

"I brought some music." Willy handed Charlie a cassette, which he jammed into the van's cassette player without looking at it. Expecting light Christian Rock, I was flabbergasted when Donna Summer flooded the vehicle. As Willy sang along, Samantha and Christine danced in their seats.

Andy had enough. He ejected the tape after the first song.

"You don't like Disco?" I asked him.

"Andy only listens to classic rock," Christine explained. "Led Zeppelin. Rush."

"I like U2," Andy added, sounding defensive.

"But not Talking Heads or the B-52s."

"They're not really rock bands."

"I was kind of surprised you like Disco," I told Willy.

"Donna Summer is a born-again Christian," Willy responded.

"It didn't sound like Christian music to me."

"She did record some Inspirational music, but it wasn't as good as the stuff she recorded in the 70s and early 80s."

"Aren't some of the lyrics non-Christian?"

"Who are we to judge?"

Samantha leaned forward to reinsert the cassette. Willy returned to singing. And Samantha and Christine back to dancing. Alice remained silent and immobile, content to live within her private world.

Charlie's focus was on the road. He abused all acceleration opportunities. Curves did not slow him down. He passed two cars before returning to his lane. Three cars. Five?

The only obstacle that was able to halt Charlie was a bison jam. Not a bread spread. It was a traffic stoppage. A hundred or so of the animals slowly crossed the road, backing-up cars for half-a-mile in both directions.

Charlie smiled. "It looks like we're going to be here for a while."

Andy, Christine, and Samantha climbed on top of the van. Charlie handed them his retractable speakers. He turned up his 100-watt stereo. Charlie joined his friends on the roof with a bag of chips in one hand and a soft drink in the other. He set them down and grabbed Christine and Samantha. The three of them begin dancing. Andy was content enjoying the view and snacking. After a single dance, the roof crew collapsed into sunbathing position. Before I could decide if I wished to join them, traffic began to move again, but slowly. Motor homes didn't have much get-up-and-go.

A campground on wheels was great for the person who owned one. For those who didn't, it was nothing but a slow-moving vehicle with old, slow reacting people driving them. I was confident there was a stick of dynamite attached to their speedometers. The driver of a motor home couldn't be that inconsiderate or passive aggressive? They were obligated to drive below 30 miles per hour, to not only save themselves and their passengers, but the other

58

vehicles around them.

We arrived at Mammoth just before the EDR closed. We ate hurriedly, wishing to ration what remained of the daylight soaking in steamy splendor. I didn't even have a second bowl of chocolate ice cream.

Two unmarked parking lots, where the 45th parallel crossed the Mammoth-Gardiner Road, was our destination, one on each side of the road. After finding the closer, eastern parking lot full, Charlie crossed the highway to slum in the overflow facility.

With towels in hand, we walked in sneakers and flip-flops down a packed, dirt trail. The Gardner River flowed swiftly on our left. A crooked tree reached across the river, a two-foot wide kink two feet up its trunk. Charlie stepped up onto the notch and clutched the tree above and out from him. He looked down into the running water. "It can put you into a trance. Nature is art, art in motion, physically and chronologically." He jumped off and rushed ahead of, like he was trying to make up for the time he wasted. The sun was just barely above the hills on the western rim of the canyon. The golden-green straw-grass between the trail and the river was already in shadows. The scent of warmth was blown into our faces every time a light breeze swirled past us.

We saw people before we could hear them, the cascading water muffling them. Steamy mist muted perception. This may have been happening, but it was just as likely a dream. The path passed above an abundance of bikinis. After the initial shock of seeing so many semi-nude women, I realized half the people in the water were middle-aged. I liked middle-aged people, but I didn't particularly care to see them in bathing suits. Some of those breasts the ladies had would have killed me if I got hit by one. The men, well, many of their bellies hung substantially over their shorts. Because men's trunks were predominantly of the boxer variety, every time they bent down the plumber smiled.

The trail wrapped around the Boiling River's subterranean origins. The river smoked like it was magma. Emerald green grass cuddled its banks. A sign warned of not disturbing the algae. Another warned of possible viruses in the water. A third, that the hot springs was going to close at 8:30.

We stripped off our outer gear on the gravel at the brink, where the hot water of the Boiling River mixed with the cold of the Gardner. It was remarkable the diversity of the female bathing suit. Alice wore cutoff jeans and a tie-dye tee-shirt. Samantha, a skimpy bikini. Christine, a one piece. Charlie, Andy and I wore boxer swimming trunks, with Charlie wearing a pair that was conspicuously too small for him. It was painful to look in his direction. Willy wore shorts.

Charlie led us into the water. Is was too hot at the brink, so we had to scuttle across the boulder retaining wall between the two rivers. Some of the cold water leaked over. More appetizer than entrée. The water was still too hot. After five more steps, the water became too cool: too much seepage. Another two, just right. We stepped into the water. Too cool again. Then just right. With calculated precision, we followed a narrow comfort zone. In the grotto at the convergence of the two rivers the water mixed more thoroughly, allowing us to spread out.

Willy got an eyeful as he scanned his surroundings. A couple was kissing beside a steamy waterfall. A second couple was playing tag. The torrent at the brink kept pushing down a woman's top. A handful of people lay contentedly on their backs in shallow water in very unladylike and ungentlemanly positions. Willy began to share his biblical perceptive with a woman who was in a bikini top a size too small for her. She was in the midst of flirting with every man present. She had started at the far end of the wading area and had nearly worked her way back to shore. Willy attempted to modify her moral convictions. She smiled silently. Her feminine wiles must have worked on him, because he became content. He gave-up soliciting and lay on his back.

Charlie disappeared. If it was anyone else I would have been concerned. He reappeared in a cacophony of water droplets. He smiled, then went back under. His head was fully submerged, but his legs dangled on the top of the water. The current of the Boiling River was strong enough to keep him outstretched. The payback was the effort required to stay anchored. Charlie had to hold onto a boulder at the bottom of the river, which was the reason his head was under.

I also made the attempt. I clutched too small of a rock. It and I were carried downstream. My second attempt was more successful, but the water assailed me so strongly I had trouble holding my breath. Through gasps I enjoyed the free-fall rush. It felt like I was skydiving while taking a shower.

I joined the girls. It was easier talking to them when they were submerged. "Do you have Yellowstone names like Charlie and Andy?"

"Sam's is Diamondback," Christine shared.

"Like the rattlesnake?"

"Suave, but hazardous," Samantha explained. "I also have this tattoo on my back." Which she proceeded to reveal by sticking her butt out of the water in my direction. There was a petite diamond there, but my gaze was focused a tad lower.

Christine blushed, then shoved her friend, all of her, back into the water.

"And you?" I asked Christine after the three of us recovered.

"Rabbit," Christine answered without enthusiasm.

"Because she's so cuddly and cute." Samantha squeezed her for emphasis.

I moved a couple of feet closer to the cooler water. There should be a sign warning girls in bathing suits from doing that.

"Who else has a Yellowstone name?" I asked.

"We call Martha Devla, The Wolf," said Samantha.

"And she actually approved of that?"

Charlie and Andy joined us.

"She loves Yellowstone and all its peculiar traditions," said Charlie. "She was honored to be compared to such a noble animal.

61

An animal that once roamed Yellowstone---before they were killed off by the government. She's vicious, but she's also protective of her young. Who else?"

"THE DOUGLASES!" shouted Christine. "Harry is called Rainbow Trout, because of his love for fishing and the colorful shirts he wears while doing it."

"Harry is so...professional."

"People can take work seriously and still have fun off the job," said Samantha. "Charlie is very solemn at work---he's completely directed."

"Iris is called Mama Bear...."

One by one we wandered off to enjoy our solitary pleasures, which meant finding the water temperature and pulsation to fit our individual needs. I saw Alice disappear underwater. I worried when she didn't reappear a couple of minutes later. She had been very quiet and reclusive since we arrived at Boiling River. Maybe she was depressed. I rushed to where I last saw her. She reappeared nearly on top of me. "Are you all right?" I asked her.

"Just doing some exploring." She brushed her long blond hair back, and squeezed it between her fingers. She leaned back to stretch, revealing she wasn't wearing anything beneath her top---tie-dyed body paint. She smiled when she noticed me looking at her. "I found a cave behind the waterfall. Do you want to see?"

"Yes."

"Take a breath, and watch your head." Alice took me by the hand. "One, two, three." We were underwater. After a few strokes, she pulled me back up. We were in waist deep water with just enough head room for us not to have to crouch. The world beyond was opaque through the waterfall.

Alice thrust herself against me, bringing her lips to mine, then attacking. Her body began to gyrate. I was afraid of what the friction might do to me. Alice was breathing as deeply as I was. I shuddered, but continued to use my torso to caress her. Alice also shuddered. She gave her body time to calm before she opened her eyes. She beamed. "The universe has many hidden niches. This is one on the physical plane. There are many more within."

16. LOVELY SHOPS

"I can't understand why more people don't want to go camping," Ryan complained.

"We found three people who did want to go," I retorted.

"But we must have asked a dozen."

"It's their loss."

Ryan and I perused the Yellowstone topographical map for the umpteenth time. "See those lines?" asked Ryan.

"No."

"That absence means we have very little elevation to climb. A thirty to forty-pound pack may feel light in a dorm room, but it will feel like a moose on our backs after climbing a thousand feet. I'm so excited about camping. Every day since I received my Yellowstone contract I have thought about backcountry camping. And tomorrow is the day. It's feels like Christmas Eve."

Kathleen O'Neel walked in. She gave Ryan a severe hug and then a light kiss on the cheek. "Do you still have tomorrow off?" she asked. "I think we should go shopping in Jackson. I heard it has lovely shops."

17. AN INTELLECTUAL DISCUSSION

A log blocked the trail---more psychologically than physically. It was easy enough to step over or around. It was purposely placed there to dissuade motorized vehicles. The trail had once been a road, and the park service didn't want tourons to challenge that decision.

"It's to keep the bear's in," I said, trying to impress the three girls accompanying me. None of us---myself included---had ever gone back country camping, so I had to be the strong, protective male. Magnolia thought the joke was funny. Rebecca was frightened. Daphnee just wanted to see a bear. A *Strong Bear Warning* sign had been at the trailhead. Everyone was edgy.

I loved the variety in women. Magnolia was fleshy feminine beneath L.L. Bean's best. Daphnee, her average built roommate, was outfitted from a second-hand store. Their lodgepole thin suite-mate was dressed in a tank top and jeans. She had to be very uncomfortable in the mid-afternoon heat. Beautifully exotic. Tom-boyish cute. Comically lanky.

We were a motley crew hiking down that oversized trail. Two parallel troughs, once gouged by tires, were gradually becoming less precise as irregular footsteps ruptured their boundaries. None of us were prepared for camping. We had two overnight packs amongst the four of us, and one of those was borrowed. The bought and paid for pack looked like it had been used in World War One. It was fatigue green, with less support than a daypack. The cloth straps dug into Daphnee's shoulders. Magnolia had the good pack, because it's owner, like a majority of the males working in Yellowstone, had a crush on her. It was an internal frame pack, as sleek and well packed as her body. Everything was hidden inside---contoured, sleek, mysterious perfection. Daphnee's army pack, having straps, not zippers, had clothing and food poking out every which way. Rebecca tied her sleeping bag to her daypack. The contraption looked ungainly, but it worked. I also wore a daypack. I carried my sleeping bag on a strap around my neck.

The girls needed a break after the first mile, not quite a half hour into the hike. They weren't accustomed to carrying so much weight, especially so awkwardly. "My bones hurt," Rebecca declared.

"Like there's not enough flesh to pad them, to provide a buffer for the pack," Daphnee clarified. An epiphany about one's weight during a hike, but not in the direction expected.

Magnolia frowned, making her even more adorable. Blemishes on a girl like Magnolia became beauty marks, accents, accessories. "I wish I could say that. I apparently have a surplus, because I don't feel anything."

"You look fine to me," I said.

"Thanks." She smiled at me appreciatively as she instinctively ran her fingers through her long, beautiful blond mane.

The trail followed a creek intermittently. Occasionally the two merged, making travel wet if detours weren't made. A swifter, but more hazardous route was on top of fallen logs. Leaping became more complicated when twenty pounds followed a second behind you. Leap. Slap. Stumble. Daphnee was the only girl who followed me across the wooden archipelago. It was difficult for me to keep my eyes off her. Her florescent green shirt was a beacon. It seemed so out of place in the pastels of the forest, yet its proprietor was the only one who followed me. Daphnee had a wonderfully pensive, yet internally joyous face. I tingled whenever that joy leaked through. I had to keep reminding myself to keep my eyes on where I was walking.

We took two more breaks during the next hour. We should be seeing Grebe Lake any moment now.   The trail narrowed to one rut. No longer were we in the safe confines of a road. The forest closed in on us. The trail dodged through it like it was being chased. Right. Left. Up. Down. We believed a bear would leap at us around the next bend, or a lion, or a tiger. OH, MY! All that worrying---half sincere---accelerated our fatigue. After ten stressful minutes, we had to take another break.

"LAND HOLE!" Daphnee exclaimed.

"We're not on the ocean," said Rebecca.

"I said land hole, not land ho. I see water ahead."

Our fatigue vanished, now that the end of our journey was in sight.

On the brink of the lake a sign directed us to our campsite. It and the other five were found along a counter-clockwise circuit around the lake. The girls looked up at me like children who must spend yet another day without food. "Our campsite is just a little farther," I reassured them.

"Which campsite do we have?" asked Rebecca.

"Number six." A chorus of groans. "The ranger said it was the best one."

The trail circumferencing the lake was soggy. We attempted to circumvent the worst of it by crossing logs, but the logs gave out before the water did. We tiptoed atop tufts of grass in a never-ending glistening delta. Most tufts supported our weight, but a few sunk partway into the liquid, soaking the sides of our boots and sneakers. As our footwear became more saturated we became less cautious. Before we were able to climb up to dry land----which occurred between campsites two and three---we no longer made even a pretense to remain dry. We sloshed through and stomped, striving to get one another wet.

Every time we passed a campsite the girls looked at me accusingly, sighed, then walked lethargically by.

We removed our shoes as soon as we reached camp. We

poured out the water, then wrung out our socks. We placed them on branches to dry. No one thought to bring an extra pair of shoes. The girls put their wet shoes back on, but I remained barefoot. I hated the feel of wet shoes.

I snatched an apple from my pack and began munching. Daphnee and Magnolia joined me. Rebecca timidly watched. "Aren't you going to eat?" I asked.

"I'm worried a bear may be attracted to my food."

"Steve will protect us," said Magnolia.

"We're probably miles from the nearest bear," I assured her.

After finishing our snack, we decided to build a fire. Having damp feet was always a preamble for building a fire. The fallen timber around the campsite had already been taken. We left our packs at camp and set off to collect wood. I retched as I put my soggy shoes back on. Rebecca joined me as I went farther counter-clockwise around the lake. Magnolia and Daphnee bushwhacked away from the water, a preventative measure to not re-saturate their footwear.

The lake was unspectacular except for the region that Rebecca and I were now in. In lush abandon, lily pads flowed into lake grass which flowed into dense lodgepole pine. The foliage followed us up the drainage for a few minutes, ultimately giving up after it was unable to sway our resolve.

Rebecca had a wonderful habit of always smiling when she spoke to someone. It was nice enough having someone pay attention to you when you spoke to them, but when they displayed bliss at every word you uttered, it felt like you were the most important person in the world. We talked of trivial things. The mood was what mattered. Perfect, but mercurial. Perpetual, but on the precipice of collapse. Living within a moment that there was no guarantee would return.

A fallen tree provided us with more wood than we would possibly need, but instead of heading back to camp directly, we continued on, towards Wolf Lake. We were too close to turn back now, especially with the pastel illumination of pre-dusk and its accompanying refreshing temperatures.

Wolf Lake was about a quarter the size of Grebe Lake, and possibly because of that alone it felt more isolated. The bigger the better was attractive for crowds, but petite originality was more welcoming for the individual. There were two campsites along the lake, and neither were occupied. They were too far in, too far from humans and humanity.

Two arms reached out from the lake to the runoff stream. They were too wide to jump, requiring wading to cross. Rebecca took off her jeans. She had also taken off her shoes, but that detail was of little importance---to me. She was halfway across before I recovered enough to follow her. Having a girl partially disrobe in front of me was much rarer than crossing a stream. We crossed the other arm, then followed the trail into the woods. Rebecca continued to carry her pants in one hand. If she had been wearing a swimsuit underneath I wouldn't have been so affected. Underwear wasn't that different. In fact, in most cases it covered more. It was the idea of seeing something you weren't supposed to see. Breaking down barriers was sometimes frightening, but always exhilarating.

I was worried it would get dark soon. We turned around after seeing a waterfall.

After we re-crossed the two streams, Rebecca continued to carry her jeans. We found our wood pile, then picked up as much as we could carry. Travel slowed. Rebecca began to drag her feet. As it got darker I became more impatient waiting for her to catch-up. Once I began moving again, she immediately fell ten paces behind me, but never more, not even when I sped up.

A fire was already blazing when we returned to camp. Magnolia smiled wickedly upon seeing Rebecca's lack of attire. "So, did you two have a good time?" Daphnee looked disappointed. Both girls neutralized after Rebecca put her pants back on.

Daphnee removed a can of pork and beans from her pack.

"CRAP ON A BISCUIT! I didn't think to bring a can opener."

"Let me see it," I said. I slammed my pocketknife into the aluminum top. The metal was soft enough that I was able to carve an opening wide enough for a spoon. Charlie would have been proud.

Daphnee looked embarrassed. "I also forgot to bring a spoon."

"We can use the plastic knives in our sack lunches," said Magnolia.

Daphnee placed the beans on the edge of the fire. "I thought we could use a hot meal after hiking."

As the beans warmed, we ate ham and cheese sandwiches, red delicious apples and barbeque potato chips.

An intellectual discussion began. Rebecca read from Cosmopolitan Magazine: "Sex and Romance in the Eighties: A Readers' Poll. Where is the most romantic place to have sex? **A)** in a soft, warm bed. **B)** in a lush meadow beside a bubbling brook. Or.... **C)** beside a roaring fire on a shag carpet? Magnolia?"

"I don't think there's any place I would rather be at the moment than here, but I also like to be pampered. I choose **A**, the warm bed."

I felt a bit embarrassed. I didn't even think girls discussed things like that. To their boyfriends, perhaps, but not to one another, not in mixed company.

"How about you, Daphnee?"

She looked at me, looking as uncomfortable as I did. "I think the specialness of a romantic situation makes it exciting. If you kiss the same way in the same place at the same time every day it may get boring. Uniqueness is what I enjoy. I think I would have to choose **B**, in a meadow."

"Steve?"

"Me? I'm not a woman. Isn't this a woman's magazine?"

"Come on, Steve," cooed Magnolia. "Where do you prefer to do it?"

69

"Let me think about it."

"How about you, Rebecca," said Daphnee. "Where would you prefer to have sex?"

"Can I choose all of the above? To be honest, it would be more like none of the above. It's been so long I think I may have forgotten how. If I had to pick I would choose **C**. I love the heat. I melt beside a fire."

"Steve?"

"The beans are boiling?"

"They can wait. Where would you want to do it?"

I blushed. I looked at Daphnee. Firelight danced on her pleasantly at ease face. Her cheeks were radiantly anguished cries of needed stroking. It would be incredible if we could lay in the grass together, just the two of us, by the lily pads....

"Steve?"

"**B**, I guess, in the grass," I burst out, nearly shouting.

"Question 2: Do you like a man with a smooth or hairy chest?"

"Steve?"

"The beans." Now how was I going to pick up the can? I found two sturdy sticks. I snatched the can out of the fire like it was a large eggroll between two chopsticks. The can wobbled, but it didn't tip over. We each appropriated as many beans as we could fit on top of a plastic knife. The can lasted many rounds.

"I hope everyone has room for a bit more." Magnolia pulled a bag of marshmallows out of her pack. We used the two bean sticks, and two others, for roasting. Marshmallows caught on fire and sticks burned, but we thoroughly enjoyed ourselves.

I removed a black trash bag from my pack. "We need to put all the food and trash in this bag. I had to see a filmstrip before the rangers would give me a camping permit. We have to hang our food so bears won't get into it. I should have thrown the rope over the food pole before it got dark."

"I'll help you look," Daphnee volunteered.

With flashlight, rope, and black garbage bag in hand, the two of us headed in the direction the food pole arrow pointed. Silently we searched. We were afraid if we spoke bears might be attracted to the sound. "There it is," Daphnee whispered.

"I don't think this rope will be heavy enough to go over."

"Why don't you tie something to the end of it. A rock...or a stick."

"Good idea." I wrapped the rope around a short, but stout branch. Daphnee shined the flashlight up at the fifteen-foot high pole. The stick hit the pole, but didn't go over. "WATCH OUT!" We ran into the woods as the branch thudded to the ground. The stick fell out of the rope on our second attempt. On our third, we were successful. The rope pulled tightly as the stick slowly fell towards the ground. Its momentum was spent three feet short. I untied the stick, attaching the end of the rope to the garbage bag. I pulled it up within a couple of feet of the pole. The other end of the rope I tied to a nearby tree.

"It's so beautiful out here," said Daphnee, looking at the stars above us. Her passion brought out a longing in me.

"A year ago, I never would have dreamt I would be in a place like this," I shared. "It's not that I didn't think I would be here, it's that I never even thought about things like that."

"Sometimes things change for the better."

I noticed Daphnee studying my face in the moonlight. "Do you sometimes wish life remained simple, like when we were kids? So full of wonder, yet safe, someone always watching out for us. Why must we work eight-to-five jobs fifty weeks a year?"

"So we may eat."

"But we are eating, aren't we? Even four miles from the nearest road. How many extras do we need? I just graduated from college. I should be going to interviews, but I wanted to have this last fling before I was trapped in reality."

"I still have two years left. I enjoy school, but it will be difficult to return after a summer here."

71

We looked at the universe, the darkness, and each other. We were quiet. We allowed nature to speak.

"Listen to the crickets," she said.

It was becoming too intense for me, more stressful than fun. I either had to make a move or…. "Let's head back. Rebecca and Magnolia are probably getting worried."

We found them in their sleeping bags. The fire was at their feet. "This heat feels great," Rebecca cooed. Their shoes were between the bags and the fire, to help dry them overnight. Daphnee and I joined the girls. We placed our bags at opposite ends of the line of sleeping bags to balance them beside the fire. It was unlikely we would get romantic this evening, but I still would have liked to be close to her.

"What's that?" someone asked shortly after we were all settled in.

"It's coming closer." We heard a rustling in the undergrowth, about 100 feet away, in the direction of our heads. The girls ducked into their sleeping bags, but I had to turn around and look. If I was going to be eaten I wanted to know by what. The animal was bulkier than a deer. It slumped past us without stopping, coming as close as 50 feet.

The girls slowly retreated from their hibernation. "What was that?"

"A bear. I think," I replied. "I couldn't see it clearly." The girls shivered, even Daphnee, who wanted to see a bear.

"Do you think it will come back?"

"No. It must be making its nightly rounds. It probably won't come by this way again until this time tomorrow. Anyone in the mood for a ghost story?"

I had trouble sleeping. The ground felt like concrete. I used my coat as a pillow, but couldn't form it into a comfortable shape. What if the bear had attacked?

I woke, which meant I had slept, but I didn't remember

when. My entire body ached. "What's that smell?" The girls were still sleeping. The morning was bright, beautiful, and fragrant. Maybe a poor night's sleep was satisfactory payment for waking up to this. The air was so fresh, except for that stench. I sat up. Rebecca's sleeping bag was smoking. "REBECCA!" It took a minute for her to orient herself. When she did, she yanked herself backwards, away from the coals.

"It's supposed to be fireproof," she said.

"It is," said Daphnee. "It didn't catch on fire."

Rebecca climbed out from her sleeping bag and assessed the damage. "It melted."

"That's not the only thing that melted." I pointed to the fire. Rebecca had also pushed her shoes into it, severely warping them. One of them even had a hole melted through it.

"What's all the racket?" said Magnolia, just waking-up. Her arboreal tresses looked like they had been in a storm. It could have been worse. No one brought a mirror.

18. RANDOMLY SHUFFLED

"Aren't you going to tell us where we're going?" I asked Charlie.

"Don't you like surprises?"

"The last surprise I had in the dark was bumping into that buffalo."

"But didn't it make your pulse race?"

There were about a dozen people piled into Charlie's van. I didn't know all of them, or even how many there were. It was dark. Charlie thought it would be exciting to drive down a side road without lights on. I couldn't see a thing. I hoped Charlie could. He entered a picnic area. "Everyone out." We emerged like grain from a silo. I could finally stretch. Ah, fresh air.

"Hold one another's hand to form a chain. I'll lead." I was the third link. Samantha was between Charlie and me. Daphnee was behind me. I tried not to squeeze her hand too tightly. I was already afraid every step, every breath would give me away. We descended at an extreme angle. Someone fell, behind me, but the support from the chain prevented him from hitting the ground.

As we leveled off we left the forest. Stars filled the hemisphere. Lake Yellowstone was on our left, the crescent waxing moon illuminating the gentle ripples. We walked upon waves of sand, our shoes filling at each trough. A small pond appeared in front of us. And Lake Yellowstone beyond it. We were on a peninsula, the shallow pool occupying nearly half of it. A handful of lodgepole pines rose from the sand, their scarcity making them look like savannah shrubbery.

"Gull Point," Charlie announced haughtily. He pulled a blanket from his backpack. He set a bottle of wine, cheese and crackers on it. He picked up a stick partially buried in the sand and rammed the cork into the bottle with it. "Now we have to finish it. Help yourself to the refreshments." The bottle was passed around. Not everyone drank, leaving enough for two revolutions.

"You know," said Christine. "If a grizzle entered this peninsula we'd be trapped, especially with that pond there. We could always swim. Is it black bears or grizzly bears that can't swim? Or is it neither? This peninsula may be a trap. Charlie was a little too mysterious, wasn't he?"

The group scattered after the food was eaten, but only in a radius of twenty feet or so from the blanket. There were as many eyes watching the woods as there were looking at Lake Hotel across the Lake. Some people played at the edge of the water. Others looked at the stars. The moon was partially concealed by clouds, causing the backside of the clouds to glow.

I looked towards the darkness, to the distant southeast arm of the Lake. What went on there when the lights were turned off? Wouldn't it be wonderful to someday be in that void---that secret wilderness? "Are you tired of having girls around?" a voice asked me from behind. I quickly spun around. IT WAS DAPHNEE! I didn't even hear her approach. The sand must have muffled her footsteps. I didn't answer, compelling Daphnee to clarify. "I'm talking about the camping trip. I don't want to smother you with my feminity." I couldn't tell in this lighting, but it looked like Daphnee was blushing. "I mean, you must have felt out of place spending so much time with three girls. I felt so sorry for you when Rebecca took out that Cosmo. I often feel out of place, so I know how it must have felt for you."

"No, I actually enjoyed myself. What man wouldn't be happy spending the night with three beautiful women."

"So, you wouldn't mind if a girl went hiking with you again sometime?"

Maybe Daphnee did like me. If I was going to ask her out I better do it now. I may never get up the nerve again. "I was planning on doing some sightseeing at Old Faithful on Tuesday. Would you like to tag along?"

"If you really don't mind. I'll try to keep up better this time."

"This will be more of a stroll than a hike. We'll take our time so we can enjoy the scenery." And so I could spend more time enjoying Daphnee.

"It's getting chilly," said someone.

"Let's form a friendship huddle," Charlie suggested. "The body heat will keep us warm." I was eager to wrap my arms around Daphnee, but she was randomly shuffled to a spot across from me. She looked at me and smiled, then looked down at the sand. On a cool night like this, nothing would had been better than cuddling with.... No. I was being foolish. I was reading too much into her desire to spend time with me. She was new to the Park, like me, and hadn't yet made many friends.

19. THE MALL

Kathleen intercepted me as I headed to Daphnee's room to retrieve her. "Do you know where the mall is? The one in the park? Jackson is too far away, and I need a new dress for the dance tonight."

I tried not to laugh. "I don't think Yellowstone has a mall."

Kathleen looked shocked, then panicked. "What am I going to do?"

"Why did you come out here? You don't seem that...outdoorsy."

"Ryan wanted to work in Yellowstone, so I agreed to go with him. I love him, so I want him to be happy. It's just for a few months."

20. MORE FUN WATCHING THE PEOPLE

Had we accidentally left the Park? Ahead was an interchange. Nope. A sign mentioning Old Faithful pointed to the exit. Old Faithful must be like New York City. Neither was representative of the greater region, Yellowstone or the United States. A two-lane one-way road took me past additional exits for

Old Faithful Inn and Snow Lodge. Not knowing where to go or what to see, I let the road to guide me. It terminated at Old Faithful Lodge's parking lot. The old-timers say Old Faithful is one large parking lot, and here was the proof. Ten-thousand people a day see Old Faithful Geyser spurt, and there had to be a place for all of them to park. Blacktop absorbs heat, making it several degrees warmer than the air temperature. It was barely past noon, and it was already sweltering.

"I almost don't want to see Old Faithful erupt," Daphnee declared. "It's such a common thing to do."

"But it will still be exciting," I added.

"Yes. That is why we must see it anyway."

A boardwalk corralled the geyser in a semi-circle. Steam escaped from a vent, but less than half of the boardwalk was unoccupied, so we still had some time before the next eruption. An experienced performer preferred a full house. The opening act was a troop of marmots. Every time a scrap of food was dropped they scurried from their hiding spots under the boardwalk, grabbed the morsel, ate it in front of the crowd, then hurried home. "Those marmots are strange looking," I commented. "Their balding heads make them look like monks."

"I think it's because they rub their heads against the bottom of the boardwalk."

"I think you're right. I wonder if Darwin would have been able to figure that one out?"

The boardwalk began to fill up. Each eruption brought up to 2000 people to watch. It was more fun watching the people. Cameras on tripods. Children on shoulders. Everyone was making their prediction when the geyser would spout. All eyes were forward. No one wanted to miss even a second of the entertainment, not after driving a thousand miles to see it.

Water bubbled out. People shrieked. Cameras clicked. The water column dropped. Murmurs of disappointment. Camera lenses were re-adjusted. Children were re-adjusted. A column of water shot up this time. Click. Click. OOOOO! Again, the water column dropped. Additional murmurs of disappointment. "Was that it?" someone asked. The voice became an exclamation in the silence of anticipation. A third column raced towards the sky. This time it didn't fall back down to earth until it rose 150 feet. Clickety, click, click. HURRAY! The column collapsed after two minutes. Congratulations were exchanged. There might not be another sight like that for another...70 minutes. The crowd dispersed.

The trail to Geyser Hill began off the right terminus of the boardwalk. The asphalt trail descended to a wooden bridge over the Firehole River. A sanctuary from the civilized horde and the chaotic middle earth belches. Cool, crisp, clear water flowed beneath us. Lush grasses and lodgepole pines were abundant. If it wasn't for the people walking by every minute, it would have been a great place to take a nap. Downstream, the banks were yellow, red, and orange, created from algae-laden thermal runoffs.

One-hundred feet beyond the bridge was the spur trail to Observation Point. It was only half-a-mile to the top, so we considered doing the hike on the way back. An additional one-hundred feet returned us to a boardwalk, to the threshold of the Geyser Hill loop.

A scene from Dante greeted us. Steam billowed through sulfur laden air. The boardwalks appeared temporary, facades to entice, brittle portals to Satan's crib. We traveled clockwise around the loop, wishing to see views of the Firehole River and Old Faithful Inn immediately. What was better, to eat your dessert first or last? The Inn was America's largest log cabin. It was constructed during the winter during the Teddy Roosevelt administration. There must had been some hardy men back then.

On our left, a depression named Anemone filled with water. When it was completely full it spurted many feet into the air. As quickly as it filled, it drained, making a gurgling sound, like the last two seconds of a toilet bowl emptying. We resumed our journey, but retreated when a couple eagerly waited next to the supposedly sated geyser. A depression behind the depression filled, then spouted. We left the geyser once again, to be startled a second later by an unnamed geyser spouting on our right. We were in a thermal minefield. Every ten yards another geyser or hot spring appeared. My favorite was Heart Pool, named for its resemblance to an anatomically correct human heart. Red algae framed its border and run-off stream.

"Where should we go next?" asked Daphnee.

"You know this place as well as I do."

"Let's head up to Observation Point. We'll be able to see the entire area from up there."

The elevation gain was just 250 feet. We made it to Observation Point in fifteen minutes. The accommodations consisted of boulders to sit on and a fence to keep people from falling off. A crowd was reforming around Old Faithful geyser, so Daphnee and I waited the fifteen minutes it took for it erupt. The geyser looked better from up there, maybe because the people around it looked like ants, and ants were more environmentally friendly than people. The insects scattered once their god had been abated.

"There's more stuff downstream," said Daphnee. Steam rose sporadically along both sides of the Firehole River. Flame-hued runoffs became a chicanery of flowing magma. Steam also built within me. Simultaneously, we looked at one another. The contact became too intense. I either had to break it or reach out. A couple walked up to the overlook. The abrupt interruption caused me to temporarily lose my balance on the boulder I was sitting on. I recovered, then laughed.

"Let's take the long way back to the geyser basin," I said to Daphnee. The long way was past Solitary Geyser, which was half-a-mile away, but similar in elevation to Observation Point, keeping us above the geyser basin.

Solitary Geyser bubbled up from a pond. It lasted just seconds, and it was only four feet high, but I still liked it, because of its uniqueness. If I had a choice of either being a large geyser in a geyser infested area, or a small geyser in its own secluded meadow, I would emphatically choose the latter.

Back on the boardwalk, Boiling River was fifty feet to our left and was being thoroughly utilized by both bison and elk. They were sunning and grazing along its lush banks. I expected one of the beasts to fall through the thin thermal crust. None did. They were either smarter than they looked or damn lucky.

At a crossroads, a small geyser called Sawmill shot out water in staccato bursts. We ignored the detour and continue north, past an inactive Grand Geyser. We were captivated by Beauty Pool. It was liquid rainbow, never ending.

A fleeting moment of insanity overwhelmed me. I considered comparing the thermal pool to Daphnee---vocally. I considered, but didn't follow through. I wasn't that bold---or uninhibitedly spontaneous.

We smiled at one another and moved on. We crossed a bridge over the Firehole River. Giantess Geyser was sleeping, but not Grotto. Water spewed in all directions from the Swiss cheese stone.

"Grotto's my favorite," said Daphnee. "It spits out what it wishes to say in no set pattern. It says what's on its mind." I now wished I would have said something. Was that the moment, the one opportunity I had to transform our relationship into something more than hiking buddies?

The trail merged with a bike path. A minute later we took a spur trail on the right to Riverside Geyser. It erupted every twelve hours, but the next prediction was just five minutes away, so we waited. The crowd in the viewing area indicated the geyser hadn't gone off early. Fifteen minutes later water shot out at us from a cone across the river. It lasted more than five minutes. It was more impressive than Old Faithful. It made the journey to the large parking lot worth the price of a quarter tank of gas.

After crossing the Firehole River once more, we climbed a

boardwalk to a railed deck overlooking Morning Glory Pool. It looked similar to Beauty Pool, except it was more cavernous and its blues were more dominant. Coins were in the pool, even with a sign warning of the damage they could do next to it. Daphnee began to cry.

I wanted to put my arm around her, but couldn't. My feelings for her were too intense. "What's wrong?"

"I once threw a coin in. I was only five at the time. I didn't feel guilty then, but…. Will you ever forgive me?"

"Of course. I know you would never do something like that now."

"I don't want you to be my friend unconditionally. If I do something heinous I want to be judged by it. I don't want to be taken for granted. I want to earn people's respect. How can I truly be appreciated if my personality and actions don't factor in?"

A dirt trail took us to the top of a hill overlooking numerous thermal pools. We walked past many of them on our way to Biscuit Basin.

Steam smothered us as it blew across the boardwalk. After passing through it, the fresh air felt as refreshing as air-conditioning. On a hot summer day. Sweat dripping from your body. Covered in dust. After mowing the lawn. On a steep bank.

Midway down the boardwalk loop a trail branched out to Mystic Falls. "Shall we?" I asked.

"It's only a mile," Daphnee responded. "Let's do it."

The trail was un-remarkable until it paralleled a creek. I sighed with contentment. Daphnee was on one side of me and a lush, clear creek was on the other. Sun danced in a wind-controlled kaleidoscope. Mystic Falls formed a veil as it splashed onto rocks. We sat on neighboring rocks far enough away from the downpour to not get wet.

"Do you miss being in a city?" I asked Daphnee.

"Sometimes. Humans are a social animal, and a major part of society is civilization."

"What do you miss the most?"

Daphnee was quick to answer. "The theater. Concerts. I love live entertainment. It's so spontaneous. The people are real. They're not third generation edits. What do you miss the most?"

It took me longer. Restaurants? Stores? "I miss my apartment. It was in a dorm, but I could cook my own food at the time I wanted to eat. I could watch TV, or read, or listen to music without interruption. I had more freedom. My apartment belonged to me."

"Should we go back the way we came, or head to the overlook?"

"I don't like to repeat myself. Let's make the hike a loop."

The trail took us to the top of the falls, then up and up, utilizing numerous switchbacks. By the time we gained 500 feet, Mystic Falls could no longer be seen. We moved away from the creek through a small canyon, eliminating any view we might have had. A half-mile later we broke into a clearing and to a spectacular view of Biscuit Basin below. A wooden fence gave token protection to prevent a sheer fall. Steam rose from numerous locations to the south. A geyser was erupting. "Is that Old Faithful going off again?"

After eleven miles of hiking, water just didn't hit the spot. Back at Old Faithful's version of civilization we entered the Hamilton General Store. Often shortened to Ham Store. Sounding like *hamster*. We bought lemonades from the fountain. Tingling. Tart. Cold. Paradise.

A trip to Old Faithful wouldn't be complete without visiting the Old Faithful Inn. The main door was ten feet high and six inches thick. Where else would giants live than in a log cabin the size of an auditorium? Odors of burning wood permeated the place. The stone chimney had openings on all four sides, but only one of the fireplaces was being used, it being nearly seventy degrees outside. An enormous pendulum clock swayed halfway up the chimney. Above two tiers of balconies, catwalks climbed eighty feet to the ceiling. Everything was constructed from logs.

I returned to my dingy white-walled room, wishing that I lived in a log cabin. I had few expectations about Yellowstone, but one of them was the rustic nature of its lodging. If I wanted to live in a dorm I could go back to college.

21. IN BETWEEN THE TWO

Knock. Knock. "Who is it?" a feminine voice answered back, laced with greeting and sweetness. It had to be Magnolia.

"It's Steve. Is Daphnee ready?"

"She's in the bathroom. Why don't you come on in and wait. The door's unlocked." Magnolia was still in bed. As I entered the room, she pushed herself up into a sitting position against the wall, which acted as her headboard. She was wearing a teddy, with a front view of a lion ready to pounce plastered against her chest. The only light in the room was sneaking in along the perimeter of the flowery curtains, beside Daphnee's bed.

"Come sit on my bed and talk to me, Steve." I felt doing so would betray my commitment to Daphnee. Internal at this moment. But that meant something. Magnolia patted the bed. I couldn't be rude. I sat very stiffly near the foot of the bed. "Will you go on a hike with me tomorrow, Steve?"

"I have to work tomorrow."

"But not the entire day." Magnolia's smile grew so large I became afraid it might decapitate her. Her blue eyes twinkled like sun upon snow. She rushed from her bed to the window. The back of her teddy was the back of a lion, tail and all. And boy could she wag that tail. The teddy was just barely long enough to cover her. As she bent over Daphnee's bed to open the drapes she exposed her yellow underwear. She slowly walked back to her bed, doing the best she could to hold back her excitement. The curves beneath her teddy kept on shifting, like an earthquake constantly ripping apart earth's contours and re-distributing them. She sat down beside me in the middle of her bed. "Why don't we see the sun rise from the top of Elephant Back tomorrow? The sun rises across the lake. It'll be phenomenal."

Daphnee walked into the room. Her face drained of all expression after noticing Magnolia and me on the bed together.

"Will you come with us to see the sunrise tomorrow, Daphnee?" Magnolia pleaded.

"I don't know."

"It will be a lot of fun."

"I don't want to impose."

"I'm going to tickle you until you agree." And she did. Magnolia chased Daphnee around the room. They fell onto Daphnee's bed. Why do guys enjoy seeing girls wrestle one another? Was it because two girls wiggling and clutching was better than one? Guys could imagine themselves with either girl, or maybe even in between the two.

Magnolia continued the onslaught until Daphnee yelled, "ALL RIGHT! I'LL GO! And I just made my bed."

22.   SAME THINGS IN DIFFERENT WAYS

The ride down from Dunraven Pass felt like being on a roller coaster. In addition to the road being windy, it was also in dire need of repair. Every few feet a pothole jumped out at Daphnee and me. A clever driver could maneuver around many of the indentations, but in doing so he was forced to cross the center line. Motor homes were additional obstacles. They were continuously pulling in and out of turnouts half their size. Tourons were attracted to rumors that grizzlies frequent the meadows below.

Daphnee had her body halfway out the window. "I don't see any," she complained. After a pothole had nearly knocked her out of the car, she sat back down.

Shortly after the road leveled off, traffic stopped. Cars were parked on both sides of the road, limiting through traffic to one lane. "Let's investigate."

We joined a mob across a meadow. "What's up?" Daphnee asked a man looking through a telephoto lens atop a tripod.

"There's a bear up a tree."

We walked a bit farther, then stopped when we saw the black bear. There were still people in front of us, so I wasn't scared of our proximity to the bear. Some of the idiots were even directly beneath the tree. The bear was asleep on a branch. It rested on its belly with its legs hanging down. It was larger than a cub, but not fully grown. A teenager? We took its picture, then left it in peace, to its warm, late-morning nap. If only everyone else would do likewise.

Roosevelt Lodge greeted us on the periphery of rolling sage. It was the least developed location in the Park, with just forty cabins, a small restaurant, and horses for hire. The latter I smelled as the Lemon pulled into the parking lot. The location was named after Teddy Roosevelt, this area of the Park being his favorite. The major disadvantage of living at Roosevelt, excluding it being so isolated, was its policy of four employees to a cabin. Maybe living in a dorm wasn't that bad after all.

The trail began on the Stagecoach Road. In addition to tours, stagecoaches were also used to transport guests to and from breakfast and dinner cookouts. The eleven o'clock coach passed us on the dusty route. It was open on the sides with benches arranged longitudinally. Basically, bleachers on wheels, but from a distance it looked authentic. Dust was thrown into the air, some of it rising above our heads. Cough. Gag. It took more than a minute for the haze to clear. We had to waste some of our precious water to clean the grit off our faces. Just walking caused the dust to be kicked up two feet. So, a cowboy's bandana was more than a fashion accessory.

The road ended at the cookout. Two employees in western attire cleaned the half-a-dozen picnic tables beneath a gazebo.

A trail began north of the cookout. We crossed a grassy field, still wet in a few places. We were careful to use the plank bridges to keep from getting wet. After a quarter of a mile the trail entered a narrow valley dotted with deciduous trees---a rarity in Yellowstone. A lazy stream carved its way through what looked like a wild apple orchard, without the fruit.

"I would love to live here," Daphnee announced. "I've always dreamt of building a house in a place like this. But what's even better is this place belonging to everyone."

The trail dropped without hesitation. In five minutes, we lost three-hundred feet of elevation. On our right was a stagnant shale cascade. Loud peeps drew our attention. MARMOTS! A dozen of the beasts were sunning themselves on the rocks. Occasionally their pleasure overwhelmed them, and they had to let the entire world know.

The trail dropped an additional three-hundred feet. The valley became a narrow canyon. If a bear met us in an unfavorable mood we would have nowhere to escape to. A third drop brought us within sight of the Yellowstone River. The water vehemently etched its way through fifty feet of granite.

A final leg brought us down to a steel suspension bridge. A thick wire mess prevented people from falling, but it was still unnerving to look down at water screaming though the stone gorge. I was halfway across before I noticed Daphnee. "Aren't you coming?"

"Give me a minute. Heights scare me." Daphnee slowly

walked across, looking straight ahead, both her arms stretched to their fullest, enabling her to touch both sides of the fencing simultaneously.

"That wasn't too bad now, was it?"

"I have to go to the bathroom."

"Scared the crap out of you?"

"I really need to go."

"Go then. I'll wait."

"It's easier for a guy. There's nothing to hide behind here."

"There's some woods up ahead. Can you wait a few minutes?"

"I guess I'm going to have to."

The sun was directly overhead. At this time of day, the trees providing partial relief. Daphnee returned with a smile on her face. "I feel much better. For some reason, I didn't think I would have to go during a day hike. I'll remember to bring toilet paper next time. Nature provides poor substitutes."

The shade was brief. We dipped into sage again. Less than a mile away was a row of trees. "That must be where Hellroaring Creek is."

Halfway to the water Daphnee stopped. She turned towards me. She looked ill. "Are you all right?" I asked her.

"I hoped it was just breakfast, but the feeling has returned. I feel nauseous, and I have a headache."

"Do you want to rest awhile?" I became concerned. What were we going to do if she couldn't make it back on her own? In the movies, the hero carried the fair damsel. I wasn't as strong as Hercules, and Daphnee didn't weigh 80 pounds. It just wasn't going to happen, especially not uphill.

"Let me just rest a minute, so I can collect myself. I think the sun is what's bothering me. That in conjunction with the elevation. The sun is supposed to be more intense at higher altitudes."

"We better head back." DID DAPHNEE HAVE HEAT STROKE!? What were we going to do?

87

"I can rest under the trees beside Hellroaring Creek. We are too close to turn back now."

Daphnee washed her face, legs, and arms with a bandana. She made a remarkable recovery. I spent the time exploring the creek. I crossed it on stepping stones. I re-crossed it via a suspension bridge that was much smaller and less stable than the one over the Yellowstone River. It swayed with every step. The protection against falling was a waist-high rope. I returned to Daphnee, and ate lunch. Although she was still a bit nauseous, she ate a little. She needed to retain her strength to hike the five miles out and the more than 1000 feet up.

"I love it out here," she declared. "It's so natural. How the world should be. I think my favorite part of hiking, and camping, is being self-sufficient. I loved bringing my own stuff to Grebe Lake, and surviving on it. Nature is so beautiful. It should be caressed with our presence, not mutilated. As the saying goes, *leave only your footprints behind*."

"My favorite part of nature is the cleanliness of it. I would rather eat a grape I drop in the mud than eat it off a table in a restaurant. Cities are so dirty. They stink. Did you know breathing the air in Mexico City is like smoking two packs of cigarettes a day?"

"That's why I like spending time with you. We enjoy the same things, but in different ways."

Daphnee crossed the small suspension bridge with me with minimal hesitation. Either she was becoming more comfortable with heights or her ambition to experience adventure trumped any phobia she might have. The campsite on the other side was trashed---by hooves, not vandalism.

Something jumped into the water, then something else, then dozens more. A HERD OF BUFFALO WERE CROSSING THE CREEK! Daphnee and I could either go farther from the trailhead or...we could run back onto the bridge and scramble to its belly. Some of the buffalo---bison---crossed directly below us. One even looked up at us. We were just a few feet above the beasts.

Exhilaration far surpassed the mild trepidation. After five minutes, it was all over, except for a few stragglers upstream. We made our escape. We found our backpacks along the shore, undamaged. We were lucky. A couple of bison had been within a few feet of them.

The trip up was uneventful. If any 1000 foot plus climb could be called so. Our shirts were soaked by the time we returned to Roosevelt.

The Lemon stalled near the top of Dunraven Pass. It too hadn't adjusted to the elevation. I re-started it. It went ten yards, then stalled again. We were stuck half a mile from the top. I looked behind me. No cars coming---yet. I coasted backwards to a turnout. Daphnee didn't shriek, but she did close her eyes. I started the Lemon, then turned around. I drove to the bottom of the incline, to get a good run at it this time. I caught up to a car that was going too slow. I was going to stall. "DAMN!" It pulled off. WHEW! I hit the gas, steadily making my way to the top of the pass. I was going a little too fast for the curves, but I didn't want to lose my momentum. I made it over this time. It was now my turn to go to the bathroom.

23. FAVORITE PART OF THE DAY

Daphnee and I walked quickly, but silently, in the cool, damp early morning haze. The only people up were cooks and waitri preparing for breakfast. It was beginning to get light, but the sun would not rise for at least another half-hour. Elephant's Back Trail was dry now. I was glad Magnolia decided to sleep in.

The morning coolness and the exertion of hiking were finally waking me up. I no longer felt like a zombie. It felt awkward not talking. Maybe Daphnee would think she was not worth the effort, or worst, that we no longer had anything in common to talk about. I had to be careful what I said. I didn't want to come across as being silly or naive.

Daphnee was first to speak. "I like getting up early. The air is crisper. There are fewer people. It's like the world starts over each dawn. This is my favorite part of the day."

"Dusk is my favorite part of the day. It may still be warm, but it's no longer hot. The sudden temperature drop is refreshing, like getting out of a shower or tub. The lighting is soft---soothing. Sunsets are spectacular, especially over Lake Yellowstone. But isn't it nice to sometimes sleep in, like what Magnolia's doing?"

"Magnolia has enough comforting. Don't get me wrong, I like her, but no one deserves that much attention. I'm tired of guys coming around all hours of the day to ask about her. No one ever asks about me."

"I'm hiking with you right now, and she's alone in bed."

"How do we know that? I'm sorry. I didn't mean to say that. You may get the wrong idea about her. The attention she receives isn't reciprocal. She isn't a girl who gets around, if you know what I mean. I shouldn't be going on this hike. Magnolia invited both of us, but I have a feeling if I didn't come into the room when I did she would have only invited you. I'm sorry if I spoiled your date with her. She is very beautiful."

"I didn't intend it to be a date." At least not with Magnolia. "I just wanted to see the sunrise. I was happy when you agreed to come along. I'm especially glad now, with Magnolia deciding to sleep in. You are here. She isn't."

Daphnee hiked up the switchbacks without stopping. I was impressed. "That thin air in Colorado has done miracles for you."

"Not as thin as the air here. I haven't done much hiking there. I had nature all around me, yet I embraced the city life. Because Fort Collins is a university town, it had a lot to offer. I didn't know what I had been missing until I came to Yellowstone.

I'm going to buy topographical maps as soon as I get home." It made me sad to think of Daphnee and the rest of my friends leaving me in a few months. I might never see any of them again.

We sat on one of the log benches and waited. We were only a foot apart, but it felt like miles.

Lake Yellowstone was covered in a fog frosting. The forest below us was clear now, but only a portion of Lake Hotel. Wisps of mist floated by, ghosts fleeing from the oncoming sun. A ray of light burnt through the opaqueness. Beginning from the shore nearest to us, the fog cleared from the lake in one fluid motion, like a barber clearing shaving cream from a chin. Once the sun had completely risen above the Absaroka Mountains, the lake relapsed into veiled obscurity. The lake had the desire, but not the belligerence to emancipate.

We had to run down the mountain to get to work on time.

24.   WAVE TO THE CAMERA

I preferred to travel with Charlie---and Daphnee. But I got off work at four, and someone had to get to the Jenny Lake Ranger Station in Grand Teton National Park before it closed. Charlie, Samantha, Tony, and Daphnee got off at two. Andy and Christine also got off about four, so the three of us travelled together, in the Lemon.

The Teton Range was seen for the first time on a flat stretch just inside Yellowstone. I had a difficult time staying in my lane. The mountains were that distracting. The highest peak in Yellowstone was barely 11,000 feet tall. The Tetons had several over 12,000 feet, including the 13,770-foot Grand. The glaciers on the mountains glistened in the sun. The peaks were jagged, textured, a stunning contrast to the smooth, weathered peaks to the north.

We lost sight of the Tetons when we dropped from the Yellowstone highlands into the forested fringes of the Jackson Hole flats. The Tetons reappeared behind Jackson Lake, and in it as a reflection. Their prominence grew when we entered the plains--- grandeur rising from nothingness.

Jenny Lake was more petite than Jackson Lake, and because it was nearer to the Grand, more picturesque. Andy had been to Lake Solitude before, so he was able to navigate without using a map. Christine and I followed him over a plank bridge that spanned the lake's runoff. I had never seen water so clear. Those rocks couldn't be real. Someone must have placed them in the water. Nature couldn't have provided something so perfectly arranged and colorful. At the center of the bridge, a spur led to the boats that took people across the lake, for a fee.

"That's the quick and easy route," Andy declared. "The part of hiking I like best is the hike. Destinations are great, but there's no sense of satisfaction. Awe, perhaps, but awe isn't always earned. I never cut short switchbacks, not because of the potential to cause erosion, which would be Charlie's excuse. I go the long way because I hike for a workout. What satisfaction would there be to be on top of the Grand, if a helicopter dropped you off? I've heard of men getting pectoral implants, because they were too lazy to exercise to create a muscular body. Exercising is as much mental as it is physical, as are the benefits."

The trail was nearly as dusty as the cookout road. The culprits were the same. Flies feasted on the festering green equine feces. I bypassed it by walking on the fringe of the trail. If Charlie was here he would say something about the widening of the trail damaging the terrain. I returned to the center of the trail, cautiously watching where I stepped.

Warm dust coated my legs. They became gray. The dust

began to stick to my sweat. I momentarily felt refreshed whenever I saw Jenny Lake through the trees. What was so wrong about taking the boat across the lake?

My backpacking inadequacies were remedied by purchasing a secondhand pack from someone who left the Park after his anticipated metamorphosis failed to live up to expectations.

The pack dropped to one side. One of the shoulder straps broke.

"I have an idea," Christine announced. She pulled out one of her boot laces and cut off a piece. The lace was long enough that even after the amputation she was still able to retie her boot. The repair was a success. It would have been…inconvenient…to carry a thirty-pound pack on your shoulder for nine miles.

The trail took us over rolling hills on the south side of the lake. A strenuous climb was rewarded with a nice view of Moose Ponds. A moose and her child were actually down there, in the marshy, lush tarns at the base of the Tetons. A trail led down to them, but we choose to leave them in peace. But not before we took photographs.

Traveling north on the western shore, we steadily dropped in elevation until we became level with the lake. We were careful where we stepped. The horse manure had companions in foot-long irregular stones partially embedded in the path. The air became more humid. Ferns flourished. For a moment, we walked on top of the lake, upon flat stones just inches above the water.

A couple of minutes after leaving the lake, the trail forked. Right led to a boat dock: the western terminus of the lake crossing. We went left, paralleling a turbulent---and very thunderous--- snowmelt creek. After climbing a half mile of switchbacks, Hidden Falls fell unabashedly before us. The watery curtain slithered down a one-hundred-foot-tall rock wall, splashing onto boulders, before dribbling into a pool that fed the creek. It wasn't Yosemite Falls, but at the top of our sweat retching climb the mist felt wonderful.

The climb continued. DAMN! A sheer cliff was above and

below. We stumbled over gravel fallen from above. Andy gained elevation like it was level ground. His foot work was flawless. "Pretty obvious now why they call you Bighorn," I told him.

Andy smirked and pointed to his lower torso.

Christine shook her head before pointing to it, specifically her proboscis.

"One of you is confused," I declared.

"All a matter of perspective," Christine clarified.

At Observation Point we caught our breath. Jenny Lake was seen in its entirety below us. The shuttle boat was crossing the lake. Plains stretched from the foothills to a less statuesque range many miles to the east. Squirrels ran over our feet looking for a handout. We declined, as much an act of stinginess as environmental stewardship. Considering the number of people that made it up there every day, the squirrels wouldn't die of hunger. Diabetes or heart disease, perhaps. Ah, to be a squirrel in summer, but what was it like for them once the snows began to fall?

Christine stared into the lake. "I wonder what it would feel like to jump off this cliff."

I looked at Andy. He knew Christine better and longer. Was she capable of doing something like this? Whimsy or potential? Andy smiled, then shook his head.

Perceiving my concern, Christine clarified. "The falling, not the landing. I don't know why I think about things like that. Skydiving and parachuting scares the crap out of me. I don't even like jumping off the high dive."

"Could it be your subconscious suggesting you try new things?" I suggested.

"That will potentially kill me?"

"A metaphor for things you are too scared to try?"

Andy stood up. "We better get moving. We're already a couple of hours behind. We don't want to get to camp after dark."

An additional gain in elevation brought us into Cascade Canyon, one of the many canyons in the Tetons carved from

94

glaciers. We had gained only 700 feet so far, bringing us up to 7300 feet. And it nearly killed me. Lake Solitude was 9000 feet in elevation. I wasn't going to make it. Seven-hundred feet felt like 7000.

The trail rarely lost sight of the creek. At times, the canyon could barely accommodate both. On our left was the Grand. Small cascades and waterfalls formed from its glaciers. The water stormed down the canyon walls, eventually finding its way to the creek. The terrain was lush. Mt. St. John was on our right. Below it the terrain was rocky and barren. The trail weaved back and forth, north and south, to each side of the canyon, and into each type of terrain. The colors---the greens of vegetation, the blues of water and sky, the browns of earth and stone---were crisper, more in focus in the Tetons than in Yellowstone. The air also felt fresher.

As the trail leveled off, it guided to the left. The creek became stagnant. It widened into a slough. It looked marshy, but it didn't smell that way. If the water wasn't so cold I might have jumped into it. SOMEONE WAS IN THE WATER! Charlie?

"ICE CREAM AND ONIONS!" he bellowed when he saw us. The rest of the gang was on the sandy shore. "Anyone coming in?" he asked. The dryness of his companions indicated no one had taken him up on his offer---yet.

"Time to go, Charlie," said Andy. "It'll get dark in a couple of hours."

"I guess I'll have to camp up wind of y'all, since I'm the only one who has bathed." He got out of the water, shook like a dog, then put on socks, boots, and a shirt. His shorts continued to drip down his leg, splattering his previously dry footwear.

"Hi, Daphnee." She smiled back at me. "These guys haven't been giving you a hard time, have they?"

"They're fun. You have good taste in friends."

Charlie bent down beside the creek and soaked his scarlet gingham bandanna in the water. He tied it around his head, pulling one end over his hair, then tied if off, forming a cap. It looked

95

strange, but I had to try it. It kept the sun off my head while keeping me cool. I hated wearing hats. They made my head sweat, and they gave me hat hair. But not this one. And it was so easy to wash.

Before we resumed our hike, we ate a snack. We hadn't eaten since lunch, and it was already past seven.

Snow crested on the pass at the end of the canyon. We entered a forest, that obscured our view. We climbed. A bridge spanned an impatient creek. A log paralleled it.

"This bridge is too civilized," Charlie declared. He picked up a stick as long as he was tall. With pack still on, and stick perpendicular to his body, he began crossing the log. Ten feet below, the water was calm, but just a few yards further downstream it banked abruptly, frothing from its steep descent.

"DAMMIT, CHARLIE!" yelled Andy. "If you hurt---or kill---yourself I don't want to carry your body back out."

"That's awfully inconsiderate." Charlie smiled. Fearlessly he completed his journey. Never was the result in doubt for him, even with the log being slippery in some places. "Anyone else?"

"I'll go," I volunteered. It was like someone else spoke. I took off my pack, being a little more safety conscience and less confident than Charlie. What was I doing? I began to walk across the log, but slumped into a crouch when the log became more slippery than it looked. It wasn't exactly a macho thing. I didn't do it because I wanted to show off. Step. Step. My hand detached, then re-attached. I snagged my shorts on a branch. I slipped. I grabbed a longer branch to catch myself. My head pounded. I was going to die of a heart attack. I did it because I wanted to challenge myself---my fear. But never again, not to this extreme. I looked down. Stupid. Stupid. My legs became wobbly. I felt like I was having a seizure.

"Smile, Steve," said Christine. I turned. She snapped my photo.

The log continued a few feet past the creek. I could safely

jump down now, but I wasn't able to. I was too frightened. I remained on the log until there was no longer any log. My legs were so unstable I could barely stand.

Samantha was next. She stalled in the middle of the log. She looked as frightened as I felt. "I can't go any farther."

"You must," said Charlie. "It's only a few feet more." He dashed to the end of the log. "Look at me. Don't look down. Now come towards me. Scoot on that cute ass of yours, slowly." Charlie grabbed her when she was close enough for him to do so.

Samantha's fright melted into bliss. "That...was...great. Let's do it again."

"Nobody is doing anything, but hiking," Andy insisted. "We have to get to camp before it gets dark."

My heart continued to pound. Daphnee squeezed my arm. "Never do anything so stupid again. I've never been so frightened. Remember that death hurts the victim far less than it hurts his family and friends. They must live with the memory the remainder of their lives. I haven't had enough time to get to know you."

"So, it wouldn't have been that great of a loss?"

"You knew what I meant." Daphnee helped me put on my pack.

Samantha's leg was bleeding. She must have scraped it against the branch that snagged my shorts. How terrible to have such beauty damaged. But what tragedy to have such beauty locked away in a padded cell to prevent it from getting damaged.

After gaining a few more hundred feet of elevation, the forest cleared. We were in another canyon. Somehow, we bypassed the snow. Charlie stopped. He turned around. The Grand was directly behind us. It was magnificent. It became the gatekeeper to that isolated valley. Shadows began to darken the canyon, but the great mountain retained its glow.

The upper canyon was rocky. The vegetation was scarce. The terrain delicate. Were we above the tree line? Nope. Still some timber ahead. Parts of the valley looked like the surface of the moon. Rocks and boulders abound.

After a mile of gradual ascent, we crossed a bridge over the creek. A sign on the far side announced us entering the *North Cascade Camping Zone*---our destination. I expected us to set up camp immediately, but Charlie pressed on. We passed pockets of snow. SNOW! And it was the middle of June. The pockets become patches. The melting snow was slushy, so even with step holes my feet became damp, almost immediately. Some members of our group had waterproof boots. I now wished I had forked out the hundred dollars needed to buy a pair. When were we going to stop? There was a good spot. There was another. Up and up through the snow we went.

Tony was a waiter---which caused me to instinctively loath him. Waitri were the cause of most dishwashers' problems. Tony was the first person to complain. "One more step and I'm going to collapse."

"Just a bit father," Charlie assured him. "There's supposed to be a group camp. Large groups are strongly encouraged to use it, to prevent damage to the environment."

"I don't remember the camp being so far in," said Andy. "The sign may be covered with snow."

My turn. "How about a couple of us scout ahead and the rest stay here, so the whole group won't have to backtrack as far. If it comes to that."

"Good idea," Charlie replied. "So, who wants to go with me?"

"It was my idea, so I guess I should go."

"I thought you might."

The patches met to form one continuous snow field. "I'm looking forward to warming my feet by the fire tonight."

"Uh...we aren't allowed to have fires in the Tetons. There isn't enough fallen timber, and the land is too fragile."

"So, it's only nine miles back?"

"People pay hundreds of dollars to go on a backcountry

camping trip like this, and we're doing it for free. They pay thousands of dollars to come to Yellowstone and the Tetons, and we get paid to be here. Don't tell me you'd rather be back in your college dorm, or in the city?"

A sign announced we were leaving the *North Cascades Camping Zone*. "I guess we're going to have to go back to one of those other areas." Charlie had a frustrated look on his face, not just frustrated, but one of pure agony. He hated backtracking. And he felt guilty camping in an area that wasn't capable of supporting us.

We set-up camp in the first clearing large enough for our group. We had dry access to the creek. Two tents were erected, with a combined occupancy of five. "I don't mind sleeping under the stars," I volunteered.

"Me neither," Daphnee rapidly seconded. We were both veterans of this practice.

While Charlie warmed spaghetti on his stove, the rest of us ate sack lunches. "Would anyone like a bite," Charlie asked as he removed the can from the fire with pliers. Only Tony accepted his generous offer. It was Charlie's dinner, and we had only ourselves to blame for not providing the means to create our own hot meal. Actually, the sack lunches weren't too bad, especially when we were as hungry as we were.

The sun still shined on the Grand Teton, but just the top one-thousand feet or so of it. We had time to play cards. A glacier boulder was barely large enough to seat seven. A bottle of wine was opened and passed around. "I guess we have to drink it all now," I said. The game we agreed on---most of us---was Old Maid.

"Kind of sexist, isn't it?" Daphnee questioned.

"It's a classic," Christine insisted.

"So is slavery."

"Why don't we just call it something else," I suggested. "It isn't the game that's offensive. Just the name. How about *Confirmed Bachelor*?"

99

"That could be offensive to homosexuals," Samantha countered. "It would be like we're saying because they're gay, they'll never want, or be able to form, a committed relationship."

"How about *Perfectly Content Being Single*?" Daphnee suggested.

"You never want to get married?" asked Christine.

"I never want to feel like I have to get married."

Was *Old Maid*---uh, *Perfectly Content Being Single*--- childish? Yes. Fun? How could trying to keep yourself and your cards on a lumpy rock not be fun? Tony and Samantha flirted with one another the entire game.

After the game ended, Charlie laid out a tarp for Daphnee and me to sleep on. He and Christine decided to join us. Andy slept in one of the tents alone. Samantha and Tony slept in the other.

Charlie grabbed the food and garbage sack and looked for a place to hang it. I tagged along. We rejected over a dozen trees before we found one with a branch long enough to hang a rope from. The trees in the Tetons were not only scarce, the weather and elevation also made them gnarled, creating branches that were both stunted and oddly angled. Charlie connected on his first toss. "You and Samantha may have an open relationship, but I'm still surprised at how well you're taking her going off with another guy, in front of you."

"Our admiration for one another is unconditional. I am happy when she's happy. We both believe in spontaneity. If one doesn't act on impulse, the moment will be lost. We only have one amazing life to live. We must make the most of it."

We lay in our sleeping bags looking up at the sky. It was so clear, so crisp, so bright. There wasn't a moon or a city nearby, so the stars were our only night lights. I had never seen so many stars. One corner of the heavens was nearly white, the density of stars so great. The light pollution of modern civilization had made the connection to the galaxy's namesake nearly obsolete. A shooting star flashed across the sky. Then another. "What's that?" I blurted ecstatically.

"A satellite," Christine replied. "Wave to the camera." She lifted up her shirt, revealing her white sports bra. "It's something Samantha would have done if she was out here."

It took five minutes for it to completely cross the sky. Another shooting star, this one dragging a blazing tail of debris behind it. Oooo. I had never seen that before. Another shooting star. I fell asleep after losing count.

25. LIVING ART

In the morning, I found myself surrounded by snow. I was really here. Still chilly, we stayed in our bags for another hour, until the sun reached our camp and began to warm us.

After breakfast, we hiked the final mile to Lake Solitude. We paused on a bridge over a swollen creek. Charlie laid down on the planking, sticking his head under the bridge to watch the water rush past him. I joined him. Soothing. Powerful. I was drawn to the water's energy. Smack. Splatter. Charlie and I were being bombarded by snowballs. The bridge was bare, so we couldn't retaliate. We risked exposing ourselves, putting ourselves in a direct line of fire, to obtain ammunition. We were both hit a couple of times. Our counter-attack was weak---we were firing uphill. We surrendered.

The lake's ice layer was just beginning to break-up. We relaxed among a scattering of bare rocks warmed by the sun, then broke into groups. The girls found a secluded spot to sunbathe. Charlie and Andy climbed a hill, which they later slid down on garbage bags. "Do you want to go around the lake?" I asked Tony.

"Sure. Maybe we can make a detour past the girls." After a hundred feet of sloshing through the snow, their hiding spot behind boulders was revealed. Two of them were just wearing bras and the other was sunbathing...TOPLESS! We were too far away to make out details. I resumed my circuit around the lake, but Tony pulled me back. "Let's get a better peek." One of them looked up at us and shrieked. They covered up, then yelled at us. Tony walked up to them. I blushed. Not being able to face the girls, I completed my hike.

Daphnee met me on the way back. I had trouble looking her in the eye, or in any other area. "I didn't try to peep, you know," I pleaded. "I was going for a walk around the lake."

"Your footprints show your little detour."

"But...." I blushed.

Daphnee couldn't keep a straight face. A giggle became a guffaw. "I know it was Tony's idea. He bragged about it. I've known guys like that in college." Another giggle. "If your face gets any redder you're going to melt a hole through the snow." Which my face immediately tested. "If I was bothered by people seeing me naked I shouldn't strip where someone could see me. I prefer to view the human body as living art, than something you should be ashamed of. I won't allow tradition, or society, to compel me into becoming uncomfortable with something innately innocent."

Now I wished I hadn't chickened out and taken an extended peek of Daphnee's *living art*. I was so shocked in what I saw that I just caught a glimpse. I wasn't even sure which girl was which. Maybe I'll have another opportunity.

26. I'M SORRY LOVE DOESN'T

Why weren't return trips never as enjoyable? Was it because people were more road weary? More sore? More tired? Yes, but that didn't explain everything. It was more likely the newness had faded. Adventures were exciting because they were unpredictable. Repetition could be enjoyable, but only when a person was expecting a familiar, comforting response. One didn't come to Yellowstone for predictability. The return to Jenny Lake wasn't memorable enough to mention.

We still had half the weekend. Adventure had been conquered. Civilization beckoned. We took sponge baths in Jenny Lake before heading to Jackson. Showers were preferred, but they weren't provided at the nearby campground. The water was pristine. We were careful not to contaminate the lake with soap. And invigorating. If a person wasn't wide awake after bathing in it, they didn't have a functioning circulatory system. In a nearby rest room we changed into fresh clothes. And reapplied deodorant.

Charlie suggested we take a detour on the way to town. A Cougar detour unaccepted was an opportunity lost. At Moose Village, we turned onto a lane-and-a-half road that led to Teton Village, a resort just outside Grand Teton National Park. After a mile, asphalt became gravel. At each ninety-degree turn, my car door swung open. I leaned out to grab it, then slammed it to its preferred position. I did all this maneuvering without stopping. I didn't want to risk losing sight of Charlie's van. That's not to say it was very visible, even a few car lengths behind it. It was cloaked in the considerable dust it kicked up. The Lemon slid around every curve and over every one-lane bridge. Shortly before the road terminated at a highway, it became blacktop again. Did the road crew pave both ends just to make the job appear complete, then pocket the rest of the money?

Being a ski resort in winter, Teton Village had many ski lifts. The largest was called the Tram. It carried passengers in enclosed cars 4000 feet to the top of Rendezvous Mountain. It was the only lift open in the summer. The last lift left at 5 p.m., so we were out of luck by an hour. Yellowstone employees rode free in June, so we were doubly disappointed.

Charlie escorted us to the Mangy Moose, a potpourri of shops, restaurants, and bars. Its slogan was *The Moose is Loose at the Mangy Moose*, in reference to Moosehead Beer. A stuffed moose on skis was in the lounge. There was also a foosball machine. We were detained, but just momentarily. There was still much to do before the day was done.

On the way out we were lassoed by the aromas of a candy shop: chocolates and caramels, cookies and cakes---made onsite. We did our best not to buy anything, to sustain our appetite, which we planned to alleviate as soon as we arrived in Jackson. But one should know better than to enter a candy store when one was hungry. Samantha, Tony---and I---surrendered. Tony tackled a caramel apple, drenching his face in goo. If I was going to be decadent I wasn't going to waste my time on anything with a hint on nutritional value. I engulfed a slab of marble fudge. Two swallows later the evidence vanished. Samantha chose a raspberry truffle. She caressed it with her lips as it melted into her mouth. She swallowed in slow motion. She was the focus of attention as the morsel slid down her throat. "Chocolate makes me feel like I'm in love."

"I'm sorry the candy didn't last longer," said Daphnee.

"I'm sorry love doesn't."

27. WE DON'T HAVE TO BUY ANYTHING

We parked near the town square. Arches constructed of elk antlers formed corner gateways into Jackson's central park. The National Elk Refuge bordered the city, providing ample construction material. We arrived during a gun fight---staged of course. It was difficult to see it with tourons ten deep around the performers. There was a bushel of bad jokes and periodic gunfire. A stagecoach full of screaming children and cameras came within a couple of feet of me. I need to pay more attention, as does the driver of the stagecoach.

The Cowboy Bar was across from the square. Parked in front were two Harleys and a pink Cadillac. We were carded at the door. Every time someone carded me I felt like a criminal. I understand why bars do it. You can't risk losing your liquor license selling alcohol to a minor. I would feel better about it if the people checking weren't so gruff. They were always expecting trouble. "You can't go in," said the doorman to Daphnee. I forgot she was still twenty.

"Can't I just go in to look?" she pleaded.

"Not until you're twenty-one."

"Why don't you guys go in without me. I'll wait outside."

Charlie jumped in. "If one of us can't go in, none of us will go in. I'm not going to leave someone out."

"Can we stand in the doorway for a minute?" Daphnee asked the doorman.

"Go ahead, but don't block the entrance if someone needs to get by." Saddle stools surrounded the bar. Silver dollars were imbedded in the counter tops. I would have enjoyed drinking a cold beer while being a butt-chair cowboy, but Charlie was right, no one should feel left out. Everyone should have fun on their weekend.

For dinner, we ate multiple whole-wheat pizzas at Mountain High Pizza Pie. We sat outside at a picnic table. It was cool enough to be refreshing, yet warm enough not to be cold. We read the free *Jackson Daily News* at a leisurely pace. It felt great to relax after an exhausting two days. Local news and ads in the paper. Lots and lots of ads. It was a free paper. Someone had to pay for it. There were also a few national stories. It was an election year. Such silliness, but most of it we could be sheltered from, for another three months.

Daphnee read the sign on the building adjacent to the pizza parlor. "Is that the company that will take us rafting tomorrow?" What a relief to see Daphnee excited again. She seemed so down after not being allowed in the Cowboy Bar. She felt she had let her friends down, especially after Charlie made the decision to withdraw.

"Yes," Christine replied. "Like the Tram, Yellowstone employees get a great deal, not free, but it's substantially less then what tourons pay. Getting tossed, soaked, and numb from the cold can be a lot of fun, but with the money I make I'm not willing to pay full price for the privilege."

"What now?"

"Shopping," Samantha responded without hesitation.

"SHOPPING?!" Andy excitedly blurted, more perplexed than irritated.

"I can't afford to go shopping," Daphnee stated.

Samantha smiled. "We don't have to buy anything."

"We could see a movie," Tony suggested. "There's that theater near the Cowboy Bar."

"When's the next show?" Daphnee asked.

"Movies are seven and nine," Charlie announced.

I looked at my watch. "That's still an hour away. Is there

another theater in Jackson?"

"Yes," Christine answered, "but the movies there also begin at seven and nine."

"Let's walk around until nine, then," Samantha suggested. "I only get to Jackson once or twice a summer. I want to do some shopping."

Daphnee frowned.

"Window shopping."

The hour elapsed expeditiously. There were a lot of nice things to look at---Jackson Hole was one of the most desirable upscale resort communities in the country---but most were too expensive, even for Samantha. Waitri were the doctors and attorneys of Yellowstone. They made that much money, in comparison to housekeepers and dishwashers. Striving to one day become a waitri was proclaimed with fervent sincerity.

Andy tapped me on the shoulder. "We're going to be late. The movie starts in five minutes." He rushed off to inform the others.

"Just a couple of more minutes," said Samantha. "I'm going to buy these books."

Andy squirmed as he waited for Samantha. "Let's hurry," he said after she checked out. He rushed off, nearly running. Turning around and seeing he was getting too far ahead, he waited up. As soon as we made up half the distance he ran off again. He didn't wait for us again until he arrived at the Teton Theater. He looked down at his watch. "It's just five after. Hopefully the previews are still playing."

It was pitch black when we entered the theater. We bumped into Andy after he stopped suddenly after walking just a couple strides down the left aisle. Someone cried out behind me. Andy shhhh'ed them. He scanned the theater. How could he possible see already? He began walking again. About two-thirds of the way down the aisle, he directed us with arm movements to a row of seats to our right. The main feature was just beginning. He sat down last, Christina beside him, me next to her. "I just don't like going into a theater late," Andy whispered to her, "being inconsiderate to all those people who were smart enough to get to the movie on time."

Christine squeezed his arm tenderly.

Daphnee was on my right. Beside her was Tony. Every few minutes he made some comment about the movie to her. Andy eventually had to shush him.

The picture we saw may not win any Oscars, but after a month without the visual stimulation that television and movies provided, the four dollars paid seemed like a bargain. Were we so addicted to civilization's diversions that nature's own were no longer satisfactory? Until today I didn't even think about watching television or going to the movies. I finally had empathy for ex-smokers who saw someone smoking.

After my eyes became adjusted to the darkness, an elk head, with a large rack, materialized on the wall to the left.

28. LET'S JUST LEAVE THE WOOD

We had to re-enter Grand Teton National Park, to camp in Gros Ventre Campground, which was just ten miles north of Jackson. Gros Ventre is French for *big stomach*. Campfires were allowed so we bought a bundle of wood, to remedy the grievous---but understandable---injustice the night before. We were so tired by the time we set up camp, the majority of us no longer cared if we built a fire. "But we bought all this wood," I whined. "We need to use it up."

"Why?" asked Charlie. "If we aren't going to enjoy a fire

tonight, let's just leave the wood for the next campers. Just because something is there doesn't mean we have interact with it. Or put our mark on it. Or destroy it."

Daphnee was Tony's catch of the day. She didn't bite, but she did slap. Samantha returned to Charlie. They slept in the pop-up section of his van. Christine and Andy slept in one of the tents. The rest of us slept outside. I had a difficult time falling asleep with Tony and Daphnee whispering to one another.

I was too late. Daphnee had already found someone. Why did I hesitate? Because she probably didn't really like me. She would rather have a relationship with a pretty, frat boy like Tony. Why did I ever think she would like a guy like me? She only thought of me as a friend.

Daphnee laughed, in reply to one of Tony's idiotic comments. I wished I could hide away in that other tent. If only I wasn't too depressed to get up.

29. THE WHIMS OF WATER

We returned to Jackson for breakfast. Specifically, to Bubba's. Their biscuits were so big one of them nearly filled the plate. It was amazing the amount of food some people could eat. Tony soaked ten pancakes with half a bottle of syrup and washed it down with two glasses of Coke. Yes, he drank Coke for breakfast. Whenever I ate a breakfast so laden with sugar I was hyper for the next hour, and felt like I had a hanger for the remainder of the morning. The sugar saturated blood felt like acid flowing through my veins.

Whitewater rafting was next on the agenda. "You're not

wearing that?" Christine was referring to Samantha's very revealing bikini.

"We're getting wet, aren't we?" Samantha retorted. "This is what I wear when I get wet."

"There's going to be families there, on the raft. Children."

"There are also families at the pool, and at the beach."

"True, but there is nowhere for them to go if they wish to create some distance. And a...distraction...at a pool or beach isn't going to cause them to fall, into rapids."

"FINE!"

We loaded a bus, carrying towels---provided by the rafting company---and backpacks. Primarily to store food and drinks. No valuables. They were left in Charlie's van and the Lemon. Lockers were provided for those without a vehicle.

A thirty-minute drive took us south of Jackson, to a rugged section of the Snake River. We were given life jackets, raincoats, and paddles.

"I need two volunteers to ride in the front," our guide announced. Daphnee jumped up and down as she raised her hand. No other takers. Samantha looked around. Seeing she wasn't going to take a coveted spot from a child, she volunteered.

After the girls took their seats in front---Samantha on the left, Daphnee on the right---the rest of us had to claim one of the ten remaining spots. Charlie sat directly behind Samantha. The rest of us stepped in behind Daphnee, first Tony, then Christine, Andy, and finally me. The other five spots were taken by a family from New Jersey.

After we were all aboard, the guide told us to push off with our paddles. The rubber raft spun slowly clockwise as the guide directed us. "Everyone must sit to the inside of the raft's wall. If you don't, you'll be thrown out of the raft once we hit turbulence." Everyone scooted a little closer to the inside of the boat. No one wanted to go for a swim in that forty-degree water. "What's your name? The young lady wearing the yellow tank top?"

Samantha answered. "How do you remember what I wore before I put on this dreadfully unattractive rain jacket?"

"White-water rafting guides have keen memories."

"Then why don't you remember my name? I gave it to you a couple of minutes ago."

"Some things we are better at remembering than others."

"My name is Samantha. I work at Lake Yellowstone Hotel. Why don't you come up and visit sometime."

"I might just do that, Samantha. You will be the leader of the left side of the raft. Everyone on the left, follow Samantha stroke for stroke. When she puts her paddle into the water, you put your paddle into the water. And you in the teal tee-shirt?"

"Daphnee."

"You are the leader of the right side of the raft. Everyone on the right-side follow Daphnee. Now, let's practice some strokes." Our guide showed us how to paddle forward, to paddle in reverse, and what to do if one of us actually fell into the Snake River. "No one has ever died while in my raft."

"How about after they fall out?" asked Andy.

"Well that's another story. Actually, no one has died while rafting with this company, but occasionally someone does fall in the water. Just follow the instructions I gave you and you'll be all right. Now, right side, paddle forward a couple of strokes." The raft straightened out. We were finally facing downstream. "Now everyone paddle forward. Let's see how fast we can move. Our first white-water is coming up. The faster we hit it the more fun it will be---and less likely we'll tip over."

The first series of rapids drenched Samantha and Daphnee. Those behind received little more than a misting. "Everyone take a break."

As we drifted, an oar-powered raft overtook us. "Let's splash them," Tony suggested.

"People who don't paddle usually don't want to get wet," our guide informed us.

"Then why are they on a rafting trip?" asked Charlie.

Daphnee answered for him. "Why do people come to Yellowstone and never go camping?"

The bottom of the raft had about an inch of icy water in it, except for those areas people applied extra pressure with a foot. A depression then formed. Water would rush to the cavity until it filled ankle high. My feet were already freezing. I gave them a respite occasionally by placing them on the safety rope in the middle of the raft. My balance was shaky in that position, so I couldn't retain it for very long.

The guide filled the down time with anecdotes and trivia. "The river is flowing at fifteen thousand cubic feet per second."

"Is that a lot of water?" I asked.

"That's 600 bathtub-fuls per second. But historically, it isn't much. A couple of years ago the flow was almost twice that this time of year. You see that rock over there on the left? Two years ago that was underwater. We had a poor snow pack this year. The moisture content in the trees is very low already. It's going to be a bad year for fires."

The next series of rapids were more intense. This time I wasn't so lucky escaping the river's wrath. After the front of the raft received its expected typhoon, most of the crew lost their concentration and stopped paddling. Losing our momentum gave the river permission to do what it pleased with us. Our raft twisted and turned, unabashedly following the whims of the water. Right side became front side became upside. I lost track of which direction we were heading. A wave crashed into the left side of the raft, throwing a little girl into the center of the raft. Her father rushed to pull her up. She was smiling. As soon as they were both sitting, the right side of the raft got hit. Water rushed into my rain jacket from the top, and bottom. They met somewhere near my belly. I was soaked from topknot to toe, with an exclamation on scrotum. My feet didn't begin to ache until the adrenaline wore off---about the time we began to drift again.

"I need two people to bail us out." And boy did we need it. The water in the raft was mid-calf level now. Andy and Charlie volunteered. They scooped up water like they were mad men. Charlie did it with more gusto, but Andy was more efficient. He pressed his weight down on one foot, forming a pool about two feet deep. He scooped up the pool with a five-gallon bucket, threw it overboard in the same motion, then returned to the rejuvenated pool and resumed the cycle. Two minutes of heavy hoisting was enough. Just in time for our next series of rapids.

We may not have repeated history, but we didn't entirely escape it either. My feet were nearly numb. There wasn't much more the river could do to us. We hit a deep depression. As the raft kicked back up, Tony was thrown into the air. He landed on one of the rubber walls, then slid into the river. Out of nowhere a hand pulled him out of the water by the scruff of his neck. Everyone was in shock. No one said anything for a couple of minutes.

The guide passed the buckets down the raft to the bailers. Charlie and Andy weren't as fervent as they were fifteen minutes ago. A snow bank crested the mountain in front of us. I shivered. Thirty seconds later the sun broke through the clouds. I began to thaw. My enthusiasm returned.

"This is our last series of rapids," our guide announced. "Let's go get 'em." We paddled madly ahead. Crescendo. Thunderous showers. Screams of glee.

The eight exhilarating miles were over. To our right was the trailer for our raft. We overshot the concrete launching dock by ten yards, then madly back-paddled upstream. After everyone was out, we tipped over the raft to drain it of water. Half of us, myself included, had to return to the river to pick up the back end of the raft. The waste high water didn't feel too bad. It almost felt warm. Numbness did wonders. After we placed the raft on the trailer, we tore off our life preservers and rain jackets.

We were a sight to behold. Clothing dripped. Feet ached. I

could barely walk on mine. Needles inflamed the thawing stumps. The New Jersey father's jeans were plastered to his legs. He walked in stiff, silent anguish. His kids, a combination of shock and glee plastered on their faces, waddled behind him---looking like the opening sequence of the Partridge Family. Samantha's bra was exposed at the sides, where her top was weighted down. Skimpy outfits became even skimpier when wet.

Daphnee was completely soaked. I was as bothered by it as she was, but in a different way. Her plastered clothing became a second skin, revealing her form. She wasn't as voluptuous as the other girls, but her sleekness accentuated the curves she did have. Her gems became more precious. She ran up to me, jumping into my arms, thoroughly re-soaking me. I didn't mind. Maybe I shouldn't completely give up on her.

We had to walk a quarter mile, most of it uphill, to reach our bus. After reclaiming our towels, and drying off the best we could with them, we sat semi-soggy for the thirty-minute trip back to Jackson.

"You don't think we'll stay wet long enough to get crotch rot?" Christine asked, stone faced. "I've heard of divers' groins occasionally having to be amputated after the gangrene-like afflictions take their toll. Most of the older divers are as smooth between their legs as the dolphins they swim with."

Charlie abruptly pulled at the top of his shorts, creating an opening. He blew down into it. Andy left his side and found another seat many rows back.

We ate at a hamburger joint next to the Cowboy Bar. Its specialty was half-pound burgers and waffle fries. But does a person really need that much beef? Does a fox need that much rabbit? Does a lion need that much wildebeest?

30. MY FAULT

Ten miles from the Yellowstone border I saw flashing lights behind me. Where did he come from? At least he didn't have his siren on. I began to perspire as I pulled onto the shoulder and stopped. With ticket pad in hand, the Teton park ranger slowly walked towards the Lemon. Do they intentionally prolong the anguish to psych out their prey? I rolled down my window after the ranger finally stepped up to it. "May I see your license, please?"

"Was I really going too fast?" What a stupid question to ask. Does anyone who asked that question really think they were going the speed limit?

"I clocked you at 62 miles per hour in a 45 mile an hour zone."

"I thought it was 55 through here."

"Do you work in Yellowstone?"

"Yes, at Lake Hotel." Maybe I shouldn't have said that. Was I going to get fired now?

"Living in Yellowstone, you should know how dangerous it is to drive too fast. Animals cross the road, frequently, and unexpectedly. There is a reason certain areas have slower speed zones." He wrote me a ticket for thirty-five dollars. I was ecstatic. I was expecting it to be considerably higher. I was very careful to go the speed limit the rest of the drive back to Lake.

"We'll split the ticket with you," said Christine.

"No, it was my fault. I chose to exceed the speed limit. I should be the one to pay. No one insisted I go that fast."

We spent the remainder of the evening washing clothes,

and ourselves.

31. THE FIRST DAY OF SUMMER

William Solomon shouted something unintelligible. What now? It was my Saturday---slang for the first of my two days off--- and it was seven in the morning. Just once I would like to sleep in. "IT'S SNOWING!" I leapt out of bed and joined Willy watching winter's invasion.

"How can it possibly snow today?" I asked. "It's the first day of summer."

There was a knock on the door. "GET UP! We must frolic in the snow before it melts." That was Charlie's voice. Only he could get that excited.

I opened the door. "I guess going to the Beartooths is out today. It's snowing, Charlie."

"Get dressed and meet me in the lobby in ten minutes." If anyone except Charlie had demanded so much of me I would have gone back to bed. I was going to have another grand adventure.

I found Andy, Christine, and Samantha in the lobby. "Where's Charlie?" I asked.

"He's looking for some things," Samantha replied. "He told us not to wait for him. He'll meet us on that road that heads to the pub through the Lake Lodge Cabins. LET'S GO SLEDDING!"

Crunch. Squeeze. Melt. There was only three or four inches of snow on the ground. It had already stopped snowing, and it was beginning to warm up. Footprints became puddles.

It was mainly downhill to the pub. We laid black garbage bags down at the top of the slope and slid. The thin layer of snow worked great, better than when we slid down Elephant's Back in May. The only problem was when we fell. Less snow meant less padding. "CAR!" We ran to one side. The car left two streaks down the middle of the road.

"I think we need a hill without a road," said Christine.

"How about the one beside Mallard dorm?" Samantha suggested.

"It's too rocky," said Andy. "The snow isn't deep enough to cover everything."

"ICE CREAM AND ONIONS!" yelled Charlie. He came roaring down the hill on a pair of skis. They scraped against the pavement. He tried to turn at the bottom of the hill, but there wasn't anything to grip into to. He fell, his momentum causing him to slide across the road.

He pushed himself up before we could reach him to help. His jacket was ripped, but the rest of him was fine. The edges of his mouth nearly met his ears. "Wouldn't it be great if one day a month it was winter?"

Samantha rubbed her finger along the jacket's tear. She shook her head.

"Let's sit by the lake and enjoy the snow before it all melts," Christine proposed. "We can reminisce. Every snowflake is a memory of a winter's tale."

After we settled down on the bluff overlooking the white-rimed lake, Christine began. "The ski to Heart Lake was the first time I went winter camping. And except for the cold, it was an enchanting experience."

"Cold?" Andy countered. "It didn't even get below zero."

"You didn't have to get up in the middle of the night to pee."

"I did. It wasn't that bad."

"Guys don't have to expose as much of themselves. Or for as long."

"It was a relatively warm evening, but not too warm during the day," said Andy. "Not enough to melt the snow." He turned towards me. "It gets treacherous when it refreezes overnight. Soggy during the day and slippery during the night isn't a great combination."

"There was even a bit of new snow on the ground," Samantha added.

"But not enough for us to have to break trail. We didn't have enough time to go down to the lake the first day, but we did reach our camp early enough to not have to rush to set it up before it got dark. Charlie heated some clam chowder he requisitioned from the EDR. Alternating bites of it with the bread and cheese we brought, it was a fine dinner."

Charlie smiled enthusiastically. "You're welcome."

"For dessert, we roasted marshmallows over Charlie's stove, and made s'mores," Samantha added.

"Sounds like you had a great time," I said.

"Except for it being cold," said Christine.

"It wasn't that cold," Andy reiterated.

"I had trouble sleeping."

"Because you had to pee," Samantha added.

"I didn't want to get up because it was cold. And the ground was too hard." Christine looked at me. "Snow seems like it would be soft to sleep on, but after it packs it feels like concrete."

"I offered to trade sleeping pads with you. I told you yours was too thin."

"After eating a hot oatmeal breakfast, we skied the rest of the way to Heart Lake, leaving most of our gear in camp. The views were breathtaking. The icy plain, that had been a lake during the summer, went on forever. Charlie was curious how stable the lake was. If it could support his weight. When we heard that crack Andy nearly peed his pants."

"Nearly?"

"Charlie stood there a hundred yards or so from shore, debating whether to sprint to shore immediately, or wait out the possibility of him falling through the ice."

"I was curious," Charlie explained. "I had never experienced falling through ice before. It would have been a once in a lifetime experience."

Andy grinned. "Once being the critical word."

"Charlie eventually headed back to shore."

"You three looked so forlorn. I was concerned something was wrong."

"On the way back to camp we made a detour," Christine continued.

"We got naked." Charlie grinned mischievously. If he was older, he would have looked like a dirty old man. On Charlie, the expression made him look about ten.

"We found a hotpot and soaked away the cold and the stress of Charlie almost dying. Samantha was enthusiastic to strip. Being more…modest, I left on my underwear."

"Which became transparent after they got wet."

"You never saw anything, and you know it. Andy also kept on his underwear."

"How about Charlie?" I asked.

"I strive to be completely honest," he said. "That includes not deceiving others by concealing my body."

"Charlie's honesty kept on popping out of the water every few minutes, every time he leapt."

"The hotpot was too hot. I had to cool off."

"After we got out, we had to dry off quickly and change, before the cold took its toll. As Charlie said, the hotpot was very hot. We had enough heat stored up to survive the sudden change in temperature. The gentlemen were kind enough to turn around as I changed."

"Or so you thought."

"You wouldn't have seen anything you haven't already seen on a plumber."

"Not the plumbers I've seen."

"My favorite part of winter is the employee Olympics," Andy

shared. "Twenty events are spread over two-weeks in February. The medals awarded are beer cans, full of course, spray painted gold, silver, and bronze. Strings are strung through the tabs, so they can be worn around our necks like medals. The events vary from the comical, like the three-legged race, to the more serious. The most prominent, and injury inducing, was the ski jump. Every winter someone gets hurts. Last year someone broke their leg."

"So how many medals did you win?" I asked Andy.

"Andy was the Olympic stud last winter," Charlie enthusiastically proclaimed. "He won nine medals, including four golds. It's tradition for you to drink all your medals, the day they're rewarded. Andy must have fell twenty times coming home from the awards ceremony. Snow is such a wonderful surface to fall in. I had to follow him home to make sure he made it. He did. I don't think he even threw up that night."

"Cleaning toilets the next morning sure wasn't fun."

"I didn't like the Olympics as well as Andy did. I enjoy competing against myself more than someone else. People come and go, but your conscience, your drive, will always be there. In February, the snow sets up. It packs. Instead of dropping four feet off trail, a skier sinks just a foot. New trails can be created almost as fast as traveling on developed trails. I loved the freedom to go wherever I wanted. Sometimes I would wander by myself in a random direction. I didn't have to worry about getting lost, because my tracks followed me. Isolation encourages one to think about certain things. There are no distractions, no outside influences. One person alone seems so insignificant. Why go through all that trouble if we're eventually going to die?"

Charlie abruptly leapt up. "We can't just waste the day away like this. Let's build a snow-grizzly before all the snow melts."

We helped Charlie, but to no avail. What remained of the snow was too sloppy to pack. Squeezing it only accelerated the thawing. Working in winter sounded like fun, another paid vacation before I had to find a real job. "So, are you guys coming back *this* winter?"

"Lifers plan season to season," Christine stated. "If they truly knew what they wanted to do with their lives, would they still be working in Yellowstone? People with full time jobs don't count, because working here is a career to them. For serial seasonals being a gypsy is a way of life. Lifers feel displaced from society. From its causes. From its moods. We are outsiders. We are heretics. We seek refuge in the cracks of the world where the grass grows."

"I think I'll return for at least one more winter," Samantha declared. "Snow Lodge has the best dances. Everyone is so uninhibited. With the dance floor being so small, it feels intimate."

"Dances are held in the employee pub, which is the snack shop during the day," Christine added. "To create space, the table tops are lifted off, leaving the posts. Plastic jugs are placed on the posts to prevent injury. The floor tends to become wet, due to the melted snow and spilt beer, adding to the explosive dance environment. Dances end officially at 1 a.m., but there have been times when they go most of the night. There are always a few people still going full speed when the music finally stops."

"The music stopped today," I said.

"But we were there when it happened," said Charlie.

"How can we make up for it tomorrow?" asked Andy.

"A PARTY!" Samantha exclaimed.

"I thought we were going on a hike," I said.

"We can have both," said Charlie. "Why not a party hike? A party hike to Mary Lake."

"How far in is it?"

"Twelve miles."

A twenty-four-mile-long party hike? Only in Yellowstone. And only with Charlie.

32. REGRETS FROM BENEATH THE STORM

After a hot shower, I lay on my bed. It was still two hours until dinner. Hopefully Daphnee will be there. I hadn't seen her all day. My window was partially opened, trying to air out the stuffiness a dorm couldn't ever rid itself of. The last of the snow dripped from the roof....

Snow white-washed visibility. Where was Daphnee? Streams of frozen perspiration cracked at each shielding grimace. We shouldn't have gone. An orange glow brightened as it enlarged. Thank God, she was wearing that florescent jacket. So out of place in nature. A fair trade for being able to remain in contact with her. I paused, allowing her time to catch her breath. My feet were becoming numb. It was getting colder. "We need to get off the Continental Divide before it gets dark. We're too exposed up here." Daphnee murmured. I gave her a push. She climbed---slowly. A couple of minutes later she stalled again. Snow was falling profusely, in grape-size flakes. My face was covered in the seconds I waited for her. "DAMMIT, DAPHNEE! WE NEED TO GO BEFORE WE ARE BURIED ALIVE!" I gave her another push. She was up and over the pass by the time she stopped again. She turned around and smiled at me. "Now let's see if we can find camp," I responded.

Daphnee began to descend, but traveled only a few yards before she lost her footing and collapsed, bottom first. She lay motionless. I rushed to her side. She opened her eyes. "Can we sleep here?"

"We need to find camp first."

"We can't even see the trail markers anymore. How do you expect us to find camp?"

Daphnee was right. And visibility was only getting worse. "All right. We'll go down to that bowl over there and set up the tent." Daphnee shook as she pushed herself up. She was exhausted.

Sealed within the tent, we finally felt safe. We gobbled something down before it got too dark to see. One good thing about camping during the winter, we didn't have to hang our food to keep it away from bears. I could barely make out Daphnee's silhouette two feet away. She was curled in a fetal position in her sleeping bag. Just her head was poking out. "I think we'd better try to get some sleep," I said. "We'll need our strength on our way out tomorrow."

"But I'm not tired yet. Give me a happy thought to put my mind at ease, so I'll be able to fall asleep."

"I was so happy to see you. You were returning to school, and suddenly...you weren't."

"I could finish college, later. I may not have another opportunity to experience Yellowstone in winter. "

"After you graduated?"

"What if the right job offer came along? And would you still be there? And Charlie and Andy and Samantha and Christine?"

"I'm so happy you changed your mind. Sorry about the storm."

"I'm just glad you're here with me."

"We better get some sleep. We'll need our strength to return to Snow Lodge tomorrow."

Daphnee and I were in a hotpot together. In our attempt to find the spot with the perfect temperature, we became tangled. The contact became an embrace, then much more.

Daphnee's image disappeared, briefly. She returned fully

clothed. She was leaning over me, shaking my left shoulder. "Are you all right? You were screaming my name loudly. You must have been having a nightmare. Was I in some kind of danger? I think it's morning. It's still dark, but it's lighter than it was. Can we break camp and start heading back to Snow Lodge?"

"As soon as I go to the bathroom. I can't wait any longer."

"It's much quieter out there, today. Do you think the storm is over?"

"Let's find out." Still in my sleeping bag, I twirled around to unzip the tent fly. Three feet of snow fell into the tent. Daphnee screamed. Both sleeping bags became covered. "We need to brush it out before it melts." Hastily we put on our boots and jackets. Snow drifted into the tent. There was still a storm out there. The wind competed with the sky to drown us. The insulation that had protected now turned against us. I retrieved the snow shovel from my pack and madly abused it. Daphnee removed the sleeping bags and shook them.

"We did a pretty good job," said Daphnee.

"I think we had to. It's unlikely we'll be able to leave camp today. Look at all that new snow, and it continues to fall. We can't even see the trail markers on the trees. If we leave now I'm afraid we won't get very far. If we stay here another day we won't have to set-up camp again."

"Then we'd better ration our food. We have enough for another day. Not much more than that."

After finally relieving myself, but still feeling bloated, we ate a breakfast of orange wedges and granola. "Let's go for a short ski," I suggested. "If we're going to spend most of the day cooped up in the tent we need some exercise first."

"Okay, but let's not go too far. I'm afraid if we're gone too long the snow that's falling will cover our tracks."

Being in a bowl, it was uphill in every direction. It was not easy breaking trail through five feet of snow, especially on an incline. We slid down eleven inches for every foot we climbed. We *did better once we took off our skis, but we sank deeper in the snow. We were soaked by the time we returned to camp.*

We stripped off our wet clothes, leaving on just enough for modesty. This was one of those situations where semi-nudity didn't feel very erotic. We madly burrowed into our sleeping bags so we wouldn't freeze to death. I had to go to the bathroom again. I was careful to zip the tent fly from the bottom this time.

"When do you think they will send out a search party?" Daphnee asked.

"We aren't expected back until tomorrow. We'll be back before a party is sent out."

"Becoming buried alive scares me, even if it's just temporary. Are we going to come out of this alive?"

"Daphnee. In case we don't...survive...I want you to know that I like you. Like you more than a friend. I think you might like me too. I just had to tell you."

"I like you too, Steve. I don't know why I waited so long to tell you. What was I waiting for?"

"I wish I would have learned how you felt about me before we came here. One final regret before we are buried beneath the storm."

"We still have time. The temperature is dropping. Will you share my bag with me? I need someone to keep me warm if these are going to be my last hours."

The rescue party arrived two days later. Beneath a snowy mound they pried apart two bodies coiled around one another, smiles frozen on their faces.

33. A SPIRITUALLY HEALTHY ENVIRONMENT

"STEVE! WAKE UP!"

It took me a minute to collect my wits. Where was I? What time was it? Was it morning already? Who was speaking to me?

"STEVE!"

"Is it snowing again?"

"THERE'S GOING TO BE A BIBLE STUDY AT EIGHT TONIGHT!" I had never seen Willy so giddy. There was something about people wearing beards that made me think they weren't capable of being silly. It might have been that facial hair was a symbol of maturity. Children don't have beards. Adults do, therefore, a clean-shaven adult appeared more child-like, and was allowed to behave childish. "It's been more than a month."

What felt like more than a month, was the last time I peed. I had to go *now* or die. Not physically, but my psyche would be fatally wounded if I peed on myself. I rushed into the bathroom. Please, hold it in, for a just a few seconds more. I opened and closed the bathroom door in one motion. I unsnapped my pants with my left hand as I pulled down my briefs with my right. The dam broke. A turbulent stream emptied onto the side of the toilet. Before I could adjust, a heavy mist flew back at me. I was fortunate. Gravity countered its rise before most of it made contact. I continued to pee. After about thirty seconds I began counting: thirty-one, thirty-two...sixty-three. Finally, the flow slowed. The straight line became curved, then intermittent. I wiped the side of the toilet, deposited the paper, then flushed. All that work down the drain.

I looked in the mirror. "OH, GOD!" I looked like a wax figure that fell on its head, in a warm room. I soaked my hair in the sink, then dried it with a towel.

Willy's glee was diminished when I came out of the bathroom. "I would appreciate if you wouldn't use God's name in vain."

What? Now I remembered. "I don't think people take it that way. I know I don't. Saying a statement like *Oh God* isn't a curse. It's more a statement of surprise or shock. What we are really saying is, *God, why did you cause this wonderful thing to happen?"*

"So, you believe that everything that happens, God has a hand in, there's a purpose for it?"

"People shouldn't be condemned for things they have no control in doing."

"Did you hear that I'm going to have a bible study in half-an-hour? You're invited." I hoped so. It was also my room. "It would benefit you to immerse yourself in the word of God." What a way to spend the evening, listening to a room full of self-righteousness.

"Is it really seven-thirty already," I said as much to myself as to Willy. "That means I missed dinner."

"We had ribeye steaks, and a sundae bar for dessert."

It would figure I would sleep through the best meal the EDR had served since I began working in Yellowstone. "So, it's three-ninety-five for a small pizza at the pub?"

"I wouldn't know." Willy sounded offended. "That's not a proper place for a God-fearing man to go. All people do there is drink, and smoke, and fondle one-another."

"And eat pizza."

"Pizza itself isn't bad, but the temptations are."

"But shouldn't a Christian be able to overcome any temptation?"

"Even I may become lost to temptation if I'm not on my

127

guard. Precautions must be taken. Please, join us in the bible study. It is a much more spiritually healthy environment than the pub."

"Maybe some other time."

34.   MARVELING AT EVERY BITE

It was the first time I had walked to the pub by myself since the bison incident. The one thing in my favor this time was it not being dark. If I walked into a bison in broad daylight I deserved to be gored.

The pub was quiet. On Sundays, it closed early, discouraging the most determined drinkers. And eradicating a late-night crowd. I was one of the first people there. That was better than arriving late. Sometimes the pub ran out of food. My eyes immediately focused on Daphnee. She had a table by herself near the bar. She waved me over, smiling in that way that made her face glow.

"I just ordered nachos," she said. "Would you join me?"

"SURE!" I liked pizza better than nachos, but I would eat a piece of cardboard if it made Daphnee happy.

"DAPHNEE!" someone yelled.

"That's my nachos," she informed me.

"I'll get it," I said. She handed me some money. "No, I said I'll get it." I must be in love for me to turn down money.

"I never let a man pay for me. I prefer to go Dutch. If a man pays, he may expect something in return. If a woman allows a man to pay, then she may feel like she must reward him. I don't want to be taken care of, like a child. If I have equal control of the situation I feel I can leave when I wish to."

I picked up the nachos, paying just half their cost, upon Daphnee's request. I at least tried. We quietly devoured the chips, cheese, and salsa. She also missed dinner. I marveled at every bite she took. Every chew. Every swallow. I followed the path of each morsel. If only it were my hands caressing her body down that pathway. Some girls were ashamed to be seen eating in public. Daphnee ate with confidence. Her actions saying, *If you think I'm going to get fat because of the way I eat, I don't want you anyway*.

"Did you get enough?" she asked. "I could eat a bit more, but I don't want a whole platter."

"Sure, I'll share another one with you." While we waited for our second round of nachos, Daphnee ate the jalapenos that I took off my tortilla chips. If I put half that many in my mouth I would be drenched in sweat, crying like a baby, and spewing fire.

After several more wonderful minutes of watching Daphnee eat, I informed her about the hike tomorrow. "It's going to be twenty-four miles long, but fairly level."

"I don't mind getting tired. It's your body's way of telling you, you have accomplished something."

For the next two hours, we talked of things others would think trivial. We enjoyed each other's company. Each new utterance was an insight into the other.

"Would you like to take a walk?" I spontaneously asked her.

"I'd love to. It's getting too loud and smoky in here."

35. ME TOO

It was nearly as loud outside as it was in the pub. There was a steady flow of tourons and employees between Lake Hotel and Lake Lodge. "Let's walk along that road beside the lake," Daphnee suggested. "After spending an hour in the pub, I could use some peace and quiet."

The narrow two-lane road bypassed most of the activity. I began to relax as the sounds of civilization dimmed. External stimuli were replaced by internal ones. The need to be close to Daphnee overwhelmed me. She was walking beside me, but that wasn't enough. I was compelled to hold her hand, but every time I extended it in her direction I pulled it back. Repeat. Repeat. REPEAT!

The lake shore was down an embankment. We found a wooded section, where the topsoil was still intact and firm. We walked along the beach until we came to a log that was washed ashore, perpendicular to the water. We straddled it, Daphnee in front. The lights of Lake Hotel illuminated the beach to our right, but directly in front of us the sky was black, and the stars were bright and distinct. A shooting star arced across the sky. We saw headlights along the western shore. Messages flashed in intermittent tree-barred Morse Code. The beach lapped up water thirstily. Slap. Pound.

My heart throbbed loudly. Loud enough for Daphnee to hear it? I couldn't continue to do this to myself. I must either act *now* or never see her again.

I reached ahead to put my arms around her.

Simultaneously, she moved her arms back to wrap them around me. We embraced in a position where we couldn't see one another. I was afraid to break contact, concerned it may never return. We finally broke contact so we could look at one another. What would Daphnee's expression be? Was her embrace an anonymous comforting, or was it a desire finally acted upon? Her expression was one of a cat waking from a nap in the sun. The kiss was tender. Neither one of us wanted to appear too aggressive, too longing for love.

"Let's get into a more comfortable position," Daphnee suggested. We dropped beside the log, our arms wrapped tightly around one another. We kissed, with mouth and bodies. We gradually became more comfortable with one another. Our contact became more passionate. We stopped before the journey stumbled into a wilderness we weren't ready to explore.

I leaned against the log. Daphnee sat between my legs with her back to me. I squeezed her tenderly. "I didn't think you liked me, not in this way," I told her.

"I've liked you ever since that drive to Grebe Lake. We could barely fit the packs into your car. We even had to put some stuff on our laps. You never complained, even with three girls tagging along, none of us with the foresight to bring a car to the Park. Being the only male on the hike you didn't try to control us, but you did act strong when we needed you to."

"And you thought I liked Magnolia?"

"What male over 10 doesn't?"

"I've liked you more since that first time I saw *you*. When you asked me if I intended the hike to be a date with Magnolia I almost broke down and said, *No, but I wish the hike could be a date with you.* I wanted to hold you on top of Elephant's Back."

"Me too. I hoped you would be next to me when we had that friendship huddle at Gull Point, but you were across from me, and between two other girls."

"I didn't even know who they were."

"I didn't know that. I wanted to hold your hand on the walk down here. I almost did a dozen times. I thought he probably doesn't even like me. I might as well give up. But if I did I couldn't bear to see you, thinking of what might have been."

We embraced, then kissed for a few more minutes. "I'm beginning to get cold," Daphnee said after catching her breath. "I wish we had our sleeping bags, then we could spend the entire night here."

"Let's get them, then. But are you sure you want to spend the night outside?"

"I slept outside at Grebe Lake, and in the Tetons."

"That you did."

We barely made it back to the road before passion overwhelmed us. I heard a coyote yelping, but chose to ignore it. No matter how strong I squeezed Daphnee, or how vicious my mouth was against hers I couldn't get enough. I would consume her if he could. Fatigue finally broke the connection.

"Did you hear the coyote?" I asked her.

"What coyote?"

36. CIRCUS PARADE

We looked like a circus parade, walking proudly, scattered in singles and pairs. The baton was a gallon jug of burgundy wine. Every half-mile it was passed on to the next person in line. Charlie had a boom-box tied to his shoulders. The rest of us brought backpacks full of beer, Yellowstone Whiskey, chips, cheese, dip, sausage, fruit, wheat thins, strawberry newtons, towels, pillows, a frisbee, a hacky-sack, and even a small rubber raft.

The trail began in the northern end of Hayden Valley. Dusty sage alternated with marshy grasslands. We stayed dry when we hiked above the muck. But bison also liked to stay dry. A gigantic bull chased us whenever we got within a hundred feet of him. Once we moved a few feet downhill, he stopped. Ahead. Stop. Drop. Stop. Ahead. We were gradually being forced into the marsh. Tony picked up a stick and chased the beast. "You're not going to make me get my boots wet. I HATE SOGGY SHOES!" So long Tony. The bison backed off. Remarkable. It's been said the most frightening beast is a madman, because he's so unpredictable. He could do anything, sometimes even contrary to his wellbeing. Tony bowed. His face soured when he didn't get any praise. What did he expect? Stupidity didn't deserve acclaim, unless it was on a sitcom.

If felt so good to be hiking again. Just thinking about sitting around all weekend made my muscles atrophy. What if it snowed again today? With Charlie around it was likely we would have gone hiking anyway.

A deep throated howl was heard in the distance. "Coyotes?" Daphnee asked.

"It sounds more like moaning," Christine replied. "Wind through the trees?" The forest was half-a-mile north of us. We traveled parallel to it so we wouldn't get lost in the fifty-square mile rolling sage valley. Our route roughly coincided with the trail markers, but the point often became moot, because we kept losing them. I wasn't too concerned. There were people here much more experienced than I, and they weren't worried. "We must be careful when we listen to the Yellowstone wind," Christine warned. "It speaks for its own benefit. It can cause delay, distraction, fear, or attraction. Mother Yellowstone might be bringing food to a hungry predator."

"Or...guiding us to an animal in distress," Samantha suggested.

"Yellowstone has been good to us," said Charlie. "Let's return the favor, even if it means filling a poor beast's belly."

133

The moaning gradually increased as we continued to hike west. Two miles later we crested a butte and saw hundreds of bison below. Their grunts drifted up to us. One thinks of bison in herds, but each beast was an individual. One was running. Another was drinking. A third was swatting a fly with its tail. A forth was lifting its tail. Charlie took out his monocular, so we could see them in detail. Bison were beautiful, with their dark brown coats, and large expressionless heads. We detoured around them, to prevent the beasts from reverting back to their potentially aggressive nature.

An emerald green creek blocked our path a few minutes later. "That's odd," said Andy. "This creek wasn't green last year, or steaming. I wouldn't even have remembered it if I hadn't jumped over it, and just barely made it." He pulled off his heavily laden day pack and dashed down to the water.

"That looks like the right temperature to take a bath," Samantha declared.

Andy yanked his hand out. "Only if you're a lobster. This creek looks strange. The water itself isn't green. The rocks below give it its color."

"Maybe they're emeralds," Daphnee hypothesized, now also at the edge of the water, along with the rest of us. "Maybe that's why Mother Yellowstone brought us here."

"They don't look like gems," said Charlie. "They look more like they've been painted. Very strange." He retrieved his velum map of Yellowstone and searched for something. "As Alice would say, it's get curiouser and curiouser. This creek has a name: Violet."

"Violet Creek is green?"

"Maybe the person who drew this map was illiterate," I suggested.

"Or color blind," said Daphnee.

"There are hot springs upstream. But they weren't this active last year. I also remember this creek. And Andy was exaggerating. He made it across with plenty of room to spare. Close to a foot. Let's do it." Without hesitation, and without much of a runway, Charlie launched himself across. His back foot landed on the lip of the far bank. He had to shuffle his feet to not fall backward.

"I think the creek has also become wider," said Andy.

"What could be happening up stream?" asked Magnolia.

"I'm going to find a better place to cross."

"We're wasting too much time," said Tony. "We're going to miss the party. Let's just walk across." He took off his boots and splashed through the thigh high water. "OW! OW! OW! OWW!!" If he was in a cartoon he would have leapt straight up into the air, and would have stayed there until the scene faded. So often hikers were tortured by fording frigid streams. Those were the good old days.

"THIS IS RIDICULOUS!" said Daphnee. "My boots are half wet already from that swamp we crossed." She stepped into the creek, boots and all, seconds later reappearing on the far bank.

The rest of us made it across one way or another. Andy found a narrower place to jump across. Others were more creative.

"Steve, will you help me across," cooed Magnolia.

"What do you want me to do, carry you?"

"That would be great." She was light enough to carry in my out-stretched arms. She wrapped her arms around my neck to prevent herself from falling off. My balance was a bit off, but other than that it was an easy crossing. My legs were beet red from the bottom of my shorts down. If the water was a couple of inches higher there would have been some Rocky Mountain oysters simmering. Girls have it made with all their secret, insulated compartments. I set Magnolia down next to Daphnee. "Thank you, Steve. I'll return the favor sometime." I used all my willpower not to laugh when Daphnee glared at her roommate, who was completely oblivious to the situation.

After seven miles, Hayden Valley finally ended. The

woods---mainly lodgepole pines, as was most of the Park---were magical, the perfect mosaic: the right lighting, the right spacing, the right odors. I could imagine myself in Sherwood Forest, the two-rut trail before me the primary catalyst of my daydream. Any moment I expected Robin Hood to jump out, onto the road, and say, "Hands up, give me your wheat thins and your boom-box."

"Stagecoaches used to use this road," Christine informed us, "when it was the main route from Canyon to Old Faithful. Wouldn't it be wonderful if they were still in the Park?"

"It probably wouldn't be much better than automobiles," said Andy. "The good old days weren't always that good. Do you realize how much of a mess horses make? With the traffic Yellowstone has today every road would become a cesspool."

"I guess it wouldn't work today, but it must have been marvelous a hundred years ago."

"If you didn't mind a bumpy ride and days, even weeks, without a shower. Time doesn't change outcomes, only the tools we achieve them with."

We heard thunder. But with blue sky above us? The ground began to shake. Trees rustled. Without any wind? I turned around. The people behind me were slowly catching up. Those in front of me also stopped. A bison ran across the trail through a gap our cluster. The trees were dense enough that we didn't see its approach. Another bison crossed. Then another. Two crossed. Three crossed. Dust was kicked up, making it difficult to see. I became concerned. I had no idea if those in the group behind us were all right. I still couldn't see them. A bison charged. We dodged up-trail. The flow of bison diminished. The dust began to settle. There was still no sign of the others. Charlie jogged in the direction of the slower group. "WAIT!" shouted Andy. "There may be a few stragglers." Moments later a bison leapt across the trail, looking more graceful than anyone had given its species credit for. Charlie dodged around it like it was a falling log obstructing the trail.

A couple of minutes later he returned with the missing members of our party: Tony, Barry, Samantha, and Alice. We cautiously scrutinized the forest as we passed through the danger zone. "You must have really pissed off that bison you chased," Barry told Tony. "He had a bunch of his boys try to rub us out."

"What I want to know," asked Samantha. "Is what where the bison running from?"

"What's a party without animal acts?" Charlie proclaimed.

"Maybe it was the same thing that turned the creek green," Alice suggested. "What else it might do to us?"

A couple of miles later there was another delay. NOT MORE BISON! I went around the people in front so I could see. Two silver-backed grizzlies were in the middle of the trail. The larger of the two was standing up. I counted the humans. Then I counted the bears. I read somewhere that a grizzly never attacks a party of four or more. I counted the humans again. We had two people to spare. Ten divided by four left a remainder of two. The smaller grizzly ran off, but the larger one didn't surrender any ground. It studied us. Maybe it was also counting. Don't chase him, Tony. This wasn't an herbivore. The larger grizzly finally ran off. Silence. Deep breaths.

"ICE CREAM AND ONIONS!" Charlie bellowed. "I never had one stare me down before, or even been this close to one. If I was alone I would have become a tale told around a campfire."

It was cold and windy when we arrived at Mary Lake. I didn't feel exhausted, surprising considering we had hiked twelve miles already, nearly continuously. But I did feel ready for a break. After many hours of walking the scenery runs together. I wanted to be able to enjoy the hike back. A bite of food and a bit of play would be more than sufficient to rejuvenate me.

We sat in the sand along the eastern shore of the lake and spread out our weighty possessions. "I'll do my part in making this lighter," said Barry as he unscrewed the gallon jug of wine. He took a swig then passed it to the next person along the row of spread out beach towels.

"Steve," cooed Magnolia. "Would you join me in performing a sun dance." She took off her shorts and tank top, leaving a skimpy bikini.

"Isn't it a little cold for that right now?" said Daphnee.

"I'm just teasing the sun."

"That's not all you are teasing," I barely heard Daphnee murmur under her breath.

We danced around in a circle, saying things like, "Come out sun. Let's play. Go away on a working day."

"We need some music," said Charlie. The sounds of the Beach Boys, Jan and Dean, and the Ventures rolled across the lake.

Tony joined the dance, then Samantha, then Christine. The rest of the recliners joined in before the first song was over, including an ever very reluctant Andy. He swayed nervously without any expression on his face. The sun shined through a break in the clouds. Screams. Congratulations.

"So, who's going in with me?" asked Charlie. He didn't wait for a reply. He walked in backwards, then dove, face to sky. He surfaced fifty feet from shore in a dazzling splash spectacle. He shook the water from his hair. "Smooooth."

I tiptoed in. Then tiptoed out. Two steps in. Two steps out. I ran in, then did a belly flop. It was easier if you got it over in one swoop, like pulling a bandage off a hairy leg, or an amputation.

No one else got in, not even the bikini-clad Magnolia. But how many girls in bikinis actually got in the water? Bikini tops have a tendency to come off in water. And who wanted that to happen?

With the sun warming us down to our souls, we found plenty to do. We played frisbee until we lost the flying disc in the middle of the lake. Wasn't plastic supposed to float? Barry paddled his raft to the middle of the lake and took a nap. He deserved it, considering how long it took him to inflate the thing. In case he got thirsty, he had a six-pack cooling at the end of a rope. It made a good anchor. The rest of us were landlubbers, but basically doing the same thing. Alice was the only person who didn't drink any alcohol.

Tony leapt acrobatically from one water crested rock to another. No one paid him any attention. He must have had continuous acclaim in high school. He sat next to Magnolia and flirted. Man to wolf, she had more ability without trying.

Samantha leaned over to Daphnee. "How long have you and Steve been together?"

"How did you know?"

"A woman who has had as many relationships as I knows. A couple looks at each other differently once a relationship has begun. The changes are often subtle, but if one knows what to look for she will see them. I never go after a man who is taken."

"I wish everyone could see as well as you."

"Just because a person is blind doesn't make them a bad person."

Charlie rolled over Samantha. "Did I hear we have a new Yellowstone couple? They must be tied."

Daphnee looked startled. Samantha explained. "No, this isn't some kinky sex game. For a couple to be tied means they must be tied together at the ankle as they leap into the Yellowstone River."

"That seems kind of dangerous," I expressed.

"There's a place near Tower Falls that is shallow and slow. I've never been close to drowning."

"And Samantha has the scarred ankles to prove it," said Charlie. "But she always comes back to me."

"That's because you're easy. After a relationship goes sour Charlie is always there for me."

Even every *great* party must eventually end. The rising sun usually marks its death, but for hikers...let's just say no one knew better than me how difficult it was to see bison in the dark.

We danced home to the gentle sounds of Jimi Hendrix. "But isn't that rude to nature?" I asked Charlie.

139

"It's our substitute for bear bells."

37. BETRAYED

Willy deleted more bible verses, something he has been doing with increasing frequency. Something like that happened in George Orwell's *1984*. Knowledge was being erased, just a little at a time, barely noticeable, but over time, significant. How long might it take for Willy to cross out every verse? It probably wouldn't be linear. More like radioactive decay. After a certain amount of time half the verses in the bible would be erased, the most obvious that needed to be eliminated. Then in that same length of time, half of what remained would also be eliminated. Iteration upon iteration, reducing, but not completely eradicating the word of God.

No sign of that Playboy. Could he have thrown it out? Once all the provocative parts were eliminated, there probably wasn't the need to keep it around. Could the same be said for the bible? How many edits would that take?

As usual, Willy entered the room while I was snooping. It was as if he knew what I was doing, but instead of preventing my action, he tortured me, by allowing me to almost get caught, repeatedly. Adrenaline flowed. I could barely speak, but I must try, so things didn't seem out of place, I becoming guilty of inconsistency. "You seem to be keeping yourself busy. You spend even less time in this room than I do."

"A lazy mind and body encourages evil to penetrate. I'm going to a picnic at Bridge Bay. Would you like to join me? A couple of dozen people are expected to attend."

"Daphnee is working late so I have nothing planned this evening. I'd love to go." A picnic sounded like fun, even with Willy. He couldn't mess that up, could he?

Some of the people at the picnic I had seen before, but most I hadn't. Before we ate we played soccer. Pretty informal. There were teams, but no one kept score. Before dinner someone said grace. The food was great. After dinner, we had to discuss how Yellowstone related to us becoming Christians.

I felt betrayed. If I knew it was going to be a religious gathering I wouldn't have gone. I no longer felt guilty looking at Willy's bible.

38. STINGING AND ITCHING

Word of a good thing made that thing grow to gargantuan proportions---like California. We had seven people go to Lake Solitude. Nine were going to High Lake. Even taking Charlie's van, we had to requisition a second vehicle---mine. Daphnee and Barry joined me, in the Lemon. The remainder---Andy, Christine, Samantha, Alice, and Tony---piled into Charlie's van.

Bison, elk, deer, moose, and an assortment of birds populated a lush valley between Madison and West Yellowstone. Barry Henry smiled contentedly. "I used to hunt those animals--- before I came to Yellowstone. I miss the exhilaration. The challenge. But beauty...that can't be experienced behind the butt of a rifle, or the string of a bow. Beauty must be observed. Participation creates anxiety. Not all of it is bad. Stress or excitement, both diminish the appreciation of the performance."

After a moment of quiet reflection, Daphnee added, "Like a

weed diminishing a plant's potential."

"We're almost out of the Park," I nervously commented. "Where is this trailhead supposed to be?"

"Northwest of the Park."

"We're hiking outside the Park?"

"I believe we go back into it."

"Twenty miles north of West Yellowstone," Barry clarified.

"Near Bozeman?"

"Same direction. Bozeman's about an hour and half further north."

"That far?"

Daphnee smiled. "Wasn't Jackson enough city for you?"

"Just curious. A new place to see."

We had to stop at the ranger station in West Yellowstone. Permits for the most popular camping sites could be obtained at any station. The more remote ones required direct contact with local jurisdiction. Current trail and campsite conditions were discussed.

West Yellowstone was not only the *Snowmobile Capital of the World*, but also the town with the most motel rooms per capita in the country. West Yellowstone was more family oriented than Jackson. Not as nice, but considerably less expensive.

The herd at the trailhead thinned as individual hiking personalities began to transpire. Charlie led, with Daphnee and I just behind. Andy and Christine were behind us, but only in sight during long, straight stretches. I wasn't sure about the rest. Please, no one get lost.

On our left was a crumbling hillside. The avalanches must be frequent enough to scare away the vegetation. On our right was a lazy creek. Dense vegetation permeated both banks. Cause or effect?

Charlie waited for everyone to catch up. He went to the end of the line to talk to Samantha, who was talking to Alice. "Lead on," he said to me. "You remember our campsite number?"

I nodded nervously. I felt uncomfortable leading. It wasn't because I didn't like to take charge. It was fun to organize a hike, and to keep it organized. The part I didn't like was being the pace setter. I had to keep looking over my shoulder to see if I was going too fast or too slow. It was easier leading from behind, where you can focus your attention in one direction. I assumed that was why Charlie was in back now. After a few minutes, I didn't have to worry about being a pace setter. The troops were spread out again.

The east fork of the creek appeared to be moving swifter than its parent creek. Because we were moving slower? Gaining elevation did that to a person. The forest became denser. It was difficult to see the creek. The grade of our ascent decreased. We crossed the creek, then shadowed it closely.

Mosquitoes were becoming a nuisance. Slapping was awkward with a thirty-pound pack strapped to your back. Only part of one's body was in reach to slap, while most of it was in reach for the mosquito. The stinging and itching became too intense. Daphnee and I were forced to strip off our packs. Frantically, I searched for my bug repellent with one hand, while slapping with my other. My arms and legs were carcass black and blood red. I finally found the spray. I drenched Daphnee, which she reciprocated after I spastically handed her the spray. It was fumbled, but she was nimble enough to recover. The mosquitoes continued to buzz around us, which was irritating enough. At least they no longer bit. We put our packs back on. My body tingled where the mosquitoes venom penetrated. I began to feel nauseous.

Five miles in we found the campsite. It was next to a slough, ripe with the insects. Daphnee and I set-up my brand-new tent. My parents' tent was too heavy and bulky to take backpacking. We immediately jumped into it, and zipped it shut. We heard the mosquitoes bounce off the nylon walls. Our defense---for the moment---was holding. I kissed Daphnee. We both sighed.

The rest of the gang arrived. Outside the tent we heard

Charlie say, "True love. They can't get enough of one another."

"Do you think they are doing it?" asked Tony.

Daphnee and I made moaning sounds and rocked the tent. Actually, we hadn't even come close to doing it. We had cuddled and kissed, but we hadn't even touched one another, not really. Being a guy, a more physical relationship was always on my mind, but liking Daphnee, *really* liking Daphnee, I didn't want to put her in a situation she wasn't ready for. Or one that might scare her away.

We emerged from the tent. We were greeted by claps. I blushed. I didn't know why. It wasn't like they thought we were really doing something.

"What do you think of the mosquitoes?" asked Charlie rhetorically. "We'd better build a fire. The smoke will help keep them away."

We rushed into the woods---all of us. The more manpower the quicker the job would be done. With nine of us, one load each ought to be sufficient.

"Don't turn around," said Daphnee from behind me.

"What?" I said as I turned around. I quickly turned back. Daphnee was squatting with her britches down, her very pale bottom exposed.

"OW!" Slap. Slap. I turned back around. Daphnee was still squatting, and now she was off balance. Every slap tipped her to one side, then the other---like a top. I turned back around, hoping Daphnee didn't see me looking at her. I didn't want her to think I was a voyeur---or a pervert.

"OW!" Daphnee pinched my butt.

"That's how it fills for a girl to go to the bathroom outdoors."

I squeezed her. "Now where did the mosquitoes bite you? Can I kiss it to make it feel better?"

Daphnee bent over. On cue, a mosquito landed on her backside. I slapped it, and her, probably harder than I should have. It left a black stain on her shorts, and probably a welt on her butt. I

144

felt terrible.

Before I could blurt out an apology, she said, "Let's start that fire." Maybe I hadn't actually hurt her. Her slight limp boldly refuted the supposition. I felt bad again.

The fire wasn't one-hundred percent effective, but the smoke did rid the area of most of the mosquitoes, even twenty or so feet away.

For dinner, we ate sack lunches and hot dogs. Barry thought of the latter, and he brought enough for everyone. We roasted them on fallen sticks, which didn't last more than one hot dog. For dessert, we roasted marshmallows. Charlie forgot to bring graham crackers to make s'mores, so we used wheat thins.

"How about a night cap?" I suggested. I pulled out a bottle of white zinfandel from my backpack. The bottle was opened and christened in the traditional manner, then consumed in one revolution of the circle of friends. Alice debated whether to have any, then took her swig. She became light-headed after a couple of minutes and had to lay down. We all laughed at her not being able to hold her liquor. Then I became concerned for her health. A couple of minutes later, she felt better, giving me permission to enjoy myself again.

"That was stupid of me," she said. "I knew how alcohol effected me."

"And you drank it anyway," I replied.

"Everyone else was drinking."

"I didn't think things like that influenced you."

"Most of the time. Everyone looked like they were having so much fun. I thought if I loosened up...."

"By getting sick?"

"I usually loosen up another way. You wouldn't happen to have any....? You wouldn't."

"It's time for the second course," said Charlie. "He passed around a bottle of wilderberry Schnapps. It was actually quite good. It wasn't too strong, but it was very thick and sweet, like

145

syrup. "How about we mix it? Does anyone have any juice left?" A dozen cans were thrown at Charlie. Most he caught. Only one hit him.

"When we run out of schnapps we can use this." Tony set a bottle of vodka next to the juices.

"And Southern Comfort," said Samantha.

"And Yellowstone Whiskey," said Daphnee. "It's the greatest American whiskey. It says so on the bottle." How did she buy that?

"And Strawberry Boone's Farm," said Andy.

"Charlie, will you take the first shot of Yellowstone Whiskey?" Christine passed him the bottle.

He took a swig, then smiled. "Smoooooth."

He handed the bottle back. Christine took her shot, grimacing as it went down. "Smooth," she choked out.

Andy skipped his turn.

Samantha coughed after swallowing, but she was able to say, "Smooooth."

"Steve?""

The stuff burned like kerosene going down, but I was able to smile afterwards. "Smoooooth."

No one else tried a shot, but it wasn't retired. It went well with strawberry wine if you didn't think about what you were putting in your mouth and swallowing.

"How about a nightcap to the nightcap?" asked Barry. He brought a bottle of peppermint schnapps to the front of the fire. "I'll supply the hot chocolate if Charlie is willing to let me borrow his stove and pan."

"Be my guest. I've never turned down hot chocolate with peppermint schnapps."

"I could use a message," said Samantha.

"Me too," said Christine.

"Let's make a massage chain," suggested Charlie. "Everyone sit down in a line, alternating boys and girls. Massage the person in

146

front, then in a few minutes we'll turn around." I massaged Daphnee, while Alice massaged me. It felt awkward being between the two people I had intimate contact with in Yellowstone. It was time to turn around. I couldn't help but see Alice as she was at Boiling River.

"Let's knock down the tent and use it for a tarp," said Daphnee. "It's more invigorating sleeping under the stars." The mosquitoes were almost non-existent, and I was too tired to balance the pros and cons, so I agreed. Charlie, Samantha, and Alice also slept outside. Barry decided to sleep against a tree. He used his poncho as a blanket. Andy, Christine, and Tony slept in Andy's tent.

I cuddled up to Daphnee and kissed her. "I'm glad we're sleeping outside," I said. "I don't like to sleep scrunched. I think I bought too small of a tent. What's that?" I felt a drop land on me. Then another.

"Time to put the tent back up," said Daphne nonchalantly. We were soggy, but not saturated, by the time we squeezed inside.

"Can I come in?" asked Alice.

I thought she was asking us, but Andy answered back. "Come on in, but wipe your feet first. Everyone scoot over. We won't get cold tonight."

It wasn't even supposed to rain. That's Yellowstone weather for you. If we knew, would we have brought another tent?

I held Daphnee until she fell asleep, then ten minutes more until my arm beneath her fell asleep. The rest of me wasn't as lucky. The rain was too noisy. It was soothing to a point, but it went on, and on, at times at a ferocious pace. I thought about Charlie, Samantha, and Barry. They were probably shivering in the rain. At least Barry was against a tree. Charlie and Samantha could be under a tree too if they wanted to be.

We heard a thud at the end of the tent. DAMN! The tent collapsed, fortunately just at one end, but that was awful enough. I waited for a slowing of the rain, then rushed out to fix the tent. It took me thirty seconds. I had to go to the bathroom for the past hour, so I took advantage of my misfortune. Barry was curled in his poncho, looking like Rip Van Winkle. Charlie and Samantha were hidden in their sleeping bags, like turtles in their shells. I rushed back into my tent, tied down the flaps, then zipped up the door. Total time in the rain: two minutes.

39. HARD TO GET AND HARDER TO FORGET

I woke to the sound of children. No, it was just Charlie and Samantha. Daphnee was smiling at me. She hit the top of the tent, sending a shower of condensation on top of me. GREAT! I bought a tent to escape the weather and it created its own. I hit the tent above Daphnee. Her hair got soaked. But I also bought the tent to have some privacy. I tackled Daphnee. We rolled, shaking the tent and causing more condensation to fall. "Who says you can't have a shower while camping," I said. Daphnee looked beautiful. Dew glistened her face and matted her hair. It dripped down to her puckered lips. She looked up at me as I looked down at her. I pressed my mouth against hers, delicately, a brushing of two petals. Then I squeezed her lower lip with my mouth, as supple as a mandarin orange segment, but much sweeter.

"EVERYBODY UP!" shouted Tony.

Daphnee opened her eyes. She frowned, then we both drifted into laughter. She hit the top of the tent again. I retaliated. The competition continued until every drop was on one of us.

"And I so wanted to sleep in this morning," I said. "At least to stay in bed."

Daphnee leaned up. She fished for something in her

sleeping bag. She pulled out a lacy, cream bra. With her back to me she reached under her tee-shirt and put it on. She fumbled with the back straps. "Can you help me please?" Just my luck, the first time I touched Daphnee's bra, it was helping her put it on. She lifted the back of her shirt. Through trial and error, I got the job done. All that biological crap taught in sex education, while skipping the important things, like bra mechanics.

Buzzing. The heat of the day and the rain brought back the pests. I smelled a fire. At least that was one thing to look forward to after getting up.

After putting on our boots, Daphnee and I ran to the flames to warm up and dry out. We were met by laughter. "It's not what it looks like," I said, blushing.

"So, you worked up a good sweat, huh?" said Tony smugly. He was jealous.

Charlie and Samantha were still in their sleeping bags. They were coated in mud. They were on their bellies facing each other, their bags aligned end-to-end.

Everyone was in a good mood, remarkable considering the mosquitoes, the rain, and the possibility of hangovers. It was remarkable no one was ill. Something in the mosquito venom to counteract the alcohol?

We left our large packs behind and took only lunches, water, and cameras in our three daypacks.

We entered a field of blazing purple and yellow flowers. "POPPIES, POPPIES!" yelled Alice as she ran through them. She fell, then rolled. With her tie dye tee-shirt on she looked like a flower child. Samantha and Christine joined her. Women were the most beautiful when they were uninhibited.

"I'm going ahead," Andy declared. "I don't want to risk not reaching High Lake before we have to head back." We spent just a few minutes in the field, but that was enough to prevent us from catching up to him.

We briefly left the park boundary. A new metal sign and an

old, worn, wooden one marked our egress. There was still no sign of Andy. Charlie displayed that boyish grin of his and rummaged through his pack. He pulled out a pen. On the wooden sign he wrote, *R.I.P. Andy Lincoln, 1963-1988.*

We found Andy sunbathing on rocks on the northern bank of High Lake, which was nestled in a mixture of forested and boulder-strewn hills. There were still patches of snow on the south shore. A cascade fed the lake from the west.

As we ate our lunches, we complained about the ten-mile hike back.

"But it's only five miles with a full pack," Christine reminded us.

"Would this view be as great if we could drive to it?" Charlie asked us.

"Like a girl that's hard to get," said Tony.

"Hard to get and harder to forget," said Samantha.

"Hard to get?" Charlie questioned. "When have you been hard to get?"

Samantha punched his arm.

"That bruise will certainly be something I won't forget for a couple of days."

40. NIPPY

On our way home, we stopped at Einos. It was a rustic restaurant and bar ten miles north of West Yellowstone, on the northern shore of Hebgen Lake. It served u-grill hamburgers, hot dogs, and steaks. On the walls and ceiling were dollar bills signed by patrons. "That 500-peso bill is mine," Christine enthusiastically informed us.

After a very welcomed dinner---why did grilled food taste so much better, especially when one was hungry?---we played volleyball on the court outside. Everyone played until Charlie rendered a proposal. "Let's agree that the losing team must jump in the lake." How far was it back to Lake Hotel? Only Barry, Samantha, Christine, and I were brave---foolish---enough to accept Charlie's challenge. I thought Charlie would chose Samantha to be his partner, but both immediately insisted to being on opposite sides. Wanting to kick someone's butt apparently superseded mutual devotion and companionship. Fondly remembering my introduction to Charlie, I volunteered to be his partner.

"ICECREAM AND ONIONS!"

One would think that even being one person down Charlie and I we would be triumphant. We were more athletic. And more skilled. The problem: the other side was more organized. Instead of working together Charlie and I tried to out-do each other as we returned the ball without setting each other up. Too often our opponents were able to place the ball where neither of us were.

"Now that that's over," said Samantha, "I'm going to put on a sweater. It's getting a bit nippy. Weren't you guys going to do something too?"

"Come on, Steve." At the edge of the water Charlie stripped down to his too tight gray briefs and leapt in. He signaled me to follow. I also stripped down to my underwear and jumped. "This way we will have dry clothes to ride home in," he said. "But maybe not everyone." He winked at me. We splashed the people on shore. Samantha, in particular, made a good target. Wait, she wasn't backing away like the others. She was moving closer. Charlie realized what she was about to do. He climbed out of the lake and tackled her before she could grab his clothes and throw them in the lake. They rolled, too long and too intensely for an audience. Charlie stood up, but with Samantha in his arms. He threw her in the water. She splashed water towards Charlie---and

151

me---but we were already heading into the building, with dry clothes in our hands. As we headed back outside Samantha entered. Her bra was askew beneath her tank top. Her red-striped underwear was boldly displayed beneath her white shorts. Charlie held up his wet underwear. "I feel so free."

41. THE WORLD'S GREATEST RODEO

The best place to spend Independence Day in the greater Yellowstone Area was Cody, Wyoming. It was home to the *World's Greatest Rodeo*, as stated on its sign. Every night during the summer there was a show. The city was named after William "Buffalo Bill" Cody, who founded the city. Also named after him, and as popular as the rodeo, was its western historical center. The tradition to spend the Fourth of July holiday in Cody was so well respected that many Yellowstone old-timers requested their days off to coincide with the holiday. Charlie and Samantha were two such employees. Andy enjoyed hiking too much to devote an entire weekend to a social/traditional event. Christine, Daphnee, and I agreed to go hiking with him, on the condition we could spend the remainder of the fourth---a Monday, our Friday---at Cody after we got off work.

We traveled eastward in Christine's car, a vehicle so cavernous that if someone passed gas it would dissipate before it reached the next person. The one disadvantage of owning such a vehicle was feeding the gas guzzler, but with the four of us to split the expense, it wouldn't be any more expensive than if Daphnee and I had ridden in the Lemon together. *Bertha*, as the vehicle was affectionately called, was a fine example of racial equality. Nearly every color of the rainbow was somewhere on the Buick's hide. It had endured numerous u-paint beautifications in its twenty years. Being the youngest of five children, it took a while, but Christine finally had the misfortune of having the family heirloom pass down to her.

"Do you have a specific place in mind when we go to that bear place?" asked Daphnee.

"You mean the Beartooths?" Andy responded, riding shotgun. "I'm going to wait until I can evaluate the snow conditions. Beartooth Pass has been open for a couple of weeks, but much of the area is probably still covered in snow. I think we're going to hit it just right if we can find somewhere dry enough. By mid to late July the mosquitoes are terribly. Much worse than those at High Lake."

"Worse?" Daphnee and I simultaneously barked.

"It's a long drive up there, especially from Cody," said Christine, looking back at Daphnee and me every time she spoke. I wished she wouldn't do that. Sylvan Pass was very windy. Sure, Bertha would probably survive, but the parasites within her weren't that durable. "But the scenery is worth the drive. The range is nearly as spectacular as the Tetons." Christine turned around again. "And there's more of it, and in every direction, including down. It's like you're on top of the world."

"Is that Avalanche Peak?" I asked as I pointed to a crumbling mountain on our left.

"It is." Andy grimaced. "Last May Charlie and I came here to play in the snow. We intended to bag down in a bowl near the top. As we traveled along Avalanche's spine, Charlie got too close to the edge. He sunk, up to his chest. He was able to pull himself out somehow, before he dropped any deeper. After following the curve of the mountain for a few minutes, we turned around to see where Charlie had been. Beneath him the snow had been undercut. Just a few more feet down and he would have fallen through, and down, two-thousand feet to his death."

153

"Charlie does seem to be reckless."

"A cougar may have many lives, but they aren't infinite."

Daphnee looked concerned. "If Charlie works next winter wouldn't that be his ninth season?"

"Yes," Christine answered. "But the symbolism is only significant if you are superstitious. Charlie doesn't believe in anything that doesn't allow him to do what he wants."

As we slowed to exit the Park, I noticed the gas gage. It was on empty. Did Christine know? Should I tell her, just in case? I didn't want to be pushy, a know-it-all, a backseat driver, but I also didn't want to get stranded, especially with just a couple of hours of sunlight remaining. We passed a resort called Pahaska, which was famous for it being a hunting lodge Teddy Roosevelt frequented. It had a gas station. We may have left the Park, but there was still national forest to travel through. This could be the last gas before we arrived in Cody, still over fifty miles away. I began to sweat. "Ah, Christine. You do realize Bertha's on empty?"

"Sure, but don't worry. We can still go another forty or fifty miles before we start running on fumes. Some of these older cars have screwy gas gages. There's a place twenty miles from here that sells gas for twenty cents per gallon cheaper. As a rule, the farther you go from the Park the more economical the gas."

"I'm sorry I was so worried."

"Don't worry about being worried. The only bad question is when someone's just trying to waste time in class."

Fifteen miles before Cody, we drove through Buffalo Bill State Park. It was the ugliest piece of recreational land I had ever seen. It was dry. It was desolate. It was softened of any character, and hardened of any beauty. Its only attraction was a turbid, still lake, devoid of any life. For people who liked to fish, or to just be on a boat, the place might have been wonderful, but only if they didn't care for any scenery. It would have been much easier for them to lay in a bathtub eating a fish sandwich from McDonalds. Its lack was its one virtue. No one could complain it was too crowded.

Just beyond the park, a canyon formed. *Danger: Dynamite* signs were plastered all over the place. "They've been working on improving the passage through here for half of forever," said Andy. "It'll take the other half to complete it."

I always felt uncomfortable going through a tunnel. It was extremely unlikely the tunnel would collapse, but what if it did? I also felt trapped. Not full on claustrophobic, but uneasy.

On the other side of the tunnel, the outskirts of Cody began. On our left was the Shoshone River. A couple of miles further up the road, also on our left, was the rodeo stadium, home of the *Cody Stampede, July 2, 3, 4.* Was the stampede that much better than the regular rodeo? Possibly. What was certain, it was an excuse to charge more.

"CAN WE GO?!" Daphnee pleaded.

"If we can get tickets," said Christine. "That's one of the reasons why people get to Cody early. There are probably some seats left, but they won't be good ones, and likely not four together."

"What time does it begin?" I asked. "It looks like the parking lot is full."

"At eight-thirty," said Andy.

Daphnee looked at her watch. "By the time we get our tickets and sit down it will be nine. Let's see it some other time when it's cheaper and it's not so crowded."

"I'm kind of surprised you gave up so easily," I told her.

"Not giving up so much as moving on. I refuse to overpay for an event I can't experience in its entirety. You wanted to see it, didn't you?"

"Yes, but not as strong as you didn't want to see it."

"Maybe I can find a way to make you forget about it." Daphnee leaned over and squeezed me, made easier by her wearing one of those old seatbelts that just went around a person's waist.

"When?"

155

Daphnee chuckled. It was cute when she did that, but it didn't answer my question. Later in the day? This week? Before the summer ended? Anyone have a female to male translator?

"Where are we staying?" Christine asked.

"Buffalo Bill Village," Andy replied. "Everyone's probably at the Rodeo, but Charlie would have told them to leave a key for us. We're lucky Charlie got here yesterday---morning. It's unlikely we'll find a room so late on the 4th."

We were surprised to see Charlie lying on one of the two queen-size beds watching television when we entered the room.

"You didn't go to the Stampede?" asked Christine.

"And miss your arrival. I've seen the Stampede before."

"You've seen us before too."

"There was also a Looney Tunes Marathon on I didn't want to miss." It didn't surprise me that Charlie liked to watch cartoons. He got up and gave us the grand tour. "There's the bathroom. As you see, it has a tub, but the plug is missing. If you can't do with just a shower, you can either sit on the drain to plug it up, or you can stick a washcloth in it. I would recommend the latter. The suction can create a doozy of a time getting back up. And this incredibly spacious room is the living-slash-bedroom. We only have two beds, but they are large. If we become creative four people can fit on each. And there is plenty of floor space. The only rule is there isn't to be any fornication, not because I'm against such things, but because it will make the less fortunate uncomfortable and/or jealous. Remember, everyone must have fun on their weekend."

We piled our stuff in the room, then cleaned-up. None of us had taken a shower after work today. We were in too much of a hurry.

"Who wants to go skinny dipping?" asked Charlie.

"How skinny do we have to be?" Christine asked back.

"I guess you can wear what you like, but it's going to be dark by the time we get there. Half the fun is knowing the person next to you is naked, and imagining what that person would look like if the lights suddenly came on."

"Will the water be warm enough to soak?" asked Daphnee.

"Plenty warm. But no details. I want it to be a surprise. So, who is going with me?" Christine, Daphnee, and I answered back. "Andy?"

"There is plenty of hot water coming out of this faucet. I'd rather take a long shower. I'll stay here to make sure the others are able to get in."

42. FREE OF ANY COTTON CONSTRICTIONS

Samantha had the van, so we took Christine's car. She was driving, but Charlie was navigating. He was being very mysterious. We retraced our route into the city, but not completely. A couple of blocks before the rodeo stadium, we turned right onto a gravel road. Once we left the lights of the main highway, it became very dark. The road forked. We guided left past a sign that said something about a condemned bridge. Christine stopped at a rickety one-lane span. "Do we walk from here?" she asked.

"Don't you want to drive across it?" asked Charlie. The people who put that sign up weren't making a judgment call. Any fool could see that the wooden floor boards were on the precipice of rupturing. But there were no bigger fools than those who allow themselves to be talked into something foolish. Christine slowly rolled Bertha down to the bridge. The grade was steep enough she didn't need to apply any pressure to the gas pedal. The bridge creaked as weight was applied to its decrepit back. It began to bend as more weight was applied to it. We should have taken the

Lemon---it was lighter. Bertha stopped. Christine gave her some gas. The bridge yelped as Bertha leapt to solid ground.

"Now I know why you took us here at night," stated Christine. I was strongly considering walking across the bridge when we left. Who was going to tell the wonderfully gruesome tale if we all perished?

We parked beside a crumbling shell of a building. Besides no longer having a roof, two of its walls were missing. "It was once a restaurant or a bath house," Charlie shared. "I've heard rumors of both. Maybe it was both. Take your towels with you. The water is warm, but the air temperature won't be when we get out. Follow me and stay together. I don't want to turn on this flashlight unless I need to. I'm looking for a No Trespassing sign." Great. "There it is."

Charlie led us to a trail beside the river. It alternated between being sandy and rocky, depending on how close to the cliffside we were. After two minutes, which seemed much longer in the dark, Charlie stopped. Ahead was a cave. Periodically, a flash of light reflected off something shiny within it---likely water. Without preamble Charlie stripped off his clothes and placed them on a rock beside the cave entrance. My eyes had adjusted to the dark by now, but details were still vague. I could see that Charlie didn't have the upper torso of a woman, but that was about all I could see. I walked into the cave, gradually sinking into oblivion. It had to be an optical illusion. Didn't it?

Now it was my turn. With my back to the girls, I stripped down to my underwear. If I couldn't see them they wouldn't be able to see me, would they? Did I really want to do this? With a final downward swoosh, my underwear was also removed. I walked into the cave, trying to be as graceful as a naked man could be. The water didn't feel too bad, but I did think it would be a little warmer---more like a hot tub than a lake in mid-summer. When I became waist deep I turned around. "We'll be there in a couple of minutes," said Daphnee. As I travelled farther into the cave I began to see light. Not bright like from a light bulb, but the illumination one's bedroom receives at night if there was light peaking under the door. At the end of the cave a billow of putrid gas blocked my way. I leapt, gagging through it into fresher air. The water was warmer, on the brink of becoming uncomfortable. I saw Charlie on the far side of a pool formed by a boulder reef. The river was beyond. The farther I got from the gas, the easier it was to breath. I could see stars above me now, and an occasional headlight at the top of the canyon, one-hundred yards upstream.

"This is the life," said Charlie, his body arched back enough to cover him up to his neck. In hot water? How could he appear that comfortable in water that was a few degrees below scolding? As I moved closer to Charlie---and the river---the water began to cool off, becoming quite pleasant.

"CHIRP!"

"WHAT WAS THAT!" Charlie bellowed.

"It sounds like Daphnee. I think she just stepped into the water. She's quite found of marmots."

"A girl who makes animal sounds certainly has its appeals." Charlie's winked. "Can't get much better than this. A warm soak under the stars, free of any cotton restrictions."

Gag. Cough. Daphnee and Christine appeared through the mist. "It gets better once you move away from the cave," I assured them.

What the.... They were carrying towels out in front of them.

"Christine was reluctant to disrobe," Daphnee explained. "I asked her if she would have taken off her clothes if there were only girls here? She said she probably would have. So, the only difference would be that boys...."

"Men," Charlie corrected.

"So, the only difference would be that *boys* would see you, I asked her. She agreed, so we came up with this plan. We can be as free as you guys, yet remain modest."

"You're taking all the fun out of skinny dipping," said Charlie.

159

"There's no longer the anticipation, the hope of see anything accidentally. Then again, those towels are so old they are practically falling apart. That one even has a big hole in it."

Christine looked down at it. She shrieked. "It does."

"Don't worry," said Daphnee. "I'm right next to you and I can barely can see anything."

Charlie coughed, then leapt into the air, revealing a modified version of what he was born with. He breathed deeply a couple of times, then settled back in the water. The girls looked annoyed. "I had to do it. The wind changed, choking me with those gases."

"CHARLIE!" Christine screeched. Nothing could diminish a guy's bravado more than a girl screaming, except maybe when she was crying.

We contemplated silently as we watched the sky and each other. Not a bad spot to spend some time alone with Daphnee, especially with what she was wearing. If we were alone.

"WHAT'S THAT?"

We looked to the north, in the direction we came. Colored lights danced in the sky as they fell to the earth. POP! Another brilliant display filled the sky. "That's the real reason I didn't go to the Rodeo," Charlie explained. "You get a better view of the fireworks from down here."

Daphnee and Christine turned towards the fireworks. The sides of their chests could be seen, but in the darkness no more than one would see on someone with a one-piece pulled tight. Christine's breasts were enormous, twice the size of Daphnee's. The larger breasts were already beginning to sag, but Daphnee's were nearly perfect---ample and perky. In the state the silhouettes had put me in I intended to remain submerged for as long as possible.

43. WHOSE LEG

I woke to chaos. Bodies were scattered all over the room. Some on the two beds. Some on the floor. Some in between. Some solitary. Some huddled. It was difficult to tell whose leg or arm belonged to whom. We looked like a can of worms. Daphnee was on one of the beds with me and a couple of people I didn't recognize. It didn't really matter. Any body heat was good, or any cushioning, when pillows were scarce. I wasn't sure who was on the other bed. On the carpet, at the foot of my bed, were Christine and Andy. Barry and Willy were at the foot of the other. They made an interesting pair. At least Willy had found a friend who wasn't heavily involved in religion. What did they have in common? I didn't see Charlie or Samantha. A girl screamed on the other bed. SLAP! Tony fell onto the ground. "I thought that was mine," he said.

"Why would you be pinching your own ass?"

"That's how I wake myself up in the morning."

The rest of us also began to wake up. It wasn't really an option considering all the commotion.

"Where can we go for breakfast?" asked Barry.

"How about Taco Johns?" Daphnee suggested.

"They don't serve breakfast, at least not a real American breakfast of eggs and bacon."

"But it's already lunch time."

Andy looked agitated, as he burrowed for his watch under his pile of clothes and toiletries. "We better get going," he said. "We've wasted nearly half the day."

"But not before we eat," Daphnee insisted.

As we turned into Taco John's parking lot, we saw Charlie and Samantha walking towards us with sleeping bags and pillows under their arms. "Can we put these in your car, Christine? The grizzlies will go wild if they smell fast food on them."

"Where have you two been?" asked Christine.

"We found it a little crowded in the room," Samantha answered.

"Then why didn't you sleep in the van?"

"When the Buffalo Bill Historical Center has such good accommodations."

"You didn't?" said Andy.

"What did they do?" asked Daphnee.

"They slept in that tepee in the parking lot of the museum. Charlie has been threatening to do that since our first summer out here?"

After picking up our food, we spread out over three tables. Andy and Christine sat with Daphnee and me, so we could make plans for the next two days. "Considering our late start, and the uncertain hiking conditions, I don't think we should go to the Beartooths today," said Andy.

"We are camping though, aren't we?" I asked.

"Remember those rock formations on the way to Cody? They're called Hoodoos. There are a lot more of them in a place called Hoodoo Basin."

"Great," said Daphnee, between bites of a soft taco. Hot sauce dripped from her chin. "Sounds like Bryce Canyon, in Utah. My family took me there when I was a kid."

"The only problem," Andy continued, "is the time required to get there, at least from traditional routes. Hoodoo Basin is in the easternmost part of the park."

"So, what non-traditional route are you contemplating?" asked Christine.

"Through Sunlight Basin, which is off the Chief Joseph

162

Highway."

"Isn't most of that gravel?"

"About fifty miles of it, not counting how far into Sunlight Basin we can go. There is an old road that goes in quite aways, but you know what old roads in Yellowstone become."

"Trails," said Daphnee as she got up. "Does anyone want anything?" We were either too full or too polite to respond. Daphnee returned with two plain tortillas. "I like them better than anything that goes in them. I like flour better than corn. But potato is the best. It's called lefse. Scandinavians eat it."

"Eaten with cod treated with lye," Christine added.

"Why?" I asked.

"Tradition, I guess. Lye was once used to preserve fish, before refrigeration."

"They need refrigeration in Norway?"

"In the summer. Even Yellowstone doesn't have snow year around."

"The Tetons do," Charlie added.

"The tops of them," Christine clarified.

"So how far do you think we'll have to hike in?" I asked.

"Five miles, but that's just a wild guess."

"Maybe we can day hike part way with you," said Charlie.

Samantha elbowed him. "We have to go back to work this afternoon, remember?"

"Maybe we can go in a little way and still have time to return to Lake."

"You'll barely get back in time as it is," said Andy.

"Maybe we can call in sick?"

Andy looked pleased with himself. "Do you wish you hadn't changed your days off now?"

"No, I'm glad I spent the weekend in Cody. I just wish work wouldn't keep getting in the way."

"Everyone ready to go?" asked Andy. He already had thrown his garbage away and was standing up, leaning against his chair. Daphnee was finishing her last tortilla.

"WAIT!" said Charlie. "Since there are a lot of us together in one place, let's create some new Yellowstone names."

"Daphnee doesn't have one," I volunteered.

"Steve, since you know Daphnee best...." Tony snickered. "Tell us something Daphnee likes."

I knew immediately what to say. "She likes marmots."

"And if I recall, she can even make marmot sounds," said Charlie. "ICECREAM AND ONIONS! It's perfect. Marmot it is. Do you accept your Yellowstone name, Daphne?"

Daphnee chirped. Or was that a burp?

Other names were created and accepted: Mantis for William Solomon, because he's religious and prays. Bald Owl for Barry Henry, because he stays up all night and wasn't growing old gracefully. And the Mosquito for Tony Whitaker, for obvious reasons. We also named Ryan Turner, Grizzly, because of him hibernating---rarely leaving the dorm. Kathleen O'Neel, Poodle, because she's a city girl that wears a lot of makeup. Magnolia Woods, Amber Fox. Alice Grunden, Dish Dove. And Rebecca Gar, Terrapin, because she's slow, in all terrains. Of course, their names weren't official until they agreed to them. Charlie said he would inform them of the...ah...good news as soon as he returned to Lake.

44. TOWARDS THE RIVER

We finally found ourselves on the Chief Joseph Highway. Andy's face soured every time he looked at the clock: 12:03, 12:09.... The road conditions varied from relatively flat to bumpy to washboard. Maneuvering around curves while losing elevation was...interesting. Nerve-wracking, but also exciting. Were we going to make the next turn? If not, would the car just go off the road, or become airborne before a terminal incendiary impact? To reduce the instability of the loose gravel, Christine dropped Bertha into *L2* to decelerate enough to make the turns. Even with the precaution, she occasionally slid.

We found our turnoff, near the Sunlight Basin Ranger Station. The road steadily deteriorated, becoming narrower and bumpier, with each successive ranch access we passed. Beyond the last, the road became barely wide enough for one vehicle. To our left was a river, just below the road. To our right, boulders, precariously balanced on the cliff a thousand feet above us.

"STOP THE CAR!" Daphnee demanded. She threw open the door and darted towards the river as soon as Christine slammed on the brakes. By the time the rest of us abandoned the car, the source of her agitation and our near accident became apparent. A mountain lion reclined on a cliff overhanging the distant shore of the river. It was less than a hundred feet away. Its eyes pried open. It was so sleek. It lifted its head. How could something that large be that beautiful? Then suddenly, it was gone. So gracefully and expeditiously was its departure, it appeared to vanish in thin air.

"I wish Cougar was here to see his name sake," said Andy.

"It's so rare to see a big cat," said Christine. "They are loners, as are all great philosophers. They know so much, but aren't capable of communicating it to us, even if they wished to---which they don't. We wouldn't understand. Did the Romans believe space travel was possible? Or the Greeks, that computers would revolutionize the information age? For all we know, large cats may think humans are cute, but sometimes not worth their upkeep."

A couple of minutes later Christine was forced to stop again. She looked behind her. "It's going to take me...forever...to back-up all the way." Fifty feet in front of Bertha an avalanche blocked the road.

"Maybe we are close enough to walk the rest of the way,"

Andy suggested. He took out a map from the front pocket of his backpack and began studying it. "Ah, maybe not. It's still about fifteen miles to Hoodoo Basin."

I got out of the car and walked over to the rocks blocking the road. "HEY! People have been past here. I see tire tracks in the dust on top."

Andy looked worried. "So, what are you suggesting?"

"Let's cross."

"I'm not driving across that," Christine insisted. "That rickety bridge in Cody rattled me more than it did Bertha."

"Then let me. If Charlie was here he would try it. Someone has too."

"You want to drive over a boulder field?"

"None of the rocks are that big."

"They aren't gravel either."

Andy was shaking too much to say anything.

"Steve," Daphnee pleaded. "Do you really want to do this? It looks pretty dangerous to me."

"That mountain lion was an omen. The spirit of Charlie is with us. Nothing will go wrong."

"All right, but let me guide you."

"Aren't you going to be in the car with me?"

"I like you, Steve, but I always thought Romeo and Juliet were two messed up kids."

Alone, I coasted Bertha to the first rock. Daphnee was in the middle of the avalanche, about twenty-five feet from the car. She pointed to my left. I turned the wheel slowly counter-clockwise as I gave Bertha some gas. Daphnee waved me ahead. The left front tire climbed. She pointed to the right. I turned the wheel clockwise. The right front tire climbed, but at a much greater rate than the left did. Bertha was tilting downhill. Daphnee waved me ahead. The back tires climbed. Daphnee back peddled off the pile of rocks. I became concerned when she stopped giving me directions, so I stopped. She shook her head furiously, but it was

166

too late. "NOW! START MOVING AGAIN, BUT SLOWLY!" she yelled at me. I pressed the gas pedal down. Bertha lunged a couple of feet, then her hind end began to slide towards the river. "STEVE!" A panicked driver often turns the steering wheel in the direction he's sliding, but I was aware all that would do would cause the car to slide even more. I had to straighten out the car. As I gave Bertha a steady, but miniscule quantity of gas I turned the steering wheel counterintuitively to the left, towards the river. The car slid another foot, but dropped no more. I had traction again. I was lower on the avalanche than I wished to be, but any alteration in the wheel positioning would cause the car to slide again. I breathed a sigh of relief when the front tires finally thumped down to level ground. Daphnee ran up and kissed me before I could get out of Bertha to vomit.

We traveled just two more miles before we came to another avalanche across the road. Experience paid off. I had no trouble with this one. I felt if a third came along someone might actually agree to be in the car with me.

A creek flowed across the road. "Let's do it," said Christine. "Bertha's so heavy she'll stick to the bedrock."

Bertha glided through the two-foot-deep water like it was butter. She hydroplaned for an instant halfway across, but she recovered so quickly no one had time to worry.

"How many more obstacles are we going to have to endure?" asked Andy, his brow beaded, and his shirt soaked.

"And more importantly," says Daphnee. "When will they become too dangerous to attempt?"

"I think we have our answer," said Christine. The new creek in front of us was much wider and deeper than the last one. A Ford Bronco was parked in a wide outcropping of grass. Christine parked beside it.

"But I see tire tracks on the other side," I said.

"Someone probably crossed when the creek was lower," said Andy. "Bertha doesn't have a high enough clearance or four-wheel drive."

"She has more like one-wheel drive," Christine whispered. "But please don't tell her. We're trying to build up her esteem."

With full packs on we walked to the water's edge. Andy set his pack down, then wandered upstream by himself. "This is as good a place as any to cross," he said after he returned. "I don't like the looks of this water, though. It's too deep and it's too swift."

"Could we form a human chain across?" asked Daphnee. "I saw it in a movie once."

"Wait, I have even a better idea." Andy shuffled through his pack and extracted a white nylon rope. "I'll tie one end onto myself and the other onto that log. When I get across I'll tie my end to a log on that side. You'll be perfectly safe as long as you hold onto the rope when you cross. The last one across can tie the rope around themselves."

Andy jerked as he stepped into the water. "IT'S PRETTY COLD!" The current forced him downstream, but he didn't fall. His legs were bright red when he got out. The water went half-way up his shorts, but didn't quite reach his backpack. Daphnee and Christine went next. They chirped and howled, respectively. They weren't as tall as Andy. Helpful when not wanting to hit your head. Less so when you wanted to keep your pack dry. If the material was waterproof the brief encounter would have been inconsequential. If.

I tied the rope around my waist. I stepped into the water. My testicles felt like they had been hit with a snow ball. The shock caused me to lose my balance. The current took me. I fell up to my neck. I was eventually able to wedge a foot against a boulder. I stood back up. Andy was on the other side of the rope. He pulled me towards shore. I allowed him to do most of the work. When I stepped onto the shore I could barely stand. I was shivering. From the cold. But also from the potentially fatal consequences of my mishap. "Did anyone take my picture?" I tore into my pack. MY EXTRA CLOTHES WERE STILL DRY!

"Should we head back to Cody?" Daphnee suggested.

My feet were burning from the sudden temperature rise, but my crotch felt much better. The cramps were even going away. "I have some dry clothes in my pack. That fall would be wasted if we turned back now."

Instead of changing immediately I put it off until we set up camp. It was a warm day. I felt fine after a couple of minutes, except for the sogginess.

Lee City was half-a-mile up the road. It consisted of two old shacks that used to be occupied by miners many years ago. Andy looked at his watch and his map. "It's going to be dark soon. This is the best place to camp in the valley. I recommend we make it a long day hike tomorrow. It's about eight more miles to the park boundary. We should be able to see Hoodoo Basin from there." We agreed.

After we set up Andy's tent I finally changed into dry clothes. I had my tent with me, but being tied to the outside of my pack, it was wet. Instead of trying to dry it out we opted to cram the four of us into the other tent. Even if my tent had been dry, we may have still all slept in the same tent. Lee City was spooky.

We hung our wet sneakers on branches to dry. Daphnee and I were clever enough to bring fording shoes.

After eating sack lunches, we explored the cabins. One had a *Lee City* sign above its doorway. It must have belonged to Lee. We saw all we needed to from the doorway. None of its original furnishings remained within the rotting wood structure. In their place was litter and human feces. Daphnee backed down the steps. "THIS PLACE STINKS! What type of person degrades a historic monument?"

"Better to corrupt a manmade structure than nature," I countered.

"You prefer people going to the bathroom in a place like this than outdoors?"

"I was thinking of the trash."

The other cabin had a sleeping bag and a box of food in it. "I wonder where he is?" asked Andy.

"How do you know it's a he?" Daphnee asked back. "A woman is just as capable as a man surviving alone in the wilderness."

"There aren't any curtains or other decorations. Women like to accessorize more than just the clothes they wear."

"Then where is *his* television to watch football, and *his* Playboy Magazine to get off with? Men have their own accessories."

"Maybe the person is transsexual or asexual," I suggested.

"He could be the original tenant," Christine proposed.

"He would be over a hundred years old if he was still alive," said Daphnee.

"Maybe that's why he isn't back yet. Old men walk slowly. Maybe he lived so long so he could better Ol' Lee in the cabin next door. Let's call this man, Grant. He competed with Lee in everything he did, but Lee always won. Lee mined the most ore. Lee built the largest cabin. Lee had the city named after himself. LEE, LEE, LEE! Grant couldn't sleep at night, tormented by his failures. But there was one way he could win in the end, and that was for Lee's end to come first. Maybe he even killed Lee. Now he laughs at Lee while he throws garbage in his home and craps where he once slept."

"It's time to leave," said Andy. "Whoever this hermit is probably doesn't want anyone snooping around in his stuff."

No one slept very soundly. Because we were crammed together like sardines? Or maybe, just maybe, it was because of the sounds we heard all night: voices and laughter, rustling and banging.

"Steve, will you get up and see what it is?" asked Daphnee, her voice dripping with honey. "I won't be able to sleep unless I know what's going on out there."

"LIKE HELL I WILL!" I whispered back loudly. "What we don't

see won't hurt us." Yes, I was being a wimp, but why did the man always have to be the brave one? Andy snored on the other side of Daphnee. He was faking. I just knew it.

45. PERFECT TIMING

In the morning, we felt more fatigued than the night before. Our bodies ached from laying one way too long. And our heads, from too much worry. Our shoes were no longer hanging on the branches. "DAMN!" I cursed. "I just bought them."

"Let's see if we can find that hermit," Daphnee suggested.

"And what? Accuse that crazy, anti-social old coot of taking them?" Andy countered. "I don't want to get shot. Or reenact that scene in Deliverance."

"Dueling banjos?"

"Yes, I'm frightened of him challenging me to a music competition. I'm talking about the scene where Ned Beatty gets raped. Let's get out of here before he wakes up."

When we walked quietly past his cabin we noticed that it was no longer occupied, if it ever was. The food and sleeping bag looked like they hadn't been disturbed.

"I don't think I want to take my overnight pack on a 16-mile hike, half of it uphill," I said.

"We can put them back in Bertha," said Andy.

"I only want to cross that creek once more."

"Why don't we leave our packs here," Daphnee suggested. "We can pick them up on the way back."

"If we do that they'll be stolen, just like our fording shoes."

"Let's hide them in the bushes," said Christine. "He can't

take what he doesn't know exists."

The first few minutes of a hike felt like that first swallow of cold water when you were very thirsty. Or that first bite of pizza when you were famished. Hiking did become an addiction after a while. Muscles begin to feel lonely after a few sedimentary days. They needed reassurances, caresses from soil, to continue in the efficient manner they had become accustomed to.

The poisons of shabby sleep soon dissipated. We became cheerful. We gained elevation, but slowly. The trail split three ways. The map just showed one route. We went on the assumption the right and left trails were spurs to the canyon walls. We proceeded forward.

The wooden plank roof of a mine seized our attention. Daphnee wandered towards it. "HOLD UP!" shouted Andy. "Don't get too close. Those boards look like they may---will---collapse."

"I'm just going to take a peek. I won't actually get on top."

"What do you see?"

"I can't see a thing. It's too dark. I think there may have been a cave-in."

"Grant is definitely not making a living from this," Christine stated.

"He's probably sells the stuff he steals," I said. "I'll see my shoes being auctioned off one day, from the back of a truck, by a smelly, old man with one tooth."

Near the top of the canyon we saw snow banks. We bypassed them, wanting nothing more to do with water, in any form, that wasn't absolutely necessary. Andy and Christine had been out of sight for nearly half-an-hour. Daphnee did as well as anyone on straightaways, but she lost quite a bit of momentum once a slope exceeded a certain grade. She chirped as she peaked over the next ridge. I rushed to her side so I could participate in her excitement. An *Entering Yellowstone* sign was posted a hundred feet below us. Beyond it, 20 bighorn sheep galloped across a snowfield. Andy was sitting in the tundra to the right of them.

Christine's face was partially concealed by a 35mm camera. For once, perfect timing. The Bighorns even stayed within sight as we ate lunch.

Looking in the direction we came, the valley looked so green and uniform, like someone took a hoe, swung it down a hillside, then planted alfalfa in it. It was hard to believe it was eight miles down to the bottom. I was confident if we had a sled we could be at the bottom of that chute in five minutes. We talked very little, but why should we? The more pristine the location, the more a person desired solitude. Noise pollution diminished perfection.

A giddiness overcame me on the way down. The excitement of seeing Bighorn Sheep? The acceptance of gravity? The lack of oxygen at 10,000 feet? Perhaps all three.

I slid down a snow bank I originally circumvented. My feet were getting soaked from the slush, but I didn't care. Chirp. I looked over my shoulder. Daphnee was following me. I turned back around. Too late. I intentionally fell to dodge a boulder. I stood back up as hastily as possible, to prevent the wetness from sinking in. TOO LATE! My butt was soaked. Daphnee left the glacier in better shape. She slapped my butt with a thud, followed by a spray. "Does Stevey need to be changed?" I grabbed her, then pushed her down into the snow. I ran away before she could retaliate. A snowball buzzed past my ear. The next one I caught. I threw it back at her. It hit her squarely in the middle of her chest. She launched more projectiles, but I was now out of range.

Seeing that she didn't have anything in her hands I let her catch up to me. She kissed me. We finally broke from our romantic stupor when we heard gravel crunching.

Andy and Christine had been in front of us. Daphnee and my more direct route, even with the mischief, enabled us to overtake them. Andy and Christine smiled as they walked past us. Daphnee and I followed them, the four of us staying together the rest of the way down.

There was still no sign of the hermit. "THEY'RE STILL

THERE!" Andy said enthusiastically. We crammed our daypacks into our overnight packs, then headed for the creek. Andy took the rope out of his pack and began to tie it to a log.

Christine looked downstream. "Andy." A man with a fishing pole was crossing the creek easily. It must be shallower there, because the water was hitting his legs about a foot lower than it did ours when we crossed the day before.

Andy untied the rope, and the four of us walked to the downstream ford. "There's a metal grate down there," he said. "It explains why he was able to practically run across the creek. If the creek was a little lower Bertha might even be able to cross it."

"But not today," Christine insisted. "She still has to recross those initial obstacles."

"Would anyone think less of me if I said I was looking forward to returning to civilization?" Daphnee enquired. "I had fun, but I'm still looking forward to...."

"Taking a hot shower?" I hypothesized.

Both girls looked at me like I said a dirty word.

Andy explained. "Girls prefer to take baths."

"But showers are quicker."

"Which defeats the purpose of taking a bath," Christine responded. "Best is drinking a glass of wine in the tub after a long day."

"I need to try that," said Daphnee, "after I'm old enough to drink."

"I'll bring you a glass---discretely---after we get home."

46. JUST A GIRL WHO MADE HERSELF AVAILABLE

"I'm bored." Daphnee began to dismantle her paper cup, tearing small pieces off it, from the top down. There was enough Coke left in the bottom of it that drops of the dark, sticky liquid flew onto the tabletop, her hands, and even me. It was one of those rare spiritless nights in the pub. There was just a handful of other people there, and they were spending more time eating and drinking than socializing. There had to be a party somewhere, one we hadn't been invited to.

"You're tired of me already? After just one week?"

"I think we should go for another walk, like that one that led us down to the beach." We both smiled at the memory of our first kiss.

"We could hike to Fishing Bridge. It's only a mile and most of it's along the Yellowstone River." Daphnee looked back with a blank expression. "What?"

"Walking to Fishing Bridge doesn't seem special enough to me. It's like we're an old married couple. The walk to the end of the block, our weekly entertainment."

"How many married couples see swans and pelicans and bison in their neighborhood?"

"You have a good point. But I'm thinking more of a spontaneous romantic getaway."

"Like Jackson? We have to work tomorrow."

"We can stay in the Park, just not here. And why did you have to mention work? Some days I think I'll rather wash dishes with you than make 600 salads."

"I'll be happy to trade."

"I guess I would just like more variety. In the pantry, we make the same salads, the same sandwiches, the same desserts, every day. Now, working in the EDR, that would be great. Serving different food every day."

"I don't think I could put up with the complaints."

"Paying just a few dollars a day, people shouldn't expect gourmet food."

"I never complain."

"You'll eat about anything put on in front of you, won't you? Sometimes I worry that you feel the same way about girls. Am I special to you or just a girl who made herself available?"

I leaned across the table and kissed her. "Does that answer your question?"

"If another girl was here would you be doing the same to her?"

My face drained of emotion. I didn't know how to respond. Relationships were confusing. Girls were confusing.

"I'm sorry. Girls sometimes have insecurities. They need reassurances. How about we go to this Storm Point you told me about? It sounds romantic. Cuddling on a blanket, on a thermal beach, under the stars. Who knows what might happen?"

Sometimes girls liked to talk about such things, but they rarely followed through. Many of those lost opportunities weren't the girls' fault. Things just happened to come up, there being a lot of obstacles between thoughts and actions. Being a guy, I preferred the direct approach: buy a four-by-four and plow over those obstacles. No matter the potential outcome, the bait was dangling. "Okay, but I'm not carrying everything." I did end up carrying everything. Somehow that always happened. It was better just to assume you would be carrying everything, so you wouldn't be so shocked about it. Everything but the flashlight. Daphnee couldn't lead without illumination.

As we left the pub, Charlie, Andy, Christine, and Samantha

entered. Charlie carried a game board and a zippered bag full of colorful strips of paper and dice. Great, now the pub picks up.

"You guys want to play *Black Friday*?" asked Charlie.

I looked at Daphnee. She had that content, just ate an entire bar of chocolate look. Her eyes promised she would do all she could to circumvent those potential obstacles.

I was compelled to watch a few minutes of the game, but I had to delicately balance my curiosity with the potential weakening of the romantic mood. A fire left unattended would eventually go out.

The object of the Black Friday was to collect the items on your shopping list quicker than your opponents. It was a game Charlie created as a child. What made the game challenging was the items in your shopping cart weren't safe until you paid for them at a check stand. The number of check stands opened varied and if someone landed on you they mugged you and stole the items in your cart.

"You don't want to do that," said Samantha. Charlie just rolled a number that could place his piece on top of hers. "If you land on me in the game, you won't land on me tonight." Charlie risked the consequences. After Christine landed on his piece the next move, Samantha apparently forgot her threat because she kissed Charlie sweetly on his suddenly sour countenance.

The game sure looked like fun. Maybe we could stay to play just one game. One glance in Daphnee's direction caused an instantaneous, acute case of amnesia. As the pub door slammed behind us, I thought I heard something about turning the game into *Strip Black Friday*. I may have been mistaken, my mind being as muddled as it was at the moment.

47. CLAUSTROPHOBIC

Daphnee and I were greeted by an empty parking lot. It was so quiet. A rising three-quarter moon illuminated Indian Pond. Rubber upon asphalt approached from the east. By the time the vehicle swooshed by, we were already on the trail. Daphnee carried a flashlight, but we saved the batteries until they were needed. Another car passed, then complete silence again, except for the patter of our feet. The breeze was just strong enough to bend our shadows on the sage and wild grass.

I yelled and clapped before we passed through a narrow contour of trees near the lake shore---to alert bears and bison of our prescience. The rupturing of the serenity was stark. Then back to meticulous silence. The breakers were so passive and methodical, they blended into the evening's ethereal ambiance.

"This is where the fun begins," I spoke quietly. The forest was just ahead.

Daphnee whispered back, "This romance stuff is sure exciting." Only in Yellowstone would someone associate romance with hiking a trail in the dark in grizzly habitat.

I yelled ahead and clapped. Daphnee switched on her flashlight. Suddenly it got dark everywhere except for where the flashlight was pointing. It was as if the flashlight consumed the light, then regurgitated it in a stronger, but thinner stream. Daphnee's flashlight went out. Was it the battery? The bulb? We should have brought a backup. Sometimes romantic thoughts made a person not think straight. It was pitch black in every direction. Gradually our surroundings brightened to gray. The flashlight came back on. "We may be ninety percent blind, but at least we can see really well with that other ten percent."

"Please don't do that again. I didn't bring an extra pair of underwear with me."

We were forced to walk single file during the densest stretch of forest. Daphnee walked ahead of me, *slowwwlyyy*. "You want me to walk ahead?" I volunteered. In addition to the daypack I carried, a brown army blanket was thrown over my shoulder, which I held onto with my right hand, leaving one hand free.

"I'm okay. It's actually kind of fun leading. If I was behind you I wouldn't be able to see everything as well."

"Especially the spider webs."

"I ain't scared of no spiders. Or snakes. Or bees. I don't know why more people don't pet bees, especially the ones with that velveteen hair." What kind of freak was I dating? I was simultaneously disturbed and awed.

A minute later Daphnee turned around. She actually looked a bit frightened as she shined her flashlight at me, a few yards back from her. "I thought something had happened to you for a second. I'm not a particularly clingy girl, but under these circumstances I need you to stay close to me. Grab the back of my shirt so I know you're there." I reached out. "That's not my shirt."

"I got confused. It's dark."

"It's not that dark." After making sure I was attached to her, in an appropriate manner, she resumed her approach to Storm Point. It was awkward trying to walk, being so close to her, but there were fringe benefits. Bumpy, sporadic movement caused my hand to bump into her, occasionally, even my body.

Fallen and partially fallen trees became a living optical nightmare. Every branch became a paw. Every knot a face. Every trunk a beast.

"What's that?" asked Daphnee, sounding a bit rattled. She wrapped her arms around me after I came up beside her.

"Animal droppings of some kind."

"Could it be from a bear?"

"It could be, but it's difficult to make out. Someone has stepped on it. We better check your shoes before you get back in the Lemon."

"It wasn't me. I stopped as soon as I saw it. That print means someone has been by here since the bear or whatever it was, so we're probably safe."

"Unless the bear is still in the area."

Daphnee punched my arm. "You sure try to make a girl feel secure, don't you?"

"You want to continue?"

"We don't even know if it's from a bear. Let's go on." She now looked determined, not someone wanting romance. Maybe when we reached the beach amorous thoughts would return.

A few minutes later we found more droppings. "Now that may be from a bear. It's untouched, and it has the human characteristics that define bear scat. But look. There isn't any animal matter in it. There's just vegetation."

"And a bear never changes its diet?"

"I don't know. I'm no expert. Actually, I know very little about scatology. Even if it's not hunting it still might attack if it's provoked or frightened, or in a pissy mood."

Daphnee began singing. "We love bears, yes we do, they never eat anyone, and they drop lovely poo."

I definitely didn't want to head back now. We were nearly there, there was that sexual desire that continued to build, and quite frankly, it was exciting being in a precarious situation, as long as I believed we probably weren't in any real danger. But I was concerned for Daphnee's feelings. "Do you want to head back? This isn't what we were expecting. I'll understand if you wish to head back. I won't think any less of you."

"Do *you* want to head back?"

"No."

"If you don't, then I don't. I'm getting a chill. Let's get to that steaming sand."

There were no more signs of bears. With all that singing and hollering there probably wasn't even a skeleton of a teddy bear within five miles of us. The forest was replaced with a bright moonlit landscape. The marmot mounds looked like monuments in a graveyard. I envisioned furry ghosts lounging beneath the evening rays.

We briefly made the detour to the tip of Storm Point. I had never seen so many stars in my life. It was amazing in the Tetons, but there was no water to reflect off, which magnified the magnificence. It was so calm. Not a single ripple in the Lake. More mirror than body of water. The silhouette of the Absaroka Mountains was seen to the east, as was the silhouette of Mt. Sheridan to the south. We embraced, then kissed. In such a setting who wouldn't be moved to do so. Not wanting to topple off the cliff into the frigid waters, we plopped down and resumed our enjoyment of the one another.

We would have kept at it...for hours...if reality imitated movies and romance novels. Rocks eventually became hard and high elevation evenings became cold.

"To the beach?" I suggested. One more embrace and intoxicating pressing of lips and we were off, hand in hand. Pressing that warm pliable flesh was simultaneously stimulating and relaxing. An exchange of electrical impulse accompanied by an umbilical of companionship.

Upon reaching the beach, I set the blanket down and removed my backpack. We searched for the warmest spot. Steam rose through the sand in half-a-dozen places. We debated whether to settle for one of the cooler ones, but decided the insulation of the blanket would dampen the heat enough that we wouldn't get burned.

I stretched out the blanket and placed the contents of the pack on one side of it: a bottle of wine, an opener, cheese and crackers left over from a sack lunch, and a cherry turnover, the latter requisitioned from Lake's Hamilton Store. No one was going to call me a cheap date. We dropped to the part of the blanket that was unencumbered. "You want some wine?" I asked.

"Maybe a little later." Daphnee wrapped her arms around my head and attacked me with her lips. I wrapped my arms around the lower part of her back. The contact wasn't close enough. Our legs intertwined. We tossed and turned and in our passion, knocking the wine and food into the sand. The pressure from our bodies was enough to force the heat through the wool army blanket. It was becoming almost too hot.

We stopped a moment to catch our breath. The moon illuminated the lake. Under different circumstances we may have taken the time to marvel at the backdrop, but there were more than just environmental wonders to explore.

We both glistened from the heat of the thermal beach and our passion. Daphnee removed her shirt, revealing a lacy robin's egg blue bra that displaced ample cleavage. It was the type of bra a woman didn't wear going to the grocery store. She grabbed the back of my neck and pulled me back down to her. I kissed her lips then slowly worked my way southward. Her neck first, then the top of her chest.

She helped me take off my shirt. As we lay facing one another on our sides, she touched my chest, then kissed it.

"Lay back." Daphnee pulled a small plastic bottle of lotion out of her shorts. She squirted a dollop in her hand then rubbed her hands together. She bent down and messaged my chest. After applying more lotion to her hands, she rubbed my legs. "Now turn over." After spending many more glorious minutes on my back and shoulders, she abruptly stopped. "Now, it's my turn."

She removed her shorts, revealing flowery underwear that was large enough to cover everything, but not too large to appear matronly. She lay on her stomach, displaying her well-defined, but not overly large bottom. The material clutched her tight enough to emphasize the cleft between her cheeks. Being overly-excited I forgot to warm the lotion before applying it to her back. She yelped, jerking up, but after the initial shock she settled back down. "Sorry." It was incredible touching her back: so soft, so smooth, so alive. And I had thought squeezing her hand was the ultimate. At first, I worked around her bra strap, then I went under it.

"You can undo it, if you like." If I like? I guess I was willing to make the sacrifice.

It came off easier than it went on during the High Lake hike. What a wonderful world we lived in. One of the sexiest things was a woman's exposed back. Sure, other areas of a woman's body being exposed had their merits, but an exposed back was both innocent and an implication of other, unseen, areas also being bare. My hands remained on her back, but edged to the boundary between front and back. The perimeter of a softer region was explored but not quite reached.

With remorse, I finally left her back and began to rub the back of her legs. From the murmurs Daphnee was making she was enjoying the contact as much as I was. There were some sounds men just couldn't make. I so wanted to reach higher, her lower protuberance jutting out at me, daring.

"Steve, lay on top of me."

"On your back? Won't I crush you?"

"I think I'm tough enough to take it, for a minute or two anyway. I just want to feel the weight of your body on me."

Crushing her wasn't the only thing I was concerned of. Messaging Daphnee had done a number on me. Unless we were going to do something about the situation---soon---I preferred not to make such close contact. Daphnee was still waiting. I gently dropped onto her. I was careful not to move around too much. I was almost to the point of no return. Behaving like I did with Alice didn't seem right with Daphnee. She was too special for me to provide myself relief at her expense.

"Uh, Steve. You're going to have to get up now. I'm beginning to feel claustrophobic."

With mixed reluctance and relief, I did what I was told. A moment later Daphnee leaned up on her forearms, exposing a bit more of herself, but not significantly. It was all a bit too much for me. With uncharacteristic boldness, I dropped back down to the blanket and caressed that area still clothed.

"Don't."

I jerked back. "I apologize. I just thought…."

After an extended moment of silence Daphnee said, "It's not that I don't want to. I just rather it not be here. It's very romantic out here but not very practical. Let's get away this weekend, and I don't mean hiking."

"Sure."

Daphnee stood up and turned around. "Here's a little down payment on what you have to look forward to." Perfection is a word too often used, but it was fitting. Daphnee's breasts drooped slightly, authenticating their naturalness, but they were also firm, jarring only slightly at her movement. Their tips reached towards me, but alas the gift was returned to its package. It wasn't as exciting to see Daphnee put her shirt and shorts back on as it was when she took them off, but it was something. Before we left the thermal beach, we embraced a final time, finishing with a brief but knee-wobbling kiss. After packing the uneaten food and the unopened wine, I snagged the blanket, still warm from the sand.

48. HAVE A NICE EVENING

A ranger, from his car, shined a spotlight into the sage near Indian Pond. "He's probably looking for us," I said without enthusiasm.

"Should we hide in the forest until he goes away?" asked Daphnee.

"He might ticket the Lemon. We better talk to him. I don't think we're supposed to be hiking after dark."

The ranger got out of his car and walked over to the Lemon. With a flashlight in his hand he searched the vehicle. We walked up to him, guilt dripping from our pores. "Hello," said the ranger.

"We went for a hike, because of the moon," I declared.

"A beautiful evening for it. Investigating the abandoned vehicle. Often its hikers, like you two. Sometimes its engine trouble. Occasionally, an illegal camp."

"We saw some bear scat on the trail," Daphnee volunteered.

"There were two grizzlies spotted here this afternoon. Have a nice evening."

49.   A GUY ON THE COVER

Returning to my room at 1 a.m., I was surprised to find Willy gone. His bed was disheveled, like has had been sleeping in it and had abruptly left. He wasn't in the bathroom. Where did he go? And why?

There was something hidden under the covers, but not entirely. A magazine? Maybe Willy hadn't thrown away that Playboy. I hadn't completely recovered from my unconsummated liaison with Daphnee. Willy had rendered the magazine less titillating, but I could make mental substitutions, my *down payment* my greatest inspiration.

There was a guy on the cover. That was odd. Sometimes there were couple layouts, but where was the woman? I opened the magazine and...immediately threw it on the bed like it had burned me. There were naked men in it. Only naked men. I looked at the cover: *Playguy*. I returned it to Willy's bed. It was under the covers, but which side? I think it was facing up, but which orientation?

If the ranger mentioning the two grizzlies hadn't completely relinquished my ardor, seeing those photos certainly had. Male nudity doesn't bother me, but there was an expectation that wasn't met. Not just unmet, but boldly countered.

I was too wound up to sleep. Reading helped. After turning off the light I began to think about Daphnee, beginning with that romantic walk. When I got to her *down payment*, instead of the most magnificent breasts exposed it was the man in the centerfold.

50. COTTON BALLS SMEARED IN CALAMINE

The ten of us piled out of Charlie's van. There were already five cars at Lake Butte. "We can see the whole lake from here," said Daphnee. Music, liquor, and snacks were in ample supply. It was a sunset tail gate party.

"BRING THE COOLER!" shouted Samantha to Charlie. She ran to a tree overlooking the parking lot. She climbed halfway up and perched before Charlie even made it to the base of the tree. Daphnee and I followed them. Charlie opened the cooler. It was full of drinks and snacks.

"Help yourself," he said. He took two cans of juice and a box of wheat thins up the tree with him.

I grabbed a Coke. Daphnee grabbed M&Ms. I had trouble climbing with one hand full. How did Charlie manage with three things?

"HURRY UP!" shouted Samantha. "You're going to miss the sunset."

The sky was red to the west, diminishing to pink as it arced above us: cotton balls smeared in calamine lotion. The colors reflected in the lake, staining it violet. The bleeding sky softened as it expanded, becoming orange, yellow, and ochre. Pastels conquered.

"Would you like a wheat thin?" asked Charlie.

"Sure," I replied. Charlie passed the box down. "Would you like some M&Ms?"

"I never turn down dessert." I passed up the candy. "My mom made me wear clean underwear whenever we went somewhere in the car."

"In case you got in an accident," Daphnee appended.

"Seems like the least of your worries when you get injured is wearing clean underwear, but you know how mothers are. It's also why she cleaned the house before we went somewhere. In case someone robbed us."

"She didn't want thieves to think she was a slob?"

"She had her pride. It's why I never turn down dessert. You never know when you're going to die."

"And the last thing you want to eat before you die is dessert?"

"More like insurance, to prevent the regret of not eating it."

Daphnee climbed down.

"You're not leaving us, are you?" I asked her.

"Just grabbing skittles. They are a rainbow full of flavor." She took off her shoes and climbed back up. "I used to climb barefoot all the time as a kid. No better way to make contact with nature. To feel the tree breathing, and its heart pumping. Becoming part of it. No longer a trespasser."

"Do I smell skittles?" asked Charlie.

"Do you want some?"

187

"No, don't send up the bag. Just hand me some." Charlie reached down in a very unbalanced manner. Daphnee poured some skittles in his cupped hand. He brought his hand back up, being careful not to tip it.

"You guys going with us to Electric Peak this weekend?" asked Samantha. "It's the tallest peak in Yellowstone that can be climbed in a weekend."

"That some of us can climb," Charlie stated.

"I climbed most of it last year. I was just five-hundred feet short of the peak. I would have made it if it wasn't for the storm. Electric Peak was named for its frequent electrical storms. This year I'm definitely going to make it all the way to the top."

"And she will," said Charlie. "When Diamondback coils around something, she doesn't let go until she's done with it. Not topping the peak last summer ate away at her all year."

"I may not have made it to the top, but I still had fun. It was just Christine, Andy, Charlie, and I, as it often was last year. That storm wasn't the first one to pass through. We were camped about four miles away. We wanted to get an early start, so we could be heading back down by noon, when the afternoon thunderstorms usually begin. It rained all morning. We waited and waited. It had been a particularly wet summer. I hope this summer is dryer."

"But we were able to enjoy ourselves, thanks to Sam," Charlie added. "Neither of the tents was large enough to move around in." I had first-hand experience with that. "So Sam took out a lightweight tarp from her pack and stretched it between the two tents, which were facing each other, about four feet apart. We stretched forward from our individual tents, playing hearts in our miniature city, while we waited for the rain to stop."

"Which it did, but too late to safely climb all the way to the top."

"Samantha collected the queen of spades more often than anyone else. It's often referred to as the...."

"And a man who leaves a frightened woman alone on the

188

side of a mountain is called a bastard. So, are you guys going to do Electric Peak with us this?"

"We thought we might spend the weekend together," I replied.

"We're going to Glacier National Park," said Daphnee. "And maybe to Canada?" she added hesitantly as she looked at me sweetly.

"That's quite aways to be driving in a weekend," said Charlie.

"We know," I said. "But we are leaving tomorrow afternoon right after work. We hope to make it to the park by midnight. We'll be back early Thursday morning."

"Enough time to sleep a bit before heading to work," Daphnee added.

"Have fun. I took a road trip to Rocky Mountain National Park, in Colorado, two years ago. I was tired for a couple of days after I got back, but it was worth it. Yellowstone doesn't have all the wonders."

51. PROMOTION

I stumbled into the EDR at seven-thirty A. M., bleary eyed and not very hungry. I ate anyway, because I wouldn't get another opportunity until eleven. Iris Douglas looked wide awake behind the steam tables. "How can you be so cheerful so early?" I asked her.

"When you get up at four-thirty you have time to build up to it."

"You go to work at four-thirty?"

"I get up at four-thirty. Work doesn't start until five-thirty."

"What time to you go to bed?"

"It depends on what time Harry comes in. I wait up for him. When we get older we don't need as much sleep. It has something to do with life becoming less stimulating. Not as many unique situations or ideas come up. As you probably have started to notice, time accelerates when we grow older. What would you like, Steve?"

"Just some French toast, please."

"Are you sure, dear? May I suggest you also eat some eggs or sausage. They'll give you energy throughout the day."

"Okay, but just a little. I'm not very hungry."

"It'll be just another minute on the French toast."

"Iris, where did you meet your husband?"

"We were both working at a summer camp in Kentucky. Harry managed the camp and I was a counselor. I was just nineteen. He was eleven years older than me, but we had many things in common. We both loved kids. We both loved the outdoors. We loved helping people develop emotionally and spiritually. It's much easier to find someone special if you look in the right places. If you are looking for a religious person you may not find one in a bar. If you are looking for a person who loves animals don't ask a taxidermist out. Many restaurants serve hamburgers, but you get faster service in a burger shop. Here's your food, dear."

The kitchen manager, Mark, sat down next to me. I looked up at the clock. "I still have ten minutes."

"Take your time. After you clock in head to the pantry." Crap. I would enjoy working with Daphnee, but did that mean we would no longer have the same days off? How likely was it that two people in the same department would have the same days off? "You've been doing a good job washing dishes and we need another person in cold prep. Sarah fell off the curb on the way home from the pub last night. She broke her ankle."

190

"Is she all right? Is she going home?"

"She's in a cast. She chose to stay, so she's now a cashier."

"Uh, I don't think I want the promotion if I have to change my days off."

"We'll work something out. You'll still get off Tuesday and Wednesday this week. We'll see after that."

On my way to the pantry I dropped by the dish room to see Alice. "I've been promoted."

"I know. Congratulations. I hope the new guy leaves me alone."

"I'm sure you'll be out of here as soon as another position opens up."

"I've already told Mark that I don't want to be moved. I like my solitude. I don't want to waste my time learning new procedures or listening to waitresses give me orders."

"But don't you get tired of cleaning crap off people's plates?"

"More crap is within."

52.   YOU SURE WE NEED THOSE?

Daphnee and I ate dinner at Mammoth. We debated whether to order sack lunches, opting out. They weren't very romantic.

We stopped for gas in Bozeman, Montana. "I'll pump if you pay," said Daphnee as she got out of the Lemon.

I met her at the pump. "I thought you liked to share expenses? Aren't you worried I might take advantage of you?"

"I hope so. Don't worry. I'll pay for groceries. That's if we

191

don't break up in the next ten minutes."

"I actually don't mind paying for a woman if I ask her out. I'm paying for the privilege of winning her over. But the same goes for a woman who asks me out."

"How often has that happened?"

"I'll let you know in ten minutes."

The pump clicked. As Daphnee topped off the tank I walked into the convenience store to pay. When I returned to the Lemon Daphnee was in the driver's seat. "Please," she mouthed at me through the window. I smiled and nodded. She smiled back at me warmly, then enthusiastically grabbed hold of the steering wheel and turned it back and forth, like a child pretending she was driving. "It's been more than a month since I've driven." She jerked the car in reverse, thrusting us backwards about ten feet. "Just kidding."

A block down the road Daphnee stopped at a grocery store. She pried a shopping cart from the metallic, avant-garde sculpture prevalent at supermarkets. "Let's pretend we're married."

"Then shouldn't you be in curlers?"

"To try to look pretty for my husband when he comes home from work, so he won't neglect me as much as he usually does?"

"Neglect you? I took you out to the grocery store tonight. This is quality time we're spending together." The shopping cart rolled into the produce section. "So, Darling, how about we buy some grapes for the kids' lunches?"

"They're on sale, Honey, but look kind of moldy. How about apples instead? And some celery and carrots."

"For when I'm gone, on one of my *business trips*?" I mimed quotations marks by curling two fingers on each hand.

"Cucumbers work better. But the mailman who makes a special delivery on those days works best."

"Well, if we're going to buy celery, we also need peanut butter."

"I've heard of whip cream, but peanut butter?"

"You spread it on the celery. It's actually quite good. It adds protein."

"Why are men so fond of protein? I don't think so."

"Come on, try it. If you can pee in front of me, you can eat some peanut butter with celery on it."

"The last time you said something that romantic was nine months before Henrietta was born."

"Henrietta?"

"That's my grandmother's name."

"We need bread." I plopped a loaf of white in our cart.

"Bread needs to go on top, so it won't get squished." Daphnee placed the bread in that part of the cart children usually sit. "And let's get some multi-grain bread, something with flavor and substance. White bread tastes like soggy cardboard." She exchanged the white loaf for one with more color. Nuts and other things were sticking out of it.

"But I like my tasteless, gummy bread."

"It wouldn't hurt you to put some more meat on your bones."

Before the discussion could turn into an argument, Daphnee got distracted. Her eyes danced as she saw the Hostess display. She settled for a box of Suzy Qs.

"You sure we need those?"

Emotion drained from her face. She took the Suzy Qs out of the cart and slammed them on top of the display. "Why are men so concerned about women gaining weight? It wasn't that long ago when large women were considered beautiful."

"You made fun of me because I looked scrawny."

Daphnee's face loosened. "You're right. What right do I have to criticize you on your perceived notion of female imperfections if I'm criticizing you on my own. I apologize."

I put the box of Suzy Qs back in the cart. I liked dessert too. Daphnee took them back out. "I really don't need them---not a whole a box. Why don't we buy one of those double packs instead? They are fresher. I hate spending all that money---and calories---on a box of sweats I won't really enjoy."

Too much time was wasted in the supermarket. After buying a few more things we ran to the Lemon, then squealed out of the parking lot.

We pursued dusk, traveling west and north. The light's escape became arduous. It wasn't even completely dark when we entered the Blackfoot Indian Reservation at eleven. Browning, its main city, didn't look much different than any other city in the country, except for the wooden crosses on its fringes: monuments to careless driving.

Daphnee became tired. I relieved her. I was also tired, but we were close to Glacier---very close. I could stay awake a little longer. The road became a roller coaster. Just in time. Who could sleep on a roller coaster?

No one was manning the gate at this late hour, so we entered Glacier National Park for free. Daphnee woke. When she saw the lake below us glowing under a full moon, she sat up fully. "Can we camp there?" she asked. We were still planning to spend a night in a room with a bed, but this first night we decided to camp to save a little money.

"We'll try."

The campground was also unmanned. We drove around for many frustrating minutes. "What do we do if we can't find a campsite?" asked Daphnee.

"We can either try another campground or we can sleep in the Lemon."

"No offense, Steve, but your car isn't very comfortable."

"But it's paid for."

"This is true, but I would rather sleep beside the road than in it."

"Well, it doesn't look like we'll have to do either." The unoccupied campsite wasn't quite level, but I was used to that after my initial night in Yellowstone.

Having room to do so, I brought my parents five-man tent.

Being able to stretch out improved the quality of one's sleep. We also remembered to bring pillows. It was impractical taking that extra bulk hiking, but in a car…. Hurriedly we reconstructed the tent. The icy, early morning wind easily penetrated our summer attire. "What's that musty smell?" asked Daphnee.

"I guess I forgot to dry out the tent after the last time I used it. At least it's paid for." I opened the air flaps. We collapsed on our sleeping bags. I leaned over Daphnee, kissed her, then fell back down.

53.   PALLID SUBSTITUTIONS

"WAKE UP!" shouted Daphnee from outside the tent. Through the open flap I saw her spinning around, her head probing the heavens. I put on my shoes and joined her. MAGNIFICENT! We were surrounded by snow-capped mountains. She wrapped her arms around me. "Thank you, Steve."

"What for?"

"For being here with me." We kissed passionately for several minutes.

"WOW! I'm really looking forward to that room tonight." Like I wasn't before.

Before heading west, on the Going-to-the-Sun Road, we saw Trick Falls. Part of a stream disappeared through a fissure, then reappeared as a waterfall halfway down another falls, reuniting with the original channel. "It's kind of like people," said Daphnee. "Couples become separated, but sometimes they get back together, often as a result of peculiar circumstances."

Going-to-the-Sun was considered one of the most scenic

highways in the United States. It was July and there was still snow at the pass near the visitor's center. Daphnee took her shoes and socks off and stepped into the icy crystals. After I took her photo she warmed her feet on me.

Not wanting to be cooped up in the car the entire trip, we hiked to a glacier at the end of a canyon so saturated with wildflowers it looked like an Impressionist painting.

We embraced and kissed. Who wouldn't be compelled to in such a setting? The spell was broken when a family joined us. The kids complained and the parents yelled---the most effective birth control ever created.

"Can we go to Canada now?" asked Daphnee. "I've never been outside the United States."

"I've been to Mexico once. My dad didn't want our car stolen so we walked across the border over a bridge. The Rio Grande River looked very polluted, but Mexican kids still played in it. At the time, I thought it looked fun. As an adult, I've become aware of the ramifications, the contributing factors why Mexico's life expectancy is so much lower than ours. Nearly everyone lived in a shack. I remember telling my dad I wished we had a house like that, because they looked like forts. My dad replied that we were more civilized than that. From that day on I wasn't too awed by civilization. I'm still not."

"As long as Canada has hot running water I'll be happy."

We approached a *Welcome to Canada* sign, but were detained before we could reach it. "Pull into stall two please," said a border patrol officer. "Please remove all your possessions so we may search your car." We only had a few things to remove, it being just a weekend trip, but what about the people who were traveling for weeks? This was ten times worse than being carded. "What country are you folks from?"

"Yellowstone," I blurted.

Daphnee strained to contain herself, not completely successfully. A smidgen of mirth bubbled to the surface, like when a person tried to suppress a cough, but couldn't. "I'm from Colorado."

"May I see some identification please." We handed him our licenses. "How long do you plan to stay in Canada?"

"We'll be leaving tomorrow," I answered.

"You may re-pack your car. Have a nice stay."

WE WERE IN! "The signs have French written on them," Daphnee squealed. "And the speed limits are in kilometers. Let's collect some Canadian money."

"I don't think we'll have a problem doing that."

"Two dollars please," said the Waterton Lakes National Park ranger.

I handed him an American ten-dollar bill. "Sorry it's American. That's all I have."

"Most businesses near the border take American currency. After the exchange rate, you receive nine dollars and ninety cents. Enjoy your stay."

"Only ten cents to enter the park," stated Daphnee. "With prices this cheap maybe we should move up here."

Before I could correct her, I noticed her smirking. I reached for her hand and squeezed it.

The Prince of Whales Hotel overlooked the Township of Waterton. The building looked like a large French chateau. Not having the type of money necessary to splurge on a room in the hotel we rented a room in a motel below the hill.

After dropping my bag in the middle of room I locked the door. In addition to turning the lock on the doorknob, I secured the dead bolt. The drapes were already shut, but I pulled them tighter.

When I turned around, Daphnee emptied a box of condoms onto the bed. What expectations did she have for me? She smiled, with a balance of wickedness and warmth. "I'm going to take a shower."

"Okay. I'll watch TV or something." I put the condoms on the nightstand beside the bed. "I'm going to turn down the bedspread. The sheets might be clean, but the rest of the bed....”

I looked back up. Daphnee had her top off, and was pulling down her shorts. She turned around as her bra became unclasped. It dropped to the ground on top of her other clothes. She leaned forward as she pulled down her underwear, stepping out of them. Under some circumstances such a posture may have been considered rude. This wasn't one of them.

I don't think I took a breath until she was out of sight, in the bathroom. Photos in a magazine were pallid substitutes for the real thing. It was not only that real women were in 3-D---they moved. If a picture is worth a thousand words, a real woman is worth a thousand photos.

I heard the shower turn on. Not exactly knowing what to do with myself, I lay on the bed. Television wasn't going to cut it. From the next room I heard, “Maybe you would like to join me.”

I nearly sprained something getting off that bed. By the time I was down to my boxers, reality set in. Was the state I was in the best way to greet a girl? After all, we were just going to take a shower. What would she think? I was also concerned if I got too stimulated too early things might happen prematurely. I tried to think about more wholesome activities, but none came to mind. I took a deep breath. Not a complete descent, but certainly less indecent. I pulled off my underwear and headed into the bathroom. Just seeing Daphnee's silhouette behind the opaque curtain was enough to return me to my original state.

I stepped into the shower. Water dripped from all the *wonders* that were Daphnee, from the hair plastered to her head, to her iridescent brown eyes, down her nose, and off her full, partially opened lips. Continuing between and over her breasts, cascading off their tips. Finally, sliding down her stomach, some of the drops being caught in the curls between her legs before finishing their journey down her legs.

Daphnee smirked as she examined me. “I hope we have enough soap.” She held out her arms. I entered them, then wrapped my arms around her. With the water flowing between us there was minimal friction. Our bodies glided over each other. It felt like being in the womb again, but after a wondrous adult metamorphosis. Our kiss became as liquid as our surroundings, an overture in miniature.

Before we reached a point of no return Daphnee subtly broke away. She tore the soap from its paper wrapping and rubbed it vigorously in her hand, creating a lather. She lowered her hands, making contact with me. If we hadn't been so soapy I may have had that premature release. Even with the soap I was getting close. "I think you're going to need to stop." She didn't. If such a thing was going to happen the shower was the best place for it. "I'm sorry. I did warn you."

Daphnee smiled silently, then bent over to pick up the soap. The embrace from behind was impulsive. Considering what occurred just a moment ago it didn't have the same connotation--- or potential---but it was close. As she leaned back up I filled my hands with her breasts. "Now it's your turn to clean *me*," she said as she handed me the soap. To say I was thorough was an understatement. I may have washed Daphnee for hours if the soap hadn't fallen apart. After rinsing off the suds, the water was turned off. Drying was brief, just enough to prevent us from dripping.

Daphnee dove onto the bed.

With less enthusiasm, I sauntered out of the bathroom. "It might be a few minutes before I'm ready again."

"That's okay. That will allow you time to focus on me."

We spent what remained of the afternoon---and part of the evening---making each other quite happy. Afterwards we cuddled and watched television. It was so wonderful just to see news when one hadn't had television the entire summer.

Daphnee became pensive. She got up and turned off the television. How marvelous it was to see a woman doing common tasks in the nude. Sexual acts were awkward at times, but run of the mill actions flowed. Natural curves, colors, and textures in motion was nature at its most beautiful, at its most wondrous.

"Can we just talk?" asked Daphnee.

"Sure."

Daphnee laid back down on the bed. She pulled the covers tight, then burrowed backwards, against me. I leaned up to look deeply into the prettiest brown eyes I had ever seen. They were the color of soil, something one could build a foundation upon. I kissed her lightly, then settled back down.

"How close am I allowed to get?" she asked.

"As close as you like." I leaned back up to kiss her, but her response was weak. I broke the contact. Her eyes were watering.

"But I must return to school in August. It's already July. How can I let myself fall for you completely when I know we'll eventually be apart? I can't put myself through that. I'm a cautious person. I'm not the type of girl who *has* to have a boyfriend. I didn't come to Yellowstone to find romance."

"Life is so unpredictable. Maybe something will happen to one of us between now and then. If I knew I could have loved you and didn't I would have trouble living with myself. I think I do love you."

"I don't know. I don't know if I'm able to love you, not at this time. Don't be sad. I'm not saying I won't love you. If I allowed myself to love anyone it would be you."

54.   I COULD HAVE KILLED YOU

Hundreds of miles of driving, on top of endless hours of sightseeing and hiking, made it too tiring for me to drive. I pulled into a rest area. "I have to sleep awhile. We'll still get back to Yellowstone in time for work."

"I haven't driven for a while. I'll drive. We're so close to Yellowstone. I don't want to stop now."

"Are you sure you're awake enough to drive?"

"I'm just a little sleepy."

"All right, but if you get *too* sleepy, pull off."

I was half asleep, but enough of my senses remained to know we were passing through Gardiner. We were climbing up to Mammoth. Now we were in Mammoth. We were heading up to the terraces. We were almost up to the Golden Gate and Swan Flats.

The Lemon swerved to the left, then screeched to a stop. Daphnee began to bawl. She opened her door and ran into the darkness. I ran after her. She was sitting beside the road, sobbing hysterically. I tried to comfort her, but she pushed me away. I sat on the ground next to her. After a few minutes, she calmed down. "I fell asleep. I could have killed us."

"But you didn't."

"But I could have. I should have listened to you and slept, but I thought I was awake enough."

"It could as easily been me."

"We almost died."

"Let's look on the bright side. You prevented us from

201

crashing."

"I do love you, Steve." Daphnee tipped me over and smothered me with affection.

55. A STRONG WIND

From Artist Point we saw the three-hundred-foot Lower Falls of the Yellowstone River. The red and yellow canyon dropped one-thousand feet beneath us. It was amazing how a few feet of distance can make things appear so make-believable. The Yellowstone River flowed in slow motion, like it was magma. It took a minute for a whitecap to move a couple of inches. Across the chasm other tourons perched, insects upon epidermis. One slap from a strong wind would bring relief to the canyon.

"Is there a way to hike down, into the canyon?" I asked Charlie.

"There's the Seven-Mile Hole trail, but it's on the other side and five miles in. We don't have enough time before it gets dark."

"You sure we can do thirty-four miles in two-and-a-half days?"

"I've done it before." We walked back to Charlie's van. He spread a Yellowstone map on the carpeting in the back. "We begin up here in the Lamar Valley, and we finish there, at the Pelican Valley trailhead."

"It looks like we're going halfway across the park."

"A safari, except we'll hunt adventure, instead of animals. Twelve people said they would go. That's over four-hundred total miles. It will be the hike of the season. What I don't understand is why more people didn't want to go."

56. SUBMERGED IN DARKNESS

As I feared, the *Hell Hike*, as we later referred to the hike, was turning into a logistical nightmare. I was ready to go, and so was Charlie, but that was it. It was already five o'clock. We had an hour and forty-five-minute drive ahead of us, and a five-mile hike to the first night's campsite. Charlie and I laid side by side, leaning against our backpacks outside Pelican Dorm. People came by to update their progress. Others came by to give their apologies. I had a piece of straw in my mouth. Charlie wore a straw hat.

Christine came up to us. "You guys look like Tom Sawyer and Huckleberry Finn."

"You look like someone who's ready to go," I said.

"ICE CREAM AND ONIONS!" said Charlie enthusiastically. "We have three."

Christine was only the first drop in the canteen. Every five minutes for the next twenty-five someone plopped down their bloated backpack: Samantha, Andy, Daphnee, Tony, and finally Barry.

"I wish we had more people," said Charlie.

"Eight is better than seven," Barry responded. "Yep, yep, yep."

We took three vehicles, one to be parked at the Pelican Valley parking lot and two to go to Lamar Valley. We began hiking at 8:30---PM.

We had to cross the Lamar River fifty feet into the hike, so we thought it best to do so without our boots. A minor inconvenience now meant dry feet later. Andy, Christine, and

203

Samantha put on their wading shoes, but Charlie opted to keep his dry, so they wouldn't drip on him. The rest of us---including me---didn't bring any extra shoes. We---along with Charlie---crossed barefoot. The water was icy and the rocks, sharp, but it was only twenty feet across the river, and early in the hike.

In pairs, we trod down the two-trough trail. I looked at the sun. We weren't going to make it to camp before dark. We spread out. Daphnee was talking to Christine, so I walked a little faster, to catch up to Andy. "This hike will put me at one-hundred and sixty-eight miles," he said to me. "I had one-hundred ninety-five last year. I got so close to two-hundred. I'm definitely going to make it this year. A certificate is given after hiking one-hundred miles. Do you think they'll give me two certificates?"

I calculated my miles. This hike would put me over a hundred and fifty. One-hundred and fifty-two miles to be precise.

We caught up to Charlie. "How many miles do you have?" I asked him.

"I never count. It takes the fun out of hiking. Some people consider mile-counters braggarts. I don't. Everyone must have fun on their weekend---in the manner they consider best for them. To those that do, it's like bragging about how much money you make."

I stopped beside the trail to allow Daphnee to catch up to me. "How you doing?" I asked her.

"Fine. Ask me again in thirty-three miles."

We had to cross another stream. When did it become so dark? The cluster of trees we entered had something to do with it. We could barely see the bottom of the water, so we all wore boots or shoes to cross this time. My wet boots felt refreshing at first, but after fifteen minutes they became just soggy. Slosh. Squeak.

The terrain transformed from sage and golden wild grass to sparse lodgepole and green bush. The trail reunited with the Lamar River. It followed its course, but from a respectable hundred feet. Through forest and occasional meadow, we concentrated on spotting the trail. We alternated between hiking up gentle slopes and moseying on restive flats. There were just two flashlights amongst us, and they were both ahead. I didn't think we would be hiking in the dark. A woman sang ahead. Samantha? Her high-pitched wane became a beacon. As long as I heard it I knew I was close to others of my party, and likely going in the right direction. We must have slowed considerably, because those last two miles took an eternity.

We saw light ahead. Daphnee hugged me. Charlie, Samantha, and Andy were waiting for us. Christine, Tony, and Barry caught up a few minutes later.

A sign pointed to our campsite. It was submerged in darkness between the trail and the river. We climbed through bushes, around trees, and over fallen logs to reach the river. We didn't see any evidence of a campsite. We spread out. A fire ring and food pole were stumbled upon a couple of minutes later.

First things first. We needed to start a fire. Not only would it bring us warmth, but also light. The flashlights could go out any minute. It wasn't cold yet, but the fire still brought comfort. We ate dinner, then set up camp. We had three tents, but we decided not to use them. It was a clear night and we were awfully tired. After working all day and hiking two tense miles---plus three easy ones---we fell asleep almost immediately.

57. THREAT OF BEARS AND BEING BURNT ALIVE

In the morning, our surroundings became evident. Why weren't we able to find our campsite more quickly? Breakfast length varied considerably. I took five minutes to eat an orange and a granola bar, and drink a can of apple juice. Other people ate sack lunches. Barry cooked himself oatmeal, and had half-a-dozen side dishes. The rest of us were packed before he was done eating. Andy and Tony were anxious to begin hiking, just slightly more than the rest of us, so they started while Barry packed. "We won't get too far ahead," Andy assured us. To re-pack, Barry had to first take everything out of his pack. His stuff was evenly scattered in a five-foot radius. By the time he was finished we were a good hour behind the scouting party.

Two miles later---two of the seventeen we allotted for the day---Charlie yelled, "BISON!" As I turned around I saw the sign, abruptly becoming aware that I had overshot the fork. The six of us clustered around our guide. Charlie took out his map. "We take the right fork. If we had gone straight we would be following Miller Creek, not the Lamar River."

"Do you think Andy and Tony saw the sign?" asked Christine nervously. "Both trails go upstream."

"We'll leave a note," said Samantha. "They'll realize they are heading the wrong way after they notice the trail heading east instead of south. We'll let them know we continued on."

"I'm going to run down the Miller Creek Trail a bit," said Charlie. "Maybe I'll find them, or they'll at least hear me shouting." Charlie took off his pack and sprinted. We bided our time by eating *gorp*: a mixture or peanuts, raisins, and M&Ms.

Charlie returned fifteen minutes later. "I went about a mile and saw footprints from what could have been Andy's boots. I yelled, but there was no reply."

Miller Creek was crossed in two clusters. Boulders and tree trunks were placed in such a manner that if a person was athletic, almost of gymnastic ability---and lucky---he, or she, could cross without getting wet. Charlie, Samantha, and I made it across. The others decided to wade. Daphnee's sour look as she stepped into the water was understandable. My boots were still partially damp from the crossing the night before. Daphnee's would be soaked for the remainder of the day.

We caught up to the Lamar River a third time. According to the map it would be some time before we left it again. Its shore alternated between sandy beaches and rocky cliffs. We were walking in paradise and there wasn't anyone---or thing---around to spoil it: no roads, no cities, no civilization. Our pace was slow. Paradise bred contentment. And contentment bred sloth. It didn't help that Barry stopped to take a photo every five minutes. He brought a tripod with him, so his photography consisted of more than pointing and shooting. We hiked just six miles and it was already two o'clock. We still had ten miles to go before reaching our campsite. It could have been worse. We still had seven hours of daylight remaining.

Smoke rose to the west. Charlie stopped and looked at his map. "That's Mirror Plateau," he announced.

"There's been a lot of fires this summer," stated Daphnee.

"It wasn't like that last year," said Samantha.

"It's dryer this year," Christine elucidated.

"Yellowstone has 2.2 million acres," Barry reminded us. "A few hundred burned is but a single leaf on a tree. As long as the fires are put out before they spread."

"But they aren't being put out," I said. "I read in the paper that Yellowstone has a *let burn* policy. If a fire is started by natural causes, such as by a lightning strike, nothing is done."

"It's a good policy," Charlie stated. "Lodgepole pines reproduce with the help of fire. Their cones won't crack open unless there's intense heat. Fire enriches the soil. Yellowstone's forests should remain as natural as possible."

"But Yellowstone is a national park, a natural crown jewel," Barry countered. "Shouldn't we have some obligation to protect the flora, and fauna, and historic structures?"

"Not too many years ago the powers to be thought like that. Every fire, no matter how small, no matter what caused it, was put out. The result was an unnatural amount of dead timber. You've probably noticed it hiking in some parts of the Park. It's become kindling. One-hundred years ago a dry spell like this wouldn't have resulted in so many fires."

To get a closer look at the fire, we left the trail, crossing a small meadow to reach the sandy shore of the Lamar River. I heard rustling. Something was moving downstream. "HEY! That looks like Bighorn and the Mosquito," Christine announced. They ran towards the trail at a diagonal. We yelled at them.

They slowed to a saunter. Tony looked defeated. "We were so close to sneaking past you."

"Where have you been?" asked Christine.

Andy's face reddened. "We took the wrong trail."

"How far did you go before you realized it?" asked Samantha. "Charlie went after you, along Miller Creek, but I guess you were too far away. Did you see our note?"

"We went two miles, I think," said Andy.

"We talked to two beautiful Norwegian girls," Tony bragged. "We found out from them we were going the wrong way."

"You didn't really talk to two beautiful Norwegian women," stated Daphnee.

"Yes, we did," Andy insisted. "And they were just seventeen, so they were girls. Here's something for you Christine. I recognized your handwriting." He handed her the note.

"We practically ran the whole way to catch up to you," said Tony. "When we saw you, we tried to sneak by, so it would look like we were ahead of you."

"You notice the fire?" asked Andy.

"How couldn't we," I said.

"Let's take a group photo," Barry insisted, "with the fire behind us." He set his camera on the tripod, focused, hit the timer, then ran to his spot. Click.

"I want a copy of that one," said Daphnee.

"Me too," echoed through the group.

"We better get moving," said Andy. "We're less than a mile from the fire. We'll be in trouble if it suddenly heads our direction."

Flames could now be seen.

With the fire so close, our pace increased. I wanted to get away from it, but a part of me wanted it to follow us. It was exciting. Every few minutes I turned around to watch its approach. We were getting farther away, which didn't mean the fire wasn't coming our way. It just meant we were moving faster than it.

Once the fire disappeared our dissimilar hiking styles came into play again. Andy sprinted ahead, then waited for the rest of us to catch up. Charlie stayed near the back, so no one would get lost, but occasionally he sprinted ahead to scout out the area, especially if a fork was coming. The rest of us were more constant in our movement, our individual paces based on both ability and will.

At six o'clock, we lost the trail at a junction of three creeks, which, according to the map, coincided with a fork of the trail. A compass didn't help. The creeks twisted direction every hundred feet. We needed a more detailed map. A fourth creek and a slough were discovered a couple of minutes later. Where were the signs? We found a trail on the southwestern shore of one of the creeks. It looked promising. Elevation was gained immediately, matching the map.

We went up, and up. The last thing a person wanted to do at the end of the day with muscles sore and feet tired was climb a mountain. When was it ever going to end? Someone screamed ahead of me. I continued climbing, afraid to go on, but anxious to help. And discover what went wrong. Andy, Samantha, and Tony ran towards me. "WE WENT THE WRONG WAY!" shrieked Samantha. I followed them down, Daphnee dragging her feet, dejectedly, a few steps behind me.

"We were heading south," Andy explained. "We should have been heading west. I thought it was strange we were climbing for so long, but assumed it was fatigue causing me to overestimate. We were supposed to go over a ridge, not a mountain."

"We must have climbed a thousand feet," said Tony.

"That we didn't have to," added Samantha. "And an extra

five miles by the time we return to that junction from hell."

Charlie smiled when he saw us coming towards him. "It was time for something else to go wrong. Let the adventure never end." He extracted his map and was able to match up the trail we were on with one on the parchment. "Lucky that we stopped when we did. We still had a thousand more feet to climb before the trail leveled off."

"In another three miles, we would have been completely out of the Park," said Samantha, peaking over Charlie's shoulder. "At Frost Lake."

"And what a cold reception that would have been when we read the park boundary sign."

Surprisingly, we were in a jolly mood again. We were no longer hiking up hill, and there was only three more miles to go until we reached camp. An hour more if we pushed.

By trial and error, we eventually found the correct trail. It was getting dark, so we opted to camp at a site near the junction, instead of hiking the rest of the way---in the dark. "I remember this campsite on the ranger station map," said Charlie. "It was closed due to the numerous grizzly sightings in the area. Water attracts bears and there is plenty of that here. We should be safe with eight people."

While looking for firewood and for a food pole, we found bear scat, just fifty feet from the fire ring. "That's pretty fresh," said Andy. "Look at all that moisture still in it. From today would be my guess. We may have guests tonight."

"But they won't attack," I stated, but not with confidence.

"Probably not."

We didn't find a food pole. It was probably taken down when the campsite was made inactive. Before it got dark, we found a suitable tree to hang food from, a couple of hundred feet from camp. After dinner, we pulled the food up, not completely confident it would still be there in the morning. Losing the food would be devastating. We needed the energy to complete the last seventeen miles of the hike.

Charlie handed out iodine water purification tablets. I heard they weren't too reliable, so I boiled my water. Who said you can't burn water? Or was it the pan that had burned? The water tasted terrible, but at least it wouldn't give me the runs.

We built a roaring fire, with a huge pile of logs and sticks stacked in reserve nearby. We huddled next to the pulsating heat, not wanting to be too far away from its protection in case the bear or one of its friends returned.

We could see the forest fire again. "It's still five miles away," said Charlie, "but if the wind picks up it can travel that far in a couple of hours. We better keep a fire watch tonight in case we have to bug out."

Another night sleeping without tents. Who wanted to spend time packing a tent when one was fleeing for his life? It was difficult to fall asleep with the threat of bears and being burnt alive. Whenever the wind changed directions someone different got their sleeping bag fumigated with campfire smoke. To remedy the situation, we hid our heads in our bags. We only poked them out for an occasional breath of fresh air, or to look at the glow to the north.

58. LIKE A ZOMBIE

In the morning, the fire didn't appear to be any closer than it was the night before. Charlie was still up. "I didn't want to wake anyone to relieve me. Everyone needed their rest. It's going to be a long day today."

"You needed your rest as much as any of us," said

Samantha.

"This hike was my idea, therefore I'm responsible for everyone's wellbeing. Everyone must have fun on their weekend."

"Including you."

"I am. I spent most of the night reminiscing."

"You must have been very concerned."

We found our food intact. Barry took as long to get ready as he did the day before. We left late, again. It was already 10 a.m.

As expected, the route up the pass was more gradual than the evening before. Near the top of the ridge, I heard a scream. NOT AGAIN! Should I hurry ahead or limit my losses? "Come on," said Daphnee.

We huddled around Andy. He was breathing profusely. "What happened?" asked Christine.

"It came at me. It was fierce."

"A grizzly?" asked Tony.

"A bison?" asked Daphnee.

"It was a grouse." Everyone who knew what a grouse was began to laugh. "It was only knee high and kind of scrawny looking, but it was ferocious. It must have been protecting its young."

"Did it attack you?" asked Christine.

"Taunted more than attacked. But it did chase me a bit before...."

"Before?"

"I taunted it back."

"You screamed."

"I scared it off."

The trail leveled off near where we should have camped. The campsite was on the edge of the meadow Mist Creek flowed through. It would have been a nice place to spend the night, but how could it compete with the excitement of the night before?

The trail rose again as we climbed Mist Pass. I spent most of the hike near the back, because Daphnee was there, but now I wanted to give it my all. I passed Samantha first, then Tony. I passed Andy as the top of the pass came into view. Andy and Tony ran to try to catch up to me, but they didn't make it in time. They hiked the last few yards in slow motion. They were completely drained.

We ate lunch on the pass---hastily. No mosquitoes, but gigantic flies that pilfered vast plugs of flesh every time they landed.

I felt cheated. I used all that energy to get to the top of the pass first and wasn't able to relax for those extra minutes I gained.

Part way down the other side of the pass, we entered a clearing, bestowing a view of Pelican Valley. Lush grass was seen for miles. The area was famous for wildlife, especially for grizzlies. The density of those bears was so great the valley was only open from 9 a.m. to 7 p.m., dissuading nocturnal encounters.

At the bottom of the hill was an unoccupied, but locked ranger patrol cabin. "It sure would have been nice to stay in one last night," I commented.

"And forego the potential for being eaten by grizzlies as a fire burned us alive?" Charlie responded, before shaking his head.

We crawled through Pelican Valley under a sweltering sun. It was late afternoon and the temperature was at its max for the day. Possibly for the year. Daphnee was beginning to noticeably slow. I became concerned. Others were also slowing, but not as much as she was. I stayed with her as she fell behind.

We were drenched with sweat and exhausted by the time we reached a creek crossing, two miles into the valley. We didn't even consider taking off our boots as we sloshed across. It felt great. It was cool, but not cold. The water was nearly stagnant, but clear. "Let's go swimming," Charlie suggested.

"But we need to get out before seven," Andy insisted.

"We have plenty of time." The rest of us concurred.

We stripped down to our underwear. We waded and splashed for 30 minutes. Then took another ten to dry off in the sun. We felt rejuvenated. We put our shirts and shorts back on, our barely damp undergarments feeling more refreshing than soggy.

After a mile, we were hot and tired again. "I think we have three miles left," I announced. Daphnee cheered up. After two more miles, we came to a fork at a bridge. A skull of an anonymous animal hung at the opposite end. A sign boasted we still had 3.4 miles to go.

Daphnee looked angry. She hit me, then began walking--- slowly.

A hairy shape was on the perimeter of the forest about a half-mile away. "IT'S A GRIZZLY!" Daphnee squealed. We hadn't seen one yet on our trip, so she was understandably excited.

I asked Charlie if I could borrow his monocular. "It's a bison."

Daphnee hit me again. "If you didn't look at it closely it would have stayed a grizzly." She walked ahead, pouting.

When we left the valley, we had just a mile-and-a-half remaining. Every time we went around a curve I believed the trailhead would greet us. Daphnee was slowing down even more. She shuffled her feet like she was a zombie. Her eyes were glazed. "Would you like to rest awhile?" I asked her. No reply. "Would you like to eat or drink something?" No reply. "I'll carry your pack for you. I can carry it on a shoulder. It's not that far to the trailhead now."

"Like when we had just three more miles to go?" Daphnee countered softly, like the whisper of a radio when the batteries were dying.

"You sure you don't want me to carry your pack?"

"I want to complete the hike on my own. I don't need anyone's help."

Thirty minutes later Daphnee complained about being cold. I was still sweating so I became *very* concerned. She might have heat exhaustion. SHE COULD BE GOING INTO SHOCK! She refused to stop. The remainder of the party huddled ahead. This had to be the end.

"There they are," said Charlie. "I was on the brink of searching for you. We have just a quarter of a mile to go."

It was close enough for Daphnee. She lay down without even taking her pack off. "Maybe we can drive the car down here," I suggested.

"Not easily," said Andy. "The gate's locked." The last stretch was on an old dirt road, so my suggestion was more reasonable than it sounded.

"Let's get up and out of here," said Charlie. "If we stay immobile for much longer we'll become too stiff to move." The rest revitalized Daphnee. She got up and actually looked energetic. To the disgusted look of my hiking companions I ran the last one-hundred yards to the gate. I had to finish this thirty-five---ah, thirty-nine---mile hike in style.

When Daphnee reached the parking lot she fell back onto her pack.

59. BETTER THAN NOT PLAYING AT ALL

"You're sure you don't want to play, Charlie?"

"I would rather live life than role play it."

"How about you, Andy?"

"I'm looking forward to it, Steve. Ryan has put a lot of time into the game."

"Who else is playing?"

"Tony and Barry."

"No women?"

"They would rather participate in reality than pretend in an alternate universe."

"Unless it involves reading romance novels."

We entered Ryan's room. He had papers scattered on his desk, including a homemade map of Yellowstone. "Who would like to be map-maker and note-taker?" he asked. No one spoke. The note-taking sounded too much like school.

"I'll do it," I volunteered. From the looks my friends gave me they were thinking *teacher's pet*.

"I guess that makes you the leader, Steve. The lives of your teammates are now your responsibility. Make yourselves comfortable. I'll keep track of all statistics and player characteristics. I'm trying to make this game as realistic as possible. If players know every minute detail about their characters, it makes the game too mechanical. I will give notice when characters progress, saying things like *Bighorn is getting stronger*. Character traits are divided into six categories: *attack, defense, ranged, damage, health, and luck. Attack* is your ability to connect with a blow. *Damage* is the severity of the blow, primarily based on your strength. *Defense* is your ability to counter attacks made against you. Your *ranged* ability determines how accurate you are with a bow, or other projectile device, and how far away your target can be. *Health* determines how much endurance you have, and is an indicator of how much life energy you have remaining. When it's down to zero you are not only dead tired, you're dead. *Luck* is self-explanatory. When you want to do something, no matter how crazy it is, *luck* determines your chances of doing it. It also can be used against you if you have a particularly low *luck* rating. You all begin with eighteen ability rating points to be split amongst the six categories. As in real life, you choose the paths of your development. Steve?"

"Well, if I'm supposed to be leader I should be well balanced. Make all my categories level three."

"Wuss," said Tony.

"Since you have all the answers, why don't you go next."

"I want to be an archer. If I can attack monsters well from a distance I will live longer. Make my *ranged* ability level eight, and all the other categories level two."

"Bighorn?"

"I'm not ready yet. Give me a minute."

"Bald Owl?"

Barry grinned insanely. "I want to be a wizard." He laughed wickedly. "I want to alter reality."

"This isn't a fantasy game like Dungeons and Dragons," said Ryan. "You can't perform any spells, and there won't be any dragons. It's a game about hiking in Yellowstone. Something unusual might pop up, like crocodiles in the Firehole River or giant eagles, but nothing too far from the fringes of reality. If you want some odd things to happen to your character, why don't you give him a high *luck* rating?"

"How high a *luck* rating can I have?"

"You have to spend at least one point in the other categories."

"Then that is what I'm going to do. Put all my remaining points in *luck*."

"So, your *luck* rating becomes 13 and your other abilities are at level one. You ready, now, Bighorn?"

"The logical choice is to become a warrior, if we must defend ourselves from wild animals: Level five *attack*, level four *damage*, level three *health*, level two the others."

"Let the game begin. You are political prisoners in the Thirtieth Century. A coup has ousted your political party, and as the leaders of your party you must be punished and kept out of the public's eye. The death penalty has been dropped from civilized thought long ago, so you are exiled to Penitentiary Planet, a terra-formed world used exclusively to house prisoners. It's lead designer had recently vacationed with his family on Earth, spending significant time in Yellowstone Global Park. To pay homage to the park many of its features were replicated in the prison. The world was left wild, forcing the criminals sentenced to it to fend for themselves. The warden is not without sympathy for her prisoners. You are provided with a bow, arrows, sword, paper, pens, compass, clothing, camping equipment, and lightweight armor. Food grows on trees. Your mission: to escape Penitentiary Planet so you can reclaim the universe. Good Luck.

"You materialize in a savannah. A river meanders a mile to the east. Forest is two miles to the south and can be seen on the horizons in the other three directions. Yelping is heard to the west. Birds cluster in the sky in the same direction."

"Is that a hint?" asked Tony.

"Play the part," Barry insisted.

"Play with this." Tony pointed to his groin.

"Should we see what all the commotion is about?" I asked.

"Maybe someone---or thing---is there to give us some information," said Andy. "We have to start somewhere."

"It makes sense to me. Does everyone agree? Good. We're heading towards the birds and the yelping. We're going at a leisurely pace, so we don't tire ourselves needlessly."

"You can now see six dingoes chewing on something. A dozen vultures circle the carrion, waiting for the canines to leave so they can eat. What is your move?"

"I fire an arrow at the dingoes," said Tony.

"You miss badly, Mosquito. The dingoes look up, then continue feeding."

"We're too far away," said Tony. "Let's get closer."

"Are you all going with the Mosquito?"

"Our first clue may be ahead," said Andy. "We must see what the dingoes are attacking."

"Let's find some treasure," says Barry, "so we can buy some herbal supplements. We can improve our abilities, can't we, from eating certain things."

"You'll have to see for yourself."

"I think it's just as likely eating something will cause a detrimental effect," said Andy. "I don't think we should risk randomly eating something. There has to be someone around, maybe a pharmacist, who knows what affect each plant has."

"We're continuing forward, half the distance to the dingoes," I said.

"I'll fire another arrow when we stop," said Tony.

"You miss again. The dingoes look up again. They study you this time, then return to their feeding."

"I think we should be careful," said Andy.

"I'll continue to shoot arrows until they are all dead," said Tony. "Or until they attack."

"Your next arrow hits a dingo and kills it. Two dingoes run towards you."

"May I shoot another arrow and still draw my sword?" asked Tony.

"Yes, but just barely."

"I do then."

"You miss with the arrow. One dingo attacks you. The other attacks Bald Owl. You both fail to hit the dingoes, but the Mosquito is bit. Fortunately, the wound is superficial."

"Bighorn and I will head toward the other four dingoes," I said. "If that's all right with you, Andy?"

"I don't know if I like the odds, but let's get on with the show."

"The Mosquito hits his dingo and kills it. Bald Owl misses again and this time he gets a superficial wound. It takes a while to reach the dingoes, so the Mosquito and Bald Owl may strike again, if they wish."

"We do."

"You both miss, but so does the dingo, who continues to attack Bald Owl."

"The feeding dingoes do not attack, but they occasionally look up."

"Shall we attack them, Andy?"

"Let's."

"Only the two dingoes you attack fight back. Both miss as does Bison. Bighorn kills his dingo. Bald Owl, the Mosquito, and their dingoes miss. Do you continue fighting?"

"Yes."

"All three feeding dingoes attack. Bison is bit. Blood is drawn, but you are still able to fight. Bighorn kills another dingo. The Mosquito, Bald Owl, and their dingoes miss again. The three surviving dingoes flee."

"Should we go after them?" asked Tony.

"What for?" I asked.

"They hurt you. For revenge."

"Let's see what they left us."

"The vultures still circle, and wait. They don't attack."

"I forgot about them."

"Me too," Andy replied. "Let's be more cautious in the future."

"Five bodies lay mutilated. They are in a mangled mass, so it's difficult to see if they have anything of value on them."

"I don't think the dingo killed them," I said. "They were no match for us, and we are rookies. I believe the dingoes discovered the free dinner, and began to feast."

"I agree," said Andy.

"Let's see what's underneath them," said Barry. "I need my herbal supplements."

"It's bad luck to forage through corpses," said Andy.

"It's only bad luck to have someone forage through your own corpse," said Tony.

"What do we find?" asked Barry.

"Bones, flesh, blood, a notebook...and a small brown crystal."

"That looks promising," said Barry. "I wonder what it does? I'm going to swallow it."

"Why does Barry get the crystal?" Tony whined. "Shouldn't we flip a coin for it, or roll some dice or something?"

"Barry has been begging to put an unknown substance into his body since we started playing," I said, taking my leadership role seriously. "The next thing we find can be yours, the third Andy's. The one after that will be mine. We don't even know if that crystal can be consumed. It might be inert. It could be this planet's equivalent of currency."

"If it doesn't dissolve in my body how long will it take to pass through my body?" asked Barry.

"We'll just have to see," said Ryan.

"I'm going to swallow it."

"Wait," said Andy. "Maybe we should examine that notebook first. It might give us a clue about the crystal."

"I agree," I quickly added, before Ryan could do something nasty to Barry. "We're looking at the notebook first. What do we find? What is written in it?"

"*It has been a daily fight to survive. I don't think this planet is done forming. Henry is beginning to change, like the others before him. He is becoming exceedingly animalistic in nature. I left during the night, attempting to flee before he attacked me. I keep on running. He and the others are getting closer. I can hear them, sporadically. Sometimes I even see them from a distance, but then they are gone again. Maybe I'm going insane. Have I also begun to change? My features look the same, but the initial changes could be internal. The only good to come from my companions turning into beasts is most of them no longer care about having possessions. I've accumulated quite a fortune picking through their human discards. I see them again, coming from the northeast, where most of them live, in caves along the canyon....*"

"Was that it?" asked Tony.

"What was legible. The rest of the notebook is soiled in mud---and blood."

"I'm going to swallow that brown crystal now," said Barry.

"You feel a surge through your veins. Your entire body tingles. You feel rejuvenated. It's difficult to stay still."

221

"I think we need to find some more of those."

"If we do, let's wait to swallow them, after we get injured or walking all day," said Andy. "I wouldn't be surprised if one of those crystals brought a person back from the brink of death."

"I think we should try to find those people who turned into animals," said Tony. "It looks like they finally caught up to this guy, and took his treasure."

"If those guys are contagious, I don't think we should go near them," said Andy.

"Didn't the notebook imply that the terra-forming process that transformed the planet is also changing the people living on it?" I said. "There might be an antidote somewhere, though. We need to keep our eyes open, and ask anyone we see. Anyone still human."

"The notebook mentioned them living northeast of here in a canyon," said Tony. "If this place is a replica of Yellowstone, then that canyon must be our Canyon."

"And this grassland we're in must be Hayden Valley," added Andy.

"Those mutants are likely to put up a better fight than those dingoes," I warned.

"We'll, I'm ready for a challenge," said Tony. "I didn't come here to talk. If that's all you guys want to do, we might as well get our dolls out too. Let's fight something."

"We're heading northeast. Once we see a river we'll re-evaluate our course of action. If this is Hayden Valley, the Yellowstone River has to be nearby."

"You don't see a river yet, but after two miles you see grazing beasts: giraffes, antelope, zebras. You also see lions. They are watching the grazers, but aren't paying any attention to you."

"Let's kill the cats," said Tony. "We'll shoot them dead before they know what hit them."

"They aren't important," said Andy. "We'll waste time and possible get someone killed."

"We continue northeast," I said.

"In two more miles, you come to a flowing body of water. It is fifty feet across and shallow---maybe two or three feet deep."

"That doesn't sound like the Yellowstone River. We cross the creek."

"The water is swifter than it looks. Everyone except Bald Owl has trouble keeping upright. He either has good balance or he is very lucky. Bighorn falls and is dragged against the rocks on the bottom of the creek. He has trouble getting up, because of his heavy pack."

"Is anyone close enough to help him?"

"He's too far downstream. But it isn't necessary. Bighorn gets up and makes it the last ten feet across the water. He is badly bruised and shaken up. He is slowed, but far from dead."

"We should have been more careful," said Andy. "We should have held hands or used rope to cross."

"We'll learn," said Barry. "Life is a learning experience. The more you live the more you learn. I really respect older people, because they know so much about life."

"We continue northeast," I said. "Do we see any sign of those people mentioned in the notebook?"

"Nothing discernible. Forest is two miles ahead. To the west is a herd of bison. There are thousands of them. It looks unreal, like from the days of Buffalo Bill."

"Buffalo Bill was a wimp," said Tony. "He used a gun. I can do just as well with a bow. I fire at the beasts if I'm close enough."

"You are, and you kill one, which causes a stampede in your direction."

"We run away towards the forest," I said.

"The bison catch up to you, but you only encounter the fringe of the herd. Tony is trampled to death."

"So, I'm out of the game? GREAT!"

"If you weren't so stupid you wouldn't have gotten yourself killed," said Andy. "You nearly killed the rest of us too."

"Wait," says Barry. "Maybe you can be reincarnated or something."

"Tony still looks dead. You all are tired."

"There you are." Daphnee walked into the room through the already opened doorway. "You still playing that game?"

"We're trying to find some mutants, so we can take their treasure," I responded. "We should be done in another hour."

Daphnee appeared both upset and perplexed, with a pinch of disappointment. "Would you rather spend time playing that game, or playing with a real live girl?"

"I need to be going, guys. If you aren't reincarnated soon, Tony, you can play my character---if you promise not to get him killed."

"So, you like to role play, huh?" Daphnee whispered to me as we headed to her room.

"Kathleen prevents Ryan from hiking. This is his substitution to exploring the wilderness. I just had to play. I haven't seen him this excited in weeks."

"I guess playing in a make-believe Yellowstone is better than not playing in Yellowstone at all. So, do you want me to dress up as a buffalo or a mutant?"

60.   AFTER THE ENTHUSIASM WANES

I sat down beside Ryan in the EDR. "I'm sorry I had to leave the game early. Daphnee needed me for something."

"I'm the last guy you need to apologize to for being led on a leash. If only it wasn't such a beautiful leash."

"It must be awful working split hours every day."

"Not really. I only have to work four hours in the morning, leaving my entire afternoon free."

"But you can't go very far."

"There's a lot to do in the Lake Area. With going to Billings or Bozeman or Jackson or Cody on the weekends with Kathleen, it's my only time to go hiking."

"Other than Elephant's Back where else can you go?"

"Sometimes I walk along the lakeshore. There's also that trail to Fishing Bridge---it's only a mile long, but it's sure pretty. Then if I wanted to go further I could take the Howard Eaten trail from Fishing Bridge to Canyon for a-ways. Why complain about being stuck in one location when there are more things to do outdoors here than in any city?" And I was worried about Ryan. His accumulative short hikes probably added up to what I did on my weekends.

"Are you going anywhere today?"

"I'm heading to Fishing Bridge. A couple of times a week I like to get ice cream from the Hamilton Fountain."

"Do you mind if I tag along? When I have to work at three or four I usually sit by the lake for a couple of hours."

"Sure, but don't expect this to be a workout. I like to take my time, looking at things as I go."

"That's fine with me. Who needs to be tired before work?"

The trail began at Lake Lodge. It meandered through the wild grasses between the Yellowstone River and the inland forest. Periodically, a copse of lodgepoles clung to the shore, but there were plenty of places open enough to see the headwaters of the Yellowstone River.

"Steve, come over here." Ryan was looking down at one of the spawning streams that crossed the meadow on its way down to the river. The steam was only a foot wide, and barely as deep. It was so well in sync with its environment that a person couldn't even tell it was there unless he was directly over it.

"There's a fish swimming in it," I observed.

"A rainbow trout."

"It's nearly as large as the stream. Why is it doing something so foolish?"

"I imagine it wants to spawn. Humans have been known to do even crazier things when they have the urge."

We were forced to make a detour a few minutes later. Three bison had strategically spaced themselves, forcing us to the bluff overlooking the river. Trumpeter Swans swam downstream, towards Fishing Bridge. South of them, near the river's mouth, pelicans mooned us as they bobbed for fish. The sky had that magical three to one ratio of blue sky to fluffy white clouds that coerced one to daydream. "Sometimes I bring my portable hammock here, lay down, and read a good book," Ryan shared. "After a couple of chapters I usually put the book down and take a nap."

"I imagine there are days you sleep right through dinner."

"Something always wakes me by five. Maybe it's the growing shadows. Perhaps the dropping temperatures. Nature takes care of us. It soothes us, then it acts as our alarm clock."

The last few yards to Fishing Bridge was down fifty wooden steps, built just this year, to prevent any additional erosion to the bluff. "Don't walk down barefoot," Ryan warned. "I learned my painful lesson last month. Some of the splinters are worn down since then, but not all of them."

There was a walkway on each side of the wooden Fishing Bridge, walled off to protect pedestrians from motorized traffic. We walked on the south side to see the fish below. The water beneath the bridge on the other side was in shadows. "There are so many of them," I said. "They cluster near the bridge."

"They know that people aren't allowed to fish off the bridge anymore."

We bought our ice cream cones in the Ham Store, a wood and stone structure much larger than Lake's general store. We carried them with us as we headed home. I needed to be at work in

90 minutes. "Did you hear about Barry getting arrested?" Ryan asked.

"WHAT?!"

"The rangers caught him smoking pot outside Pelican. He had enough on him that he was not only arrested for possession, but for intent to sell."

"How can someone be so stupid?"

"He was very upset about something he didn't want to talk about. He wasn't thinking, but I guess that's what most drugs do to people."

"What's going to happen to him?"

"He's in jail up in Mammoth right now. I don't think he's going to come back."

"I bet Martha Devla helped with that."

"No, the Wolf did all she could to keep him out of jail. *Why should he be put in jail for doing something that doesn't harm anyone?* she reasoned with the rangers rather loudly. Nothing helped."

"I guess this is the time of year people begin to leave."

"But they shouldn't be forced out, against their will. Everyone should be able to choose their time for departure. End games should only occur after the enthusiasm wanes."

61. LIKE A BIG HOT TUB

Another quiet night at the pub. If the state legislature really wanted to make a moral statement, why didn't they forbid the sale of alcohol completely on Sunday, instead of after ten? Token gestures still got people re-elected. With the pub closing about the time it normally began to pop most people decided it wasn't worth showing up at all---except for when the EDR had a particularly bad meal. After the first tooth was cracked on the pork chops, people flocked to the pub. In contrast, the nachos and pizza served there were always of the highest caliber. It was sad but true, prepaying diminished quality.

Daphnee, Christine, Andy, Tony, Rebecca, and I shared a table.

"I have an idea," Rebecca announced. "Something we can do tonight. Let's go hotpotting."

"Isn't Boiling River closed at night?" I asked.

"We don't have to go there. There's a hotpot north of Old Faithful called Ranger Pool."

"I've never heard of it," said Daphnee.

"That's because it's illegal," said Andy. "Any thermal pool that doesn't have a cold-water source to regulate its heat is unsafe."

"I've been there many times," said Rebecca. "It's like a big hot tub."

"With algae growing in it," added Andy.

"If it's so unsafe why is it called Ranger Pool?" asked Christine. "How many hotpots do you think the rangers know about, legal or otherwise, they keep to themselves?"

"Let's go hotpotting," Tony declared.

"I'm up for it," I seconded.

"Me too," added Daphnee.

"We shouldn't stay up late tonight," said Andy. "We have to hike nine miles tomorrow after a full day of work."

"Let's see if Charlie and Samantha want to come along," said Tony.

"They probably want to go to bed early," said Daphnee. "They're traveling to Denver tomorrow to go to that wedding."

"We can at least ask them," I said.

"You sure you want to go hotpotting?" Andy asked Christine.

"You remember what happened at Three Rivers?"

"We're going at night. You'll be surprised what I'm willing to do in the dark."

62. RETURNING TO WHERE WE SPAWNED

"Sure, we would love to go," said Charlie. "Nothing helps a person to fall asleep better than a hot soak in a hotpot. That's all right with you, Sam?"

"Did you have to ask? I haven't been hotpotting at all this summer. To glide unhindered by cloth or social barrier through pulsating liquid heat...."

So, it was going to be another skinny-dipping thing. It explains why Christine was so hesitant. The hotpot was probably more out in the open than the one in Cody. And probably not as deep. Am I going to be able to do this? What if I become excited? If I was low enough in the water and the water wasn't too clear. Andy said something about it being covered in Algae. I wouldn't mind seeing the girls naked, especially Samantha. It was hard not to imagine her in that state. Why didn't such things have an on and off switch? I was even...curious...about Christine and Rebecca. I should have just been thinking about Daphnee. Why did guys think about other girls being naked? The only girl I wanted to have a relationship with was Daphnee, so why did my mind occasional wander to other girls? I looked at Daphnee. Something just came to me. It's just as likely Daphnee was going to see guys naked as it was for me to see girls.

We traveled an hour before turning onto a side road called *Firehole Lake Drive*. There was steam all around us. We passed a parking lot beside an *S* curve. Charlie continued for another mile, before stopping at a second parking lot where the road turned back towards the highway. "The hotpot is a half-mile back," he said, "but parking right next to Ranger Pool would draw attention."

"Doesn't seven people walking down a road at night with towels in their hands look conspicuous?" asked Daphnee.

We could barely see the blacktop beneath us, but we didn't want to risk turning on a flashlight. "Now, where is that sign?" said Charlie to himself. Every few paces he jumped off the road on the left to examine the terrain. "Here it is." He risked a brief illumination from his flashlight. A sign boldly stated: *Dangerous Thermal Area. Do Not Go Beyond This Point*.

Charlie pushed his way through the trees beyond the sign. We followed. The landscape was barren beyond the foliage. Charlie changed directions in a seeming haphazard fashion. Steam rose around us. Most of the time there was about an inch of water beneath us. I was careful to step where Charlie stepped. I feared a one-foot deviation meant falling into a boiling cauldron.

Charlie stopped, then laid down a tarp. "Here we are." The spot didn't look any different than any other. He put his towel on the tarp and began undressing. "You'll want to put anything you want to keep dry on the tarp. The steam will get them wet. Will the last person fold the tarp over, please?" Charlie's bare butt walked into oblivion. A splash, then the sound of someone moving through water.

Samantha was next to disrobe. I tried not to appear like I was watching her. It was so dark and misty she was more ethereal than flesh. A dark patch was at her midsection and two smaller patches were slightly above. They looked like the eyes and nose of a ghost. When she bent down to organize her clothes on the tarp, her firm breasts and their acute tips gave her true identity away. She had transformed into a succubus.

Rebecca also undressed without hesitation. Her form was nearly shear. She walked into the water like she was stepping into her own tub.

Tony began to undress. My cue to follow his lead or be left behind. I did, as did Daphnee. The three of us stood shivering in our underwear. We looked at one another's blurry forms. This was ridiculous. We couldn't even see one another---not really. I yanked my underwear down and threw them on the tarp. Tony's underwear and Daphnee's bra came off just as quickly. We walked together quickly in the direction Charlie and Samantha went. Why did it feel morally wrong to be doing this? Humans didn't always wear clothes. What was so sinister about bathing? In many Asian cultures, groups bathed together. It seemed so natural to being doing this, yet part of me still felt uncomfortable. The steam began to get thicker. One foot dropped a foot into hot, murky water. Startled, I yanked it up. I dipped it back in. "Not bad," I said. I held Daphnee's hand. It looked strange for her to still be wearing something on the lower half, but not on the top. Together we walked into the unknown.

The water got deeper the farther we went into it. It was only murky on the bottom. The water's depth stabilized chest high. Christine finally stepping in. HEY! She had a bathing suit on.

"Good idea, Rebecca," Charlie's voice declared. "The water temperature is perfect." I aimed for that voice. Samantha was riding on Charlie's back to keep her feet out of the sludge.

"Would you like to get on my back?" I asked Daphnee.

"I won't be too heavy for you, will I?"

"Impossible." I bent down. Daphnee wrapped her arms around my neck and raised one leg. I grabbed the limb, then reached behind for another. Grab. Lift. Walk. It was easier than I thought it would be. There was still enough of Daphnee in the water for her to be buoyant. The most difficult part was having to lean forward so she wouldn't slip off.

"How about a little competition?" asked Charlie. Charlie didn't wait for a reply. He charged us, the water significantly dampening his movement. Samantha pushed Daphnee. My better half lost her grip on my neck, but didn't fall. Her legs continued to wrap around me, sustaining the connection. She pulled herself back up to my neck. Now it was Daphnee's and my turn. Daphnee went for Samantha's legs. Charlie's hand was ripped away. Samantha slumped to one side. They recovered. Combat continued for many minutes with small battles won by both sides, but without any knockout punches. It felt so natural having Daphnee on top of me. She had become an extension of my body and mind. THAT WAS IT! We had to work together to win. I backed away.

"CHICKEN!" yelled Samantha. "SEAGULL! GROUSE!" How soon she forgot about that fearsome bird.

I ran towards Charlie and Samantha as fast as I could. A wake followed me. "RAMMING SPEED!" We crashed into them. Daphnee claws were outstretched. Samantha was yanked from Charlie like a nail from a board. She was thrown backwards. The counter-force knocked Charlie forward. They both went under. Wet hair was as significant in this competition as a splatter of color in a paintball war.

Daphnee and I explored the hotpot. Daphnee screamed. She swam spastically to get behind me, then clutched my shoulders tightly.

"What's wrong?" I asked her.

"Go that way."

"How far?"

"You'll know."

OOOO! Shivers ran down my spine. A furry wall was on the edge of the pool. I thought it was a dead animal at first, but nothing could be shaped like that. I touched it. It felt firm, yet slimy. I felt it again to see how large it was. "It's an algae wall. Come feel it."

"WHAT ARE YOU DOING OVER THERE!" yelled Tony. "Can I watch?"

"No conjugal activities," Andy's voice warned from

somewhere in the mist. "You don't want to risk your peckers---or your peckerettes---falling off from the diseases you might get from this bacterial soup."

Daphnee answered by throwing a piece of algae in the direction of the voice. The algae was returned. Chaos ensued. One didn't know where or when the mortar would land. I was hit in the head from behind. "Sorry, Steve," said Daphnee. She and I closed in on the enemy, which wasn't easy because the return fire was coming from three directions. I saw Tony first. I threw. He ducked. He blitzed. A huge piece of algae slapped me in the head. I surrendered.

Charlie looked at us, then shook his head. He didn't say a word, but I knew what he was thinking. I felt horrible. We'll probably all die of some disease we received from the algae. We had actually rubbed the stuff on each other's bodies. I may have even swallowed some of it. But that wasn't the worst of it. If we were hurt from our own actions so be it, but.... we ripped algae from nature's garden. We mutilated. We raped. We had fun at nature's expense. We were guilty as those who littered. We were guilty as those who cut down virgin forests. In Charlie's eyes, I saw a parent who wished he didn't allow his children to play in the living room. It was too late to clean the grape juice off the white shag carpet. It was too late to glue together the Ming vase.

Not wanting one event to ruin the entire outing, Charlie's silent admonishment was brief. "I need some warmer water." We followed Charlie to a slightly warmer stream that flowed into the pool. He climbed out of the pool and crawled upstream. We followed. The water wasn't deep enough to cover us, so most of our naked forms were exposed. An elderly waning moon rose. A few rays found their way through the steam to our glossy flesh. Natural shading intensified, but identification remained blurry. We stayed low to the ground to absorb what heat we could, and to retain our balance. We crouched. We crawled. We were pink and helpless. We were uncertain, returning to where we spawned.

Charlie dropped. He found a steaming pool much warmer than the algae pool, and more importantly, the stream. It was clear. Charlie rested his back against a log in its center. The rest of us climbed into the pool. There was enough space for all of us to lean against the log. The wind blew just enough to free steam in one direction. STARS! The moon shined from another direction, illuminating the steam, but not our bodies.

My groin itched. I reached down to pry the small stones from the hair there, not caring if anyone saw. Others also appeared secure with themselves. Samantha was slumped with her legs comfortably apart. Tony was asleep with his manhood partially exposed. Charlie stretched, contorting his. The eroticism that permeated our disrobing had evaporated. We had regained our innocence---young children bathing together.

Daphnee removed her underwear. "It's kind of silly, isn't it?" she said. "Taking my top off, but not my bottom. What do I expect someone to see? It's not like someone looking between my legs can gape at my exposed soul."

Christine began fidgeting---under her swimsuit. Discretely, at first, then frustratingly, less so. "IS A WOMAN'S SWIMSUIT INTENTIONALLY DESIGNED TO COLLECT SAND?!" she screamed, before violently stripping. "This is the first time I have ever done this," she explained after calming down. "Even my mother hasn't seen me naked since I was a small girl."

"You have a beautiful body," said Daphnee. She did. Her heavy breasts were beginning to sag, and she was far from skinny, but her skin was smooth and everything perfectly proportioned.

"My mother never wore a bikini. I don't think I even saw her or my father even in their underwear."

"And that's bad?" said Andy. He was the only person who hadn't transformed---who hadn't lost his inhibitions. Nervously he soaked three-quarters deep at the perimeter of the pool, his eyes looking away from the bodies in the pool.

"So, what are we doing Wednesday?" I asked Daphnee.

"Someone asked me to work for him. We were going to be back from Sky Rim Tuesday evening, so I thought it would be all right. It means more money for my trip home in two weeks."

"But we don't have much time left to spend together."

"It's only one day."

"Is money more important than spending time with me?"

"Come on, Steve. It's only for one day." Daphnee held my hand, but I took little comfort from it. It reminded me of what I soon would be missing.

I thought it would be cold getting out of the water. It was, but for only a minute. Once I dried off and dressed, I felt warmed to my soul. Mountain air rushed against my body, cooling, but not chilling. Every ounce of flesh tingled.

63. GIVING THE SPECTER ITS SUBSTANCE

"Why are we stopping here?" asked Rebecca. Charlie turned into the parking lot of the West Thumb Geyser Basin. He turned off the lights and cut the engine. Silently we coasted through an empty parking lot. There was a brief jerk as he hit the brakes at the end of the pavement.

"There is something I want to show you," Charlie finally answered. We heard water percolating when he opened his door. It disappeared momentarily as the door slammed, its echo reverberating into the still night. It returned when the other doors were opened.

"I need to pee," said Christine, as she walked away from us. "I'll meet you back at the van."

"The rest of you guys stay right there. Samantha?" They

walked together hand in hand into the swirling steam below. A column of light pierced the mist, the water droplets giving the specter its substance. A second column appeared. The two energy rods entangled, creating a dazzling visual display. "You can come down the boardwalk now," Charlie insisted. As we each entered the steam we were struck by the irradiated columns. I had to momentarily feel my midsection to confirm I was still in one piece. The warm, moist air felt soothing. Charlie and Samantha left the mist, coming out the far side. Their energy swords vanished, then momentarily flickered as the wind blew an arm of steam in their direction. As I left the comfort of the steam I felt a sudden, unexpectant chill, like I had been thrown out of the womb. It felt much colder than it did before we entered the cloud.

Daphnee grabbed my hand. We walked faster so we could catch up to Charlie and Samantha. Rebecca and Tony walked quietly side by side, about five paces behind. They must have felt out of place, being brought together by the pairing off of their companions.

Between the vanishing steam of hot pools and thermal runoffs we saw Lake Yellowstone to our right. The moon illuminated Fishing Cone, a thermal pool fifty feet from shore. Steam rose from its crater. I looked back at Rebecca and Tony. It looked like they were holding hands.

Samantha turned on her flashlight. She screamed. Both she and Charlie ran back towards Daphnee and me, which caused us to run. Better safe than sorry. After the four of us caught up to Rebecca and Tony, the six of us backtracked all the way to the parking lot. It was remarkable none of us slipped on the wet boardwalk and fell into a boiling cauldron.

"What happened?" asked Christine, as she met us at the van.

"I don't know," Daphnee answered. "I was just running, because Charlie and Samantha were running. What did you see, Charlie?"

236

"I didn't see anything. I ran, because Samantha screamed and ran. Samantha?"

"I think I saw a bison, but I'm not sure."

"You're not sure?" Tony whined.

"It could have been a bison."

"I think it's time we head home and go to bed," I said.

Most of us were comatose during the half-hour it took for us to return home. The notable exception was Tony and Rebecca. Whatever relationship they had initiated in the geyser basin progressed in the back of the van. Nothing that required them to get their own room, but enough to make those around them uncomfortable.

What did the two see in each other? Tony was an overly-aggressive chauvinistic pig, and Rebecca was the type of girl such guys normally did not find attractive. Rebecca was plain and gangly. She had an almost complete lack of the curves normally associated with post-adolescent females. But she was also confident in the shell genetics gave her, and that may have been enough to catch Tony's eye. Although she didn't have much to show off, she did the best with what she had, wearing tops that would have revealed a substantial part of most women's upper anatomy, but on her revealed just a trace.

I looked over at Daphnee beside me, trying to picture her in such a top. Her head lay against my shoulder. She snored lightly as she drooled on my shirt. She snorted loudly waking herself. "Huh, did you say something."

"Nope. Go back to sleep. We still have a few more minutes before we get back to Lake." Maybe no one's situation was perfect. Why should I find fault in Tony and Rebecca's relationship? Maybe the common ground they found in one another would trump any differences they had.

64. CORRUPTING YOUNG MEN

Sky Rim could be reached by one of three trails. We choose the easiest, but longest. It began at the same trailhead as High Lake. But instead of going straight at the two-mile fork, we veered left. We walked silently beside a creek. While distracted by the thralls of daydreams, a moose leapt across the trail, finally settling down in the lush grass across the creek. "Moose are like people in some ways," said Christine. "They can't wait to soak their feet after a hard day's work."

"What do moose do all day?" asked Daphnee.

"Their work varies, as does ours. Moose work very hard. They are the manual laborers of the forests and meadows. They clear branches away from animal paths and occasional add them to human paths. They aren't practical jokers, but they are practical. The more difficult it is for humans to travel through the forest the fewer that attempt it. Moose also lift other animals up on their antlers. That's why they are so wide. Old and handicapped squirrels need to get into the trees somehow. Moose sometimes give birds rides, when their wings are undeveloped or damaged. Moose do many things for many animals. They even help beavers build dams."

As we began to ascend, Sky Rim formed above us, to our left---jagged, light gray granite resting upon shoulders of dark green pine. The grade became steeper as we got closer to Shelf Lake--- the first day's destination. Two-hundred feet above it the *Top of the World* taunted. We were going to have to earn our view. The trail became narrow as it snaked even steeper upwards. We had gained two-thousand feet already, with nearly five-hundred remaining.

Something was in the middle of the trail. A BLACK BEAR! It ran off before anyone but I could see it. "We need to make sure our food is secure tonight," Andy insisted. "We're just half-a-mile from Shelf Lake. Bears have a tendency to ascend into the high country in the middle of summer, to escape the heat, and people."

Shelf Lake was appropriately named. Mountains surrounded it on three sides. Water emptied abruptly on its fourth, down the canyon we had just climbed up through. Shadows completely engulfed the lake, but Sky Rim still shined. We set-up two tents, then ate.

"Let's hike up Sheep Mountain before it gets dark," Tony suggested.

"Do we have time?" I asked.

"It'll just take a half-hour if we rush."

"You also going, Andy?"

He shook his head. "By the time you top the peak and return it'll be dark."

"Daphnee? Christine?"

"I like to rest at the end of a grueling hike," Christine answered. "Not begin another one."

"Me too," said Daphnee.

There wasn't an official trail to Sheep Mountain, so we had to climb the first two-hundred feet through unmarked forest. Being close to timberline, the undergrowth was manageable. The last five-hundred feet up was through steppe, easily traversable, but a bit self-defeating, because we could easily see how far we still had to climb. With the endurance we had developed from the hiking we had done so far this summer we were able to jog up the moderate and consistent slope. Periodically, we had to detour around boulders embedded in the grass. They were adequately spaced to give ample warning of their prescience, so we didn't have to go too far out of our way to circumvent them.

A three-story reflecting tower sat on top of the mountain. It looked like a drive-in movie theater screen. Tony threw a rock at it. It bounced off with a ding. Deducing we couldn't do any real damage to it, I also threw and connected. "Do you think we cause static every time we do that?" I asked Tony.

"I hope so."

"This has to be the tower that reflects Bozeman's signals to Gardiner and Mammoth."

"Your map tell you that?"

"Just an educated speculation. Do you remember how clear that station gets when we drive north of Norris?"

Tony's eyes followed the signal's path, from the north to the southeast. We were near the top of a kaleidoscope of contrasting elevations. Mountains, ridges, and valleys enveloped us. The highest peak in the area caught his eye. "Do you know what mountain that is?"

"I think it's Electric." I looked for it in my hiking book, eventually finding it. "It's high iron concentration acts like a magnet for electrical activity. When a storm approaches it would be wise to not be on top."

Tony looked pensive. So uncharacteristic of the undeveloped face that might be making mud pies one moment, and stealing a kiss from an unsuspecting young woman the next. His thoughts finally became too full to be contained. "Steve, do you think I'm too young for Rebecca?"

"I'm a little surprised that you are interested in Rebecca. Nothing against her, but she doesn't seem your type. Don't you usually go after the young, unfairly attractive type?"

"Then you don't really know me, Steve. I'm a non-discriminating chaser of women. I'll go after anyone with boobs that breaths. That's not to say if given a choice I wouldn't go after the most beautiful girl. Rebecca definitely wouldn't be my first choice in a woman, but she is in her thirties, and that's when women reach their sexual prime. We began to talk on that boardwalk at West Thumb. Strange forces sometimes bring people together? She loves to do fun, crazy, uninhibited stuff---just like me. She was actually the first one to make a move. She grabbed my hand while we passed through one of those steam baths. I was flattered. Who wouldn't be flattered anytime a woman is attracted to you? Our first kiss was the most incredible of my life. She not only made contact, she consumed."

"So, what's the problem? It sounds like you enjoy each other's company."

"She's much more experienced than me, if you know what I mean. What if I'm inadequate for her?"

"You seem like the type of person who could write a book on the subject."

"Sure, I've had sex with a lot of girls, but they were just girls. They were easy to please, because they didn't know any more about it than I did. But Rebecca is a woman, with womanly needs. I don't think she would be satisfied with a quickie."

"You could just ask her what she likes. I'm sure the experimenting will be fun for both of you."

"But do you think she'll want to waste her time on a sexual bumpkin until I get it right?"

"If she didn't want such a relationship with you she wouldn't have provoked one. She probably likes the challenge. She may get kicks out of corrupting young men."

"Well, this young man wouldn't mind being corrupted. I'm getting tired of the games girls play. By the time I finally get them into bed I just want to do them and go home."

The sun began to set behind Sky Rim to the west. It was the most intensely red sunset I had ever seen. It was as if the sun had pricked the earth and the blood dripping from it had stained the sky. The sun was still partially visible, and it too was vermilion. I felt sorry for the lazy people below who weren't seeing this spectacle from our vantage point.

We started back down before the sun completely set. We

had to get back to camp before it got too dark to see. From the top of Sheep Mountain, we saw an easier, more direct route down. We were mistaken. It was heavily forested. We nearly tripped with every step we took from the vegetation that entangled our feet, but we still had fun. Challenges were entertaining. We were a bit careless in our swift descent, causing some bruises and scrapes, but no real injuries, like a broken leg.

Before turning in I walked to the rim of the canyon. Warm air struck my face. How did I become so lucky to be in a place like this? Daphnee hugged me from behind. We sat down and held one another. The silhouette of the valley was below. Mountains embraced us. We kissed, gently at first, progressing to passionately. "Let's head back to the tent," Daphnee murmured.

65. THE BACK OF A SERPENT

It was wonderful to get an early start. Within an hour of the time we woke we were off. In three long switchbacks, we reached Sky Rim. Feral pasture surrounded us. The *Sound of Music* flowed through our pores.

The terrain changed drastically and often. We entered a forest, then stepped onto a rocky spine. We watched our steps. A tumble of a thousand feet, to the right or left, would severely dampen the mood. Like the back of a serpent, Sky Rim weaved up and down, but the up was what concerned us the most. It was extremely hot, easily into the eighties, maybe even ninety---a rarity for Yellowstone. At our elevation, the solar radiation bombarded us at twice the level we experienced at sea level. We dripped with sweat, especially from our backs, where our packs clung to our bodies.

Three miles from camp we had our worse climb. We gained eight-hundred feet in half-a-mile. The trail looped in such a manner that the speedier hikers could see the slowest, and vice-versa, many minutes apart. I was delighted I was so close to the top, but felt guilty about. Daphnee must have hated my guts. Why couldn't she be at the top instead of me? I wished I could trade places with her.

Tony, Andy, and I read the journal beside Bighorn Mountain while we waited for the others to arrive. Various prose was written, announcing personal achievements that precipitated arrival at this particular spot. And of spiritual enlightenment awakened, such beauty not occurring without divine grace. Tony wrote:

Not another mountain. Where's the coke machine? I wish I hadn't come up here. I see elk below. Where's my rifle?

Tony could be clever, if you were willing to weed through his post adolescent foolishness to recognize it.

Daphnee stumbled to the ground beside me. I attempted to comfort her, but she shoved me away.

We ate lunch. Why was food so tasteless when one was hot? All I wanted to do was rest in the shade a couple of minutes with a bottomless glass of ice water. The bottle I had left---half full---was almost as warm as I.

After an unsatisfying two minutes of closing my eyes beneath the broiler, I climbed the remaining twenty feet up Bighorn Peak. It was a sheer drop down, with brief outcroppings to break the fall. Something was moving. "A BIGHORN SHEEP!" I yelled. Tony came running, but the others were less hasty. We were the only two who saw it before it disappeared. "It's underneath the outcropping," I insisted.

"Sure," Daphnee responded. "Just like the bear you saw yesterday."

"I did see a bear. And I have proof with the bighorn. Tony also saw it."

"Guys have this oath of solidarity," Christine countered.

"They protect one another, never divulging the lies they constantly tell women." I wasn't sure if the girls were kidding. I didn't care. I actually saw the animals, and they didn't.

Sky Rim was nine miles long. There was so much beauty along it, beneath it, on both sides it, it all became a blur after a while. Wild flowers upon meadows a mile long. Mountains near. Mountains far. Textured stone. Crumbling cliff. Sapphire sky. Emerald forest.

What I really wanted to see was a level trail. Was the next hill the last? Will I have any moisture left in me when I returned to the Lemon? My back got a break while I ate lunch, the evaporation of the considerable moisture on it cooling me. Once moving again, it took just minutes for it to become saturated, as it did for the bandana around my head. I was completed out of water. The trail ought to be renamed *Sun Rim*.

Our relief was a freefall run down a meadow, dropping a thousand feet in minutes. We permitted gravity to take over, slowing ourselves just enough to be able to dodge the minimal rocks and trees that were in the way. By the time we reached the bottom we were going quite fast. The extra weight of our packs made it difficult to stop, so we didn't even try. We ran part way up the next hill, our momentum acting as our propulsion. Nothing was free. What went down had to come up, but in this instance just five-hundred feet. Since Bighorn Peak we've had more downhill than up.

Because Sky Rim was on the border of Yellowstone, the trail occasionally carried us outside the Park. I found a thin piece of petrified wood. "This will make a good letter opener."

"It's against the law to take petrified wood from a national park," Andy stated. "I think it's even illegal to move it."

"But I took it from outside the Park."

"The rangers won't know that."

The end of Sky Rim didn't mean the end of our hike. It was another five miles down to the highway, beginning with steep switchbacks. It was highly eroded near the ridge, and in some places, it had collapsed, the top soil being poorly supported.

A herd of elk were in the meadow below. Before we could reach them, they ran off. Animals in the Park weren't usually that skittish around humans, so it may have been a predator, a grizzly, perhaps, or a mountain lion. Whatever it was, I never saw it. Dessert after a long day, taken away.

Tony looked like he was about to fall over. "Anyone have any more water?"

No one responded.

"How much farther?"

"Two miles," Andy hypothesized.

"Is there a creek, or a lake, any closer?"

"You're not planning on drinking untreated water, are you?"

"Everyone talks about getting giardia, but I haven't heard of anyone actually getting it."

"And you want to risk it?"

"I guess it's like religion," commented Daphnee.

66. JUST A DANCE

"Would you like to dance?" cooed Magnolia.

"Uh...."

"It's just a dance. There is nothing for Daphnee to worry about."

"All right."

About once a month a dance was held. This month there was actually a live band. Dances were held in the Rec Hall at Lake Lodge. Daphnee had gone to the rest room. If I had any luck at all she would return after I finished dancing. When Magnolia danced her entire body moved. If I guy made those motions he would have looked foolish, but when Magnolia did it….

"You're a good dancer, Steve."

"Thanks."

"Would you like to go hiking with Alice and me tomorrow?"

"Where are you going?"

"Mt. Sheridan."

"That's over twenty miles. I just got back from hiking twenty-five."

"So, you don't want to go?"

"I didn't say that." A slow song began. "I better get going."

"But Daphnee isn't back yet."

"I have to go."

Tony grabbed me. "I'm having a party after the dance. Will you come?"

"When?"

"1 a.m."

"That's awfully late."

"How much fun is sleeping? When you're sixty years old you'll regret not coming to this party. You won't regret the sleep you missed."

"Okay. I'll be at your room at one, but I may not stay long."

"Fair enough."

It was Daphnee's turn to grab me. We danced for an hour. "I have to leave now," she said.

"But it's only eleven."

"I work tomorrow morning." Why did Daphnee have to pick up that shift? We had just one more weekend together before she left. "Will you walk me home?"

I gave Daphnee a kiss outside her dorm room, then returned to the dance.

"STEVE!" Magnolia cheerfully skipped towards me.

"I've decided to go hiking with you tomorrow. What time do

you plan on leaving?"

"Can you meet Alice and me in the EDR at six-thirty?"

67. THE BOOK OF WILLIAM

Willy's stuff was scattered across the room. Suitcases were opened on his bed with an appetizer within each. He hadn't mentioned he was leaving. There wasn't a magazine---of any variety---present. I picked up his bible. I thumbed through it. There didn't appear to be any additional changes. Except.... Willy had written something at the end of the book, on a blank page, intended for notes. *The Book of William* was underlined at the top of the page. Below it was:

The man I admired the most has chosen not to admire me in the same manner. God, forgive me for what I put him through. I feel the fires in Yellowstone is the Lord's way of making my life a living hell. I must depart this land before I become trapped. I still believe in salvation, but I don't know how to achieve it.

68.   GRRRR!

Every waking hour Charlie seemed to have something planned. And many of the non-waking ones. When did he sleep? Mentioning sleep, I didn't have any the night of the dance. After Tony's party, it was time to meet Magnolia and Alice in the EDR. As long as I was moving I did okay. Those five-minute breaks to catch our breath were brutal. They were just long enough to tease my body into thinking it was finally time to go to bed. I HIKED 40 MIILES WITHOUT SLEEP! It took me the rest of the week to recover, but it was a wonderful memory. Back to Charlie. For his first night off after returning to work he chose a smorgasbord approach to post-dinner entertainment, stopping first at Norris Geyser Basin.

"Steamboat is the world's largest geyser," Charlie announced with a swooping arm, like he was one of those women who revealed products on *The Price is Right* or *Let's Make a Deal*. "It can erupt up to 400 feet."

"When will it erupt?" asked Daphnee.

"How long do we have to wait?" Tony hastily added.

"It varies," Charlie answered. "From four days to fifty years between eruptions."

"Years?" the rest of said in unison, but in varying degrees of intensity.

We gave it another five minutes, then rushed past the other geysers and hot springs of the southern basin.

To get to the northern geyser basin we passed through the Visitor Center's breezeway. Steps descended into rising steam and translucent milky-blue pools.

"Where's the dragon?" I remarked.

"Dragon?" Daphnee questioned.

"You know, the one the wizard would summon from a place like this."

Daphnee slapped the back of my head playfully.

"Why do women get away with doing something like that and men arrested?"

"Because men merit the thrashing."

"It looks like a miniature of Yellowstone, doesn't it?" Samantha commented. "Smoke rising from beauty. What will be left of the Park when the fires burn themselves out?"

"I heard over 100,00 acres have burned already," I threw out. "Now that we are fighting the fires, why do they keep growing?"

"There is too much dead undergrowth," said Charlie. "It's like trying to put out a fire in a match factory."

"When will it all end?" asked Daphnee.

"Maybe when there's nothing left to burn," said Samantha.

"I heard Grant has been evacuated," I said.

"Where will all the employees go?" asked Daphnee.

"Some will return home," said Charlie. "Those who wish to stay will be distributed to other locations. August is the time people begin to leave to go back to school. We can never hire enough people at the end of the season to sustain a full staff. There will be plenty of positions available. Next stop, Apollanaris Spring. We still have a lot to see before dark."

Halfway to Mammoth we stopped at a pullout. Stairs led up to a patio. Water tinkled out from metal pipes in a stone wall. It fell into a pond with stones spaced close enough together that a person could reach the flowing water without getting wet. A plaque presented a history of the spring.

"Let's partake of the magic nectar," said Charlie.

"But the sign says it may not be safe to drink," I responded.

"We've drank from Apollanaris Spring many times," said Samantha. "And we've never gotten sick from it. Do you believe a sign or your friends?"

"Authority shouldn't always be trusted," Tony agreed. "Even experts can be occasionally wrong. Blind faith is dangerous."

"The sign says the water may not be safe to drink," said Charlie. "I'm going to drink, but I'm not forcing anyone else to. If you make someone do something for their own good, they are either going to not enjoy it---for spite---or they will come to expect their enjoyment to be derived from others."

Charlie and Samantha walked to the two miniature waterfalls. Each placed their head beneath the nectar and allowed it drip into their mouths. "Smooth."

"Smoooooth."

I had to try it. The water was tangy, a little bitter, like soda water without any syrup added to it. "Smooth. It is invigorating."

"It will bring you health and long life," said Samantha.

Next to try it was Tony. He was so spastic he had trouble staying in one place. Water soaked his face and shirt. "Smoooth. This stuff is making me tingle. How much do you think I have to drink to get a buzz?"

"Aren't you going to drink any, Daphnee?" I asked.

"I don't want anything to happen to me. I'm going to be leaving in a week." Did she have to remind me?

We didn't make it to Mammoth in time to eat at the EDR, so we bought junk food at the Ham Store there. Charlie's idea of junk food was an apple and some whole wheat crackers. We had a picnic on the lawn in front of the store. "You're not really a veg-head, are you, Charlie?" I asked. "I mean, I've seen you eat meat before in the EDR."

"I try to eat healthy, which means not eating any red meat. There is also the moral issue of eating something with a brain. It's difficult to be faithful to either concept. Vegetarian dishes are few and far between in the EDR, at least ones that are edible.

Vegetarians couldn't have created those recipes. The EDR also considers fish and chicken to be vegetarian, which isn't a problem for me, but true vegetarians can't eat them."

"How can you survive on just a salad?" Daphnee asked Samantha.

"I don't want to get fat. I used to go on diets all the time, but they would never last. I would lose ten pounds, then gain it back in a month. I felt terrible with the constant changes my body had to go through. A woman's body goes through enough changes already. My remedy was to eat relatively low calories many times a day."

"And that works?"

"The key is keeping something in your belly. Low calorie snacks. Water. I drink a full glass before I eat a meal."

"I'm tired of putting myself through misery just to please others. I like myself just the way I am."

"I wish I had your attitude. I like guys to look at me. I like the attention. In ten years, I may be comfortable with myself, but not right now."

We parked at a pull-out along Mammoth Terrace Drive. "I hope I can remember where the caves are," said Charlie. We hiked into the forest. Charlie darted away from us every couple of minutes. He always returned. "This way." We stopped at the entrance to a cave. Water dripped down rock into an algae-tinted pool. Ominous signs were everywhere: *Do Not Enter. Danger. Poisonous Gasses.*

"We're not going down there?" questioned a terrified Daphnee.

Charlie laughed. "I may be foolhardy, but I'm not suicidal. But it would be fun to explore someday, with an oxygen mask."

Charlie brought us farther into the forest. We followed a shallow ravine. Charlie scurried in and out of it. Three times he disappeared into holes. The last time he reappeared with his trademark grin. "Come on down." It was no Mammoth Cave, but it was huge, relative to the cavities we had previously explored. The five of us could stand-up inside with enough room remaining to turn around. Two tunnels led into darkness.

"That's not bear hair, is it?" Daphnee shivered. She picked up a clump of the stuff from an alcove below the entrance. It was entangled in needles and moss.

"It probably is," said Charlie. "It looks like a bear slept here."

"If it returns we'll be trapped."

"I'm sure it won't return until fall."

"We are the invaders," said Christine. "It has the right to return to its home."

"Let's check out those other two areas," said Charlie. I followed him into a space we had to walk sideways to fit into. After ten feet, the passage widened. I turned to face forward, then stretched. I was beginning to feel claustrophobic. Charlie explored the chamber with his flashlight. Glittery specks shined back.

"WE FOUND A DIAMOND MINE!" I shouted back to the others.

"Wouldn't it be wonderful if we actually did," said Charlie. "Then we could buy land somewhere and start a commune." I could think of better ways to spend millions of dollars.

We squirmed back out. "Where's Daphnee?" I asked.

"She went outside to use the little girl's tree," Samantha answered.

GRRRR!

Charlie and I looked at one another, smiled, then chortled. So uncontrolled was the release, it was surprisingly either of us was able to remain upright. "That...ah...bear sure sounds frightening. What do you think, Steve?"

"I nearly peed my pants."

Daphnee stomped into the cave. The sight of her stern disappointment made us lose it again.

"Don't pay any attention to them," said Christine. "It was a valiant attempt." Becoming pensive, she added, "What if today was the last day of your life? All those other days would have been practice, preparation for that one day that mattered. Then again why not consider today the first day, because history is trivial. Every new today becomes the only day---the beginning and the end."

"I don't think life is that simple," said Andy. "The purpose of life is to be comfortable with yourself and the environment in which you live."

"Well, the only way this person can be comfortable is to use the little boy's tree," I said.

One good thing about going where there's no trails is knowing that there aren't people around. When nature calls a bathroom is always near. I walked a few feet from the entrance to the cave, then dropped my shorts. "Ahhhh." Maybe if I gave it some altitude I could hit that tree.

"Hello." Instinctively, I pulled up my shorts. The one thing I forgot to do was stop peeing. I turned around. Daphnee was laughing so hard I wouldn't have surprised me if she too had peed her pants.

Our commotion brought the rest of the gang out of the cave. The only way to deflate an embarrassment was to make it apparent. "Does anybody have any water I can borrow?"

"I think you've had enough water," said Tony. "You're overflowing with it." Everyone began laughing, except for me. Maybe after a shower I could laugh about it. As a minimum, after an exchange of clothes.

"You can borrow my water, Steve," said Charlie. I applied the water liberally and close to the source. "You can keep the water bottle when you're done," he added.

"Now I need to think of something for Charlie," said Daphnee.

"You'll never see me drop my britches," he said.

Samantha laughed. "At the first whiff of estrogen...."

"I still have my amateur status."

"That's one thing we can both agree on."

"We better head back to the van," said Andy. "It's getting dark."

By the time we hit pavement it was pitch black. "LOOK AT THE SKY!" Tony bellowed. A splash of color pulsated north of us.

"It's the Aurora Borealis," said Christine. "I've only seen it once before."

"First and last?" questioned Daphnee.

"Well, maybe it's okay to experience more than one day. Epics are often more rewarding than short stories."

69. SOMEONE ELSE'S STUFF

Willy was gone when I returned to Lake. Someone else's stuff was on his bed. I tried to picture my new roommate, based on his possessions, but couldn't. There were too many variables. Nothing stood out like that bible of Willy's---or his magazines. It was probably one of the Grant evacuees.

70. LIKE TAKING A FINAL

Daphnee and I drove into the Gros Ventre Campground at 1 a.m. We had to make a 200-mile detour through Idaho, because the fire near Grant closed the South Gate. The rest of the gang spent the day in Jackson, but we wanted to spend some time alone. It was Daphnee's last weekend. "Are you sure you want to climb the Middle Teton tomorrow? Don't you want to relax your last week in Yellowstone?"

"I can relax when I get home."

"But this is going to be the most difficult hike of the season. We'll be gaining over six-thousand feet in eight miles."

"Then it'll be like taking a final. I need to get into practice. A hiking final will be much more enjoyable than the college variety."

Everyone was asleep when we arrived in camp, except for Charlie, who was tending the fire. "How many?" I asked.

"You guys make ten."

"That's more than we thought. Who else showed up."

"Ryan."

71. RUNNING OUT OF TIME

Charlie hoped we could be at the trailhead by 6 a.m. I thought if they were lucky, maybe seven. By the time we packed the cars, got our climbing permit, and unpacked our hiking gear, it was after eight. In addition to Charlie, Ryan, Daphnee and me, there was Andy, Christine, Samantha, Tony, Magnolia, and Rebecca. Remembering Grebe Lake, I was concerned about Rebecca's ability of making it to the top. I looked at my watch. "The ranger told us we should be at the summit by noon, because of afternoon thunderstorms," I reminded Charlie.

"I know," he replied.

"Do you think we'll make the deadline?"

Charlie shook his head.

The first four miles consisted of a mixture of lodgepole pines and aspens, with the occasional wild flower speckled meadow to break-up the monotony. Sure, we were going uphill most of the time, but the occasional views of the Tetons made the climb worth it. After we rose a thousand feet, we were high enough to see Taggart and Bradley Lakes to the southeast of us, and the Snake River farther east. At each switchback Andy and I waited for the others to catch-up. We didn't want such a large party to become separated.

The beginning of the fifth mile brought us into Garnet Canyon. A mile away, near its termination, was the characteristic black stripe that marked the Middle Teton. WE HAD JUST 4000 FEET LEFT TO CLIMB! The canyon was a series of boulders, scattered trees, steppe, and marmots---very much like what we saw in the Upper Cascade Canyon. Daphnee chirped a welcome to her namesake. They chirped back.

A quarter of a mile into the canyon, a boulder field blocked our route. The stones varied in size from one to ten feet in diameter. Cairns---piles of rocks used as markers---showed us the way across. We were led over and under and in between. The creek crossing was the most stressful part. It was strange. I feared getting wet more than a fracture from a hard fall. Wet shoes would make a tiring day even more so. Discomfort was as detrimental to endurance as an extended hike and a steep climb.

At the base of the mountain, a dozen tents were scattered over a petite meadow, between boulders twice their size. This was where we would have camped if we chose to make the trip an overnighter. Above us were two saddles, both covered in snow. The right led to the 13,770-foot Grand. The left, our route, led to the South and Middle Tetons, both about a thousand feet lower.

I should have bought waterproof boots. I looked up to the cloudy sky. Sun might be nice too. A drop of rain landed on my nose. Why couldn't it do that up north?

Charlie looked to the top of the gray haloed Middle Teton and shook his head. "We need to be careful," he warned. "If we walk across that glacier we could slip, which would likely result in falling off that cliff. It's wiser to go around, to the right."

"Didn't the ranger say the best route up was to the left?" Andy commented.

"I don't remember that. Anyway, it looks better on the right side."

"It doesn't look that far up," said Ryan.

Ryan was the first one to take off. It must have felt great for him to finally be set free. We climbed up a rock cascade. Sometimes the stones were boulders. Other times, gravel. It was easier to climb the boulders. Not only did one have better traction on them, they also caused one to gain elevation faster. I paused on a boulder to catch my breath. Everyone but Ryan was spread out beneath me. Andy and Christine had nearly caught up with me. It looked like Rebecca had just started. I began again, before my legs tightened. It helped me to pick a focal point, then tell myself I couldn't stop to rest until I reached it. It was usually the biggest boulder in the area. I had to cross a creek, but there were enough boulders within it that crossing was easy. After climbing up the far bank, I lost Ryan. I quickly scanned behind me to see if I could see anyone. I couldn't see those right behind me, but I could see Rebecca and a couple of others. I began climbing again. I was blocked by a wall of snow. I looked to my right and saw my mistake. I didn't go far enough over. I had to backtrack, meaning I had to go down---which wasn't a problem---but that meant also going back up. I thought for an instant that it might be better to cross the snowfield. I looked at the boulders below me, concluding it wasn't worth it. When I reached the bottom of the snow I saw Ryan above me and on the correct route. When Ryan reached the top of the snow bank he took a handful of the frozen precipitation and lobbed it at me. I took a handful and threw it back. It didn't go very far. It wasn't fair, me having to overcome gravity, and gravity helping Ryan. After Ryan hit me he allowed me to climb up. We had to direct everyone up the proper route, which we chased with a snowball. We waited to resume our climb until everyone was up.

It gave me time to interrogate Ryan. "So, Kathleen left you behind?"

"She hated the smoky air. She's house hunting."

"So, you've been accepted into Yale Law?"

"I begin in two weeks."

"Isn't it premature to be looking for a house until you are married and have a job?"

"That's the strange part. Kathleen has decided she can't wait to get married now. Her father is going to buy us a house, as long as it's in New Haven."

"And she's letting you cavort with the likes of us?" asked Charlie.

"*We will spend the rest of our life together*, she said. *Have some fun.*"

"What is she doing with her free time?"

"What else? Shopping."

We continued, after allotting Rebecca a few minutes to rest. How was she going to make it all the way to the top? I was surprised she made it this far. A glacier creeping closer forced us to move closer to the rock face. "Uh, oh," said Andy. "Maybe we should have gone to the left." The snow and ice finally converged with the canyon wall. It was a few feet higher than our heads.

"Wait," said Samantha. "I think I see a way." After exploring, she waved us towards a tunnel, half rock, half snow. Light shined into it from its termination.

"The sun must have heated the rock enough to melt most of the snow against it," Ryan explained. "But not enough yet to collapse the tunnel." At the end of the tunnel there was still snow beside us, but the roof was missing.

We passed through a bee infested meadow, hastily. We thought we may have reached the saddle, but we could still see a ridge ahead of us.

So we wouldn't lose any elevation by dropping into the canyon floor, we stayed high, near the canyon wall. The going wasn't easy, but at least we didn't waste any energy going down, then back up. We ate lunch at the six-mile point. It was already noon. A ranger, on his way down from the Middle checked our permit. "It's an easier climb on the canyon floor," he advised. I thought he might give us a lecture about starting so late. He didn't.

Andy was a good substitute. "Maybe we should cut our losses," he said. "If we aren't going to make it to the top maybe we shouldn't even try."

"That doesn't sound like you," Christine admonished. "You want to give up?"

"If we aren't going to make it to the top...."

"Sometimes the journey is more important than the

destination."

"Without a goal...."

"You can't fail."

"I didn't come all this way to not reach the top," Charlie declared. It was so uncharacteristic of him to be this serious.

"Me neither," Ryan seconded.

We looked at Rebecca.

"I want to straddle the Middle," she said, sounding very determined. "I won't give up."

"The sky is about ready to let loose on us," Andy warned. "Are we going to risk getting hit by lightning?"

"Lightning has far better things to do than tap us on the shoulder." Charlie resumed climbing.

"What's wrong with him?" Daphnee asked.

Samantha answered. "He feels he's running out of time. Most of the trails are closed in Yellowstone. It won't be long before the entire park burns down. It's like his entire way of life is being destroyed."

We chased after Charlie. It was much easier traveling on the canyon floor than one-hundred feet up its wall. We were moving at least twice as fast now, before being slowed by another boulder field. The creek in the center of the canyon disappeared beneath it. I couldn't see the water, but I could hear it, rushing beneath the rocks I was climbing over. JUST AHEAD, ABOVE THOSE BOULDERS WAS THE SADDLE! I was mistaken. There was still another ridge. The going was easier again. I saw Charlie looking down at me from the top of the ridge. I was hesitant about getting too worked up this time. Charlie waved. I waved back, then smiled weakly, too worn out---as much emotionally as physically---to commit fully to the task. We had finally made it to the saddle. "It's one-fifteen," he announced.

I looked down the other side of the saddle. It dropped a thousand feet, straight down. Directly below us was the florescent blue Iceflow Lake. Its rim was garnished with glaciers. Farther away was golf course green Alaska Basin. And beyond it was the amber farmland of Idaho. "DID YOU SEE THAT!" I shouted. A piece of ice fell into Iceflow Lake. It bobbed back up to the surface. A new iceberg had been created. Charlie nodded, then smiled sadly.

The last of our party arrived at two. After resting for a few minutes, we headed towards the peak. Charlie said, "If anyone doesn't wish to go all the way to the top, you can wait here, and we'll pick you up on the way down." Everyone wished to continue. Charlie smiled the widest he had since beginning the hike. "ICE CREAM AND ONIONS! Isn't the air at 11,000 feet invigorating?"

A snowbank forced us to straddle a spine between the snow and the thousand-foot drop. At times, the rocky path was only a few feet across. Every little gust of wind made me clutch the rock. Our reward for making it safely across was a brief steppe meadow of gradual slope. As we got closer to the peak a trail formed. It wound its way, in steep, short switchbacks, through the cat-size rocks towards the chimney---a narrow, steep, box canyon that guided us to the top of the mountain. As the elevation increased, and the air got thinner, we spread out again. Charlie and I were in front, followed by Ryan, Christine, Andy, Samantha, and Daphnee. Tony was in the rear encouraging Rebecca. The rocks were extremely unstable. Every few steps Charlie kicked something down at me. A rock the size of my head almost landed on my foot, the rocks on either side of it preventing it from making contact.

"YOU ALL RIGHT?!" Charlie shouted down at me.

"I think I'll let you get ahead a bit, to give me more time to react."

Charlie paused at a sheer incline, about halfway up the chimney. He waved me up. "There has to be a better way up. We can probably make it, but I don't know if everyone can. Let's find an alternate route."

"How about to the right. It's less steep there."

"Kind of close to the cliff though."

Charlie looked down at the string of climbers. "We've got

time to investigate."

We followed the gentle slope away from the chimney. Our easier route terminated at a five-foot wide ravine. Two-thousand feet below was the canyon we spent most of the day climbing. On the other side of the ravine, the gentle incline continued. Charlie jumped across without thinking. I hesitated. What if I fell? I knew that the odds were greatly against it, but what if? Charlie waited. Okay, but this was the last time I was going to do something so stupid. I landed without incident, and we continued. We could see the top of the mountain. We hooted and howled when we reached it.

"Whoa," I said. "What is that over there?" To the northwest was a peak at least a hundred feet higher.

"GRIZZLY SCAT!"

By the time we backtracked to the chimney, we heard someone else's exclamation of triumph. Ten minutes later we reached the top ourselves, finding Christine, Andy, and Ryan already there.

"What happened to you?" asked Andy.

Charlie answered. "Someone moved the mountain just as we made it to the top. Who was the first one up?"

"Ryan was," said Christine.

"Then you are the *King of the Mountain*. How may we serve?" Charlie bowed.

"How about giving me your Oreos."

"What proof do you have this is the *top* of the Middle Teton?" Charlie countered.

"There's a benchmark," said Christine. Engraved in the metal was *Middle Teton 12,804 feet*.

Charlie handed Ryan his four-pack of Oreos.

Christine extracted a leather-bound book from a metal canister next to the benchmark. "It's a log." After browsing through it she handed it to Charlie, who, after a couple of minutes, passed it on to someone else.

Fifteen minutes later Daphnee, Samantha, and Magnolia arrived. I kissed my girlfriend, after she caught her breath. "It looks like you passed your final."

"We still have to get back down."

"Have you seen Tony and Rebecca recently?" Christine asked.

"Not since we entered the chimney," Magnolia answered.

"That's too bad," said Samantha. "I don't think there ever has been a group this large before on the Middle Teton. The record is invalid if everyone doesn't make it."

"They still might make it," said Charlie. "Rebecca has the determination. It's getting late though. It's already four-thirty. No matter what, we need to head down by five."

At four-fifty Tony came into view. "Where's Rebecca?" Christine asked.

"She's coming." At four-fifty-five she appeared, looking completely exhausted. Everyone cheered.

"I have to get a picture," said Charlie. "Everyone press together." Charlie set his camera on a rock, triggered the timer, then ran back. He slipped, but Andy was able to grab him before he fell off the mountain. Click.

Charlie slowly rotated, taking photos of the entire panorama. To the east was Garnet Canyon and the plains of Jackson Hole. To the south was the South Teton, nearly as tall as the mountain we were on. To the west was Alaska Basin and Upper Cascade Canyon. Where exactly did we camp? And finally, to the north was the majestic Grand Teton, the highest peak in the range.

Charlie stowed his camera, then pulled out a bottle of Boone's Farm. There was just enough for a couple of small swigs each. Charlie toasted everyone and finally, with bottle outstretched, he toasted the Grand.

"That curtain of rain is so beautiful," said Magnolia.

"And dangerous," said Andy. "We need to be below the summit before the storm reaches us."

"Look at your hair, Magnolia," said Samantha laughing.

"It must look atrocious."

"It's standing up."

"You hear that?" I said.

"The crackle?" asked Tony.

"Lightning's about to strike," said Ryan.

"Everyone pack your bags," said Charlie. "We need to get down from here---NOW!"

By the time we reached the chimney, it began to hail. It took just seconds for the ground to be covered. We slid down the icy marbles as fast as we could. We didn't stop until we were beneath the chimney and onto the meadow. Above us we saw lightning strikes behind the Middle.

"I hope everyone has gotten their money's worth," said Charlie. "Now let's see if we can reach the trailhead before it gets dark."

It sprinkled on us about where we ate lunch. We got damp, but not soaked. It let up when we reached the camping zone. The sky began to darken as we were climbing the boulders blocking the trail. It was completely dark when we left the canyon. "Did anyone bring a flashlight?" asked Magnolia. No one replied.

"I didn't think it would take this long," said Charlie.

"How are we going to make it down?" asked Andy. "The rocks embedded in the trail are going to make it difficult. Awkward and dangerous."

"We're going to have to move very slowly," said Charlie. "We must stay together so no one gets lost."

"How can we do that if we can't even see?" asked Tony.

"I have an idea," I said. "Rebecca's wearing a white shirt. She'll be our night light."

"But I don't want to...."

"You're our only hope," said Charlie. "You can do it."

And Rebecca did do it, but very slowly. She had trouble staying on the trail. And every time she fell off, a vulgarity was released loudly into the darkness. The moon finally rose, but not until we were less than a mile from the trailhead.

"What time is it?" an invisible voice called out from behind me.

"Midnight," a voice answered in front of me. WE'VE BEEN TRIPPING IN THE DARK FOR NEARLY THREE HOURS!

Before we drove back to Yellowstone through Idaho, we learned that the South Gate had re-opened. Those of us who weren't driving would have liked to sleep on the way home, but it was impossible with the sky glowing in the direction we were heading. What if there was nothing left to go back to? Near Grant we saw blackened trees, many of them still smoking. The sign at the West Thumb junction was so charred we could no longer read the words on it. "Is that Lake Hotel?" asked Daphnee. She was referring to the flames on the horizon.

"No, Lake is further to the west," I answered, but I wasn't sure.

At two-thirty we drove into Lake Village and found it untouched by nature's fury, but there was always tomorrow.

72.   ADAM TAKING EVE FROM THE GARDEN

I carried Daphnee's bags down the hallway. When I reached the door at the end I turned.   A nudge from my backside opened it. The door scraped shut against me as I squeezed through. I tried to keep Daphnee's bags from hitting the steps as I walked down them, but the drops came too suddenly. I was as equally inept as I was competent. I walked past five cars before arriving at the Lemon. I wasn't able to park any closer. This was my third, but last trip.

Daphnee said goodbye to her friends, but I was the one taking her to the bus depot in Livingston. I felt like I was committing suicide. I didn't want her to go, yet I was the person taking her away. I was Adam taking Eve from the garden. But if I didn't take her, someone else would, and *he* would be the last to see her.

Daphnee skipped up to me. Her eyes were moist, but she was smiling. She was happy to leave minimum wage toil and to see her family. She was sad to leave her new friends and beautiful surroundings....and me? "Are you ready?" I asked her.

"I've said my goodbyes. Let's get out of here before I change my mind." Daphnee squirmed in her seat, poking her head out and behind to see everything one last time, adding to her mental library.

We didn't talk much. Just being in each other's presence---possibly for the last time---was enough. Each creek, each thermal spring, each tree, was cherished. I would see them again, but they wouldn't be the same. When one peruses, time slows, which was my intent.

Traffic was backed up at the beginning of Hayden Valley---again. Even when bison didn't cross the road, movement was lethargic. Tourons don't wait for a pullout when a dividend on their vacation expenses materializes. I used the opportunity to kiss Daphnee. She smiled, then sighed. Yes, it was a fleeting moment. Does love enhanced by brevity balance its inevitable departure?

Daphnee shuffled in her seat. "There has to be a better way of doing this," she said. "The roads in the Park are deplorable. There are more potholes in some spots than pavement. It's like we're white water rafting."

"That was kind of fun, wasn't it?" I interjected, an attempt to make a suddenly serious moment jovial. There wasn't enough time remaining for it to be wasted on grim subjects and somber moods.

"You wouldn't think it was so fun if you had a new car, or a

266

flat tire."

"Getting wet and cold rafting is a tolerable risk. I'm not going to wear dirty hiking boots to an interview. People should know better than to bring a new car out here."

"But don't you think there is room for improvement? How about having some shuttle busses?"

"That might diminish the traffic, but the road will still be hazardous. Road deterioration in Yellowstone is caused by harsh winters as much as by heavy loads."

"How can we limit that? The damage it does?"

"Get above it? Above the snow?"

"Trains?"

"That would be too noisy."

"No noisier than twenty-thousand vehicles per day."

"How about a monorail, like at Disneyland?"

"That would be awfully expensive."

"But there wouldn't be deteriorating blacktop trashing the Park."

"And we could travel from one trailhead to another without hitchhiking or taking two cars."

DAMN! We were already at Dunraven Pass. We had just enough time remaining for one last hike together. To the top of Mt. Washburn. Where did the time go? I knew we shouldn't have discussed something serious.

The hike up the mountain was a continuous incline, but gradual. 1200 feet up spread out over three miles. We receded into mutual solitude. Just a few hours of happiness remained.

After an initial straightaway overlooking the rise to the pass, the trail became a series of quarter-mile long switchbacks. Occasionally, a slab of asphalt poked its way through the dust, a clue to the route's prior purpose. We never paused. Time was fleeting. We could relax tonight.

A fire-watch tower perched on top of the mountain. It resembled the *Wicked Witch of the West's Castle*. The drawbridge was stone. Rock spires were the railing. A thousand-foot drop was the moat.

Daphnee stopped suddenly at the beginning of the spiral to the pinnacle and tower. I bumped into her, not minding the contact. She squeezed me, while muffling a scream. She pointed ahead and to the right, to a grassy knoll. A dozen mountain goats grazed upon its left flank, the one nearest to us.

It was windy on top of the mountain. We rushed into the tower. I excused himself to use the rest room. The toilet wasn't much better than a pit, but at least it was away from the wind.

Daphnee was talking on the phone when I returned to the observatory. I didn't see any telephone lines, so it must have been wireless. She was talking to her mom. She missed everyone at home and was anxious to return. I became depressed. It was inevitable sometime during the trip. Would I feel happy if I was going home and leaving Daphnee behind?

I looked out the 270 degrees of windows. I saw Canyon, Hayden Valley, and Lake Yellowstone. Metal plaques informed tourists of viewpoints through words and silhouettes. I looked through the mounted telescope, trying to spot bison in Hayden Valley.

Daphnee hugged me from behind. "Isn't the view wonderful? It's so romantic." And Daphnee wasted her time calling home? She'll be there soon enough.

There was a log, but my emotional energy was too low to think of anything to write.

The trip down the mountain was quick. Daphnee held onto my arm to steady herself on the loose rock and to make contact with me. I wished she didn't. I was in agony. It was a single raindrop before a drought.

In the picnic area at the trailhead, an animal scavenged in the garbage beneath a picnic table. "Is that your dog?" Daphnee asked the family at the table nearby.

"No," they replied, shocked. I laughed until my belly hurt.

That's just what I needed. Daphnee hit me, for laughing at her expense. Preemptive, because I hadn't yet shared the details.

"It's a fox, Daphnee." Its fluffed-out tail was half the length of its red body.

I found the solitude I sought earlier in our journey. Three months passed during the two-hour drive to Livingston. Memories of the summer, and then some. Few words were said, and those that were seemed forced. "I'll call every day," Daphnee said behind emotionless eyes. It was the thing to say, and what we both wished to be true, but reality was a chameleon. Other things would come up. Expenses would mount. Flames would inevitably flicker as stoking became more sporadic.

We stopped at a local fast food joint and ate hungrily. We still had an hour before the bus departed. We released our passion in our food consumption. We ordered another large fry. We sighed simultaneously as the last piece of food was spent. All that remained on the wax paper on top of the plastic tray was a smudge of ketchup.

Daphnee squeezed my hand. "I must be going." I bent over the table and kissed her. I got too close to the tray, dragging my shirt through the ketchup.

I helped Daphnee bring her bags into the bus depot. Her ticket was pre-paid so all she had to do was check in. A half-an-hour to go. Tension mounted. I felt claustrophobic. "Let's wait outside for a few minutes."

We stood next to the Lemon nervously, like we were two teenagers on our first date. Simultaneously, we leaned in and embraced. It was that evening beside the lake all over again. I looked into Daphnee's eyes. They were as lost as mine. We kissed. I looked at her again. My eyes begin to water. She placed my head against her bosom. "I love you," she said.

"I love you," I replied softly, through somber emotion.

"It'll be all right. What happens, happens. Enjoy the prelude to events that may never occur." Daphnee hugged me one last time, then rushed into the bus depot.

I made it into the Lemon before I lost control again. Five minutes passed before I could drive away. I was relieved I didn't have to immediately return to Yellowstone. I didn't want to see anyone I knew. I didn't want to communicate, even to myself.

My itinerary was pre-planned. A backpack was in the Lemon. A camping site was chosen. I had nearly forty-eight hours before I had to be back to work.

73. WRITING ON THE LAVORATORY WALL

Four miles south of Livingston, on US 89, I turned onto East River Drive. A poor excuse for a paved road, but better than a gravel one. Mountains pressed down on me from both sides of Paradise Valley. Before the day was over I would press down upon them. After passing through seven miles of lush farmland nourished by the Yellowstone River, I turned left towards the Pine Creek Campground. The road climbed immediately, then leveled off once it entered Gallatin National Forest two miles later. An additional mile brought me to the campground.

Where was the trailhead? There should have been a sign. But wasn't. Not one I could find. Maybe I'll just head home. My roommate had returned to Grant, so I would be alone. I drove through the campground, finally finding the trailhead beyond the last R.V. I had a hard time finding a parking spot. It wasn't going to be the solitary hike I was looking forward to.

I took my pack out of the Lemon. I checked each compartment to make sure I hadn't forgotten anything. I always forget something. Food? Check. Sleeping bag? Check. Tent?

Check. Water? Check. Good enough. At least I would survive.

Pine Creek Falls 1 Mile, was engraved on a metal sign. And four miles after that was Pine Creek Lake, my destination. That wasn't too bad. Why was Charlie worn out after doing this hike? I looked up, to the top of the mountains, where the trail seemed to be heading. How far up would I have to go? I opened the front pocket of my pack to retrieve the national forest map. It wasn't there. THAT'S WHAT I FORGOT! I remembered putting it in the glove box. I found it. My luck was improving.

I found the lake on that map. What was its elevation? 2700 meters---that's about 9000 feet. A sign at the campground said 5600 feet. DAMN! I wasn't going to make it, not with a full pack. Yes, I was. I would make it to the lake, and through the remainder of the summer without Daphnee.

I passed twenty or so people on the fairly level first mile. I spent more time saying hello than watching the scenery, which wasn't as unfortunate as it may seem, because the forest was too dense to see much of anything, including the creek a few yards away. I wanted to be alone, but it's been said that the loneliest place is in a big city, where everyone you meet is a complete stranger. I should have spent the weekend in Bozeman.

I crossed the creek at the base of the falls, where the water forked. The one-hundred-foot falls was underwhelming---to someone who spent the summer in Yellowstone. To those people who drove to work every day it was---certainly---more magnificent.

The trail rose once I no longer could see the falls. I was the only person to pass through the invisible barrier below the waters that apparently ricocheted everyone else back to the trailhead. They would probably head to Yellowstone tomorrow and see the entire park in one day.

Switchback upon switchback took me first above the falls, then up the creek's accompanying canyon. I was determined not to stop. After five minutes, the worst of my agony was over. My body was becoming adjusted: my heart, my lungs. The incline was so

271

great that my legs began to cramp. I had to stop after forty minutes to allow the lactic acid in my muscles to dissipate, but I was halfway to the lake. A minute was long enough to recover. It felt great resuming hiking, for the first minute, then my legs and chest began to burn again. In five additional minutes my body began to re-adjust. The grade lessened a bit as the trail crossed the creek. A five percent grade felt like I was going downhill. The steep grade resumed, forcing me to rest after just twenty minutes this time. My endurance was waning, but I had just a mile to go---I hoped. I wished I could see where I was going, but the forest was too dense. The trail's grade decreased as it passed a waterfall. I saw the pool at its base at a passing glance---I didn't want to stop again. The grade increased---again---forcing a third defeat. I should have taken the time to pause at the beautiful pool. Five minutes later the trail terminated on a shelf. I unhooked my waist strap and pulled the shoulder straps out and to the side. My pack fell onto the lush grass with a thud. It felt like I was rising to the heavens, my shoulders no longer carrying their burden. I DID IT! And I only had to stop three times. If I could survive climbing 3400 feet, and do it in less than two hours, I could survive anything.

Time to explore my mountain motel. Jewel Lake was at the precipice of the shelf. It drained slowly, but abruptly, forming the waterfall I saw a few minutes ago. Beyond the falls, Paradise Valley, once lush, transitioning to ashen, was framed in pine green by the dense foothills flora. Jewel Lake's source was Pine Creek Lake, ten times its size. They were connected by a chain of two-foot waterfalls. The larger lake's banks were rocky, like most of the shelf, in contrast to the soft vegetation surrounding the smaller lake. The 10,900-foot Black Mountain was directly south of the shelf, intimidating the two pristine, alpine lakes.

I pitched my tent near Jewel Lake, where my mattress could be natural. After eating a cold turkey and cheese sandwich from one of the sack lunches I brought with me, and drinking an apple juice, I sat on a glacier boulder within sight of both lakes and their tether.

I felt very alone, but did I really need someone to feel whole? It seemed so silly. But was it? The wonders of diversity was what made life interesting---and that included having others in your life. Why was a place like Pine Creek Lake enjoyable? The land was textured: jagged mountains, chaotic creeks, irregular angles. People were textured too: their faces, their bodies, their personalities. About the only place on earth that wasn't textured was a padded cell. Did people become insane before or after they entered?

The sky was becoming textured. Opaque blue was attacked by pulsating puffy white sequins. Orange, yellow, and red explosives converged on the battlefield. Then silence. Calm. Colors faded.

Warm air rose from the canyon. Cold air fell from the mountain tops. My bare legs suddenly felt cold. It was time to leave, but that meant abandoning the ambiance of solitude. I wished Daphnee was there to enjoy this with me.

Back at camp, I hung my food in a tree. The idea of seeing a bear while in complete isolation was worse than that re-occurring dream of sleeping through my finals. I zipped-up the tent behind me, attempting to lock out the infinite wonders of nature for just this one solitary night.

FALL SLEEP, DAMMIT! FALL ASLEEP! Doctors may make the worst patients, but one's subconscious definitely becomes one's worst enemy. I heard wind. How long would it take before it reached me? Wind was like lightning. It has its blatant precursors. The tent swayed gently, then abruptly, shaking so violently I believed it would not only collapse, but rupture into shreds.

After a couple of hours of intense insomnia, I left the tent to pee. Anxiety---positive or negative---accelerated my urine production. I was about to explode. As my bladder emptied, robustly, I read the writing on the lavatory walls: dark, irregular clouds, grotesquely human-shaped, animated flora, nature howling from cramps. Fear. Loneliness. Futility.

I crawled back into my tent. I didn't want to die. Will all life cease when I did? Will it be total extinction for not only myself, but for the entire universe? If I was the center of the universe and I ceased to exist, would everything cease to exist? I shuddered. I couldn't even create non-existence in my mind. If I didn't exist in the future how could I exist now? I was scaring myself. I tried to change the subject. What if I wasn't really human? Life for me just an experiment, to see how I would interact with other artificially created organisms. Too preposterous. What if life for me was just a dream? I may wake at any moment and find myself in a strange bed in an alien environment. What if reality for me, at this moment, was a dream continuation of reality? A dream within a dream within a dream. Each dimension was minute growth, a larger exoskeleton.

The tent brightened. I don't think I ever fell asleep, but I wasn't sure. Thinking and dreaming all seemed to come together for a while. I broke down camp, then ate a hasty breakfast: a muffin, an apple, a bag of potato chips, and two swallows of water.

I was eager to see someone---anyone. A thousand feet down I met a man and a boy fishing. How did they get up here so quickly? There were a half-a-dozen more---people---beneath the waterfall. It felt like I was in a city.

Around a curve in the trail I came eye to eye with something black and bulky. A BEAR! Did it have the bristly coat and humped shoulders of a grizzly? No. Good. It was probably just as scared of me as I was of it. Probably more scared, because men hurt and kill for entertainment. I looked for a tree to climb, instinct overpowering reason. Black bears were supposed to be good climbers. It was going to run away any second. IT DID! My heart was pounding so loudly it drowned out the crickets and the birds. A bear had been just thirty feet away from me, and I had been alone. I could have been killed. I was never going to camp alone again.

Four teenage boys entered the trail as I left it. Should I warn them of the bear? I wasn't that heartless. I couldn't deprive them of their reception when they returned to school in the fall. Surviving adolescence is easier when you become a hero.

74. PAYMENT ENOUGH

Charlie fell forty feet from a rock ledge into a ten by ten-foot lagoon side-swept by white water. COME UP! Maybe he didn't jump far enough out, and he was up to his neck in mud and can't break free. Or he jumped too far, landing on those rocks, his lungs compressed, his body smashed. Water exploded at my feet on the rim of the Firehole River. Charlie burst from the water and shook like a dog.

"Let's go body surfing." Charlie grabbed me. We tripped over girls---and guys---sunning themselves on the lush grass beside the river. Most of them appeared to be employees. The water must have been too cold for the tourons. By sure coincidence, Charlie's route took us past the sexiest women on the shore.

I had to agree with the person who said mystery was what made a woman most beautiful. Sure, women in string bikinis with half their breasts exposed turns a man's eyes, but a woman in a sleek one piece will make the man fantasize about what's underneath. A one-piece appears more natural. The body retains its fluidity, rather than becoming a segmented, garbled mess. Looking at a one-piece's silhouette is like looking at the woman not wearing anything at all, but with all her flaws airbrushed out.

We hooked Andy, Tony, and Rebecca on our way upstream. We lost sight of the river for a few seconds as we went around a rock leaning in towards the channel connecting the rapids to the pools. A line of people climbed to the top of the boulder. They jumped off one by one from half the height Charlie jumped, into a pool twice as large as the one he landed in. There were signs posted---everywhere---that jumping from the rocks was unsafe and unlawful.

Upstream, the river carved a narrow canyon through bedrock. A foot below, the gorge screamed towards the five-foot-wide maw one-hundred feet downstream. Without hesitation, Charlie jumped across. He landed on an uneven spot, tripped, but caught himself two steps later without falling. He looked back at us, smiling with that mischievous little boy grin of his. The corners of his mouth fell when he realized no one else was leaping after him. DAMN! I couldn't disappoint him. Charlie's disturbed childhood might affect him when he became an adult.

I stepped back four steps, then ran as fast as I could. Now, was it best to jump from your right foot or from your left? How did I do it when I played basketball? I stopped two feet from the water. I backed up. Let's see, I went to the hoop with my right hand, that meant to get a full extension I had to push off with my left foot. I ran towards the river. Now, don't run into the river without even leaping. I made sure my takeoff was at least a foot from the edge. I landed about where Charlie landed, and did a similar hop, skip, and jump.

Tony was next. He landed much better than either Charlie or me. He shuffled a half-step to complete an exclamatory termination.

Andy shook his head with disgust, then walked upstream. Fifty paces in that direction the river became shallow and widened. He crossed it vehemently, upon stepping stones.

Rebecca backed up about ten paces. With a determined expression, she sprinted towards the river. By the time she reached the brink her endurance was exhausted. She leapt about halfway across, then plopped into the river. "THIS WAY!" shouted Charlie. "Keep your feet out in front of you." Rebecca traveled close enough to the far side of the river to grab a tree branch sticking into the water. After Charlie caught up to her, he snatched her arm and pulled her to safety. He gave her a hug. "What were you trying to do? Go down the rapids by yourself? Are you trying to have fun without us?" Tony kissed her. Rebecca hugged him back, rubbing against him to dry herself. He slapped her backside, then wiggled free.

We returned upstream to join Andy at the beginning of the rapids. The last fifty feet we had to climb over boulders. Charlie was in the lead. His legs wobbled as he propelled himself over the boulders. He was still pretty shaken up. Charlie was an enigma. He never got frightened for himself, or even when others tried something precarious. But at the first sign of danger he became that concerned, distraught mother who was able to lift that multi-ton vehicle to save her child. His lack of fear was countered by his unfaltering compassion.

We looked downstream, toward the rushing water and the maw. Charlie displayed one of his rare stern expressions. "It's hard to have fun on your weekend if you get injured---or killed. To prevent that from happening when you're running the rapids, put your feet out in front of you. Feet will heal. A skull may not."

"I'll go first," said Andy. "Watch what I do." He jumped in the water. He disappeared for a long second, then emerged thirty feet downstream. He lay on his back. His feet were stretched out in front of him. He was getting too close to the left shore. To remedy he kicked away from it. Two seconds later he squeezed through the maw. He vanished beyond the river's curvature.

The same adrenaline that made him the Mosquito propelled Tony into the water. Only his head popped up. He was rapidly approaching the maw. HE WAS GOING TO CRASH INTO THE LEFT INCISOR! His face looked like a skydiver's whose parachutes didn't open. At the last instant Tony thrust a leg ahead and to his left. He kicked free. He too passed from view.

I went next, as much to get it over with as any amusement

to be received. I aimed for the middle of the river. Being fully emerged was startling. As soon as I hit water I was pulled forward. RISE DAMMIT, before I hit something. I was jolted as I saw the shore rush by. The opaqueness of the water left me nearly blind. I remembered to put my feet out in front of me, then feared if they actually made contact with the rock they'll either break or be ripped to shreds. I tried my best to keep myself in the middle of the river. Here came the maw. For some odd reason, the experience reminded me of childbirth---my own. Did I feel a similar terror and exhilaration? Andy and Tony hit the left side, so I had to go farther to the right to compensate. OH, NO! I had overcompensated. I was approaching the right side of the river. I paddled towards the center. I closed my eyes, then immediately re-opened them. If I was going to die I didn't want to miss the climax. The price of admission would be wasted if I walked out after the previews. I swooshed just inches from the right incisor. I shot past the leapers to my right before I lost momentum. The water was nearly stagnant now. I tried to stand up. My feet pressed into soft sand and muck. The water was just chest high.

I turned around so I could see Rebecca and Charlie pass through the gauntlet. Rebecca was laughing hysterically as she came into view through the gap. Five seconds later Charlie shot through. They came to a stop in front of me. "Are you all right?" Andy asked Rebecca. He and Tony were also within a few feet of me. Rebecca's left arm and leg were bleeding.

She pulled them out of the water for everyone to see. "I see worse every month."

"Let's do it again," said Tony. The second time didn't have the giddy fear of the unknown, but it did have fewer mishaps, and less encumbering worry, so I was able to fully enjoy the rush.

One-hundred yards downstream from where I watched the others emerge, was a three-foot drop. The cascading wall was just the right height to be used as the back of a lounge chair. We leaned against the natural shower massager, and allowed it soothe us into delirium.

"Are you going to jump off the high rock, Steve?" Tony asked, cushioned between Rebecca's legs.

"I don't know. What if I don't land in the right spot. I don't know if the exhilaration is worth the risk."

"You guys should have been here last year, when Charlie jumped off in the dark," said Andy.

"Did you really?" asked Rebecca.

"It's less scary if you can't see where you're going to land. If you know how far to jump it doesn't matter if you can see your target. Once you leave the cliff it's too late to control your jump."

"Did you ever jump?" Tony asked Andy.

"For me the risk is too great."

"But you went through the gauntlet."

"I could control myself floating down the river."

"I don't think I would want to do something like that in the dark either," said Rebecca. "There are plenty of other exciting things to do in the dark. Reduced sight makes the typical mystical. Isn't it more romantic making love to someone in shadows than where every detail is on display. It leaves more to the imagination. And I have a good imagination. It sure was fun hotpotting at Ranger Pool. Anyone been to Huckleberry Springs?"

"I've heard of it," said Charlie. "But I've never been there. It's south of the Park, isn't it?"

"Isn't it supposed to cause spinal meningitis?" asked Andy.

"I'm still living," Rebecca replied. "A friend of mine took me last year. It's half-a-mile into the woods and very secluded. The moon was out, and the water was steaming. We looked more like spirits than people."

Tony scowled. "You went with some guy, didn't you?"

"You do know you aren't the first guy I've dated."

"I know. I just don't like to think about such things."

"And you lived the life of a monk before you met me?"

"But that's different."

Charlie interrupted. Strategic or inconsiderate, it changed the subject. "Rebecca, can you take us there tonight?"

"I have to open tomorrow."

"Do you think you could give us directions?"

"I'll try, but I'm not that good at it?"

"It'll be an adventure. Like we're looking for buried treasure. You coming, Andy?"

"I would prefer not to get spinal meningitis."

"Steve?"

"If Rebecca can survive Huckleberry, so can I."

"Tony."

"Even if I didn't also have to work, Rebecca being there with another guy has ruined it for me." Rebecca snugged up to him. With a half-hearted effort, he attempted to push her away. He was still upset with her, but she was wearing a bathing suit.

"When we get back to Lake, Rebecca will draw us a map, won't you?"

She nodded as she nibbled on her boyfriend, whose resolve to be apathetic began to weaken.

"But we still have another hour, don't we, before we have to head back?" Tony pleaded. He had finally given in to Rebecca's affection, after an impassioned embrace and kiss. "So, who will jump first, Steve? You or I?"

Tony and I swam to the far side of the river and climbed to the top of the forty-foot-high cliff. If I didn't do this now I would never be able to. "I guess I'll go first." I stepped to the tip of the rock. Charlie, Andy, and Rebecca watched us from the other side of the river. Most of the sixty eyes below were upon me. From this height, the rocks beneath the water all looked the same. How far did Charlie jump out? It looked like I could jump to the other side if I tried. It was just an illusion, but that didn't make it less unnerving. I didn't really want to do this, so why was I doing it? Everyone was watching. I had to jump now. It won't be over until I jumped. I stepped out. Air rushed. Too late. I promised myself if I landed safely I'll never do something like this again. I landed askew. My feet slapped the water, then my chin. My face was on fire, but because I could feel the sensation I had to still be alive. When was I going to hit the bottom, so I could push up? This pool must be really deep. I broke through the surface before I realized I was rising. I swam towards my friends. Charlie helped me up and out. I smiled, painfully. Then I felt my jaw. No blood. No broken bones. If I was the type of person who fainted I probably would have.

I looked up to the top of the cliff. Tony was ready to jump. He looked as frightened as I felt. "DOWN FROM THERE!" someone shouted from behind us. I turned and saw two rangers. "If you jump you will be fined."

"How much?" asked Charlie.

Before the ranger replied---potentially replied---Tony crawled down the cliff, probably relieved he didn't have to go through with the jump. Did the ranger see *me* jump? Being as scared as I was, was payment enough.

75. SUB-HUMAN AND SEMI-ERECT

We left as the sun was setting. I never knew anyone with a better sense of timing than Charlie. Somehow, he always knew where to be, physically and chronologically---the exact location and time, to achieve the greatest overall pleasure, sense of wellbeing and self-worth, for all involved. What more apt wonder could Charlie have taken us to than the setting sun reflecting off Lake Yellowstone. By the time we were no longer beside the lake it was too dark to see anything. By the time we would begin to get bored we would arrive at the unmarked trailhead to Huckleberry Hot

Springs. Even the people whose company Charlie kept on these excursions seemed appropriate. Charlie was the least discriminating person I knew---he invited everyone to go on his outings---but the people who accepted always fit the situation perfectly. Samantha sat in the passenger seat of Charlie's van. Alice sat beside me, in the back seat.

We turned onto the Reclamation Road, which began in the middle of John D. Rockefeller Parkway, that six-mile-long strip of land that connected Grand Teton National Park to Yellowstone. "Everyone start looking for a gravelly hill after we cross the bridge," said Charlie, remembering what Rebecca wrote down. "It should be at the first bend in the road." Thump. Thump. Bzzzzz. Thump. Thump.

"THERE IT IS!" shouted Samantha. "And there's even room to park beside the road."

"Be sure to bring everything you think you'll need," Charlie advised. "I don't think we'll want to make too many trips back to the van." I brought a towel and a flashlight. I wore a light-weight jacket, sweat bottoms, and hiking boots. Charlie and Samantha wore shorts, sweaters, and sandals. Charlie also shouldered a large day pack, which if consistent with past excursions, had a little bit of everything in it. Alice wore jeans, a denim jacket, and sneakers.

Charlie switched on his flashlight. Our dim surroundings became black. "I wish we had a full moon tonight," I said. "It's like we're walking down a tunnel. Something could be twenty feet to either side of us and we wouldn't be able to see it."

"Without sight, one must trust other senses," said Alice.

"Like hearing," Samantha added.

"Like instinct. Walk forward, or turn left, or make peace, or leave, because that is the way."

"Did your instincts tell you to quit?" asked Charlie.

"The Grateful Dead is the paradise that will most enlighten me the remainder of the summer."

Charlie handed Samantha the map Rebecca made for us. "Would you like to be our navigator?"

"Women *are* better at following directions."

"I thought they were just better at asking for directions," I said. "Aren't guys supposed to be better with spatial relationships."

"Guys are oblivious to all forms of relationships. When was the last time you called Daphnee?"

"I've written a couple of times. She could call *me*."

"You know how difficult it is for someone to reach us here, with there being just a couple of pay phones in each dorm, and us never being around, and no one ever wanting to answer the phone." I looked blankly at her. "Maybe not. You are a guy, after all…. Unless Daphnee already has a new boyfriend, she'll probably want to hear from you, maybe even if she has someone else to snuggle up with." If that was her attempt at a pep talk, Samantha would make a terrible coach.

She glanced at the captioned map Rebecca drew. "We follow that clearing until it splits. Then we take the right fork." The only thing we could see as we proceeded, other than the blaze directly in front of us, were the silhouettes of trees, primarily their crowns. "We should be coming up to a creek."

"I see something shimmering," said Charlie. "That must be the creek."

"Anyone have a portable boat?" I asked.

"I don't think it's very deep." Charlie stepped in, then quickly backed out. "But it is cold."

"It looks like there's a lot of rocks in there. How are we able to navigate around them if we can't see them?"

"Sense where they are," said Alice. "What we can't see won't hurt us unless we allow it to."

"We must feel our way across," Samantha added enthusiastically. "Feeling with our feet before accepting our footing as real and secure."

Charlie splashed through the water first. Samantha

followed. I now wished I didn't bring my sweats. Alice started across, her jean bottoms getting soaked. I rolled up my sweats to my thighs, and crossed. I watched where Alice was stepping, and how she reacted to her environment. It was easier crossing than I envisaged. With my eyes being nearly non-functional, my sense of touch was greatly enhanced. My feet became feelers. Brushing against an object of improper shape forced a reaction of more to the right, more to the left, sometimes even more up or down. Once Charlie made it across he shined his flashlight towards the rest of us, partially blinding our sense of touch. The last few yards we stumbled. My left leg felt sticky. I looked down and saw that that side of my sweats had slipped to just below my knee. I didn't feel cold yet, especially with it feeling so good to get out of the freezing water, but it was likely my sense of cold would supersede all other senses on our return trip. I felt particularly bad for Alice. Jeans were warm only when dry.

There was a similar tree-cleared corridor on the far side of the creek. "In a quarter of a mile we'll come to a fallen log," Samantha informed us. "We'll head northwest through some trees, and then through a meadow. We stop when we hit water." We were heading due north, so northwest meant veering to our left a bit.

"There's the log," said Charlie. "This is a great map. We must remember to thank Rebecca when we return to Lake. Everyone ready to find that treasure?"

I haven't been scared up to this point, but the idea of going through a dark forest really began to frighten me. If something came at me in a clearing I would have time---and room---to maneuver. In a forest, at night, I felt trapped. Fortunately, the forest was just a few trees deep. My spirit soared.

"FOLLOW THAT STEAM!" Charlie pranced across the meadow, towards the whispering billows. He stopped on top of a hill between a bubbling pool on his left, and a hissing creek on his right. A rising half-moon splattered just enough light upon him to reveal a featureless madman. He stripped off his clothes, raised his hands to the starry canopy, then darted, testing a foot here, then a foot there. By the time the rest of us topped the hill he had completely circled the water. He scrambled past us, oblivious to our prescience. He stepped into the steam, crouching as he slowly scampered downstream. He dropped down and out of sight.

"Do you think the water is affecting him?" I asked.

"Before he even got in?" Samantha responded. "Charlie's enthusiastic fervors often enthrall him."

"Time to drown this cold bod into some hot water," Alice announced.

"Time to drown this *hot* bod into some hot water," Samantha echoed.

Both women stripped, leaving their discarded clothing wildly scattered upon the hill. They scurried off, like Charlie. They were female, yet sub-human and semi-erect, nearly quadrupedal. They slipped into the primeval steam and disappeared.

I heard laughing. Instinctively, I flung my clothes away and sauntered towards *the calling.* Three bodies lay three-quarters submerged in the fiery creek below. I dropped into the water, a few yards upstream from them, where the bank looked more secure. The water was nearly too hot, but not for someone passing through. I moved crab-like towards my friends, feeling like a crab about to be boiled alive. The water gradually cooled as I moved downstream. The moon had climbed above the trees now, igniting the neon steam. My friends looked like angels bathing in the clouds. Alice leaned against the mossy-muck bank. Charlie and Samantha were in the middle of the creek back to back. I struggled to achieve comfort, first sitting with my knees held, then by crouching. My companions didn't have as much difficulty. Their eyes opened and closed sleepily, like cats upon a sunny window sill. "It looks like the carnivorous bank has you for good," I told Alice.

"It can have me for as long as it likes. It's a little gunky, but it sure feels good."

"May I join you?"

"The wilderness belongs to no one and to all."

Assuming that meant yes, I slid against the bank. I indented the ground beneath me, but I didn't sink. It felt like clay. I leaned back. The bank also yielded, but it didn't indent, like a hard mattress. I was more comfortable than I had ever been in any bathtub or bed.

"Are you guys afraid your playful madness may cross the line? That you may not be able to return to sanity?"

"All creativity is madness," Alice answered. "The most creative people go insane."

"There's a higher proportion of homosexuals in the art community than in the general population," said Samantha. "To be creative one must be different. Anyone who doesn't follow the prescribed method of doing something, including following an approved lifestyle, is considered to be insane by our homogeneous society. Homosexuals are therefore insane. Many people think working more than a summer in Yellowstone is insane."

Charlie piped up. "The only people truly insane are those who decide if a location in Yellowstone should be closed. Why even re-open Grant if they are going to evacuate it again a week later? They should have kept it closed so they could use the employees to fully staff the other locations. This time they're going to send the Grant employees home."

"Who could have predicted another fire would attack the area?" I asked.

"We no longer need those employees if tourons are afraid to enter the Park," Samantha declared. "Lake is at seventy percent of capacity and dropping."

"What are we going to do this weekend? Most trails are closed to camping."

"We can go to Bechler," Charlie suggested.

"Isn't that kind of remote?"

"The greater the difficulty, the greater the reward."

"That sounds like something Andy would say. How will we get there?"

"We have to go through Ashton, Idaho," said Charlie.

"That's halfway to Idaho Falls. Fifty miles from West Yellowstone?"

"Give or take," Samantha confirmed.

"Or we could take the Reclamation Road," Charlie hesitantly suggested. "But I wouldn't recommend it. This van doesn't really have the clearance. The only time I took it on it, it's belly must have scraped a dozen times."

I wasn't sure what Charlie and Samantha could have been doing back to back, but it didn't take them long to wander upstream together. They were cloaked in the mist by the time they traveled twenty feet.

I was alone with Alice now. Skinny dipping with a group of friends was fun, but being alone with one naked woman, felt indecent. "I hope Samantha and Charlie aren't foolish enough to do anything in this bacteria...enriched...water," I whispered.

"Sometimes risks must be taken to feel alive." Alice's eyes were shut, but she still made a connection. She had scooted up enough to allow her breasts to float on top of the water. She moved her body often enough that it was unlikely the dance was incidental.

"Don't you think certain precautions and self-control must be exercised in this day and age?"

"If I don't want to get my feet dirty I shouldn't play in a landfill. And isn't it wonderful to be the first one to eat some freshly popped popcorn?"

Daphnee was still on my mind. Even if she wasn't I still didn't think I would want the kernels in the bottom of the bowl.

I hope I can find my clothes.

76.   INFECTED WITH HUMANITY

Steamed billowed from the West Thumb Geyser Basin. Normally the sight was impressive, but not when smoke plumes were behind it and drifting hundreds of feet into the sky. The wooden junction sign hadn't been replaced, remaining charcoal black. South of Grant, trees burned beside the road. "I don't think we'll be coming back this way," I said. "I don't have asbestos tires."

"Regrets about volunteering to drive?" Charlie asked.

"Regrets I didn't volunteer sooner. Keeping the Lemon experience to myself was a crime against humanity. Or was it insanity?"

A mile beyond the Huckleberry Hot Springs trailhead the gravel road became nasty. Pebbles became rocks, which become small, jagged boulders. Steep ascents and descents were connected by sharp turns. The Lemon shook so much from the washboard road that I feared it would fall apart. The Reclamation Road wouldn't save us any time if we had to walk the rest of the way to Bechler. The Lemon had higher clearance than Charlie's van, but just barely. It scraped a few times. Part of me worried about how much it would cost to fix it, if something broke or was punctured. The other part just wanted me to enjoy the experience. If I had to eventually deal with the repairs, I didn't want to live through them twice. Charlie, in the front bucket seat, and Samantha and Christine, in the back, were loving it. The girls rocked from one side of the vehicle to the other. They had *volunteered* to be back there. "It will be safer when we have an accident," Samantha explained. When, not if. "Backpacks are as good as any air bag."

The road improved near its termination at Ashton, Idaho. What pissed me off was our route to the Bechler Ranger Station being nearly parallel to the Reclamation Road. Why wasn't there a cut-through road? Over farmland and forest, we took half-a-dozen side roads before finally reaching our goal.

Andy picked up the camping permit already, so we were able to bypass the ranger station and head directly to the trailhead. We were cut off by a man in green. "Can I see your permit please?"

"Andy Lincoln picked up a permit yesterday," Charlie announced.

"Where are you camping tonight?"

"Bechler Meadows. We'll also be camping there tomorrow night."

The ranger called in the information on his radio. "Everything checks out. Enjoy your stay."

We had just five miles to go today, so we were in good spirits. The first two miles were through forest, relatively flat and less dense than we were accustomed to. Being one of the lowest sections in the park, the ground had retained moisture, and in many areas, was still swampy. Planks, connected erratically, functioned as boardwalks above the water. Attention had to be paid to keep from stepping off. We crossed a putrid dollop of water, called a creek, via a suspension bridge. Mosquitoes swarmed from the water and attacked. We attempted to rush across the structure, but gained ground sluggishly. The bridge swayed from its unstable foundation and our unstable, massive packs. We ripped off the packs as soon as we touched solid ground, then drenched ourselves in bug repellent. It helped, but not perfectly.

Beyond the creek was savannah. We were occasionally attacked by mosquitoes, but they never got as bad as when we crossed the water. Three miles later---through a hodgepodge of grassland and pines---we arrived at another wobbly bridge. Our campsite was on the other side. We saw people there, but nobody we knew. "Could this be the wrong campsite?" Samantha conjectured.

"Let's head up the trail a bit more," said Charlie.

Someone yelled at us as we walked away. "UP HERE!" It was Andy. He rushed down a hill and greeted us at the bridge. We followed him to the top of the hill where Tony and Rebecca were cuddling beside a fire. "We thought the mosquitoes wouldn't be so bad up here," said Tony.

"They are bad enough," said Christine, slapping behind her knee.

"Why are there so many people here?" I asked. "Did they just decide this site was better?"

"It's a multi-group camp," Andy explained.

"Loss of solitude in exchange for a single campsite to become infected with humanity," Christine elucidated.

We ate dinner after setting up one more tent. Andy, Rebecca, and Tony already had theirs up from the night before. If the mosquitoes got too bad, we needed a place to escape to quickly. With the smoke from the fire and the temperature dropping they became almost non-existent.

"It's too bad you guys can't go with us to Ferris Fork tomorrow," Samantha announced. "It's the hot pot I fantasize about when I take a bath."

"Don't feel too sorry for us," said Andy. "We went to Dunan Falls this morning. There's a thermal pool below it. We soaked for more than an hour."

"I didn't come to Yellowstone to work six days a week," Christine complained a few minutes later.

"Tourists prefer clean beds and hot food," Samantha retorted.

"Did so many employees have to leave?"

"Probably afraid they'll become trapped by the fires."

"Or burned alive," Andy added.

"That's a gruesome thought."

"But they signed a contract," I grumbled. "Agreeing to work until a certain date. Don't they care how leaving will affect others? They should honor their contracts?"

"They don't expect to return," Charlie explained. "So they don't care what anyone in Yellowstone thinks of them. We become short-handed every summer after the college kids leave."

"If it wasn't for Rebecca I would consider leaving," said Tony. "I love the Park, but hate the work. If all the trails close what is the point of being here?"

"There are still some trails open," Charlie stated.

Tony looked at Rebecca. "What are we going to do when I leave?"

"You don't have to leave."

"I do. You could also leave."

"I can't. Not while there is the ability not to. I may never come back after leave."

"You can work next season," said Samantha.

"I'm thirty-three years old."

"There are people here who are older."

"I don't wish a fling to become a career."

"I'm not going to work in Yellowstone forever either," Samantha declared. "One day I'm going to finish school. I love learning, but I hate studying. Why can't we just go to lectures and labs, and write a paper or two for each class. Tests are too often multiple choice, which reveals more what we don't know than what we do. The things put on tests are usually the things people will forget a year later. Memorizing a list and regurgitating it on a bubble form is idiotic."

"But there's so much more to college than academics," said Tony. "Living in a fraternity builds brotherhood and character. It's practice for living on your own and becoming part of the community."

"Only if you expect to have someone cook and clean for you," said Christine. "Belonging to an organization or a club is a way to make yourself believe you are better than others. There is even a club for intelligence called Mensa. Just because a person is more intelligent than me or is more beautiful or stronger doesn't make them a better person. It's a form of prejudice. I think I have nice feet. Should I then establish a club for people who have nice feet, so I can prop myself up by not accepting people who don't?"

"I don't think anyone who pledged at my frat got rejected. I didn't join because I felt superior. I just thought it would be more fun than living in a dorm."

"There's nothing wrong with that, as long as anyone can join. It hasn't been that long ago that women weren't allowed to join most clubs."

It was a tight squeeze, but Charlie, Samantha and I fit in Charlie's tent. Whenever I traveled I usually forgot something. This time I forgot my tent. At least I didn't forget my sleeping bag. It was my mistake, so I was willing to pay the price, which meant sleeping under the stars, and, potentially, a swarm of mosquitoes, but Charlie insisted I sleep with him and Samantha. "You'll be eaten alive if you sleep outside. There's plenty of room in my tent. It will be cozy. Sam will be in the middle. She'll enjoy that. Everyone must have fun on their weekend."

It was not easy falling to sleep. Cozy is as cozy does, and I sure didn't, not since Daphnee left. But Charlie and Samantha.... I didn't want to ease drop, but when one is an inch away it was kind of hard not to read one's mind, not to mention one's body language. All I could say was they were quite efficient with the space available. After they fell asleep, I heard loud voices from outside the tent. First, a male voice, "BUT WHY NOT?!"

A female voice responded, "BECAUSE I DON'T WANT TO RIGHT NOW! Let's talk about it in the morning."

77.   CLEANSING TO THE BODY, MIND AND SOUL

In the morning, Tony left with Andy and Christine. Rebecca explained a couple of miles north of camp. "Tony proposed to me. It was the only way he could think to keep us together. I'm too young to be married. I still have a lot of stuff to do before I'm tied down. And Tony needs to see more of the world, including women, before he can decide to settle on just one. It would be quite a compliment if he decided I was the perfect woman for him. In five to ten years. But now.... I'm just a passing craze. He'll realize in a couple of years how lucky he was not to marry me." Years? Is that how long it will take me to get over Daphnee if I never see her again?

We entered Bechler Canyon. The trail rose slowly, but steadily. Ouzel Falls, one-hundred feet tall and lithe, was the western sentinel. The forest was the most fertile I've experienced so far in Yellowstone. The cooling humidity created by the falls rendered the canyon refreshing, even in August. There were actually ferns---something so common in the Cascades, but a rarity in the more arid Rockies.

We were running low on water, but I brought a surprise: a water pump. Refreshing, cool, sweet stream water could be consumed seconds after being pulled from the water. No more nasty iodine-tasting water. No more waiting for boiled water to cool. My companions nearly cried. After filling their water bottles with the icy cold liquid, Rebecca wanted to drink directly from the source. She placed the hose in her mouth, then slid it in and out. The pumping action caused the water to come out in spurts. Liquid dribbled down her face and chest.

We were too mesmerized to speak. Finally, Samantha said, "You take great pleasure in drinking."

"I take great pleasure in everything I do," she responded.

It was ten miles of rushing water and waterfalls. We became completely immersed in the primordial, Dante's Inferno becoming a distant memory.

An A-frame backcountry ranger station was spotting off-trail. A half-mile beyond, three rivers met, at a place appropriately named *Three Rivers Junction*. We crossed a bridge over the easternmost river. The trail straddled the peninsula above the two forks for a hundred yards. A quarter of a mile after the rivers separated, a sign announced *Ferris Fork*. Two minutes later we saw steam. Another five, steaming water. Sizzling liquid cascaded into the river. We leapt---successfully---onto a partially rocky/partially grassy island.

Charlie didn't hesitate to strip off his clothes. He put them on top of his rain poncho. Samantha joined him. They leapt into the water. The crystal-clear water left little to the imagination. Surprisingly, I was less aroused seeing Samantha in this state than I was when her body was more shrouded. Did the mystery, the incompleteness of those contours, make it more erotic? Or was this far reaching natural place more wild? A place where animals, beasts and humans, should frolic in the garments they were born with? Rebecca and I looked at one another. We took off our clothes, wrapped them in the rain poncho and joined our wilderness siblings.

The water felt cleansing to the body, mind, and soul. It was so clean compared to Ranger Pool. It was probably cleaner than most bath water. Sand and soft pebbles cushioned our feet. The water was deep enough to fall between stomach and chest, but to enjoy the pulsating womb to its fullest we slouched down to our necks. We were in the circulatory system of the wilderness. We were in tune with its every move, with its every thought, with its every emotion. No one spoke, the water and our surroundings being entertaining enough.

Thunder boomed. The connection was broken. Rebecca looked concerned. "Shouldn't we get out before it rains?"

Samantha laughed. "I don't think a little rain will hurt you in here."

"I mean the lightening. What if it strikes while we're in the water?"

Charlie smiled. "Rain in Yellowstone, this year? Don't worry, Rebecca. If we were in a swimming pool, lightening might be dangerous. But in a river…. The electricity will dissipate. I guess there is a chance we might get electrocuted, if we are very close to the strike. But the risk is slim. Doing this is more dangerous." Charlie leapt across bubbling water.

"Why does it seem more dangerous when naked?" I asked.

"It isn't really that hot," said Charlie. "Feel it." I did. It was just a little warmer than the rest of the hot pot. "The bubbling is due to gases, not to water boiling."

It began to sprinkle, making dull drum taps on the water. We relaxed and frolicked, for hours it seemed, just taking a break to eat lunch. After it stopped sprinkling for the second time, I got out of the water and looked at my watch. "It's five o'clock already."

Rebecca got out next. Then Samantha. And finally, Charlie. We looked hilarious: naked men and women wrapped in towels, surrounded by steam. Romans in a Roman bathhouse.

It sprinkled once more, briefly, on the way back to camp. "Do you think the rain will help the fires?" I asked.

"If you think this is rain then I'm a corporate lobbyist," said Charlie. "There's more moisture running down my back. A little rain will just make those people fighting the fires uncomfortable. It will do more harm than good. To put out these fires we need a drenching rain."

"Or a flood," said Samantha.

"Or winter to arrive four months early."

Fatigue set in. Waterfalls and cascades were no longer highlights. They became backdrops, background visuals.

"I've been thinking," said Rebecca. "Why don't we go all the way out today."

"But that means hiking another five miles. And most of that in the dark," I complained. "Don't you remember coming down from the Middle Teton?"

"I was also thinking about going out tonight," Samantha admitted. "It's just two more hours of hiking. I don't want to camp with mosquitoes tonight."

Charlie added, "If it's not going to be fun we might as well head back."

Five miles didn't seem too bad when we had day packs on. It was grueling with an extra thirty pounds on your back. Crossing the planks was nearly impossible. Charlie had our one flashlight and he was in front. I was third in line and had to feel with my feet to work my way across. Rebecca fell further and further behind. She didn't even try to use the planks. She sloshed through the water, cursing each time she got her feet wet. Every few minutes Charlie waited for her to catch up, but she immediately fell back once he began moving again.

"Nobody talk as we pass the ranger station," Charlie warned. "We aren't supposed to hike in the dark. If the rangers know, we may get fined." The Lemon rolled quietly away, crushing gravel. Rebecca's Ford Bronco followed a little more exuberantly. She made up in metal and plastic what her flesh and blood wasn't capable of.

Charlie traveled with me, and Samantha with Rebecca. I appreciated Charlie's willingness to slum with me. A couple of miles into the drive Rebecca passed me. Northeast of Ashton, on the West Yellowstone Highway, Rebecca pulled off onto a side road in the National Forest. She stopped after half-a-mile.

"What are they doing?" I asked Charlie.

"Getting ready for bed." The backs of their seats bent down.

They grabbed blankets and pillows from further back in the vehicle. Charlie shook his seat.

"I'm sorry, the seats in the Lemon don't go back. You should have brought your van."

"ICE CREAM AND ONIONS! We'll sleep outside. It's dry enough here that the mosquitoes won't bother us."

Feet from the Lemon, we placed sleeping bags upon sleeping pads. I was very tired. I walked a couple of steps away and peed, making sure I was at least facing away from my bed. The sky sprinkled back a few minutes later. We laughed uncontrollably. We burrowed into our sleeping bags and hibernated.

78. ONLY A HIKE

Magnolia sat across from me in the EDR. I chose to sit at her table, so it was my own fault for my anguish. I sat quietly, delaying. "Come on, Steve," she said. "We should go on at least one hike together before we leave Yellowstone, and maybe each other forever."

"It's getting late. It gets darker much sooner now than it did in June."

"We'll go on a short hike."

I did wish to go hiking, but it felt wrong going with Magnolia. It was only a hike though, wasn't it? I shouldn't feel guilty even if something did happen between us. I may not even see Daphnee again. We never agreed not to see anyone else. "All right. Do you have a particular place you want to go?"

"No, just to hike with you, Steve."

"We have to go somewhere close. How about Hayden

Valley? There's a lake called Wrangler on the northern end of it, four or five miles in. We'll see how far we can get before it gets dark."

"It sounds like fun. Let me fix my hair, then we can go."

79.   A DISTRACTING EFFECT

There wasn't a bison jam through Hayden Valley today. If there was I might have thought about turning around. I was already feeling pressured beginning a hike so late in the day. A hike should be relaxing. How could it be if you had to worry about finishing in the dark, and wondering where and when you had to turn around to get back before that happened?

The trail began at the Chittenden parking lot, a crossroads of trails that headed south into Hayden Valley, and north towards the cluster of small lakes near the southeast rim of the Canyon. The parking lot was strangely empty. When was a parking lot in Yellowstone National Park ever empty? The air was smoky, especially to the north and west, where one of the largest Yellowstone fires was consuming thousands of acres a day. I looked at Magnolia. My eyes asked if she was sure she wanted to do this. I hadn't fully recovered from the Hell Hike, but I was willing to tempt fate again with some motivation.

Magnolia grabbed my arm and smiled. "Let's go." We chose the most easterly route, the shorter of the two trails---by a quarter of a mile---that would eventually take us to Wrangler Lake. The smoke in the air moderated the temperature. What should have been a late summer swelter, felt more like autumnal bliss. The trail was level for the most part, but it had enough twenty foot dips and rises in it to make the scenery varying. We were currently in sage, but one-hundred yards to the north it was forested. Hayden Valley stretched to the southwest of us. There was another forest on the eastern horizon. Somewhere in there was Wrangler Lake.

"What are you going to do after the season is over, Steve?"

"I don't know. Go back home to look for a job."

"I'm going to take a semester off, to travel. There's room for another person."

"I don't know."

"You're that anxious to get back to the *real world* and find a *real job*? You know it'll be hard to come back here and travel once you settle down."

"So, you think I'll be one of those people that will wish to come back here as soon as I leave?"

"I'm already missing Yellowstone."

"I'm not sure I want to work in the kitchen again. I have a college degree."

"Doing something requiring a degree doesn't always make a person happy. Or prevent them from doing it at a later date."

"Charlie and Andy both have degrees and remain underemployed."

"They're happy though, aren't they?"

"How long does working just one more season become routine? I don't want to risk becoming trapped."

"Promise me that you'll think about returning."

"I need to start earning some money."

"Snow Lodge is hiring for the winter."

"I can't afford to work another minimum wage job."

"Don't returnees get an extra ten cents per hour?"

I stayed in the lead as often as possible. A woman like Magnolia hiking in shorts had a distracting effect on me. I didn't want the hike to turn into anything but.

After a mile, the trail forked north and south. We guided right. I looked at my watch and then to the sun, where it should be, if it wasn't behind the smoke. It wouldn't be much longer before we had to turn around. A mile-and-a-half later we took the Wrangler Lake spur trail to the southeast. A few minutes after that we came to a creek just barely too wide to jump across. Magnolia took off her shoes and socks. I knew it would come to this---just four more pieces of clothing and she would be completely naked. The water was cold, but was padded with sand. It took just seconds to cross. We put our socks and shoes back on, over wet feet. We continued. After a few paces, we were halted by mud. I looked at Magnolia. *Do we head back now?* I asked with my eyes. Round two of strip water poker. Slosh. Slurp. Slosh. The mud felt great. The straw was tender enough that it messaged my feet, instead of cutting and tearing them. The water was cool, but not cold. Somehow Magnolia got ahead of me. Mud splattered all the way up to her.... I better catch up.

"ANOTHER CREEK!" Magnolia cried out as she ran towards it. Actually, it was the same creek we crossed five minutes ago. Couldn't a less demanding route be created? The most direct route was a straight line, but a slightly modified one would have not only kept me dry, but ultimately, saved time. Magnolia soaked part of her shorts and splashed her shirt as she enthusiastically crossed the creek. The frigid creek water was a shock compared to the more tepid watery mud.

I shivered as I sat next to Magnolia on a small hill overlooking the creek. She slid her hands up and down her legs, in an attempt to dry and to warm them. Foot. Ankle. Shin. Knee. Thigh. Then back down again.

A large pterodactyl-like bird flew out of the trees behind us. It's screeching caused goose bumps, replacing those I received from watching Magnolia. It flew directly over us, then past the creek. It faded into the medieval, misty horizon. The sun began to set, poking through the smoke just enough to add color to our prehistoric setting: reds and oranges of erupting volcanoes and flowing magma.

Magnolia placed a hand on my leg.

We heard rustling behind us. We stood-up and turned around. A black, bent shape walked through the woods, ten feet from the meadow. It was time to head back. We re-crossed the creek. I didn't turn around to see the bear's progression---what could it have been but a bear---until we had the two crossings between us and it.

Magnolia held onto my arm. I allowed her to, but I didn't display any affection in return. I felt so conflicted. I was attracted to Magnolia, but didn't want to betray Daphnee. Was I even going to see her again?

There was another rustling, this time in the copse we just passed through.

"What is it?" questioned Magnolia.

"A porcupine, I think."

"It's climbing that tree like a cat. It's so cute." Only a female would think something with poke-your-eyes-out-sharp needles was cute.

Magnolia clutched my arm again. If felt comforting having someone so close.

The lack of illumination had bottomed out. We could still see a bit. I turned on my flashlight. The smoke particles in the air made anything twenty feet away or more opaque. I turned it back off and waited for my eyes to re-adjust to the darkness. The trail was well enough marked that it was inevitable we would reach the trailhead---eventually.

"Are you ever afraid of dying, Steve?"

"Sometimes. I try not to think about it."

"Do you believe we will actually go to heaven, or is that just a comforting fairy tale to protect us from the reality of death?"

"I hope it's true. I don't believe we will go to a physical place. I think it's more mental, more spiritual. What if heaven is what you create it to be? Don't a lot of people consider death an eternal sleep? If that is true, then heaven must be your dreams

301

during this sleep."

"So, it doesn't matter what type of person you were when you lived? You could be a mass murderer and still go to your own personal heaven?"

"Yes, but one's dreams are manufactured from one's subconscious. If one's life isn't something to be proud of, it can return to haunt, as nightmares."

"Eternal nightmares. I wouldn't care to have those."

"It's just a theory. No one living really knows what death is like."

"So, this wonderful, romantic walk with you could be replayed over and over again after I die?"

"Or your psyche may transform it and have that bear catch and eat us."

"Those birds over there are chasing one another. They're beautiful. They look like tubs of vanilla ice cream with wings."

"They're owls. Small ones. They must be babies."

"Or teenagers, cruising the main drag."

The snowy owlets kept pace with us, doing acrobatics the best World War I dogfighters would be proud of. A hooting from the forest sent the little ones home. Mama had finally discovered her children had snuck out.

"I SEE A LIGHT!" I shrieked. Magnolia wrapped her arms around me, pulling me towards her, then squeezing intensely. The Lemon was still in the parking lot. I knew it was extremely unlikely someone would steal it, but it would be just my luck not to have it there after returning from a scary hike in the dark.

Magnolia kissed me on the lips as she got out of the Lemon. It was brief, but there was nothing platonic about it. "See you tomorrow, Steve," she said sweetly, skipping back to the dorm. "I had a wonderful time."

80. SUMMER TAKES ITS TOLL

"What can we do this weekend?" asked Charlie while eating dinner in the EDR. With the fires limiting activities I tended to spend a lot of time in the EDR.

"We can go to Union Falls," Andy suggested.

"The South Gate is still closed."

"Are they allowing any camping in the Park?" I asked.

"I don't think so," Andy replied. "They're afraid what happened to us on the Hell Hike might happen to someone else."

"How about a day hike?"

"There are still some trails open in the north," Charlie responded enthusiastically.

"We've never done the Yellowstone River Trail," said Andy.

"There are still some trails you guys haven't hiked?" I asked.

"A few remote ones. And others we never had time to do because something better always came up."

"You've mentioned some trails you do every year. If you eliminated some of those you'll have more time to do the ones you haven't gotten to yet."

"Why?" Charlie questioned.

"Why?"

"If you know a trail will be great, why risk hiking an unknown one, if doing so eliminates the time that could have been spent on the better trail?"

"But you don't know it's the better trail until you try the new one."

"True. But that new trail could be much worse. There are

also the memories. The anticipation of reliving a memorable event."

"How about you, Andy? Would you rather have the satisfaction of hiking all the trails in Yellowstone or repeat the ones you've enjoyed the most?"

Charlie answered for him. "Andy is still working on it. Deciding if he wants to stay on the trail he hasn't been able to complete. Or trying something new."

I smirked. "We're not just talking about hiking, are we?" Andy blushed.

"To answer your initial question," Charlie continued. "I haven't dated every girl in Yellowstone."

"Yet," Andy interrupted.

"If given the opportunity to do so, I would decline most of those relationships in exchange for spending more time with Sam."

"Not all?"

"You have to occasionally break up the monotony."

"So, how many of us are going hiking? And when *I* say hiking, I mean *hiking*. Walking in the woods. Climbing mountains. Crossing creeks."

"Great euphuisms."

"That wasn't what I...."

"Just the three of us," said Andy. "Samantha is having trouble breathing in the smoky air, and Christine won't go alone with us. She's afraid we'll go too fast."

"No one else?" I asked.

"They're all gone," said Andy. "A summer takes its toll. It's always difficult the last month or so to find people to hike with--- even when there aren't any fires."

Magnolia entered the EDR. It took her ten minutes to get her food and sit down. She had to socialize and flirt with everyone she met. She knew who was the center of attention. By the time she did sit down, Charlie and Andy were gone, making it easier on me.

"You going to take me to the dance next Saturday?"

"I don't know."

Magnolia pouted. The only thing more persuasive than a woman pouting is when she cries, and Magnolia wasn't going to risk her make-up running in front of all these people. "I thought I was someone special to you?"

"You are, but so is Daphnee. I know she isn't here now, and I may never see her again, but she is still very much on my mind."

"Aren't I also on your mind? It's only a dance."

"Even if I never met Daphnee I don't think I could ever be your boyfriend."

Magnolia was on the verge of tears now. I didn't want to do this to her, especially in front of all these people, but I had to be honest with her, didn't I? "Aren't I good enough for you, Steve? Aren't I pretty enough? Or pleasant enough to be around? Everyone likes me."

"That's the problem. Everyone likes you, and you like everyone. I don't want to feel like I'm always competing for you."

"But you're the one I want to spend time with."

"I believe that, but your...interactions...with other guys sends certain signals. I don't want to date a woman who I must share, even if she never acts upon any of the advances. Someone will always be trying to win you away from me. You're like a celebrity."

"But I don't want to be."

"I know." She kind of did, but I believed she also wanted an authentic existence.

Magnolia began to cry. I gently placed her head on the inside of my shoulder.

"I can change."

I wiped her face with a dispenser napkin.

"Don't change for me. You must be true to yourself. You have a gift. Don't be ashamed of it. You will meet someone who will love you because of it."

Magnolia snatched the napkin from me and finished cleaning her face. "Someone who isn't ashamed of me?"

"There are plenty of guys that will get an ego boost having their girl being lusted after."

"I need to use the rest room."

"I'm sorry."

Magnolia kissed me on the cheek and left.

81. THREE GRUNGY MEN IN THE DARK

It rained for about an hour that night, clearing the air of smoke, momentarily. In the morning, we could see across the lake for the first time in more than a week. And we could take robust breathes of air without choking. It was like the first day of spring after a nuclear winter. Crisp, clear, clean precipitation was followed by glory-to-the-soul rays of sunshine. After breakfast, the smoke came back. We drove north in a continuous reddish-gray haze. Death had returned.

The only other vehicles on the Grand Loop Road were fire trucks and the occasional RV heading for the nearest exit. Canyon Village, recently evacuated, had more fire fighters than it ever had guests. With the North Fork Fire approaching, Canyon was a gathering spot for the next line of defense. There were nearly 10,000 fire fighters in the Park already and more were expected to arrive. We saw no one at all at Tower. It had been evacuated for more than a week. Roosevelt also looked deserted.

We parked next to the ranger station there, to ask about trail conditions and fires in the area. It was possible the Yellowstone River trail had closed since we last checked. The door to the ranger station was locked. No closure sign or announcement when the attending ranger would return. We knocked. No answer.

"This isn't a good sign," Andy declared.

"A worst sign would be the one announcing the closure of the trail," said Charlie. "Let's see how far we can go before a ranger, or a sign, tells us we can't go no further."

"Do you think your van will be safe?" I asked.

"Nothing in Yellowstone would hurt me, not even a fire."

"I still think we should have brought an additional vehicle," said Andy, "to leave at the other trailhead. I would prefer to not be stuck out here during Armageddon."

"When have we ever failed to be picked up while hitchhiking in Yellowstone? The day I don't get picked up hitchhiking is the day I have to spend the night with the two of you instead of with a beautiful woman."

We didn't see any closure signs on the trail, but we did see smoke, plenty of it. We attempted to pinpoint where it was coming from and settled for everywhere. The friendly Pleasant Valley of two months ago had turned into a canyon of foreboding. There were no shadows, just a constant, continuous murkiness. If it wasn't for the endorphins being produced by hiking, I might have felt depressed. Instead, I began to understand what manic depression might feel like. What if we didn't see anyone again--- ever? What if we never died? To walk in slow motion through the eternal mists of limbo forever. We spoke very little. The battle had to be fought alone.

We perked up a bit as we crossed the Yellowstone River suspension bridge. But the excitement was short-lived. It was so hazy we could barely see the water rushing below. Was it even possible to experience fear in our emotionless shroud?

Next was the shaky suspension bridge over Hellroaring Creek. No one even tried to shake it as we stumbled over the uneven planks. I feared if we weren't careful we might just lay down somewhere and not care to get back up.

I began to get excited once we entered territory new to me. "Do you guys still get excited the second, third...or tenth time you hike a trail? And I'm just talking about hiking, not girls. Everything is so new to me, but you guys have been here for quite a while."

"A good trail, one that's scenic, varying, that doesn't have too many people on it," Charlie replied, "is always a pleasure to hike on, no matter how many times you've hiked on it before. Think of all the good books you've read, or the good movies you've seen. You don't mind seeing them again, do you? In some ways, it's more exciting. The anticipation of a dramatic cliff or a beautiful meadow. Details I didn't notice last time because I was distracted, or too warm, or constipated."

"Girls are the same," said Andy. "Some of them."

"I thought we were done talking about girls," I interrupted.

"You were done talking about girls," said Charlie. "My thoughts are constantly intertwined with them."

"And apparently, Andy's."

Andy continued. "It's exciting when you first meet a beautiful woman, but because you are nervous, because you don't know the person, you can't fully enjoy her presence. It takes a while before you can be totally comfortable with her. After you know what pleases her, and she, you, you can be truly content in a relationship. You feel safe when the outcome is predetermined."

"Like your relationship with Christine?"

Charlie laughed. "Whatever relationship he has with Christine will never be comfortable, for either of them."

Andy frowned, but he also didn't refute what Charlie said.

"So, what is the outcome of this trail?" I asked.

"I guess we'll have to hike it to find out," said Charlie.

"Who wants to open all their presents on Christmas Eve?" Andy added.

"Me," Charlie responded enthusiastically. "The sooner I unwrap them the sooner I can enjoy them."

"Are you talking about presents or girls?" I asked.

"Yes."

"For me, half the excitement of receiving a present is the anticipation of what I might find after I open it."

"I guess it's your lucky day, then."

A couple of minutes later, Charlie said, "This doesn't look right. I think we took a wrong turn while we were talking. I haven't seen a trail marker in a while. We've probably stumbled onto an animal trail."

"Time to cut our losses and turn around," Andy announced.

Charlie had a determined look on his face. "You know what I think about turning around."

I took out my map and compass. "It looks like we're heading in the right direction. Maybe this trail will merge with the correct trail again."

We hiked another mile. We stopped when we came to a foaming creek. I got out my map again and spread it out for the others to see. "It's either the Little Cottonwood or the Cottonwood," said Charlie. "Either, we are too far north. See where the trail crosses the creeks, near where they empty into the Yellowstone River. We're at least a half-a-mile too far upstream."

We crossed the creek on some rocks, then made our way hastily downstream along the western bank. We found the trail, about a hundred yards from the Yellowstone River.

We hastened our strides, to make up the time we lost. We didn't stop for lunch until we arrived at Crevice Lake, a quarter of a mile beyond the Blacktail Fork. We now knew where we were--- precisely. We had just eight more miles to go.

Crevice Lake was just over a hundred feet from the Yellowstone River, yet made no physical contact with it. We watched ducks race across the five-acre lake as we ravenously consumed cheese and crackers, peanut butter and jelly, Oreos, and apple juice. I was surprised there was still some wildlife remaining in Yellowstone. There were some animals as stupidly stubborn as humans.

A mile down trail we were entertained by the spectacle of Crevice Creek. It's only connection to Crevice Lake, its proximity. It had its own lake, many of them, small pools connected by yard-tall waterfalls.

Charlie looked at Andy, then at the pools, then back at Andy. "Okay," Andy finally responded. "But for only ten minutes. We still need to get out of here by dark."

"ICE CREAM AND ONIONS!" Charlie stripped off his clothes and settled into a pool a couple of tiers above the trail.

Andy was next. With less enthusiasm he stripped, neatly stacking his clothes. He dropped into the pool with the most powerful flow---nature's masseuse.

"ISN'T THE WATER COLD?!" I yelled at them. The water was rushing downward at a thirty-degree angle, so it was difficult to hear.

"FEEL FOR YOURSELF!" Charlie yelled back. "THERE MUST BE A THERMAL RUNOFF UPSTREAM SOMEWHERE!"

I stepped down to the stone bank and dipped in a hand. It wasn't exactly warm, but it wasn't that cold either. A couple of degrees cooler than the Firehole River. "I THOUGHT YOU WERE AGAINST SKINNY DIPPING!" I yelled at Andy.

"ONLY WHEN GIRLS ARE AROUND!"

"AND IF SOMEONE WALKS BY?!"

"YOU WEREN'T THIS TIMID AT FERRIS FORK!" Charlie commented.

"WE WEREN'T NEXT TO A MAJOR TRAIL!"

"WHO IS GOING TO WALK BY? WE HAVEN'T SEEM ANYONE THE ENTIRE DAY!"

The water felt great. It was like it was this morning, for that brief period after it rained, before the smoke reclaimed its turf. But even better, because my entire body could feel the massaging purity.

After we dressed and were on our way again, Charlie said, "Each summer in Yellowstone feels like a lifespan. I don't mean it's duration. It doesn't feel like it goes on forever. I'm referring to the emotional aspects. We arrive in May. We go through orientation and training. We meet new people. We begin to go hiking as the snow melts. Our desires change as the conditions in the Park change. We begin to go camping. Our endurance builds. We go on longer hikes. People begin to leave us. Obligations curtail our hiking. More people leave us. Old friends become more important. We try to regain youth, but we are no longer capable."

"I hope that doesn't mean you think we won't make it back alive?" I asked.

"Are we three old friends sitting together in a park?" asked Andy. "After everyone else has passed away?"

"Maybe for this season. Hopefully there will be other seasons. It's wonderful to relive life each year. Each season begins with the same potentials. As babies pushed from the womb we enter Yellowstone. Each person you meet changes your course a little, beginning with your parents. Next year I might meet a woman who I will marry. Or maybe I will be fed up with work and quit. Or a bear will eat me. Wouldn't it be great to live our lives over again?"

"Not all of it," I declared. "I don't think anyone looks too fondly at their adolescence. What if life is worse the second time around? I don't want to relive my struggles."

"But wouldn't you like to live forever? To be someone slightly different each time?"

"It frightens me to be reincarnated," said Andy. "It's like my soul is being tasked again and again without any reprieve. It makes me feel tired. When I finally rest in peace, I want to stay that way."

I added, "To lose your family and friends, again, and again? They should only have to die once. It was bad enough when Daphnee left two weeks ago."

Knowles Falls was disappointing. It dropped only thirty feet. It was going to be the highlight of our hike.

An hour later we came upon our true highlight. The trail left

311

the Park briefly, and at that instant the smoke abandoned us. It was amazing. Back across the border the sky was charcoal, but directly above us it was blue, with puffy, white clouds smiling at us pleasantly, stupidly, like in a child's book.

Timing was perfect. We ran out of water as we entered a sage flat. For three miles we had to endure thirst under a hot, bright sun. Gardiner was 2500 feet lower than Lake Yellowstone, so even on a uniformly sunny day this desert trek would be ten degrees warmer than what we were accustomed to. THERE WERE ACTUALLY CACTI BESIDE THE TRAIL!

A mile from Gardiner, the river---and trail---entered a narrow barren canyon. Our route was cut steeply into the canyon wall. Because of the scarcity of vegetation, the trail was eroding, creating dust. Every step brought a cloud of it up. In contrast, in a shadowed section of the canyon, the trail was muddy. We attempted to circumvent the funk, but in some places, there was no safe route around it. Our feet became heavy. Every step became a chore. After we determined the gunk was safely behind us, we used whatever sticks and rocks we could find to scrape off as much mud as possible. Our boots were lighter, but they still looked terrible.

The last half-a-mile, the trail was quite pleasant. We were back down beside the river. A scattering of aspens caressed its bank. After seeing lodgepole pines everyday it was refreshing to see some trees with leaves.

"CIVILIZATION!" Andy bellowed. Only in Yellowstone could seeing a bear on a building signal a departure from the wilderness.

The trail terminated at a private campground. We filled our water bottles from a tap at one of the campsites. People sitting in lawn chairs stared at us as we walked down the hill to Gardiner's main road. Hadn't these people seen anyone hike before?

A gas station food mart was across the street. We bought a quart bottle of Gatorade each and miscellaneous junk food. It was almost not worth hiking, considering all the crap you put into your ravenous body after you finished.

We hiked to the north entrance of the Park, about half-a-mile away. For every vehicle entering the Park there were ten that left. We hitched a ride after five minutes. It was an Old Faithful employee coming home from a wild weekend in Bozeman. He dropped us off in front of the Mammoth Hotel. He regretted not going through Roosevelt. We regretted it more.

Across the street from the hotel, the Mammoth to Roosevelt leg of the Grand Loop Road began. It was dusk. We waited for a ride. And waited. A dozen cars and trucks passed us. No one wished to pick up three grungy men in the dark. Who would have guessed?

"I don't think we're going to find a ride tonight," said Andy. "It's too late."

"What can we do?" I asked.

"I think we should wait here, just a little longer," said Charlie. "I'm sure someone will pick us up."

We waited another half-an-hour. Still no luck.

"Why don't we see if they'll put us up in Mammoth tonight," Andy suggested. "There are supposed to be transient rooms available for employees who must travel around the Park as part of their job."

"*Juniper Residence Hall*," I announced. "You think the RC is still up?"

Andy knocked on the RC's door. A girl, who looked barely old enough to drink legally, opened it. We told our tale and she put us up for the night, even supplying pillows and sheets.

We threw our backpacks on the three beds, then washed up. Our room didn't have a connecting bathroom, so we had to walk down the hallway to a communal facility to improve our hygiene. None of us had enough energy left to take a shower, so we did the best we could with bandannas and water.

Back in our room we fell onto our individual beds. "So, Charlie," said Andy. "Which one of us would you like to do first?"

313

"Go to sleep." And we did, a few seconds later.

82. PARSLEY

Every community had its indigenous, peculiar traditions. One of Yellowstone's is *Christmas In August*. Many years ago, there was a snow storm on August 25th. Everyone was stranded in the Park---tourists and employees. Instead of begrudging the isolating snow they used the occasion to celebrate the enjoyment of sharing one another's company. Trees were decorated, and presents were exchanged.

Christmas in August 1988 meant a dance and decorating Lake Yellowstone Hotel. There were also isolated Christmas parties. I was fortunate to be invited to one of the best---Charlie's.

I was greeted by a kiss from Samantha. I blushed. "That's what you get for standing under the mistletoe," said Charlie.

"It looks like parsley to me," I shot back.

"Charlie said he was going to kiss every girl," said Samantha, "so I decided to kiss all the guys."

"Can I come in and out more than once?"

"Would you like some eggnog?" asked Charlie. He pressed a cup into my hand before I could reply. I choked a shallow down.

"He hasn't perfected the right ratio of rum to nog yet," said Christine, sitting on the edge of Andy's bed. She was the only person there so far except for the two greeters.

Hundreds of lights hung throughout the room, including the three-foot high artificial Christmas tree on the nightstand between the two beds. Christmas music played softly in the background.

"I'm surprised you don't have a full room," I commented.

"Have a seat," said Samantha. "Christmas is a time to relax." I sat on the floor, leaning against Charlie's bed. I always felt more relaxed when I wasn't fighting gravity.

Andy attempted to sneak in. Samantha grabbed him and generously planted kisses. Andy's face reddened. "That's the third time. I'm not even safe entering my own room."

"That's what you get for leaving the party," said Samantha.

"Did you round up anyone?" asked Charlie.

"There's a couple of people from housekeeping that say they will show up later."

"I guess everyone wants to show-up fashionably late," I remarked.

"The cartoons begin promptly at eight," stated Charlie. "Empty room or packed house."

One by one people did show up. Magnolia showed up with a date. She was cordial to me, but I knew it would be difficult for us to remain friends. She cuddled with her new beau in the corner. Harry and Iris showed up, but stayed for just a few minutes. Their awkward excuse made it apparent they didn't feel comfortable being three to four decades older than everyone else.

"*The Grinch Who Stole Christmas* will be shown first, followed by *Frosty the Snowman* and *Rudolph the Red-Nosed Reindeer*."

After the cartoons, Christine showed the video she shot of people at work. Everyone liked to see themselves on television, so it was a crowd pleaser. Someone made a Christmas tree out of the ends of a pineapple, a cheese star topping it. Cherry tomatoes were attached to the fronds with toothpicks. At the end of the video was some random footage of the Yellowstone fires. Before the tape ran out, the last few seconds of a Looney Tunes cartoon played, left over from what had been previously recorded on the tape. It ended with *That's All Folks*!

83. CAR!

Andy watched for car lights as the rest of us climbed the metal rungs to the roof of the Fishing Bridge Hamilton Store. "You sure that this place is completely closed down?" he whispered to Charlie, who was leading the pack, and had just reached the roof.

"Fishing Bridge closed last week," Charlie shouted down, a little too loudly in Andy's opinion, evidenced by his grimace. "You don't see any lights on do you?"

"No, but what if they're using night goggles?"

The rest of us climbed to the roof. Andy nearly fell, his overly aggressive surveillance making him unstable. We spread out to explore. Samantha followed Charlie to the far edge. They peered over the side precariously. Tony climbed up the chimney, then looked down it. Andy watched east and west for headlights. Magnolia leapt across the roof like a ballerina. She noticed me watching her. She smiled, then motioned me to join her. I did acrobatic leaps and direction changes like I was a dancer in a Broadway musical. Charlie and Samantha were drawn to the motion. In tribute, or an attempt to outdo me, they performed an aerobics routine.

"Car," whispered Andy loudly. We all dropped to the ground, laying as flat as possible, so no one could see us from below. The sky and trees south of us began to brighten. The buzzing intensified. Seconds later the storm passed, leveling off into solitude.

"All clear," Charlie announced. "The Nazis have returned to Germany."

"You don't think they saw us?" asked Andy.

"If someone did, they didn't care," Samantha reassured him. "They didn't even slow down."

"It doesn't feel right being up here. We're trespassing."

"Not if everything was community property," Charlie countered. "As it should be. There are millions of acres of beautiful forests and prairies and mountains, but there are fences. Why?"

"Because of liability," Andy answered. "If someone gets hurt on their land they can be sued."

"That's stupid. Anyway, fences are the most dangerous part of most properties."

Magnolia added, "Did you hear about the home owner who was sued because a burglar tried to enter his house through its roof, fell and was injured."

"TA DA!" said Christine loudly. She stood proudly by her masterpiece: a very abstract picture of a woman above a caption stating, *Martha Devla Was Here.*

Andy looked partly angry, but mostly nervous. "Wipe that off before anyone sees it. We'll first get fired, then sent to prison to spend the rest of our lives in a cell with a man covered in tattoos of naked men. I'm not ready for a lifestyle change."

"No one will see it," said Charlie. "It was done in chalk, so it will wash away in the rain."

"Martha would write that up there herself if she wasn't location manager," Samantha stated. "We're just doing her a favor."

"CAR!" shouted Magnolia. Everyone dropped flat on the roof again. The vehicle stopped in front of the store, paused, then headed off again.

"That was too close," said Andy. "We better escape while we still can."

"Just a bit longer," said Charlie. "I want to see if I can spot a bear." We headed to the far side of the roof. We looked into the woods north of us, along the course of the Yellowstone River.

"Anyone else imagining the Yellowstone River flooding?" Christine asked. "There is so much water that only this roof and tops of trees are visible."

Andy snorted. "Only you."

"And the only way we can travel from place to place is by boat," Magnolia added.

"Or we could swing from one tree to another by a vine, like Tarzan," Christine countered.

"I don't see any bears," said Charlie. "The fires have probably scared them all away."

"Then let's get down," Andy begged.

A car rushed by after half of us were down. Those still on the ladder climbed back onto the roof and lay flat. Those on the ground hid behind columns. Magnolia lay next to me. I asked her, "Are you having fun?"

"I always do." And so she did. And apparently, she didn't hold any grudges that derailed that enjoyment. Magnolia and I could still be friends even after I rejected her.

"Would you like to go to Natural Bridge with me tomorrow after dinner?" I asked her. "I've never been there, and I would like to see it before I leave Yellowstone."

"I haven't seen it either, but I'm working late tomorrow."

"How about after you get off?"

"But it'll be dark."

"I don't mind if you don't."

"I would love to."

We climbed down, then headed towards Charlie's van. It was parked a couple of blocks away, next to Fishing Bridge. We didn't want to park in front of the Ham Store and give ourselves away now, did we?

Charlie's eyes twinkled as we passed a condemned building. "NO!" said Andy firmly as Charlie approached the building.

"Those who don't wish to participate in the discovery of these ruins, can return home."

"I don't mind driving them back," I volunteered.

Charlie's mouth widened into that little boy grin of his. He handed me his keys.

"I'll come right back."

"You don't have to do that. We can walk back."

"And miss out on this archaeological discovery?"

Charlie grin became even wider. "Oh. And if you can remember, bring the bag of chips in the van back with you. I'm all of sudden very hungry."

Samantha stayed with Charlie, but the rest of them headed back. "You too?" I asked Magnolia.

"I have to sleep at least one night this week."

84. ONE-HUNDRED TOILETS

When I returned to the abandoned building I couldn't find Charlie and Samantha. "BOO!" someone yelled from behind. I dropped the chips. Half of them fell out. Charlie ate them anyway. "A little dirt won't hurt me. In fact, this dirt is a lot cleaner than the chemicals spayed on fruit and vegetables you find in the supermarket."

"We found a way in," said Samantha. She bypassed the chips on the ground for a clean one in the bag. I looked at the building. It was two stories of rotting wood. All the windows were boarded up. I tried a door. It was locked.

"Over here." Samantha removed a board from one of the front windows. It came off easily. They must had done most of the work before I arrived. The window was half open, just enough space for a person to squeeze through. Inside was a room littered with scattered papers.

Charlie went in first. The window was high enough that Samantha and I had to hold onto his legs to prevent him from falling onto his head on the other side. Samantha went next. With one of us on both sides it was easier for her to climb through. The only trouble she had was with her chest. "There are times like this when I wish I was flat-chested." I was able to force open the window a couple of inches more, which was enough to force Samantha through. I was practically dragged through. The last foot they both got beneath me and carried me away from the window. We pulled the window down. No easy task with the condition it was in. "So no one will suspect anything," said Charlie.

"What if someone nailed that board back in place?" I asked.

"Then we will kick our way free," Charlie replied. "In a few more years this place will fall down on its own."

"I don't think we can wait that long," said Samantha. "The chips are almost gone."

We picked-up the papers thrown about and read them with the flashlights we brought with us. "It's like we're in a tomb. All this stuff is six to eight years old."

"Grant Village was built to replace Fishing Bridge, after it was torn down," said Charlie. "They are still in the process. Just a few years ago there were cabins behind here."

"They are going to remove the bridge?" I asked.

"Just most of the village," Samantha assured me.

"Do you think bears will really return to this area after most of the buildings, and people, are gone?"

"You remember the bear and her cubs who were in this area this spring? A river entering a lake is prime grizzly habitat."

Charlie passed through a vacant doorway to the back of the building. "OVER HERE!" he shouted. The next room was unbelievable. Dozens of toilets were scattered throughout the room. "They must be from the cabins that were torn down."

"They could have at least cleaned them first," said

Samantha. One of the toilets had crap in it. It wasn't fresh, but it wasn't six years old either.

"It looks like we weren't the first ones to explore here," I said.

"Let's find a way up to the second story," said Charlie. "There has to be a staircase somewhere."

"I don't see anything."

"How about behind those boards?"

We pulled the boards away from the wall, revealing an L-shaped stairway.

The still night amplified the creaking up the stairs. "Anyone have a wooden stake to stab Dracula through the heart?" asked Samantha.

"We have an almost empty bag of chips," I volunteered. "Maybe we can suffocate him."

"But can't he turn into a gaseous state?"

"Then we will trap the gas in the bag and pop him, like this." I popped the bag, with the few remaining chips still inside. In the dark, tight tomb, it sounded like a gun shot. Something bumped into a wall at the top of the stairs.

Charlie said an expletive, then asked, "What was what?"

"Sorry. Just checking if we're still alive."

The second story was a dorm. Twenty rooms were up there, plus two bathrooms. "It looks like that person had to go again," Samantha informed us. The walls in some of the rooms had names and dates written on them. They were mainly from the sixties and seventies. The rooms were completely barren: no beds, no dressers, not even any windows you could see out of. They were boarded up like those on the first floor.

Charlie shined his flashlight through a hole in the ceiling. "Help me up." He stepped on my back, then pulled himself up. Samantha was next. She stood on my back as Charlie pulled her up. I jumped up and caught the lip of the opening. I kicked against the wall, giving me the leverage I needed to make it the rest of the way up.

There was nothing in the attic but rafters. Charlie held onto one of them and swung over the hole. Being the lemmings that we were, Samantha and I followed his lead. Why did I always do these stupid things? Sure, the odds were greatly in my favor, but there was always that miniscule risk. If I did these foolish things often enough double zero will eventually come up.

"Do you still have that pen?" Samantha asked Charlie.

"Yes. What do you want it for?" Charlie fished for it in his pants. He gave it to Samantha.

"So we can leave our mark on this place. Explorers leave a flag. These are our flags."

We wrote our names and 1988. Charlie also drew a small sketch of the earth. We looked inquisitively at him. "It's about time we earthlings claimed the earth."

"How long do you think our names will be here?" I asked.

"Hopefully not too much longer. It's detrimental for an animal to stay in one place for too long. He over-grazes, he over-uses, he abuses. Gypsies are more environmentally friendly than squatters. Over indulgence in anything is unhealthy. Haven't you read those medical reports?"

"One day a muscular demolition man will pick up that rafter and see the name Samantha Salsa and fantasize about who she was?"

85. PALS

It wasn't too startling that Magnolia and I found ourselves alone at Natural Bridge at midnight. Magnolia took her shoes and socks off before she left the Lemon. "What are you doing?" I asked her. "Aren't you afraid of hurting your feet?"

"Not these feet. I was born barefoot. I grew up barefoot. I'll probably die barefoot." Now that Magnolia saw me as only a friend she seemed to be more open with me, more herself. It must be awful for a person to feel like she must put on an artificial sugar and spice facade to be considered a proper and desirable young woman.

We followed a nearly dry creek bed. What liquid remained was now in my less-than-waterproof sneakers. I switched on my flashlight, illuminating a glass enclosed display informing the public of the natural bridge. I looked upstream. It was so dark I could barely see the formation. I shined the flashlight to the top of it. Its most prominent feature was a tree growing on top of it. One trail appeared to go through the natural bridge. The other went around and up.

We took the more direct route, but were stopped by the sheerness of the climb. The water running below the arch was definitely a creek. One learns such things after falling in up to the bottom of his shorts. With her clinging feet, Magnolia arrived at the beginning of the other route completely dry. The second trail consisted of dirt instead of rock, but it was nearly as steep. Magnolia's toes were like cleats as she clawed her way to top of the ridge. I slipped one foot for every two I climbed. Magnolia actually

323

had to help *me* up in a few places. Every time she gave my butt a shove, she followed it by a curt slap, saying, "There you go, pal."

The bridge was a precarious five feet wide, so I opted to illuminate it with my flashlight as we crossed. In the middle of the bridge, next to the tree, was a hole, a one-foot wide by three-foot-long gap in the stone. Magnolia sat down, sticking her legs through the hole. I waited for her to get up as I held onto the tree that may uproot any second.

"You don't want me to be here all by myself, do you?" she asked.

"I feel safer up here."

"Even if you did fall down the hole you probably wouldn't fall all the way. The hole isn't very large." Getting stuck wouldn't be much better.

We looked towards Lake Yellowstone, which we couldn't quite see over the trees. The smoke seemed to almost disappear at night. It still had to be there, but it eased my mind to have it out of sight for a few hours. "The Wolf made an announcement tonight," I said. "She assured us we aren't going to be evacuated, so we should continue to do our best."

"I heard it from the host's stand. I don't believe it. A week from now I'll be on the road with Rebecca."

"So, you're going to travel with Terrapin?"

"It'll be fun. Rebecca is fun. We'll go to Glacier, then into Canada to see Lake Louise in Banff. If it was October the weather would be questionable, but in September.... There are some good things to come out of the Yellowstone fires."

"You're ready to head down?"

"Just lead the way."

The trail on the other side of the bridge was similar to the trail we took up. I slid down on my boots. There were a couple of sudden switchbacks, which I just barely managed to maneuver in time. Magnolia wasn't as fortunate. The slippery slope caused her to drop too quickly, mitigated her natural abilities, blinding her connection with the earth. She tripped on something and slid on her butt.

At the bottom of the slope she pouted, but just for a second. "Pal, can you clean my back for me?" I did what was requested of me. "You missed a spot." I brushed off her protruding posterior, as precipitously as possible. She had to slide on *that*, didn't she? She grabbed my hand and shook it. "Thank you, pal."

86.   SERIAL SEASONALS

Andy and Christine lounged on the bare bed my two ex-roommates once occupied. I searched for a cassette tape that I hadn't listened to three or four times already this summer.

Andy looked frustrated. "Too many trails are closed."

"We could take a road trip," Christine suggested. "To the Wind River Range. Or Glacier. I've heard of people going as far as Colorado to escape the smoke."

"Even if we find a way out, we may not be let back in."

"I love traveling. Exploring exotic locations. Camping in national parks. Hitchhiking across Europe."

"When have you ever hitchhiked across Europe?"

"I would like to."

"No, you wouldn't."

"I like the idea of it."

"Travelling isn't free."

"That's why work in summer and winter, to support our habit."

"We could go to rehab."

"You would miss hiking."

"People who work real jobs hike."

"Not as often, or as far. Aren't you looking forward to travelling?"

"Do you remember us breaking down in Idaho?"

"On our way to Craters of the Moon."

"We stayed in Idaho Falls for two days, and spent a week's worth of traveling expenses fixing the car."

"That's because we bought a beater car."

"We always buy beater cars. Because they're the only ones we can afford earning barely better than minimum wage for only part of the year."

"How about Bertha?" I asked.

"I inherited her a couple of years ago," Christine answered. "Before the trip to Idaho."

"Do you remember Ghoul?" asked Andy.

"Ghoul the Gremlin."

"Why did you name it Ghoul?" I asked.

"Because pieces of it broke all the time," Andy answered. "Sometimes completely off, like the limbs of a rotting corpse."

"We repaired that door before we went back on the road."

"Then the brakes went out in rush hour traffic. The following week one of our bald tires had a blowout. Have you ever changed a tire on a twenty-degree slope, Steve, in the Mojave Desert? We ended up running out of money two weeks before we were scheduled to return to the Park."

"The friends we stayed with worked as we loafed. Lifers are the modern American gypsies."

"I prefer the term *serial seasonal*. Life is a series of choices. Every action has a consequence. Paradise isn't free."

"What should we do tonight?" Christine asked a moment later, after everyone had to time to digest the conversation, and masticate the memories.

"Just because Charlie isn't here to direct us doesn't mean we can't have any fun," I responded. "What would he suggest if he was here?"

Andy replied, "He would probably suggest some mischief, like climbing on top of a building."

"But we already did that," said Christine.

"Then how about doing just the opposite," I suggested. "Why don't we go under a building."

"Which one?" asked Andy, becoming suddenly excited. Crawling on hands and knees was much safer than climbing ladders and peering down sheer drops.

"*The* building."

"Lake Hotel?" Christine asked. I nodded. "Where can we enter?"

"There's supposed to be an entrance across from the small building that looks like a bomb shelter," said Andy.

"Let's check that out too," I said.

87.   NO LONGER IN THE MOOD

The door to the square stone building, half buried in the ground, was closed. "I think we could really get into trouble if we break into this," said Andy.

"It's not private property," I retorted. "If we were high enough in the chain of command we would be allowed to enter it whenever we wished. Maybe one day we will be promoted into such a position. So, as I see it, we are just doing some training on our own time. We should be commended for our action." Of course, that didn't mean we didn't watch for voyeurs as we entered.

I swung my flashlight. The building did look like a bomb

327

shelter. Jars of food were on shelves on one side. On the other, there was firewood. In the middle of the room was miscellaneous equipment lying on benches on the floor. Christine found a light switch and used it, successfully. The door slammed shut. "We're going to have a really bad day if we can't get that open," said Andy.

"If not, we do have an ample supply of food," I said.

"I don't think so," said Christine. "The food doesn't look edible. It must have been sitting here for quite a while. Some of the bottles are even broken."

"So that's what's making this place smell so bad," Andy commented. "I was hoping it wasn't a corpse."

"What is this?" I held up a large bottle with a swirling mass of dried vegetation inside.

"I think it was once a potato," said Christine. "You can see a bit of its remains in the bottom of the jar."

"Let's get out of here," said Andy. "This place is spooky. I don't want to end up like that potato---bits of vegetation growing out of me like I was manure."

We *were* able to re-open the door. We were careful to leave the place as we found it: lights out, door closed.

Under the pantry, near where the dining room began, was a small opening. For once we didn't feel too intrusive, since we didn't have to open anything to enter. It was like we were going into a cave. We had to crawl on dirt. At least it wasn't wet. Metal columns connected the floor above to cement blocks along eight-foot intervals. Twenty feet inside were a series of pipes that nearly blocked our way. Through a series of climbing over and squeezing underneath we were able to successfully navigate the obstacles. To our left we saw light. Getting closer we discovered a crack in a wall. Beyond was a hallway. Someone walked by in a dirty tan uniform. "That must be maintenance," Christine whispered. "It's under the EDR." The building's eastern boundary ended, so we had to turn right, heading south. We heard voices above us. We stopped and listened. Nothing that interested us.

I whispered, "So, you guys are going to work at Snow Lodge this winter?"

Andy whispered back, "We would like to, if there is still any of the Park left in December. We are still waiting to hear if we are hired."

"But you've both worked there last winter. Surely they will hire you back."

"That doesn't always matter with Snow Lodge. Because there are only one-hundred people working there, and it's so isolated, the management is very careful who they hire. Winter employees not only have to be good workers, but they also have to get along with people, especially with the management."

"But we got along well with everyone last winter, so I think we will be hired," said Christine. "Those that make the hiring decisions are just waiting to see what happens to the Park. Charlie and Samantha also want to work there again. It will be a great winter. You put your application in, didn't you?"

"Yes, but I don't know what I want to do. I probably won't even get hired."

"In a normal year," said Andy, "but with so many people quitting, because of the fires, your odds of getting hired have greatly increased."

A couple of familiar voices quieted us. "It's not fair that we have to evacuate," said Harry Douglas. "There isn't even a fire in the area."

"Mammoth thinks we might get caught off guard and become stranded," said Martha Devla. "Business hasn't been good anyway. Tourists are afraid to enter the Park. No one is more upset about abandoning the Park than me. I've been here for twenty years. When I first came to Yellowstone I was younger than most of these kids who are spending their first summer away from home. To see my home go up in flames…. It's as much of a spiritual loss for me as it is a physical one."

"When do we have to leave?"

"The guests are to leave tomorrow. The majority of the employees are to leave the next day."

The shock and grief on Christine and Andy's faces mirrored my own. We sat for five minutes in silence, reviewing what had transpired this summer, dreaming of what might have been, thinking ahead of what still must occur. We knew this day would come, but not this suddenly.

"Should we see if we can get to the far end of the Hotel?" I asked glumly.

"I'm no longer in the mood," Andy replied.

88.   UNTIL THE KITCHEN CALMED DOWN

After all the guests had left, we opened a case of champagne. Then another. Every other person seemed to have a bottle in their hand. Charlie and Andy dragged Samantha down to the Lake and threw her in. She tried to splash back at them, but she didn't have the range. One of the waiters was walking through the kitchen barefoot. He had an apron on, its pocket full of raw eggs. He threw them at people randomly, like he was a mass murderer on a shooting spree. Someone dumped a gallon of ranch dressing on him from behind. A streak of black filth began at the cook's line, where the cooks were doing deep cleaning, and spread throughout the kitchen in well-trodden paths. Someone turned on the jet sprayer, but did more harm to people than to the filth. An egg barely missed me. It looked like cleaning would be a wasted effort until the kitchen calmed down, so I escaped to the EDR.

I grabbed a coke then sat down to relax. Iris wiped down dirty tables from lunch. "You're not back in the kitchen making a mess?" I asked her.

"I raised five kids. I've had my fill of messes."

"Are you disappointed about leaving early?"

"It's so beautiful here. Even the fires are beautiful in their own way. And it's great talking to you kids. But extra time off means I can spend more time with my family. I have a new grandbaby I haven't seen. This early departure will give Harry and me two full months before we head to Flamingo, in the Everglades."

"Is it nice there?"

"In the winter it is. In the summer it's hot, wet, and infested with mosquitoes. Winter is the dry season."

89. PUB PRIVILEGES REVOKED

The pub was wild. It was the closing party. One might think with all the champagne that was consumed earlier in the day people wouldn't want any more liquor for a while. I was mistaken. Charlie snuck in a half-gallon of Yellowstone Whiskey. He even had the guts to ask the Wolf if she would like a swig. She actually took a swallow. "Smooth," she cooed.

Not being sated by the mischief he created, Charlie climbed up to the central beam, which he haughtily crossed. One look from The Wolf prevented the procession of acolytes from following him. She didn't smile until Charlie was safely down, then proceeded to revoke his pub privileges for the remainder of the season---which meant for the next two hours.

As Charlie left he grabbed my arm. "Come on."

"Where are we going?"

"If you really want to know you probably shouldn't be

going," Andy warned. "I feel safer here, in a room full of drunks." He faced Charlie. "She should have kicked you out after you snuck in that whiskey."

"She was the one who introduced it to me," Charlie responded. "Who else can we get? You grab Christine. And I'll grab...Samantha." Which he did---physically---as she was leaving the pub.

Magnolia came up to us as we began our hike back to the dorm. "Where are you guys going?"

"To Fishing Bridge," Charlie responded. "Want to come along?"

"Sure."

"Can I come too?" asked Rebecca

"All right, but no one else. We need stealth."

90. A FINAL PLUNGE

We piled into Charlie's van. At the Elephant's Back trailhead, Charlie turned around. "We better head back to get our bathing suits. And towels. It's going to be cold." Bathing suits and towels for what? No one asked, and everyone consented.

Charlie parked where he did during our archaeological exploration. Instead of going directly to the River, Charlie walked across the bridge. The squinty, rectangular headlights of a ranger's SUV was coming towards us. We ducked beneath the benches on the south side of the bridge. The vehicle passed us and continued.

"So, who would like to go first?" asked Charlie as he stood back up. I looked down at the water. It looked as dark as tar, except for the smattering of stars that were reflecting off it.

Everyone had their sweats and jackets off, priming for the inevitable. Samantha's suit was surprisingly modest---a one-piece that covered most of her body. Function over style? A dramatic, but apropos nail in the coffin of summer.

Charlie climbed over the wooden guardrail. All he needed to do now was lean forward to fall. "So, who would like to jump with me?" I didn't want to do it, but to get to the end of a tunnel often required passing through it. The longer the delay the greater the likelihood of an obstruction, psychological more prominent than physical.

I relived the summer. My hesitant arrival. Meeting Charlie and Andy. Samantha and Christine. Daphnee. Alice and Magnolia. The hikes. Camping. Hotpotting. And finally, that leap into the Firehole River. Why was I still doing something so stupid? Peer pressure? To challenge myself? There were less complicated methods.

Charlie fell. I dropped a split-second later, no longer caring about the consequences. I simply followed Charlie's lead.

I COULDN'T BREATHE! Either the fall knocked the wind out of me. Or the cold. Or both. I was simultaneously numb and in pain. I couldn't tell if I was still underwater. It felt like I was being dragged. A biting wind whipped my face. So, my head was at least above water. I saw the white of a concrete support beside me. Never again....

Traffic thinned as we drove farther from Seattle. Why were vacations more tiring than work? The kids calmed down after we climbed into the Cascades. Even children could appreciate beauty. It was late afternoon when we arrived at our small ranch outside of Missoula, Montana. The kids ran through the wild flowers to the horses. I wrapped my arm around my wife. Together we looked to the snow shrouded mountains just beginning to release their bounty.